D0269985

Also by Chaz Brenchley:

The Samaritan
The Refuge
The Garden
Mall Time
Paradise
Dead of Light

Dispossession

Chaz Brenchley

NEW ENGLISH LIBRARY
Hodder and Stoughton

First published in Great Britain in 1996 by Hodder and Stoughton
First published in paperback in 1997 by Hodder and Stoughton
A division of Hodder Headline PLC
A New English Library Paperback

10 9 8 7 6 5 4 3 2 1

A CIP catalogue record for this title is available from
the British Library

ISBN 0 340 65992 0

Printed and bound in Great Britain by
Cox & Wyman Ltd, Reading, Berkshire

Hodder and Stoughton
A division of Hodder Headline PLC
338 Euston Road
London NW1 3BH

Of what am I newly possessed?
House, cats, friends.
This comes ex Fenham View,
from Sophonisba and Artemisia and me,
with love to Gail-Nina and Gavin.

• ONE •

PHILOXENIA

Everyone does this once, at least, or should do:

where you wake up in the wrong bed with the wrong body nestled close, unfamiliar smells on the sheets and in their hair and a beat of blank in your memory before their name comes to mind, a touch of strange where you touch them because their touch is so different to what your skin is used to, what your bones expect. You listen to their breathing as they sleep, and even that's out of kilter with rhythms long established in your head; and you're so, so glad they're still sleeping, because you realise suddenly that you have no idea what colour their open eyes will be, or how your face will look reflected in them.

They say we fall in love to reinforce our own self-image; perhaps we sleep around to do the opposite, to remind ourselves that others see us differently, or can do. That we all have other faces, the possibility of alternate lives.

Whatever, it's a thing that happens, we're not a naturally monogamous species; and once, yes, once is terrific. Once in a while is okay, though you don't want to make a habit of it. But every day, every *day* I wake up with a stranger.

I'm getting to know her well.

*   *   *

Doing it once, doing it the first time made the best sense. Waking was hard that day, consciousness was something to be clawed at, fingers too weak to grip; I clawed and it tore, it frayed to ribbons under my weight and couldn't hold me, so that I slithered down into easy dark and had to start again.

And did, and struggled up and felt far worse for doing it, felt so bad I only wanted to slide again.

That was my first coherent waking thought, that waking *hurt* and I wanted none of it now that I had too much.

Didn't open my eyes, nothing so foolish; if it was daylight out there – and it had to be, surely, I felt as though I'd slept forever – then that was only going to hurt more. My head was murder already. Spears of light in the eyeball I could live without.

Second coherent thought yet, and already I was making plans for the day. *Don't open your eyes, sunshine.* This was excellent. Proactive and sensible, and what more could anyone ask of a man first thing in the morning?

Presumptive morning. Might be afternoon, but I wasn't going to enquire. Not that much interested in clocks just now.

Curiosity, famously fatal to *Felidae*, is not dangerous to cats alone; but it was a sluggish poison in my blood that day. Took a while, took the longest time for me even to start measuring where I hurt, let alone wondering why.

Head, yes. Head was the worst. Bad head in the morning traditionally meant hangover, but this was a blinder, and I couldn't believe I'd drunk enough to earn it.

Wasn't just my head, anyway. All my joints were aching, my ribs were seriously sore; trying to be dispassionate, I concluded that I must have spent a couple of hours on a rack last night, doing stretching exercises before or after some kind lad in hobnails kicked my head in.

Trying to be sensible, I went back to the tradition again: bad head plus bruises meant being well pissed, getting into a fight perhaps, staggering home from one hard-edged lamppost to the next and falling downstairs a time or two before finally crawling to the top and so to bed.

That I couldn't remember drinking last night – that I couldn't remember *anything* about last night, where I'd been or what I'd been doing, even what night of the week it must have been – was only another confirmation, alcoholic amnesia doing its stuff.

Okay. I got stotious, though it wasn't like me; I got hurt, though it really wasn't like me. That just about covered the damage, the internal situation my body was reporting.

External situation: I was in bed, obviously, but not lying flat. Propped up against pillows, I guessed. Pillows and something else, warmer and firmer, tucked tight against my side. Something that moved, a little, when I turned my questing, tormented head . . .

Ah.

Jonty, my brilliant mind deduced, *you are not alone*.

Nor should I have been; what is a helpmeet for, if not to succour the wounded partner and comfort the beloved?

Her fingers touched my forehead, and it hurt. I jerked away, and that hurt also; when I moaned I heard a chuckle close by my left ear, and a soft voice murmur, "That's my man. Why be stalwart?"

Dry tongue, dry lips; hard to talk, but I managed her name, at least.

Said, "Carol . . . ?" and felt her arm tighten, where it lay around my shoulders.

Her voice tightened too, acquired some edges; but she was still laughing, and all she actually said was, "Jonty, you're a pig. But welcome back, anyway. I missed you." Then she laid her cheek against mine and moved it gently, cool softness catching on bristles. This also hurt.

Her perfume caught in my nose, acting like sal volatile to clear my head a little after so long sleep. Perfumes, plural, at second sniff: I could smell fresh-washed skin too, conditioner on her clothes, toothpaste on her breath. But over all was the scent she was wearing, which was light, sharp, a little aggressive; expensive, for sure. It was also utterly unfamiliar.

Lances of light; my eyes had opened, regardless of earlier and wiser decisions. Squinting into the pain, they found her face and focused.

Unh.

Uncertainties about the voice and the perfume, even about the way her body felt against mine, although my skin was registering little but its own discomfort: all doubts were resolved in a moment.

No, this was not Carol. Not at all Carol, not even a little bit. Whoever this was, she was only half the size. Petite, elfin, *gamine*: my mind might be running slow, running pretty much on empty here, but I was having no problems with vocabulary.

And she was younger than Carol by three or four years at least, which made her younger than me also, by pretty much the same distance; and her hair was black and cropped short and spiky, where Carol had tumbling mouse-brown curls; and she had a crucifix on a chain around her neck and three or four silver rings in each ear and the glint of a tiny jewel in one nostril, where Carol habitually faced the world quite unadorned.

Oh, and she was also Chinese, this girl. That was the clincher. No English rose, no Carol; and a very poor attempt at a doppelgänger, so why was she cuddling me so close?

"Hullo," she said, smiling at me. Small mouth, neat teeth. Sharp, I thought, most likely. She didn't look the type to grind them.

"Hi."

"Are you back for real this time?"

"Sorry?"

"This is the third time you've woken up in the last half hour. First time you just looked at me, and sighed a bit; second time you were very polite, you said good morning and your head hurt, and then you snuggled up and went to sleep again."

"Did I? I don't remember . . ."

"Never mind. How are you feeling?"

"My head hurts," I said, and felt her chuckle. "Apart from that, sore, mostly. Confused . . ." Questions on this level I could cope with.

She nodded briskly, with the air of someone ticking items off a mental list. "You will be, for a while. The doctors said. Don't worry."

Doctors? I let my eyes drift from her face, and lost a few more assumptions very quickly. This was not my bed, nor was I at home in it. Small room, off-white walls, ugly curtains pulled against the glare of the day: okay, could be in a hospital, could well be, though I'd only ever seen or been in public wards before and didn't understand this solitude, though it was welcome. On a table by the window, a dozen vases'-worth of Interflora's best warred with each other for absent insects; looking down, I saw my own arm lying on a curtain-matching coverlet, bare but for a plastic name-band round the wrist and a cuff of bandage with a trailing tube. That led to a drip, hanging from a stand the other side of the bed.

An exercise in quick mental revision: the lad in hobnails was suddenly favourite again. I might or might not have been drunk, but my best guess now was that I'd been beaten up. And knifed, perhaps? Knifing was popular . . .

"Oy." Her hand laid itself against my cheek – *ouch*, but I wasn't going to say it – and turned my head gently towards hers. "Don't worry, I said. I'm in control, all right?"

That much, I could believe. I opened my mouth to speak, but managed nothing more than a croak; she reached around and produced a glass of something tinted faintly amber, ignoring the feeble movement in my arm and holding the glass directly to my lips, while her other hand supported my head.

"Just sip it, okay? Take your time, there's no hurry in the world."

Stuff independence; if a beautiful stranger wanted to nurse me – and she was irredeemably beautiful, this unknown girl, as well as being irredeemably not Carol – then I wasn't about to argue. I sipped, and almost choked; she pulled the glass away, scowling.

"Take your *time*, I said . . ."

Time had nothing to do with it, only surprise. I'd been expecting medicine, not whisky-and-water. But I sipped again when she allowed me, and swallowed till my mouth and throat were moist and my belly warmed; then I settled my head back – into her shoulder, purely because the world was suddenly spinning a little and her shoulder was there and not spinning, not going away – and said, "What happened to me?"

"Don't you remember?"

"I don't remember anything." *Don't remember you*, only I didn't know how to tell her that. Didn't want to upset someone who wanted to sit this close, who thought she meant that much. Maybe she'd come back to me along with everything else that was missing, if I could just find something to act as a trigger. One blinding flash, maybe, and the ragged edges in my memory would all be neatly hemmed . . .

She nodded. Another tick on the list. "They said you might not. I'm not supposed to help you, not till they've done some tests; but, hell, I'm not supposed to be giving you whisky either," and the smile was sheer mischief now, shared devilry that I was sorry I couldn't properly share. Just her name, that might be enough, if I could only find or figure out her sodding name . . .

"You were in a smash," she said slowly, earnestly, eye to eye and very close.

"What, in a car, you mean? An accident?"

Her lips twitched, *what else, stupid?*, but she only nodded.

"Who was driving?"

"You were."

"Shit." There went my no-claims bonus. All these years with never a shunt, never a scrape, I'd always been so careful; and now . . .

Now something cold and living was uncoiling itself in my spine, stretching through my bones, worse than any hurt. I'd been in an accident, and it must have been a bad one; I'd woken up in hospital, with only a stranger to comfort me; and where in hell – no, not that, but where the *fuck* was Carol?

I gazed at this comfortable stranger, tried to ask, couldn't find the words; and then didn't need them, because I guess she could read the question in my pallor, in my fear.

"Just you," she said quickly, "there wasn't anyone else in the car."

A long, slow breath of relief, and then my conscience pricked me towards another worry, before I could try again with *where the fuck is Carol?*

"What, then, was there another car?" Or a truck, perhaps, something big enough to crunch my cautious Volvo?

"Nah. You're just a crap driver," smilingly, while her hand smoothed the stubble on my cheek. I shook my head, *not true*, though moving jambled my brain; and she read that also, because the smile faded a little as she went on, "You came off the road, Jonty, that's all. Over in Cumbria it was, middle of nowhere. Maybe you swerved to miss a rabbit or something, we don't know, there weren't any witnesses; but you must have been going a hell of a lick, because there's a barrier on the corner where you came off, and you flew over that without touching it, as far as anyone can see. The car was on its roof, down in the gulley, and they never found you till morning . . ."

Again I shook my head, just not believing any of this. Volvos don't fly. But she'd turned away, she didn't see.

"If I crashed in Cumbria," I said slowly, "where am I now?"

"Home. Well, in hospital, but home. They brought you straight here from the crash, it's further but you had to have a CT scan to make sure your brain wasn't slopping about like mushy peas in your stupid head . . ."

And then she slipped out from under, easing me back onto a heap of pillows. And drew the curtains with a flourish to show me I was home, and stood smiling brightly by the bed and said, "You finish that drink quick, and I'll go get the doctors, okay?"

"No, wait." Hide what she liked behind a smile, she wasn't fooling me. I'd heard the remembered fear in her voice, *they never found you till morning*, and I didn't want to play charades any more. Time to be truthful. "Tell me one more thing," I said quietly. "I'm sorry, but I can't remember your name."

She hissed and stood motionless for a moment, biting her lip hard, I thought; then she looked at me quizzically, looking for a joke and not seeing it.

"Straight up?" she asked.

I nodded.

"So much for bloody scans, eh?" And suddenly she was nothing but amused, trying to swallow little bubbles of laughter. "I *told* them, what does that machine know, I said, there was plenty wrong with his brain even before he shook it all up like that. But – oh, you *bastard* . . ."

"Sorry," I said again.

"No matter. You know who you are, yeah?"

"Yes."

"Tell me."

"I'm Jonty," I said patiently.

"Jonty, right. And I'm Sue," she said, or I thought she said; but it didn't seem certain on the face of it. Not with that face. Soo, perhaps she'd said? Or Tzu?

"Er, how do you spell that?"

"The usual way," she said. And then, helpfully, "It's short for Susan."

Right. Okay, I'd put my hefty feet right in it. Damn it, I used to know some people from Hong Kong – or we did, rather, they'd been Carol's friends more than mine: *like all our friends*, a stray thought obtruded – and they'd had English Christian names. Come to think of it, they'd been Christians; and she did have that crucifix round her neck, that might be more than decoration . . .

"Susan what?" I asked with a gesture of surrender, hoping at least for Wu or Wong, if I couldn't have Manchu.

"Marks," she said. And then, slowly, visibly uncertain whether she should still be laughing, "I'm your wife."

No. Not possible. Demonstrably, not possible. If I'd cracked my head in a car smash – and certainly there was some heavy bandaging round my skull, my reaching fingers found that instead of the floppy hair they wanted, they needed to play with – I could imagine enough mental scrambling to make me forget a new friend temporarily, or a recently-joined colleague, perhaps. But a *wife?* No. I was Jonathan Marks, LLB, solicitor; fathered by the Reading Festival, raised by the sort of woman who would tell a small boy that his father was a festival; employed at the firm of Hesketh & Jones, with my eye on a partnership before I hit thirty; and talking of partnerships, I had lived for seven years with Carol Carter, and so far as I was aware neither one of us had ever thought of marriage, even to each other. Bachelor of Laws, I was a bachelor in life also and meant to stay that way.

Sorry, girlie. This was some kind of scam, it had to be; unless she'd slipped away from the psychiatric wing, perhaps, when the attendants had been distracted. Maybe she claimed a relationship with every new patient who was in no state to refute it, maybe that was her thing. Like someone who got off on confessing to crimes they hadn't committed, and God knew, I'd met a few of those . . .

Except that what she did then, smart girl with a natural sense for the dramatic moment, she slipped out of the room before I could deny her; and she came back a minute later with a couple of doctors in tow. Okay, that was in character; confessors always go to the police. But these two seemingly serious-minded souls called her Mrs Marks, and gave me no high-sign to suggest they were only humouring a loony till more men in white coats came to claim her.

Gave her a bollocking, though, they did, for the whisky in the water, that I hadn't had wit enough to finish; then they gave her another for preempting their memory-tests by telling me about the crash.

Never mind the crash, I said, I wish someone would tell me about the marriage.

That had them curious, concerned, asking what I meant; she only stood and looked at me, not a muscle in her seeming to move.

It's a fantasy, I said. Look, I said, I'll give you name, rank and serial number, I'll give you the story of my life; whatever it is she's told you that doesn't gel, I said, she's making it up. I don't know the girl, I said.

So I took them through all the details of my cv, just as I'd taken myself through those same details before they came. Jonathan known as Jonty, bachelor at law and in life, I said; sharing said life with Carol Carter. No wives, I said.

Um, they said. And then they asked me what the day was, and what the date.

*   *   *

Actually, I'd been wondering about that myself; I was half prepared for the question, and for the obvious thoughts behind it.

"I've lost some time, haven't I?" I said, trying for a wee grin as I spoilt their surprise. "I really don't know where in the week we are, you'll have to tell me. How long have I been unconscious?"

Funny thing about doctors, they're interrogation-proof. It was definitely my turn to ask something, but the question slid off them like water off oilskin, and they didn't seem to notice it at all.

"What about the month, then?" one of them demanded. "Can you tell me the month?"

Yes, of course I could, or nearly. "Come on, guys," I said, "you can't con me. I haven't been in a coma for weeks and weeks, there aren't enough machines going beep in here. I'm a bit muddled, I know; but if this isn't late January, it's got to be early February at the very latest, right?"

The two docs looked at each other; one of them twitched an eyebrow, the other made a note on a clipboard. It was Sue who risked their wrath once more, by treating me like a human being with the right to know what a fool I was making of myself.

"April," she said. "Thirteenth, which makes it the Ides of. Cute, eh? And I thought it was going to be so lucky for me. Just lucky it's not a Friday on top, I suppose . . ."

She was lying again, she had to be. I looked to the doctors to tell me so, and all they did was nod. "It's the thirteenth of April, Mr Marks."

"Christ." So much for machines that went beep. They must have wheeled them all away, when I started waking up . . . "So how long have I been here, then?"

"Three days," Sue said, perching herself on the side of the bed and taking one of my hands in both of hers. "And I don't care what anyone says, you're getting shaved tonight.

Scabs or no scabs. You look disgusting. If you won't do it
and they won't do it, I'll do it myself. Can't stand prickly
men, I like 'em smooth . . ."

"Please, Mrs Marks," one of the doctors butted in, bless
him. "I know this isn't easy for you, but you'll only confuse
your husband more."

Damn right. I was trying to equate three days – or what
she said was three days, though she'd shown herself an
utterly unreliable witness, and I wished to God they'd stop
supporting her – with what, ten weeks? Maybe twelve weeks
since I could find a solid, dependable memory with a date
attached to it. This did not compute. Nothing was hanging
together, nothing made sense. *Things fall apart; the centre
cannot hold*, and it felt like all that was holding me to Planet
Earth right now was the hard grip of a stranger, except that
she was the most muddling thing of all, and every time I
thought something was coming clear she gave the whole
mess another stir . . .

The doctors weren't too much help just then, though fortunately I wasn't really expecting any better of them. Slowly
and patiently they told me what was known or obvious
already: that I'd been in an accident, that I'd sustained a
significant jolt to my brain – an insult they called it first,
before catching themselves in jargon and correcting for the
layperson mentality – which had scrambled everything up a
bit. I'd experienced some memory loss – *no, really? Gosh,
tell me about it* – and once they'd checked me out physically,
what they needed to do most urgently was to establish the
range and depth of that loss.

Which actually meant that after they'd poked and prodded
and shone lights into my eyes and such, they just needed
to ask me a lot more questions. We dealt quite efficiently
with the President of the United States and what had been
the Christmas number one, but I couldn't help them at all

with who'd won the Five Nations this year or what was the score in the last Newcastle game. The last I remembered was one-all away at Stamford Bridge, but that had been a January cup-tie and I couldn't tell them who'd won the replay.

Sport and politics seemed to confirm the time-lag, that I was missing near enough three months of my life here. Unless the doctors also were lying to me – which would make them not doctors at all, I supposed, only actors in white coats and this not after all a hospital, just a room dressed up to look the part as they were. Some grand scam this could be, though the purpose defeated me . . .

Except that I knew the view outside the window. The hospital grounds had been a regular short cut for me, when I was a student and living this side of town; I knew that building, that path, those trees. This was where they said it was; which made them necessarily what they said they were. Too much to believe that they'd hired or stolen time in this place to turn a disused room into a stage-set, an operating theatre for some bizarre conspiracy.

The men at least, what they said they were. Not the woman, no way the woman . . .

So okay, I'd had a crack on the head and lost three months'-worth of memories. I wanted them back, I was ready to riot if they told me I'd never recover them; but I didn't even get the chance to ask just then. The doctors were homing in on personal stuff, and they weren't giving out information, only questions.

"What car do you drive, Jonty?"

"Volvo. Grey, 650, three years old." Sensible, boring, safe. Should have been safe, at least. No previously-recorded tendency to fly.

"Uh-huh. Do you ever drive anything else?"

"Yeah. Carol's got a 2cv, she lets me out in that sometimes." I saw the way they glanced at each other, one doctor to the other to Sue; and I sighed, and said,

"Okay, you might as well tell me. What was I driving when I crashed?"

"James the Second," Sue said.

"Eh?"

"You bought him, you named him. An MR2? In British racing green?"

I shook my head helplessly. What the hell would I be doing with a car like that?

"Who was James the First?" one of the doctors asked. Trying to catch me out, I guess, me or my memory or both.

"A Scottish king," I said flatly.

Sue looked at me and said, "Writer. Ghost stories. Christ, you really don't remember, do you?"

"That's right. I really don't remember."

"Okay. M R James wrote ghost stories; the car was an MR2; so, obviously, James the Second. It was obvious to you, anyway."

"I've never read M R James," I said, still trying to put distance between this girl's version of the world and my own.

"You read them to me every night last month. Dead spooky. I wanted candlelight but you wouldn't do that, you said you couldn't see to read, but I reckon you were scared . . ."

Layers beneath layers: teasing on the surface, she was angry underneath, or wanted me to think it. How dared I not remember what was so potent, so shared? But I thought the anger was as artificial as the tease, with something tight and frightened hiding down below.

I could get angry now myself, I thought; but I thought it would be just as artificial, and what it hid in me would be just as craven. I knew what I was scared of – and yes, you could call it a ghost story, this mythical life she claimed for me, that I had never lived – but I was less certain about her. I wanted to think about that, to try to draw some sense out of a skein of impossibilities; but more even than that I simply wanted to be alone, to answer no more questions for a while, neither to be faced with questions that I couldn't answer.

So I let my head topple back and roll into the pillow, and there was nothing artificial in this, I felt completely shagged. And said so, said, "I'm shagged. Can we save the rest till later?"

"Yes, of course, Jonty." My God, considerate doctors? "You sleep awhile, and try not to worry. Experience shows that most memories are recovered, sooner or later. We can't force nature in this respect, but she does a pretty good job on her own account."

They left, conferring in low voices before they were even out of the door. Sue hesitated a moment, made half a move to come back to the bed, half opened her mouth to speak; but I only looked at her, offering no encouragement and certainly no help, and in the end she just twisted away and walked out.

She might be short, but she did okay in proportion. Nice legs, neat bottom. I barely registered, though, was in no mood to enjoy.

A nurse looked in an hour later, to check that I was sleeping. I wasn't; I'd not felt so exhausted, so drained and confused, so very far from sleep since the first night I ever spent in someone else's bed, nervous and daring and massively, monstrously pleased with myself and with her. The emotions this time were as different as their causes, but the effect was similar.

"You're supposed to be resting," she said, fussing with my pillows and my pulse. "It's no good battering your head against a brick wall, you know, that won't bring things back any quicker. It's like when something just slips your mind, you know? You have to forget about it, and then suddenly there it is. Think about something else, and I bet you'll start remembering what you've lost. You're trying too hard, that's all. Do you want the telly on? Or the radio? As you're obviously not going to go to sleep?"

"No," I said, relieved to find myself positive about one thing in my life. "Thanks," added a little belatedly; and then, "Do you know where my clothes are?"

"In the locker there, what's left of them. But you're not getting up, sonny Jim, so don't you think it."

I smiled thinly. "Last thing I want to do, believe me. My legs ache like fuck," which I said only to hear her cluck; I don't much like being ordered about by strangers. But she never twitched an eyebrow, and that was points to her, so I explained more reasonably, "I only want to see what I've got in my pockets."

Just my luck, to land a maternal Tolkien fan. She hissed softly as she opened a drawer in the bedside locker, and whispered "What has it got in its pocketses?" And then she tipped the drawer upside down over my knees, and said, "That's the lot. Anything missing must have got left in the wreck. I don't know if Mr Coffey would approve of this or not, but it sounds like a good idea to me. Maybe something here'll trigger your memories."

That's what I was hoping also, or a part of it. She put the drawer back into the locker and stood there, arms folded, watching with interest; I kept my face neutral and my hands still, and said, "I thought nurses were all desperately overworked?"

"Touchy," she said, tutting at my manners. "If there's anything personal in there, lad, I've probably seen it already. I'm the one who undressed you – well, cut the rags off you, mostly – and sorted out what was savable."

"Was I that much of a mess, then?" My body might be an awkward and uncomfortable vehicle just now, but it didn't seem to me so badly damaged. Not from the neck down, at least. I wasn't in traction, or even in plaster so far as I could see.

She shook her head. "Cuts and bruises is all. But you looked worse than that when you came in, and we couldn't take chances. What I say is, if you're going to throw your car off the road, you shouldn't wear Calvin Kleins to do it."

"I haven't got any Calvin Kleins," I said automatically. Levis were my limit, I didn't give a toss about designer labels on my clothes.

"Well, you haven't now, that's for sure." I guess it was becoming clear to her round about then that I'd make small talk for the rest of the day and all night too, but I wasn't going to look through my things until she was gone. That realisation still didn't shift her, though. She glanced at the flowers in the window, and said, "Did that little wife of yours show you the cards that came with these?"

"No." *And don't call her my wife* – but I didn't want to say that aloud, I just beamed it as a sullen message of denial which penetrated not a millimetre into the woman's skull.

"No? She'll have been too much relieved to think of it, I expect. Three days she's been sitting by your bed, you know, even in the ICU where she was just getting under people's feet, and so we told her. We've sent her home at night, of course, but she's straight back again in the morning, first thing. Ruining her beauty over you, she's been, so I hope you're properly grateful . . ."

I said nothing, though Sue's beauty didn't seem to me to have taken noticeable damage. Meanwhile, as she talked the nurse was gathering up the florists' cards from all the separate bouquets.

"Hard enough time we had of it, getting her to go and clean up when you started to wake. It took Mr Coffey himself to tell her that it'd be an hour or two yet before you made any kind of sense, you weren't coming to in a hurry; and besides she looked a mess, he told her, and she didn't smell nice. I think that was what shifted her, in the end. Went running off for a shower and a change, and she was still back inside half an hour. Now, you'll want to know who else has been thinking of you," she went on, in defiance of the facts. Right now I wasn't bothered, I didn't give a damn; but she clearly did. Rather than giving me the cards – "you don't want to be fussing your eyes over these, not with your bad head" – she read them to me.

Here at last, for the first time since those early thoughts registered that I was waking into pain but that there was a woman there to cuddle and kiss me better, some things started to make sense. Or to sound sensible, at least, to conform to the world that I lived in. These were names that I knew, colleagues and friends.

But nothing lasts, nothing is reliable. Though there was nothing from my mother, which again conformed to the world that I lived in, one card read 'with best wishes from Father and Mother Chu'. And apparently they had been to visit, twice: a solemn, concerned and very Chinese couple, the nurse said, who had sat almost without speaking, smiling apologies if they seemed the least bit in the way, while their worried eyes shifted constantly from Sue to me and back to Sue again. Their daughter, obviously, if anything in this crazy mess was obvious; and so whatever was going on here, I wasn't facing a single nutcase but an inscrutable conspiracy.

And no, there were no flowers from Carol; but the last and largest bunch, the brightest and the brashest bouquet was from Vernon Deverill, and what the hell, what the giddy *hell* was he doing sending me flowers? Vernon Deverill spent a good deal of his time – and hence his solicitors' time – in and out of court, though so far as I knew he'd never been convicted of anything more serious than speeding; but he wasn't one of our clients. We had something of a reputation for honesty, for straight dealing with our clients and with the courts; Vernon Deverill wouldn't recognise a deal unless it was helical. The only time I could recall seeing him in the flesh, he'd been standing on the steps outside the court building giving sound-bites to the media, talking about police persecution and harassment after his latest acquittal. Myself and ninety per cent of his auditors simply assumed that he'd nobbled the jury again, though not even the stupidest reporter there showed any signs of suggesting it.

And this man, this leading light of our business and criminal fraternity who didn't or shouldn't know me from Adam, was suddenly sending me flowers to wish me a speedy recovery? Well, it was just one more on the growing list of impossible things that I was apparently expected to believe; but it was a big one, that. Bigger than cars and clothes, at any rate.

As big as being married, maybe. All these things were impossible, but some were more impossible than others, and I wasn't even close to giving those credence. One thing I'd known all my life, that people would lie and lie again for their advantage – you had only to look at my mother – and florists at least were easy people to lie to. Not their job to check up, to be sure that the name on the message was the name of the sender.

γνῶθι σεαυτόν, *know thyself* was the motto of the Seven Wise Men, at least according to Plato. I'd seen it for myself, inscribed on Apollo's temple at Delphi. Seen it with Carol, indeed: we'd both done a Classics option at university, that was where we met, and we'd spent a long summer in Greece after, getting to know each other. I hadn't needed to take it on board as a personal motto also, because it was already there in my head, had been a part of my private philosophy long before I ever thought I had one.

I knew myself fairly well, I fancied; and even if I'd lost a large chunk of memory, my personality hadn't gone with it. I was still the same man I used to be. I could feel that; every thought fitted to the old familiar grammar, my abiding image of myself. Which meant that things done during the time that was missing would have been done according to the same rules I'd always set myself, an imperfect man trying to deal honestly with the world; and that meant that there was fraud and deception here somehow, though I couldn't understand it. I was who I was, who I always had been: and the Jonty Marks whose life I had lived would no more have got involved with Vernon Deverill than he would have left Carol in order to marry a stranger . . .

I was drifting, daydreaming almost, trying to construct this impossible world to see how it would look, and denying it even as I built. Perhaps the nurse thought that I was sleeping at last. At any rate she left me, as quietly as her heavy body would allow; and the click of the door's closing brought me back, and with no audience, no distractions, I could turn my fingers and my thoughts, my spindizzy mind in my aching head to the scatter of stuff on the bedspread.

Not the car keys, they presumably got mangled along with the car and me; but my house keys were there, or I thought they were. Briefly. My key wallet was: worn black leather, anciently familiar to eyes and touch. I'd won it on a tombola stall at a church bazaar when I was thirteen, and always used it since. But when I popped it open, most of the keys inside were wrong. Wrong colours, wrong lengths and the wards made unfamiliar patterns against my palm.

For a minute, two minutes, five I played those keys between my fingers, and recognised only a couple of them, the ones that would let me into my mother's house. Otherwise it seemed I could only open doors that were strange to me, I knew not where. If this was a con – and surely, surely it had somehow to be a con – then it was a mind-bendingly efficient one.

We might have changed the locks, I supposed, Carol and I, in these two or three missing months. New keys for our old home, I might have; but I didn't think so. Especially when the next thing I picked up was my old purse, just as certainly my own, and the first thing I saw when I opened it was a photo of Sue smiling out at me from behind plastic. I felt like Patrick McGoohan, waking to wicked if invisible chains. As an exercise in brainwashing this was superb, except that everything they wanted me to accept was impossibly out of tune with who and what I was. I'd never carried a photo of any girl in my purse; didn't see the point. I always had better and more intimate pictures in my head, ever ready for private viewing.

The picture was a head-and-shoulders shot cropped from a larger photograph. I slipped it out of the pocket designed to hold it, and wasn't at all surprised to find it inscribed on the back. 'Jonty – all my love, Sue.' Plain, simple, affecting, and I didn't credit a word of it. Efficiency, that was all. And Christ knew, if she'd sat at my bedside for three days she'd had time enough to fiddle unobserved with everything that was mine. Except my mind, except my mind, except my mind . . .

Her luck, perhaps, that my mind was letting me down; she couldn't have anticipated that. Which being the case, I didn't see how she'd ever expected this scam to work, whatever its purpose; but she'd worked so hard, there must have been something. Some benefit to her in deceiving other people, perhaps, even if she couldn't have hoped to deceive me. And then I woke up and my memory had holes in, and she thought maybe she'd have a try at the big one . . .

Did I believe that? No. It didn't work. Nothing worked. I had the pieces of two separate jigsaws in my head, and try as I might they would not fit together.

But perhaps they didn't need to. One of them was mine, and the other definitely not; I could throw that away, perhaps, and never heed it. Sue had gone, I knew not where; she might not even come back. Please? Then I could simply get on with recovering the life I knew, and not worry . . .

A quiet voice in my head somewhere, the whisper of reason reminded me that there were too many questions unanswered that I couldn't very well walk away from; and it reminded me also that there was no sign of Carol here, nor any message from her. No flowers, from a long-time partner who valued all the traditional gestures: Christmas stockings and Valentine cards, Easter eggs and birthday bonks and definitely, very definitely flowers and grapes in hospital. I tried grandly to ignore that massive absence, with little success until my eyes fell again to the personal knick-knacks spread across my lap.

After the photo and the keys, it was no major surprise to find a ring also. Plain gold, the inside cut with initials, a date and a promise. JM & SCM, 29 FEB AND FOR EVER. Expensive business, setting up a scam: this was a good ring. And it fitted. They hadn't managed to make a paler mark on my finger, where presumably I was supposed to have been wearing it, but perhaps I was supposed not to have had time to acquire one. Less than two months, after all, and only weak spring sunlight to take a tan from, even if my job ever gave me time to see the sun . . .

My job or my new wife, of course, they had that also to argue with.

There was other jewellery here, though I never wore any. A single long, dangling earring, cheap and attractive and undeniably female: not Carol's, of course, but Sue would presumably claim it as her own. More verisimilitude, I supposed. A fine gold chain that might have been meant for a man or a woman, though Sue only wore silver, at least so far as I'd seen in one meeting; and if there was a message in that, *this one's yours, boy*, then there was a terrifyingly subtle mind at work here. A stud and a ring also for pierced ears and in gold again, heavy enough for a bloke; but they'd fallen down there at least, because my ears weren't pierced.

At least . . .

No mirror within reach, but my fumbling fingers found a little dimple in one lobe and then in the other, where they stuck out below the bandaging. I wasn't even surprised. I'd gone beyond that, somehow, so far that only their failure in a matter of such crucial detail could possibly have surprised me. Cue the theme for *The Twilight Zone*, and hear me hum along.

A practical man, a dependent man in a hell of a muddle, I did what came naturally to me. There was a phone by the bed; I picked it up, and called Carol.

At work, where she should still be: I got a colleague and a mutual friend, who sounded strangely hesitant when she realised who she was speaking to. She said, "I'll try," not "I'll get her"; and she came back a minute later to say, "I'm sorry, Jonty, she won't speak to you."

I left it an hour, then tried again. Dialled our home number this time, and heard Carol's voice recite it, as she always did; said, "It's me," and heard the sudden silence, and the click thereafter as she hung up on me. Dialled again, dialled many times and got nothing but the engaged signal each time.

I should phone a friend instead, I thought, see what they could tell me; but the timing was bad. People would be getting in from work, maybe dealing with fractious babies or starting to cook dinner, certainly wanting to relax. Leave it till later, I told myself, make it easier on them. I needed someone I could talk to, not someone who had one eye on a crawling kid and the other on burning toast.

A couple of hours, I thought I'd give them; but after a couple of hours *The Twilight Zone* was in my head again and playing so loud I could barely hear anything else, except for Sue's voice calling me husband, lover, friend.

She had come back, contrary to hope or expectation; and when she came, she brought photographs with her.

And yes, that was me in the middle there: despite the unfamiliar suit (Issey Miyake, she told me) and the glint of an earring, that was unquestionably me. And yes, that was Nick Beatty beside me, known of course as Warren, my oldest and closest friend doing a friend's duty here and holding me up with a hug; and yes – alas! – that was undeniably Sue beside me, her arm slipped laughingly, possessively through mine. And these to this side were my friends and family, whom I knew and could name, every one; and those to that side were hers, whom I didn't and couldn't. And the background might look like a warehouse but it wasn't, she said, it was her parents' church, Catholic Chinese; and apart from that, she said, everything was exactly what it seemed.

That was the two of us, she said, getting married; and here was another picture of the two of us setting off on our honeymoon – Hong Kong, she said, and it rained all week, so no tan; but at home she had photos of that also, which she'd bring next time to show me – and that was James the Second I was driving, the sports car I'd totalled on an empty road in Cumbria just six weeks later.

My car, she said, not hers.

Then she kissed me, and she tasted of smoky tea and spices, alien to me.

And then, maybe seeing that this was too much, that I really couldn't cope any longer, she changed the subject.

"I saw your friend Luke on the telly last night," she said. "Luke the angel. Falling," with a giggle that was more nerves than amusement. "I'm sorry, I never believed you before, not about him. Not till I saw . . ."

And if I'd never believed her before, I believed her then. Suddenly I believed it all, though none of it made sense yet. Luke was not exactly private, not a secret, but still he was special to me; not for sharing unless with someone who ranked also as special, a lover or a good close friend.

• TWO •

SIGHTS FOR SORE EYES

So did I sleep that night?

Bet your sweet life I slept. No point enduring hospital food and hospital hours, no point taking up a hospital bed at all unless you take also every possible advantage of the facilities. I whimpered and fussed, I said every part of me hurt, I told them I was scared of the dark – and no lie that, I was terrified of its implications: the long sightless hours where your thoughts blunder heedlessly in circles, lost among landscapes extrapolated from known anxieties into horrorshows of anticipation – and at last they gave me a jab, if only to shut me up. One needle into the left buttock with what seemed to me unnecessary vigour, the payback for my being awkward, and I slept like a chemically-saturated log until a male nurse came to wake me at some godforsaken hour of the morning.

An insipid cup of tea clattered onto the locker; he gave me a practised smile to go with it, the promise of breakfast in an hour and in the meantime how about a blanket bath?

"Any chance of a real one instead?" I asked plaintively.

"Not a hope in hell," and oh, he was cheerful about it. "You don't shift from that bed till Mr Coffey says you can. Besides, I'm not replacing all your dressings for you. Settle for a bed-bath, eh? You'll be getting nice clean sheets in a bit, shame to lie on them all mucky . . ."

Truly, I did feel dirty: or stale and greasy, rather, with gunk clagging in the corners of my eyes. What I wanted was a long soak in scalding water, to wash me all the way through to my bones; but we clearly weren't operating to my agenda here and I didn't want to make enemies to no good purpose. So, "Okay," I said. "Better than nothing. But just give me a bowl of water and some soap and let me get on with it, yeah?"

"I wasn't suggesting anything else. Any patient with one good hand gets to wash their own goolies. Even when they go private . . ."

A grin, more genuine this time, to acknowledge that this relationship was already headed the way he wanted it to go, two young blokes joshing together on an equal footing; and then he left me. Left me wondering and uncertain, and wanting to ask a question that was going to sound stupid, whichever way the answer went.

But hell, stupid I could manage, I could live with; God knew, I must have sounded stupid enough yesterday. *'Who are you?' 'I'm your wife, darling, I'm the woman you're in love with.'* Words to that effect, at least; and I'd sooner remember the effect than the words themselves. Sooner still be sitting in a barrel going over Niagara, I thought that would probably be a more comfortable experience, but *one thing at a time, Jonty* . . .

The good news, I supposed, was that I could remember all the words from yesterday, and their several effects. It wasn't seemingly an ongoing thing, this memory loss, I wasn't going to wake up every morning with no recollection of the day before. I could start building a life again, at least, on this bank of the river. Though I thought I'd be spending much time, too much time, maybe all my time for the foreseeable future gazing at the further bank, and trying to build bridges.

Any information could serve as a rope, or a plank, or a concrete pile; so when the nurse came back – to fill a bowl at the basin in the corner, to lay out bowl and towel, soap and flannel on the locker where I could reach them and to add shaving gear and a small mirror because Sue hadn't made good her threat to shave me last night, I'd been too upset, but the scabs on my face were twelve hours less fresh now and the hospital didn't like stubble any more than she did – I asked him straight out, "Is this a private room?"

"Yes, of course," he said, startled, smiling. "Didn't you know?"

No, I didn't know. I'd had to work it out. Good practice, I suspected, for a whole lot more upcoming that I'd be expected to know or to remember, that I'd have to work out on my fingers. But all my time in hospitals, whether resident or visiting, had only ever shown me two standards of accommodation: solo rooms for the rich, and wards for the hoi-polloi. I was prepared to believe that there might be provision to put NHS patients on their own, when their condition required that; but a bad head and bruises were surely not enough. Neither a lapse in memory.

Nor was one question, one answer enough. Answers breed questions, inevitably; every step forward only shows us new horizons, just as far away.

"Who's paying for it?"

"I wouldn't know, would I? Aren't you?"

There at least was one answer that I knew already. No, I wasn't. My company had offered private health insurance in my contract, but I'd turned it down in an excess of political zeal. Carol had been angry, I remembered: wanted to know what was the point of saying no to something that would cost me nothing, that would give me regular check-ups and have me high-stepping over the queues whenever I needed treatment. Me, I'd wanted to know what was the point of the company paying for something that I was entitled to for nothing; every private patient, I'd said, costs the people more than the Exchequer saves. It's a trickle effect, I'd said: private work saps quality staff from where they're needed more, and the more people go private the more they endanger the whole future of the NHS. What will be the need for it, after all, when the majority of the population has made other arrangements? Slippery slope, I'd said; and down at the bottom there are ambulance drivers wanting to see a credit card or a policy document before they'll scrape you off the tarmac . . .

All of that I'd said; and here I was, scraped off the tarmac myself and hustled off into a private room without the chance to gainsay it, and if Sue were responsible for this she'd be in trouble next time she showed her face around the door . . .

The nurse was called Simon, he said, and he didn't have any problem with the idea that I wanted to be alone while I washed, for all that he and half a dozen others had presumably had me naked under their hands often enough in the last few days. I'd been unconscious then; now I was back in my body, and not actually being foolishly modest about it, despite appearances. I wanted to rediscover it, I guess, to take possession again: to learn exactly what the damage was, and to do it unobserved.

Simon seemed to understand that, without my having to explain. At any rate, he left me to peel back the covers on my own, and check out as much as I could see for dressings.

Hadn't felt up to this yesterday, the mental shocks had been enough. But my whirligig mind had run somewhat out of whirl, during seven or eight hours'-worth of drug-induced coma. I didn't like it, that I had apparently total memory loss for a significant period – no, more than significant, a Richter-scale earthquake of a period – of my recent life; but acceptance had at least settled like sediment, if it hadn't dissolved like sugar. It was a fact that inhabited my head like a tumour, like a stranger, but it was at least there and I could handle it. I could mediate all my thinking through that, not to make too great an idiot of myself hereinafter.

Getting that sussed, getting – you should excuse the expression – my head around it, however temporarily (no illusions here: I could think myself perfectly in control of the situation, and five minutes later be a shrinking, whingeing wreck again for no material reason at all, only that some synapse in my brain had gone zip instead of zap, and thrown me into panic mode): even if I was only suppressing questions that would have to be confronted later, that suppression still left me free to be curious at last about my physical condition. Everything was functioning well enough, that much I'd gathered; I didn't even have the tube in my arm any more, now that they could feed me their slops by mouth. But at the same time, everything hurt. I hadn't been lying to the nurses and the night sister to get my sleepy-jab, only exaggerating for effect.

So I threw the covers back – or I didn't, to be honest, I pulled them gingerly aside; and the gingerliness wasn't only due to my sore arms and aching shoulders not wanting to work that hard, I was chicken too. And I worked off the hospital robe they'd made me wear in lieu of the pyjamas that Sue said I didn't have, that she hadn't wanted to shop for until I was conscious. Robes were easier for the nurses, she'd said, and if I was going to have to wear stuff in bed at least I was entitled to a choice. Cotton or silk? she'd asked; and what colours would I like? Christ, I'd said, I didn't care. Bog-standard Marks and Sparks would do fine, I'd said, might as well keep it in the family.

No relation, she'd said, you can't catch me that way.

Actually I hadn't been trying to just then, but she wouldn't believe me; and to go on from there to ask what had happened to the several pairs of pyjamas that I did indeed own, that I wore every night in bed with

Carol, had seemed suddenly just too much trouble to contemplate.

But that was last night and this was still abominably early in the morning, and I was still wearing a hospital robe. Easier for the staff, and actually easier for me too, with the stiffness and pain of every movement. It fastened with bows, for God's sake, all down the back; I rolled onto my side and worked a hand slowly along my spine, tugging them undone. Then I slipped it off my shoulders; and then I flopped flat and lay still for a couple of minutes, only my head raised up, only looking at my skin and not trying to see any deeper. Trying not to, indeed. Skin was enough, skin was plenty.

I guess my skin that morning was only showing me what a body, what any body might look like after undergoing wicked deceleration in a tumbling, tearing, buckling metal shell; except that I had a lucky body, because ordinarily you'd be looking more than skin deep and still finding damage, unless you were seeing things not skin risen to the surface, bones and wet things being worn externally for a change. Only talking bodies here, of course, not talking heads. I couldn't see my head without picking up the mirror, and that was for later; but bodywise, no question, I was lucky.

Lucky to be all black and blue where I wasn't fading gently towards yellow, almost every visible inch of me a bruise, and no wonder I felt so sore. No little wonder if I'd blocked off the memory of its happening, either; that was a major wonder, and I was wonderfully grateful, though I'd have preferred not to have lost so much baby with the bathwater.

Looking more closely, even between the metres of sticking-plaster and cotton padding that made a patchwork man of me I could see a diagnostic pattern to the weight and colour of the bruising, and I was monkey enough –

monkeypuzzle man – to work it out slowly. Black diagonal like a heraldic bar, drawn from right shoulder to left hip, two or three inches wide with a herring-bone texture and strikingly distinct edges; that must be where the seat belt had caught and held me. Bless the thing. I might apparently have been driving a fast car crazy-fast on a dangerous road, but at least I'd retained that much sense, to wear a belt. Or more likely it wasn't sense at all, it was pure instinct: just something I did every time I got into a car, and surviving even when my famous common sense seemed to have died the death.

Blurring the centre of that strong diagonal was a massive disc of dark, which must have been the steering column slamming into me as the car folded up, in spite of the seat belt's good retentive work. No air bag, presumably, in this MR2. Which was yet more evidence of how wrong the story was, for all that I had to believe it; because I couldn't believe I'd buy any car without one, let alone a car built purely for speed.

Unless you just bought it to impress, a quiet, suspicious voice murmured in the back of my mind. *Like to impress a girl, maybe? Young, beautiful, and you with some kind of seven-year itch going on?*

I didn't remember any itching, I'd thought myself settled and content; but something had happened to deny that. So much was clear, undeniable.

Only that it had happened to someone else, effectively. I didn't recognise either the actions of this supposed, this apparent Jonty Marks or the motives that had driven him; he was as much a stranger to me as Sue was. Myself and my wife, and I didn't know either one of them . . .

Finding myself straying into abstraction again, drifting into muddled and misty tales that I couldn't get a finger's good hold on, I pulled myself sharply back to what was actual and solid and very much there, very much attached to me in a way that these stories were not: my body, as it lay in this bed.

The torso told the tale, seat belt and steering column vividly marked out. For the rest of me, my arms and legs were where most of the patching-up had been done, as I guess you'd expect from a man strapped into a rolling car; it's got to be flailing limbs that take most damage. I couldn't see the damage, for all the dressings; nothing too horrendous, though, by the feel of things. It hurt to move them, but that was more wrenched joints than anything else, I thought, whiplash-equivalents for elbows and knees. Lucky again, when you thought of the fragility of bone within a failing steel cage . . .

Fragile bone in manky skin, and I had hot water at my side. Reached for flannel and soap, and grunted sharply as something stabbed and twisted in my shoulder.

Nothing, I told myself, *it's only muscles yanked about too hard, maybe a bit of ripped tissue, that's all, barely more than a stiff neck from sleeping wonky . . .*

Maybe so, but it felt like flexible steel, it felt like a blade buried between bruised flesh and battered bone. I'd stretched and shifted about in bed hitherto, and thought I'd learned the extent of my discomfort; but now I was actually trying to *do* something, I found out just how wrong I'd been. My fingers had problems enough picking up the flannel; getting my other arm across to handle the soap was agonising.

If I hurt this much now, I thought maybe I should be grateful for having spent three days unconscious, having slept through what must have been worse.

Would have been grateful to have slept through this also, to have been cleaned up in the night. And though I didn't, I wouldn't ring the bell for help, I was nothing but grateful when Simon put his head around the door after ten minutes or so and said, "How are you doing, then? Need any help?"

I'd have waved the white flannel at him like a flag of surrender, only that I rather thought I'd drop it. Instead, "Bit of a problem bending," I muttered, gazing all the length of me at the impossibility of feet.

"Thought you might. You tell me how far you've got, and I'll do the rest."

He washed my feet and legs for me as briskly and efficiently as an undertaker washing a corpse, except that undertakers don't presumably keep up a constant stream of chatter with their clients as they lave; then he helped me roll over and did my back, brought me a clean robe and knotted me into it, settled me against a mound of pillows and shaved me neatly.

"Anything else now, before I bring your breakfast?"

"Yes," I said, running a hand slowly over smoothness of skin between scabs and thinking how much I liked being shaved, how much I hated shaving, "are you available for hire?"

"Bar mitzvahs, weddings and funerals," he said cheerfully. "Bar mitzvah boys don't shave, and you're already married. You could hire me for your funeral, I suppose. Money in advance."

He waited, I suppose for a smile or a swear-word; but got neither, because he'd caught me in the gut unintentionally, sent me plummeting back into confusion. Married I was, I accepted that, but acceptance made none of it any easier to handle. Married to a stranger, I was still in love with Carol if with anyone. I hadn't thought about it, I supposed, for years; not in those terms. But if knowledge and understanding, comfort and affection and concern added up to love – which I thought they did, pretty much, I felt that would be an adult definition of the word – then yes, I was in love with Carol.

And she with me? I would have said so, by the same definition. Three months ago – the latest I could remember

– I would definitely have said yes to that, and so I thought would she. But she hadn't so much as sent me flowers, and Carol sent flowers to bare acquaintances who found themselves in hospital. Could be she didn't know I was here, of course; but she'd also slammed the phone down on me without saying a word, without giving me the chance to tell her. Carol, I thought – knowing her, understanding her – was deeply, deeply angry.

That was one of the two certainties I could find in my life that morning, and neither one gave me much to hold on to. First, Carol was angry with me, and no blame to her for that; and second, by whatever definition you chose to measure it, I was certainly not in love with my wife.

Oh, *God* . . .

What I wanted that morning was metaphorical dressing-gown, teddy bear and cocoa, all the comforts of childhood against an adult world: I wanted to curl up in some fœtal space, to know that I was safe and someone else was out there coping for me, sorting all my problems.

What I got instead was doctors and nurses, my sheets changed and my mind only a little reassured. The amnesia should pass, they said, but I would have to give it time. Meanwhile just rest, they said, watch telly or listen to the radio, don't try to read if your head's still aching . . .

Then they left me alone again. And no, I didn't watch telly or listen to the radio, neither did I read or rest. I only lay there fretting, wondering, too sore to move and too confused to sleep.

It was almost a relief when Sue turned up.

Almost? Nah. It was definitely, absolutely a relief. She got me out of there, if only on a limited licence.

Breezed in, she did, just after lunch, wearing black denim and a baseball cap, black again with a silver-blue logo, *Q's* above the peak. She kissed me quick but unhurried, which is a neat trick if you can do it, which she could. I guess the quick was in case I showed signs of pulling back, the unhurried was purely for pleasure. Then she patted my shaved cheek approvingly, picked a little at one of my scabs and hissed apologetically when I winced, laughed when I pushed her away; and said she had permission to take me out.

"Only for a bit, mind. And if you act weird I have to bring you straight back again, so mind you behave yourself."

"Where are we going?" I asked cautiously.

"Just out. Out and about."

Out was good, out was great, a temporary release the closest I could hope to come today to dressing-gown and cocoa. *Out with Sue* was more problematic.

"Tell me," I said.

"Trust me," she countered instantly. "We'll go for a drive, here and there, and then I'll bring you back. It won't hurt, Jonty. Promise." Then she grinned, and added, "I already had to promise them, twenty miles an hour and no sharp stops, and nothing you could bang your head on. We're going on a tall person's drive."

She said that, she said that and *Trust me*, and then she helped me dress. Clothes she'd brought with her, nothing I'd seen before: silk shirt and soft baggy cotton trousers, thin warm socks and moccasins. All in black, matching outfits; and all a perfect fit, all showing signs of having been worn and washed.

Nor was that all. At her quiet insistence, by virtue of her clever fingers the stud and the ring went back into my ears; she fastened the chain around my neck, and I tried not to see a symbol in that; she put the wedding-ring onto the third finger of my left hand and said, "With this ring I thee wed *again*, Jonathan Marks, and don't you forget again . . ."

A nurse fetched a wheelchair; Sue pushed me through the corridors to the exit, and out to her car; and I said, "A tall person's drive, you told me."

"Okay. A tall person's drive in a small person's car. I'll drive like a tall person, I promise. Well, not like you. I won't drive like you, you crash things . . ."

It was no big surprise, I guess, that Sue drove a Mini Cooper. It suited: a short, aggressive little car, gloss black and gleaming clean, all the windows tinted as dark as the law allowed. What was more surprising was when she helped me up out of the wheelchair, and really was a help to me. She was small, but she was springy; I leaned on her more than I meant or wanted to, and she showed not a sign of buckling.

"Duck," she said, hand firm on the back of my neck to encourage me. "Duck and fold, don't you *dare* bang your head or I'm taking you straight back . . ."

I didn't bang my head. What I did, though, I caught a glimpse of my face reflected in that darkened glass, as I ducked and folded.

Caught a glimpse, and couldn't believe it.

Once I was in and she'd slammed the door on me I pulled the sun-visor down to get at the vanity mirror, looked again; and was still staring as she got in the driver's side and caught me at it, and I didn't know what the hell to say.

Not a problem. She did. She'd probably been practising, only waiting for the moment.

"Bad hair day, huh? Never mind, we all have 'em," touching the peak of her cap in a conspiratorial gesture, *me too, why d'you think I'm wearing this?*

"It's not my hair," I said wearily, stupidly. She knew that. Neither one of us could see my hair.

She smiled, with I thought a little effort, and tried again. "Is this the face that lunched on a thousand chips? I kept telling you they're bad for the complexion. You wouldn't listen, and look at you now."

"No, thanks," I said, shoving the visor up again, hiding from myself.

I looked monstrous. The bandage around my head I knew about already, but I had two appalling black eyes to go with it, like I was trying for the fashionable panda look, and all the flesh of my face was dark and swollen and a nest of worms, thread-like scabs clinging to mark where the windscreen glass had scarified me.

"Shaving didn't help much, did it?" I said, actually wondering how the hell Simon had navigated the razor around and between all those cuts, without slicing the scabs off and setting the blood to run again.

"Vain pig. Did it hurt?"

"Everything hurts," I said grumpily. She patted my knee and I could have bitten her, except that my teeth also hurt. "But no, getting shaved was okay. Simon did it."

"Did he? That's nice. That's service, I guess. But don't worry about your face, the doctors said there's nothing permanent. You'll play the violin again. On my heartstrings," grinning at me sideways, pleased with herself.

I was already off on another track, impatient with banter. "Sue, who's paying for the room I'm in? Who sent me private?"

"Vernon Deverill. Soon as he heard about the accident, he had you transferred. I guess he's picking up all the bills, unless you've got some arrangement . . . ?"

I shook my head slowly. "I don't know Vernon Deverill. Not like this." Again I was thinking *scam*, thinking *set-up*, thinking how easy it would be to black a solicitor's name with gifts when he was unconscious, and wondering why the hell he'd want to, why pick on me?

"You've been pretty thick with him, the last two months," she said. "For a man who doesn't know a man, I mean."

I don't know you either, and I married you. But that was evidence for the prosecution, not the defence. I felt very ill-defended: caught in possession, with nothing to offer but feeble denials – *not my life, not my wife* – and even my own mind turned accusatory, no longer believing myself. This would be the fast track to schizophrenia, I thought, if I allowed it.

"Where are we going, Sue?" Second time of asking, and I don't think I expected an answer this time either. Nor did I get one.

"Okay," she said. "You don't want to talk about Vernon Deverill, that's fine. I don't like him. Where do you want to go?"

"Away from here is fine. I'm not ambitious, just curious. You're taking me somewhere, and I don't like surprises."

She snorted at that, and I was aware of the irony myself, a moment too late. Right now, all my life was a surprise to me. It was true, though, I wasn't enjoying any of it.

"I thought I'd show you some of the sights," she said, "try if that jolts your memory at all. That's what I told the doctors, anyway, it was the only way I could get you an exeat. Might work, you never can tell."

"Uh-huh. So what's the real reason?"

A flicker of her eyes, and then she was totally inscrutable of face and voice both as she said, "I just want to spend an hour or two with my husband, all right? Just the two of us, no nurses banging in and out, no visitors, no nobody."

"Sue, listen . . . Okay, you've got some photos, and I guess they're proof of something. But whatever happened, that still doesn't make me the man you married. None of what you're saying fits me, or anything I know about myself. It's not just that I don't remember doing this stuff, it doesn't make sense to me that I ever would have done it. I'm sorry, but the man inside here," and I lifted a hand to tap my head, only just remembered in time not to do that, "is not your husband. Whatever I look like, inside I'm just not the same person . . ."

"Actually," she said, "you don't look the part either, right now. My Jonty's pretty, wouldn't have married him else. That makes it easier, a bit. So all right, let's just play the doctors' game for them. You be what the hell you want to be; I'm the tour guide. I'm supposed to be driving you around to see what you recognise, so don't ask where we're going. I want you to tell me, soon as you figure it out."

It wouldn't, it couldn't work, and so I told her. I knew the streets of the city too well; they'd been my playground as a student here and my workplace since, they held many memories from many years and I could summon up all of those with no effort at all, and of course none of them was a memory of her.

She just nodded, shrugged, told me not to worry about it.

And took me somewhere I'd never been in my life.

It wasn't that mysterious really, only a suburb that was too dull for students and too posh for any of my clients, too far from the centre and too insulated for me or anyone ever to have passed through it on the way from somewhere to somewhere else. It existed *sui generis*, encircled by roads and its own smug contentment, a bourgeois province that needed no more than its own reputation to keep it so.

Semis to the right of us, semis to the left of us, no access to the motorway ahead; and if this wasn't the valley of the dead that we drove along, it was a pretty fair imitation. Me, I liked the quiet life, but this . . .

This was the main shopping street, for all those souls who preferred not to take the Metro to M & S and Bainbridge's in town. There were local equivalents, clothes shops catering for no one but the middle-class, middle-brow, middle-income Middle England; I even saw one emporium that still bore its title in gilded letters on the window, *Draper and Haberdasher*. Every shopfront carried an individual trader's name; there were no chains here, no video stores or supermarkets, nothing so common.

And we parked right there, on this Street that Time Forgot, and her ladyship looked at me expectantly, teasing and hopeful both. Something here, then, something I was meant to see or react to. It had to be the shops, surely, there was nothing else; I looked more carefully. An ironmonger – and yes, again, it still called itself an ironmonger, and I wondered if they still sold screws loose by weight, from little wooden drawers – and a bakery where surely they still baked their own bread on the premises. And a delicatessen with small ill-lit windows and a display of tins so drab it didn't even tempt me out of the car; and a Chinese takeaway, and . . .

Ah.

Sue had wound the window down on her side, and was resting her elbow on the rim.

"Take your time," she said, taking a pack of Gauloises from her jacket pocket and tapping a cigarette out, finding a brass Zippo in another pocket, lighting up.

A smoker. I'd married a smoker . . .

"It's the takeaway," I said. "Right?"

"Bingo."

Made sense. She was a Chinese girl, after all. That was the only conceivable relationship, between this girl and this street. I supposed that I could live here, or make some shift at living; a creature of habit I, and already too many of the habits of age. But not she; she'd be as much an alien here as she was to me. Even her car didn't belong in this traffic.

The Sunniside Chinese Takeaway, it was called, no clues there. But I felt confident enough to chance my arm.

"Your parents?"

"Yes! Brilliant, did you . . . ?"

But the enthusiasm that made scrutable all her feelings on her face died quickly, as she read my own on mine.

"I'm sorry," I said, "that wasn't fair. I didn't remember, I was guessing."

"Unh. Well, good guess, then."

"It wasn't hard. Why are we here, Sue?" Not just so that she could show me her parents' place of business; I'd guessed that also, it had to have some greater significance than that.

"This was where we met," she said.

"Oh. Right. Uh, how, then?"

"Over a No 37, with fried rice and a Coke," she said, straight-faced.

"I never ordered anything by number." And this time I really was certain, or wanted to be. I might have married a smoking stranger, three impossibilities in a single incredible act; but surely not that, not so ignorant and patronising. Please . . . ?

"No, all right," she said, grinning now, *only winding you up, Jonty*. And maybe making a point also, that she knew me well enough to do it. "It was a Special Chop Suey, actually. Which is No 37, but no, you didn't ask for it by number."

I nodded, sat back, gazed blankly at the takeaway's frontage for a minute while she ostentatiously blew smoke out of the car, and either I was being hypersensitive here or this was also a message, or the same one again, *see how well I know you, Jonty? Husband mine? You hate the smell of cigarettes, but you married me anyway . . .*

Then, "What the hell was I doing here?" *Never been here in my life, guv, can't think of a reason why I would.*

"I don't know. You didn't say."

"So what did I say?"

"'No 37, fried rice and a Coke. Please.'" But she glanced at me, shrugged a quick apology for more than the number-slander, and said, "Seriously?"

"Seriously."

"You don't want to go in, try to remember? Mum'll be there, if Dad isn't . . ."

"No. I'm sorry, Sue, but . . . No. I don't want to do that. Not yet."

"Fair enough. I suppose."

"To be honest," I said, "I don't want to move at all, unless it's back into bed."

She looked at me sharply, anxiously. "Not feeling good?"

"Not very."

"Shall I take you back?"

I shook my head, slowly and carefully; my neck was as stiff and sore as the rest of me. Lucky not to be in a surgical collar, I thought; but that was only a side-effect of the big one. The bone-deep discomfort of sitting in a cramping car was a constant and increasing reminder, how lucky I was to be alive.

"No," I said when the headshake didn't seem to be enough, she didn't look persuaded. "Truly, I don't want to go back. It's only the body getting through to me, nothing to worry about. The head's fine. And I hate hospitals, I'm dead glad to get out."

"Yes, but you hate being driven, too," she said. Scoring points again, I thought, making demonstration, how well she knew me.

It was true enough, normally I loathed being a passenger in someone, anyone else's car; but, "I'm in no condition to drive," I said, "and I'd sooner be out than in. Besides, I've just discovered one major advantage to sitting this side."

"What's that, then?"

"The seat belt goes the other way."

It took her a second, but she caught on; she'd seen the diagonal bar of bruising on my chest, when she helped me into these utterly comfortable, utterly unfamiliar clothes. I'd tried to chase her out, but, "I'm your *wife*, for God's sake,

Jonty," and I couldn't argue with that. Or with her, really, she was adamantine with spikes on.

Come to think of it, she'd have seen all the damage before that. Three days she'd sat by my bedside, they'd told me; and I couldn't see her leaving the room at their request if she wouldn't leave at mine. She'd have seen them washing me, changing the dressings, whatever; likely she'd have joined in, if she was allowed.

So yes, she'd know where I was hurting; she'd understand how relieved I was, not to have the belt lie tight across the worst of it. And of course she'd accuse herself, I could see her doing it; she would say, as she did say, "Have I been driving too fast?"

"No. It's just the nature of seat belts, you feel them. Stop fretting. You were going to tell me, how we met . . . ?"

"Oh. Yes. All right . . ." She gazed across the street at the takeaway, and a smile touched her lips; genuine amusement, I thought, rather than just the romance of nostalgia. And sure enough,

"You were awful," she said. "Or I thought you were, at first. It was late, it was my night off so I was helping here, I used to do that. Back then, I used to," with a sidelong glance at me, *before you changed things*. "And you came in, it was only ten minutes before closing and there was no one else in, it's quiet here even at the weekends. Not like the other side of town, we don't get the closing-time trade out here."

"No, I can imagine." Looking up and down the street, I couldn't see a pub. A hotel down on the corner, yes, offering B & B no doubt to the genteel; they'd have a public bar, but probably little enough custom.

"Right. Anyway, there you were, coming in and asking if you were too late. Which you were, almost; but it was nice of you to ask, I thought, so I said no, it was okay. And you looked knackered, and you ordered dead quick, first thing you saw on the menu, almost, so I figured you were starving hungry with it.

"So I called the order through the hatch to Dad, and turned the telly back on to give you something to look at while you waited; but when I turned round it was me you were looking at. Staring at. It was creepy. I mean, I'm used to it, sort of, you weren't exactly the first; but with you being the only person in, and it was dark outside and there was no traffic on the street or anything, and you just stood there not saying anything, just watching every move I made, catching my eye every time I looked at you, not even blinking when I tried to stare you down . . . And you weren't even smiling, just, just *looking* . . . I got scared, a bit."

"I'm not surprised," I murmured. I couldn't relate this to me at all, it was a story about a stranger; but I wanted to know the ending, so, "What did you do?"

"Went back to help clean up in the kitchen, and asked Mum to take your meal out when it was ready." Smiling again, she added, "I told her you were another kinky white boy hot for little yellow sister. She still doesn't like you very much."

Well, no. I could see that. Six or eight weeks was not very long to win over a doubting mother-in-law, especially one who'd been however briefly encouraged to think of you – of me – as a toe-rag only interested in her daughter for the basest of reasons. Parents and children traditionally have problems with each other's sex-lives; no blame to her if Mrs Chu still saw only slobber and lust when she looked at me, still watched my fingers and wondered where they'd been and what they'd done, on or inside her daughter's blessed body . . .

Me, too. I looked at my own fingers, and wondered. Like everything else, my sex-life had been settled and familiar for a long time now, comfortable and contented, no risks sought or taken. It seemed unlikely somehow that the same would apply or be allowed to apply with Sue. Sleeping with a new partner was always different; but this was not only a question of a different body, a different nature, different habits learned. Sue's soul, I thought, inhabited another realm from Carol's. Their genes, I thought, were perhaps the least part of their difference; and *vive la différence*, I thought, and . . .

And what the hell was I doing, thinking this way? Proving Sue right, perhaps, showing that I was after all only a kinky white boy with the hots for little yellow sister; because Sue might impossibly be my wife but Carol was my partner still, I'd been faithful to her through all the years we'd been together and maybe I'd had a brainstorm a couple of months back but I'd recovered now, the knock on the head had maybe knocked things back into shape again and I wasn't, I was *not* even going to fantasise about sleeping with Sue.

Even if I'd already done it. Some crazy variant on wanking with a mirror, that would be, fantasising about my own sex-life . . .

"So was that it?" I asked, dragging my attention back to the story before she read my thoughts on my face, infinitely scrutable Westerner that I knew myself to be. "You sold me a meal and then hid out in the kitchen, and that was that?"

"No," she said, "that wasn't that. You were really going for the dirty-old-man act that night, I could've called the cops on you. We got everything ready for next day, and then we locked up. Mum and Dad went off home, they only live round the corner from here; and I walked down to where I'd parked, and on the way I had to walk past this Volvo, and I got the shock of my life because I was just doing that when the door opened and you jumped out. With all the wrappings and containers in your hands, you'd bought a fork from Mum and eaten your dinner in the dark, just sitting in your car there watching for me. I think you

were trying to pretend you'd just finished and you'd only
got out to dump the leftovers, but you didn't do it very well.
Just stood there staring at me again.

"And I wasn't going to scream or run away, I've got my
pride and I've done defence classes, and anyway I figured you
weren't that much of a threat with your hands full of rubbish.
So I glared at you, fierce as I could manage, and said, 'Well,
what, then? What do you *want?*' And you said you were sorry,
you couldn't think straight and you knew you weren't handling
this very well, you must look like a right creep, you said. And
I said yes, you did, and you said you weren't really, really you
weren't, you said, only you just desperately wanted to talk to
me but you couldn't think of anything to say.

"That made me smile, at least. And then you asked if I'd
go for a drink with you, right then. So I said the pubs were
shut, and you said you knew this place, sort of a private club
we could go to; but I didn't fancy that, not with a stranger.
I didn't trust you at all, only you looked so defenceless
suddenly, all broken was how you looked, like Humpty
Dumpty. So I said no, I wouldn't go to your club, but you
could come to mine. I'm safe there, with people who know
me, and I didn't mind that."

"What club's that, then?" I asked. I knew where she meant
when she talked about my club; if I wanted to drink late in
the city, I went to Salome's. I was curious to know where
she went, what circles she moved in.

"I'll show you," she said. "Next stop on the tour."

And she put the car in gear and pulled out into the traffic,
taking her time about it, not going until she could go nice
and slow and easy: sick person's drive, this was, and very
obviously not her usual style. I could hear her muttering,
cursing under her breath, "Come on, get *on* with it, bloody
Sunday drivers, what are you doing out on the road, it's not
even bloody Sunday . . ."

                    *   *   *

Next stop on the tour didn't at first appear to be clubland.
Next stop was Chinatown.

It wasn't a big place, this particular Chinatown. Lacking
a large community to serve, it wasn't a significant factor in
the city, unless I guess if you happened to be Chinese. Or
married to a Chinese girl, perhaps . . . ?

Basically what we had here was just one long street, lined
with restaurants. One gable-end overlooking a car park had
a neon mural twenty feet high, a pair of Chinese dragons
who glowed brilliantly at night but looked only dusty and
rather drab by day. Pagoda-like arches surmounted the
entrance and exit of the car park, but that was about
the limit of public decoration except at the New Year
celebrations, when they hung lanterns all along the street,
there were firecrackers and burning incense and a dragon
danced for the punters. Probably nine out of ten punters
were white, and I'd always avoided the festivities myself.
Too much of a feeling of Indians dancing for tourists on
the reservation, perhaps, though my boycott on their behalf
was probably as patronising as the TV cameras and the
gawping Caucasian faces. They had their own sensitivity;
in my rational moments, I figured that they probably didn't
need mine.

On one side, all those restaurants backed onto what
remained of the old city wall; there was nothing between but
a dark, dank, evil-smelling alley, slimy cobbles underfoot
and blackened stone on the one hand, blackened brick
and high barred windows on the other, fire exits and
loading-doors that were next to useless because you couldn't
get a truck within fifty metres, everything had to be dragged
along here on a trolley. Any time I had visitors seeing the
city for the first time, this was always a necessary part of the
tour: very Gothic, very mediaeval, and a delicious contrast to
all the glittering, savage modernity upthrusting elsewhere in
the city.

The other side of the street, the restaurants themselves made a wall, a final barrier to the encroachment of that rapacious new development. Even here there were a couple of new car parks, where buildings used to be; visible through those gaps was pale new housing, built with narrow mullioned windows and set around a quad of patchy grass in poor imitation of the fourteenth-century friary just beyond, converted now into a café and craft centre.

I hadn't realised that there was anything here bar places to eat, and a couple of Chinese supermarkets supplying the stuff in the raw for those who knew what to do with it. But Sue twitched the Mini into the kerb and parked it, then got out before I could ask questions. She walked around to my side, opened the door and stood there, very obviously waiting to help me up; I said, "I'd rather not. Really."

"Come on, Jonty," she said gently, implacably. "If it's just muscles and skin that are hurting, a bit of exercise'll do you the world of good. Besides, I want to show you something, and I can't bring it down."

Down didn't sound so good, *down* implied *up* and I wasn't in any condition; but she wasn't brooking any denial on this one, so eventually I levered myself slowly out of the car, she tucked herself under my shoulder for a welcome and necessary support, and she brought me to a door between *King Crab* and *The Peking Wall*.

God alone knows how many times I'd walked that street, and never seen the door. No major surprise, perhaps. I was always hungry, coming down here, always in a party and arguing where to eat: there were probably a dozen, two dozen similar doors I'd never thought to look at, to notice or remember. But it was big enough, in all conscience, and it had half a dozen business plaques screwed to the wall around it, and not all of them were in Chinese. The transom was of darkened glass, with a silver-blue Q's cut into it; lit from behind at night – and it always was night, when I came down here – it would blaze like a beacon.

And I'd been so cocky, *you can't show me anywhere new, not in this city* . . . I winced a little at the memory as we shuffled sideways through the door, and for penance didn't even groan when I saw nothing ahead of me but a steep flight of stairs, rising.

There were a couple of doors on the first landing. One was blank, the other held a sign picked out in ideograms, with an English translation below: *Oriental Herbalist*, it said, *Please ring buzzer and wait.*

"Uncle Han," Sue said in my ear. "As soon as you're out of hospital, I'm taking you to see him. He'll fix you up."

As soon as I'm out of hospital, I thought, *I'm going home to Carol.* But I said nothing, only grunted and turned my attention to the next flight of stairs.

On the second floor, I had to stop to rest. I leaned against the banister, breathing hard, and tried to disguise that with a question. "So what's *Q's*, then, what does it mean?"

"That's the club. It doesn't mean anything to you? Snooker club?"

I shook my head. "No, nothing. Sorry. Why *Q's*?"

"Look," she said, sighing hugely, "just because you've lost your memory doesn't mean you can act stupid. It's a pun, get it? Snooker cues?"

"Oh. Right." *Sorry again*, but I wasn't going to apologise for missing that. I didn't play snooker, and even my mind wasn't looking for puns just now. Wasn't looking for anything, really, was only trying to make sense of what it saw. "Do you work there, or something?"

Her face twisted, just a fraction, before she nodded.

"And this is where you brought me, that first night?"

Another nod.

"So that's what you're taking me up to see, is it?" She was wasting her time and more, wasting what little energy

I had. If nothing had rung any bells so far – hell, if her *face* rang no bells with me – then no snooker club was going to work the magic. That much I was sure of, and so should she have been by now.

And maybe she was, because this time she didn't nod, she said no.

"No, not that. Come on, up we go. Be a hero, be a man, you can make it . . ."

I could and I did, though not without her help. On the third floor, dark double doors had the *Q's* logo again, but we didn't go through.

"That's work," Sue said, with a sideways motion of her head; "this is home," with a forward motion, a nod towards one more bloody flight of stairs.

At the top of that was a single door, blank and unrevealing; to one side was a bellpush, with a name engraved on a wee plaque below it.

I bent closer, to see.

Jack Chu, it said. Not Sue Marks, or even Susan Chu.

"So who's Jack, then?" I asked, as she worked keys in locks to let us in.

"My brother," she said. "*Jack Q's*, get it?"

I got it, though I didn't think I got it all. It was a pun again, and presumably it meant something to her because her face was fierce and intent and dangerous as she said it; but I couldn't see the point myself. From *Q's* to cues to snooker, sure; but *Jack Q's* gave you *J'accuse*, which was properly groanworthy but nothing else, not relevant.

Not as far as I could see, at any rate. And neither presumably could her brother, or he'd have used the whole thing on his logo. No, I thought this was a private, a personal pun, peculiar to Sue and with a meaning that she didn't mean to share.

"So does he live here, then? Your brother?"

"No," she said flatly. "We do. Welcome home."

• THREE •

HOW LIKE AN ANGEL

Home to Sue – to us? – was the building's loft expensively converted, more New York than Newcastle: it made an extraordinary flat, all odd corners and angled ceilings, light and air and space you wouldn't need to swing a whole coven of cats.

There was no hallway. The door from the landing led directly into the living-room, long and broad and bent in an L-shape around the stairwell. There were windows in two walls, front and back; there was an open fireplace, with a massive cast-iron surround; the floor was stripped and polished and scattered with Bokhara rugs and kilims. There were also a couple of gaudy beanbags and enough books and magazines lying around, enough used teacups and ashtrays to make the place look lived-in.

There was a long black leather sofa under the windows to my left with another at right angles to it against the wall, a black-and-gilt uplight in the small space between them and a square coffee-table close enough to both. On the floor by the opposite wall was a snooker-club employee's annual salary in a few black boxes and LED displays, the smartest hi-fi set-up I'd seen in private hands. A big wide-screen television and a video too, all wired in to give incomparable stereo viewing.

Walls and ceiling were plain and painted white, sweetly simple and freshly done, I thought. No scuff-marks, no nicotine stains. There were pictures here and there, hung in careful disorder: a couple of abstract originals in handmade wooden frames, otherwise art posters and photographs, mostly behind glass.

There was a door in the wall opposite me; to my right the room changed direction and aspect and intent. Around the corner, there were no more rugs on the floor. There was a long, heavy table with wrought-iron candlesticks and a fruit-bowl for an epergne, ten upright chairs around; against the near wall was a fine Victorian sideboard, which at least presented every appearance of containing napery and cutlery, place mats and napkin-rings.

In the end wall beyond the table were two doors, each standing open. Glimpses of a professional-looking stainless steel cooker through one, sea-green tiles through the other: kitchen and bathroom, but neither one quite the usual offices, judging by what I could see from here.

On the floor by the sideboard, I suddenly noticed a black leather shoulder-bag, buckled tight around something chunky and rectangular. I took half a step towards it, only to be held up short when Sue didn't move with me. I suppose I could have pulled free, but instead I just gestured, said,

"Is that . . . ?"

"Yes," she confirmed, doing an easy mind-reading act. "You can't have it, though."

"What do you mean, I can't have it?"

"Jonty," said slowly and with infinite patience, "you've spent three days in a coma, this is your first hour out of hospital and I have to take you back very soon, you've got a bad head and you've forgotten everything that's happened to you in the last couple of months. Do you seriously think you're in any condition to work?"

"No, but . . ."

"But nothing. If you take that into the hospital," with a contemptuous gesture, "you'll sit up all night fighting with it, trying to make it tell you what you can't remember. I haven't a clue what you've got inside it, you never let me see; but it'd be the worst thing in the world for you just now. You need rest, you need good food and sunshine and lots of sleep-time here where I can look after you, not more stress and worry and your brain trying to crank faster than a bloody computer. Am I getting through to you here?"

Up to a point, she was; her prescription sounded infinitely tempting. Except that if she thought she could provide it, she was only pissing into the wind. Or the nearest female equivalent, perhaps. Her presence gave me stress, her simple existence had my mind giddy with effort, trying to understand.

I made some vague noise, didn't try to reach for my bag again. She nodded, slipped free of me and gave me a little push, back towards the other half of the room. "You get sat down, get comfy. I'll make some tea."

"You wanted to show me something, you said?" Not just her flat, presumably; obviously not my bag, she hadn't wanted me to see that at all.

"Later. Sit down."

She collected up dirty mugs and ashtrays, disappeared into the kitchen and made appropriately wet clattering noises. I didn't sit down.

Instead, I walked or hobbled or shuffled over to that door in the far wall, and went on exploring.

A door to the right, a blank wall ahead of me; to the left a corridor. At the far end a window, letting in light enough to show me one more door.

The one on my right stood ajar, so I pushed it wider open and stepped inside.

Bedroom, no surprise. Master bedroom, surely: the size of a small swimming-pool and again furnished sparse but practical. The bare floors seemed to be common throughout; on this one stood a stripped pine chest of drawers against the near wall, next to another open fire, and a massive mahogany wardrobe opposite. Centre-stage between them, a king-size futon was rolled like a loose sausage on a low timber frame stained black. The futon was dressed in a bright red cotton cover, the duvet tossed over a chair by the windows was in golden yellow, and the pillows heaped atop it pink and green and lilac.

On the floor also were scatter rugs in more contrasting colours and patterns, and a radio one side of the futon, my teddy bear the other.

Adolphus Bear: named I knew not how or by whom, more commonly called Little Hitler by my mother, in response to my shrill and constant cry, "Dolphus *needs* it! *Now . . . !*"

I didn't in fact remember that, I only remembered her telling me about it often as I grew, ladling out the guilt in heavy, sticky measure, *see what you put me through, you wretched infant?*

What I did remember, I remembered how crucial Adolphus had been in my childhood, a constant and reliable companion, both qualities sadly absent in my home life; how he had been outgrown in my teenage, hidden but not discarded; how he had been rediscovered almost – *almost* – as a joke in my student years, and then laid aside again, I thought for good this time, when Carol proved a better comfort, constant and reliable and much more fun in bed.

And suddenly here he was again, like a statement of recent need: *don't believe everything she tells you, Jonty*, she had to be letting me down somewhere. Fun in bed

I was prepared to take on trust; but constancy? Reliability?

Maybe it was only the short time I'd been with her, not long enough to be certain. Maybe I'd rooted Adolphus out as a precaution, or maybe again as a joke. Almost a joke. Whatever, he was here; and never mind how I'd been feeling when I brought him here, I was exceeding glad to see him now.

Had him cradled where I liked him best to be, snug in the crook of my arm, when Sue walked in and found me so.

"Hah!" she said. Not sneering, just teasing. "Having a cuddle, huh?"

And she stepped up close and made it a three-way without invitation, just assuming; and I was physically knackered and emotionally overwrought and didn't even act unfriendly, never mind push her away.

Then, her head short of my shoulder and gazing up, she said, "Do you want to take him back to hospital with you? When we go?"

"Yes." No question, no doubt in my mind.

"Okay. I guess I should've brought him in before, yeah? Only I wasn't sure, I didn't want the nurses laughing at him . . ."

"Oh, and I suppose you never laughed at him, right?"

"That's different," she said. "I'm entitled."

And she tucked her arm through mine and urged me – us – gently out of the bedroom; and en route she said, "You don't remember, do you? Me laughing, I mean?"

"No. I was hypothesising." Then I nodded down the passage, and said, "What's there?"

"Spare bedroom. Your wardrobe, and it's doubling as a study, sort of, all the bloody books and paperwork you brought home from your job. And no," she said, holding fast, "you can't go see. I'm not letting you anywhere near till you're a hell of a lot better. Work doesn't matter."

"It does to me," I murmured, thinking seriously for the first time about financial matters. Sick pay and insurance and such. The joint mortgage I'd held with Carol, what had happened to that? Was I still paying my share? And then, moving on from there because I didn't want to linger, but with my mind running on tracks of money, "So what, are you renting this place off your brother," *getting it dirt cheap*, "is that it?"

"No," and her voice was clipped and tight suddenly, almost wary, almost angry, somewhere between the two. "It's mine. Why?"

Come this far, might as well be blunt about it. Besides, I had a habit of honesty, though it had never done me much good in my profession and rarely in my private life either, and looked like doing a little more damage now. "Because you couldn't possibly afford a flat like this on the wages they'd pay you downstairs." I'd never done a professional conveyance, that wasn't my area of interest; but none the less I was professionally very well informed about property prices in the city, and this flat wouldn't come in under six figures.

"Jonty," still with a bite in her voice but I couldn't see her face now as she talked, as she steered me back into the living-room and pushed me onto the nearest of those long sofas, "you're not thinking. Sweetheart. I'm Chinese, yes? Triads, Jonty. Drugs and vice, Jonty. The club is just a cover. Actually I'm a gangster's moll," and she had her back to me now and was walking away, and just from the way she walked I could see that all wariness was gone from her now, and she was nothing but angry.

Fair enough, I supposed. I hadn't been thinking Triads, that was too lurid even for my mind or for this city, for both; but I guess I had been thinking scam, one way or another. My mind made these calculations automatically, probable income against visible expenditure, and right now alarm-bells were clattering and jangling, and I thought I'd married a crook.

Only she was so mad with me, so scathing, suddenly it didn't seem likely at all. *Open mouth, insert foot.* Not such a hot beginning, to a life of wedded bliss . . .

When she came back, with a black lacquer tray of fine porcelain tea-things and none of that looked cheap either, she still wasn't looking at me. She hitched the table over with one foot, put the tray down and sat cross-legged on the floor, the other side from me. And I said,

"Oy."

"What?"

"Thought you were supposed to be my moll?"

At least that brought her head up, gave me the benefit of her baleful stare full-frontal. "I'm your *wife*," spat out at me, and for a moment nothing more than that; but then, "I suppose you can't help being a suspicious sod," she said. "In the circumstances."

"Maybe not, but that's no excuse for being an offensive sod. I'm sorry, Sue. It's none of my business anyway, where your money comes from."

"Of course it is, fool," she said, smiling a little now, but only a little. "We're partners, and *I* don't mind sharing," with a stress there that obviously meant something, though I didn't know what. "I did offer to go halvers on everything. You wouldn't wear that, but we are running a joint account. Besides, this is family stuff, you need to know. I nearly said 'family history' there," she went on with a little sniff, "can you believe it? That's how it feels, almost, 'specially with me having to tell it like a story that's over; but it mustn't, it's too soon for that . . ."

"You don't have to," I said quickly as she broke off, turning her face away to watch her fingers fumble for a cigarette. If it could do this, if it was so oppressive that it could smother her fires and have her muttering and evasive, saying anything now to avoid telling it straight, then I thought maybe it was a story I didn't want to hear. Not yet, at any rate, and not from Sue.

But, "Yes, I *do*," she said, lighting up and scowling at me through the smoke. "I *said*, it's family. Pour the bloody tea."

She got to her feet with an easy twist of her body, *look, no hands*, and walked a few paces over to the fireplace. I checked the tea tray: pot, strainer, fragile handleless cups on saucers. No milk or sugar. Okay, I was on top of this, at least. I filled both cups and held one snug in my hands, inhaling fragrant steam, as she came back with an ashtray in one hand and a framed photo in the other.

"What is this?" I asked, watching her settle neatly down again.

"Gui Hua," she said neutrally.

"Smells good."

"That's nice. It's your favourite. Here, look," holding the photo out across the table; and, "Take it, for God's sake," as I hesitated, trying to kink my head at a difficult angle to do what she'd told me first, what I thought she wanted, to look without touching. I was getting ahead of her here, suspecting the story and half afraid that a smeared fingerprint on a picture-frame might turn out to be a blasphemous transgression against a sacred relic.

But I took it when she swore at me, teacup in one hand and frame in the other; and the photo in the frame was an informal portrait of a young Chinese man, all leather and shades and posed casually leaning in the doorway of his club; and he really did look Triad, he looked lean and dangerous and deeply, deeply dodgy.

"My brother," Sue said, unnecessarily. And, "He's dead now," she said, and that was unnecessary also.

"It was his club," she said, "he bought the top two floors here when they were nothing, just a shell. He worked like shit, he hired builders to do the conversion downstairs but he worked with them, just an unskilled labourer but it meant he was there all the time, he knew what was happening. He got muscles and the work got done, he used to say, that made it worthwhile twice over. And he was learning all the time too, so when the club was finished he could start up here and do most of it himself, him and a couple of mates. He loved this flat . . ."

And you loved him, I thought, only that wasn't strong enough, or didn't seem to be. I'd say she'd worshipped him, near enough. And her face was twitching again, control starting to crumble as she gazed around this place her brother had made, likely untouched since he had made it and the whole damn flat was the relic, we were sitting in a shrine.

"How the hell did he finance it?" I asked, the question deliberately intrusive and factual both. Call me a sweetheart, as she had, albeit nastily; or else call me a martyr, probing known sensitivities purely to achieve a response already tasted once. Didn't matter whether she chose to answer, or simply told me to fuck off. Either one would give her a moment of emotional distance, a chance to catch her breath.

Her lips tightened, her eyes narrowed; briefly, the salt of martyrdom was on my lips. But then she shrugged, *what the hell*, and told me.

"He got backers. Not the banks, he tried them and they wouldn't, not so much for a guy his age. But we're a community, right? That's how they always talk about us, the Chinese community, they say; and there aren't that many of us. Anyone I don't know, I know someone who does. And a lot of us are successful, lots of businessmen, entrepreneurs. You know. The sort of people who are always looking for another slice of the pie. And this was right in our own territory, and that made a difference too; so he did it, he raised the money a piece here and a piece there. And the club was a hit from the start, he never had any problem with repayments. And then he died, and he had loads of insurance, that paid everybody off; and he'd made a will, hadn't he? Bastard never told me, but he made a will and left it all to me. So the club's mine, and this flat is mine, and all of it free and clear, no mortgages or anything . . ."

She'd be a rich young woman, then, at least on paper. And she clearly enjoyed that for its own sake, and just as clearly hated it for the thing that had caused it, her brother's death; and I wasn't sure how thin this ice was that I was treading now, but, "Did I," I said hesitantly, "God, I'm sorry I have to ask, but did I meet him?"

Her eyes widened for a second; she'd obviously forgotten that that might be a factor. Then, "Oh. No, you never knew Jacky. It was just after Christmas, he was killed. Before I met you."

Killed, she'd said this time. Again I didn't want to ask, but again I did. "How did it happen?"

"He was killed," she said, "murdered." And took a breath to tell me how, though it wasn't the air that she needed, it was the time between, the space the air allowed; and I made use of that time myself, unexpectedly remembering. I'd been waiting to hear of an accident; but murder triggered memory, because this was very much my area of expertise and yes, I did know already but no, I didn't say so, I only sat quiet and let her tell me.

"He was *dragged* to death," she said, using what was obviously her own bitter word for it, because there wasn't an obvious one in the language. "They put handcuffs on his wrists, and tied them to the back of a van; and then they drove him all round the ring road at three in the morning, going down the fast lane good and hard."

Yes. What I remembered mostly was the jokes, murmured around the Magistrates' Courts for the following week or two: all the cracks about a Chinese takeaway, and No 24 to go, and 'If you don't like the way I drive, why don't you get out and wok?' Neither clever nor funny, but that's how it takes the trade sometimes: something dreadful suddenly becomes a source, a pattern-book for any weak pun that can be dredged up. Maybe that's just how we deal with it. How we men deal with it, it's generally the blokes – and the more blokeish women – join in with this.

The jokes, and the photographs. I remembered the photos too, which was maybe why I remembered the jokes. Maybe why there'd been so many of them, because we'd all of us seen the photos.

In my mind, in my memory the pictures came in order, like a zoom in slow motion. Whether that was how I'd actually seen them, I couldn't say; it seemed unlikely. More probably this was my own job of sorting, keeping things neat. But how I remembered them, the distant shot was first, was top of the heap.

A van pulled up on a stretch of hard shoulder, photographed from above and behind, seemingly from a bridge across the road. Cold morning light, low sun and long shadows; and nothing to see at this distance except the van and what it trailed, something dark and shapeless, only a blotch a few metres down the tarmac. A line, a thread suggested its tether, didn't prove it.

Next photo. Ground level, and closer: the tether visibly a rope now, tied around the van's back bumper. What was tethered was still undefined, still nameless, but it had form enough to be a threat, to work on deeper levels of the mind, to whisper darkly below the threshold of voice or reason.

Next photo. Closer still. What the van had dragged filled the frame, and declared itself at last. *Suckered you this close, didn't I, drew you closer than you wanted to be, before you were certain? Before your eyes could find me out, or your brain allow it?* A body it was for sure, it had all the attributes a child paints in for identity's sake: two arms tied, two legs, a torso to join them with a head atop. But this was a body most unbeautiful, a body stripped down to its most bare essentials. Skinned and shredded like meat under a tiger's tongue, rasped down in places to the bone beneath and that chipped and broken where it showed.

It showed too much in future photos, very much closer than I'd ever wanted to be. The hands still in their cuffs and the rope *in situ*; the elbows, the knees, the ribbed back all pin-sharp, all eroded; the face and the back of the head, two pictures almost indistinguishable, almost impossible to tell which bloodied mass was which . . .

Barely enough flesh remained to say that this was a man; certainly nothing from the photos I'd seen could ever have said that he was Chinese, or young, or anything pertinent to the discovery that he was my brother-in-law, albeit only by prolepsis. It had taken three or four days, I remembered, to prove his identity by fingerprints and what was left of his teeth, what remnants of his jaw hadn't been ripped away while he presumably screamed and screamed against the hard road.

That had been Jacky Chu's prolonged departure, his difficult way to death: scraped and grated and dragged at speed behind a stolen van, one lap of the city and then abandoned before the police could catch up, though motorists had been phoning all along the route to tell them what was going down. Rumour said that the first callers had seen young Jacky running behind the van, that it was going just slow enough to let him keep his feet for a minute or two, before he fell one time too often and couldn't recover. Then they'd shifted to the fast lane and put their foot down, and not even the pathologists could say how much of that our Jacky had survived, how far round they'd got before he died.

Dead he was, when the good guys found him; and now his sister my wife sat opposite me, smoking and staring deep into her tea, and even these months on she was distressed enough not to be thinking straight, not to be realising that if I'd known about it before – and she'd know that I had – then I knew about it now, because that knowledge didn't fall into the weeks that I'd lost.

She stared and smoked, and breathed a bit hard, a bit sniffily through her nose; and said, "He'd have been so scared, too. He wasn't any kind of hero, wasn't Jacky. He disappeared from the club early evening, and they didn't do, do that to him till much later; so he will've had hours of whatever they did to him before, and he must've known it was going to get worse. Hours of being scared out of his wits, he must've had; and that's worse, almost. For me, anyway. Knowing he had all that to go through, even before they killed him . . ."

"He doesn't look the kind of guy who scared easily," I said, uncertain of my ground here but interested, ready to take risks.

"What, that photo? That's just show," she said, shrugging. "He liked to look cool. Anyone can put on a pair of Ray-Bans and a leather jacket; and he had the muscles for it, but it was only ever for show, not for real. Did him good, I guess, with the club and stuff, but he was soft as shite under his clothes."

Not like his sister, then. She had the same predilection for coolth in appearance, that much was clear, and she had the muscles too, in appropriately female form; but I thought she was tough as wire underneath also, hard and sharp to the core.

If I had to marry anyone – if I'd had to marry someone – and it couldn't be Carol, then I thought I'd picked a pretty good candidate. The more I saw of her, the deeper I dug, the more Sue impressed me.

But that was a remote feeling, a stand-back-and-admire

sort of feeling, and nothing to make me hotfoot towards
an altar.

My mother always said that nothing could ever stop me
asking questions, short of a hand across my mouth. I was
slightly more sophisticated now, perhaps, but legal training
and an all-consuming curiosity still meant that I tended to
hammer away at something, anything I was interested in,
until I was directly told to shut up.

So: "Who was it, did that to your brother?" I asked. "Do
they know?" They didn't, last I'd heard; but I was near three
months out of date, and things change.

She shook her head, though, and gave me another of those
dispirited, desolate shrugs. "Not a clue, as far as I know. As
far as anyone's said. You said you'd ask around for me, see
if the police had any ideas they weren't going public with,
but you never came up with anything. Can we talk about
something else now? Please?"

"Yeah, sure. Sorry." This must have been doubly hard on
her, I realised suddenly, mentally savaging myself for being
so slow on the uptake. She hadn't just been telling the story
of her brother's death; she'd been telling it to a man to whom
she'd undoubtedly said it all at least once already. And then
having to tell him what he'd done in response, which must
feel deeply strange. And cope with the fact that that man,
her husband – me – had suddenly become a stranger: as
weird for her, I supposed, as it was for me, and probably
more disturbing.

"Sorry," I said again, trying to apologise for what was
non-specific but all-encompassing: *sorry I drove badly and
crashed the car, and started all this off*, or maybe *sorry I
came into your parents' takeaway that night, and started
all this off*.

And what the hell had I been doing out there in Limboland,
starving hungry at midnight and not going home? It wasn't
only other people I needed to be bullying with questions,

if I was going to resolve any part of what had happened to me. I'd be having myself on the rack also, necessarily. There were answers to be squeezed out somewhere in my subconscious, there had to be: motivations that had nothing to do with memory. I needed to understand myself, a whole lot better than currently I did. I'd thought I knew it all; and I'd proved myself so very, very wrong . . .

Sue smiled, shook her head, glanced at her watch and reached for a remote control unit on the table, only faking a little, truly connecting other gears and turning her mind to other things.

"I have to take you back soon," she said, "but I didn't drag you up here for the view. This was on the BBC last night and I thought you'd want to see it, so I turned over for the News at Ten and they had it too, and I taped it . . ."

She had it all set up already, the right tape in the machine and at the right place, rewound and ready to go. She punched buttons and there was a click and a whirr, TV and video coming to life simultaneously; and the screen showed a news presenter behind a desk, and behind her the magic of television faded the prime minister's face into a helicopter-shot of broad-leaved English woodland.

"At the Colburne Valley protest in Cumbria," she said, "an environmental activist had an amazing escape today, surviving a fifty-foot fall and walking away apparently without a bruise to show for it. Malcolm Hardy reports."

The woodland filled the screen and started moving, as the helicopter carried the camera down the valley to zoom in on a long scar of cleared trees and rutted earth, giant yellow machines standing idle.

A man's voice, laid over the pictures: "An uneasy peace has returned to this remote spot, after the violence and confrontation of the last few days. But it's the false peace of a stand-off, both sides shocked and disturbed by what took place here at first light this morning . . ."

Cut to a camera on the ground, showing a small group of men clustered at the foot of a tree, just where the ravaged ground met still-virgin wood.

"The under-sheriff and his men, assisted by police and professional climbers, were continuing with the operation begun on Monday. The idea has been to clear protestors and their makeshift shelters from the wood tree by tree, cutting their skyways of rope and bringing them down by force if necessary. Officials insist that safety has always been the prime consideration, and that nothing would be done to endanger life; but this morning that assurance had a hollow ring to it, as something went dangerously, desperately wrong . . ."

The camera panned slowly upwards, looking for action and finding it high in the branches. Close to the trunk, a man bedecked in bright orange look-at-me gear was clipping his safety harness to a rope that ran at handrail-height from that tree to the next. Another rope made the bridge, the skyway for those who dared to walk upon. The camera watched the man set his feet judiciously on the rope and begin to crab across; and then it moved ahead of him, to find another man already halfway over.

Much younger he looked, this second man, little more than a boy from this distance; and he wore no harness, no safety ropes, and he didn't bother to cling or sidle. He walked the rope bridge without a handhold, with total confidence, like a circus act, all show.

And he fell.

He fell without warning, without any effort to save himself from falling. He rolled and tumbled in the air, and though it was a long way down it seemed to take him longer than was natural, he seemed to fall in slo-mo.

And he hit the earth rolling, tumbling, and right in front of the camera; and in the appalled silence around him there was nothing to hear but the impact of that fall and the

scuffing sounds of his body bucking on soft earth. Even
the reporter had had wit enough to be still, to add no
commentary now.

And then, full in the camera's stare and just as distant
voices began to clamour – in oddly foreign tongues, I
couldn't hear a word of English spoken – he pulled himself
slowly and impossibly to hands and knees, and then up onto
his feet.

And again there was silence, those people who'd been
rushing to help stood frozen, and even I felt a chill as his
eyes met the lens and moved on.

He looked around, then turned around, and didn't say a
word; only walked slowly and deliberately away into the
wood, and not a person there lifted a finger to delay him.

Sue hit a button and the picture died, the slight sound of the
winding tape clicked off.

"That was him, wasn't it?" she said. "That was Luke?"

"Yes, that was Luke." No mistaking Luke. I'd known
him, even up on the rope, too high to see; I'd known
him falling, only a blur of impossible motion; and now
all the country knew him by his dirty-blond hair and his
chill, beautiful face, his ice-green eyes and his anger and
his eternal, untouchable youth.

"I thought it was. Just from what you've said, and him
being there. There couldn't be two of them. But, but even
if he's what you said he was, how did he . . . ?"

"Luke hates to fly," I said, quoting him indirectly, "but
when he must, the air will bear him up." And then, against
her doubting look, "Time that fall with a stopwatch, if you
want to. It's too slow. Like he's falling through honey.
That's how. He fell fast enough to look good, not fast
enough to do him any hurt."

I didn't think any fall could actually hurt Luke, but if he
hated to fly, he must hate more to fall. Too much resonance

in that. No surprise if he'd reached for and found that mongrel compromise, neither the one thing nor the other. That was Luke all through, in this his second life.

"Well. I thought you'd want to see it, anyway . . ."

"Yes. Thanks."

She nodded, and we were both of us mute for a moment, both caught up in separate concerns; then she stirred, shook her head slightly against whatever thoughts had clouded it, and pushed herself lightly to her feet.

"Come on, invalid. I have to get you back. Do you want to go down and see the club first, though? Just in case?"

In case it fires some circuit in your dim head, she meant. Privately, I thought there was little point in hoping. Visual stimuli clearly weren't going to work, or something would be happening by now, surely. If Sue and her flat together could trigger nothing, her club wasn't likely to be any more effective. But I shrugged an acquiescence, and levered myself up from the sofa; shook my head at her offered hand, resisting the habit of dependence; and followed her slowly down the stairs and through the emblazoned double doors where she held them open for me, into the hush and half-dark of a snooker club all but empty in mid-afternoon.

One vast space it was down here, though the ceiling was propped up on fat brick pillars at judicious points, hinting at interior walls now gone. Directly ahead of us was a long bar, with a computer in among the bottles; otherwise nothing but snooker tables and the walls lined with scoreboards, cues in racks, zoetropic photographs of impossible shots in action. Only a couple of the tables were lit up and in use.

Behind the bar, a Chinese boy grinned at me broadly, said, "Lookin' good, Jonty. Dig the bandage." And then he added something I couldn't follow in a language I didn't speak, guttural and tonal and signifying nothing. And he was still looking at me as he said it.

"It's no good, Lee," Sue said from behind me. "He doesn't remember a thing."

A stare, a grin less certain, *you've got to be joking*, followed by slow acceptance as his eyes flicked between us. "What, *nothing?*"

"I'm sorry. Not even your name," I said, with a depressing suspicion that this would prove to be a scene all too familiar in the next few weeks. Right now I was embarrassed, but soon I'd be bored and embarrassed both, telling it and telling it again . . .

"Christ on a bicycle. What, that bang on the head let all your brains out, did it? Well, hullo, Jonty. I'm Lee Kwan Yu," holding a hand across the bar to shake mine. "I've been teaching you Cantonese for the last month. Wasted effort, I guess. Start again tomorrow?"

Which was not a bad recovery in the circumstances, and I was sorry not to give him more than a vague smile and a slight cock of my head, a murmured, "Maybe. We'll see," which we both knew meant *almost certainly not*.

And then he turned to Sue, slipping back into Cantonese again; she replied in the same, which meant they were surely talking about me.

I let my eyes stray around the club, I listened to the solid, irregular *thunk!* of ball striking ball and thought that that also could drive you mad, a contemporary version of the classic water torture if you were listening for it; and I wondered how Sue and her brother before her and apparently I now could bear to live above it. But I'd heard not a thing, upstairs; and glancing upward I saw a false ceiling of polystyrene panels in an aluminium matrix, and deduced the existence of efficient soundproofing above it.

The incomprehensible sing-song went on beside me; I turned back to face them, frowning now, but Sue stilled me with just a touch on my elbow. "Are you feeling all right, Jonty? Maybe it's the lighting in here, but you look disgusting. Colour of a dirty bandage . . ."

I've no idea whether that was adroit or simply accurate, but it had what was probably its desired effect, whichever. On the verge of asking for a translation, I stopped for a moment to consider myself. And say I'd been nobly ignoring it hitherto or say the other thing, say it was all psychosomatic and came on only because she'd asked and I was looking for it; or what the hell, say it was pure hypochondria, because I liked being fussed by a beautiful girl; but she did ask and I did look inward, and I did find that my head ached momentously and my legs were trembling with the effort of balance, there was a cold slick of sweat on my skin and a sickness in my stomach, and I urgently wanted to sit down.

Which I did, Sue's strong shoulder helping me over to the nearest banquette. Lee fetched me a glass of water – ice and lemon going in there more by instinct than intent: he was at work, he was behind the bar, of *course* he put in ice and lemon – and I sat and sipped and she sat beside me with her anxiety hidden behind a cool efficiency, a cool hand on my brow; and Lee fidgeted, his eyes moving uncertainly between us.

"I could nip down," he said, "fetch Mr Han . . ."

I shook my head, *don't need a doctor*; and Sue reinforced that, with her own reasoning.

"Not while Jonty's still at the hospital. One or the other, but not both at once. Soon as he comes out, Uncle Han can look after him. There's probably a herb," she said to me, "brings your memory back. It'll taste vile, mind. How's your rotten head?"

"Rotten," I confirmed with half a smile, the best I could manage.

"Poor lover," with a touch of her lips to my ear, the closest she could come to kissing the sore bit better. "Are you going to manage those stairs for me?"

"I think so. I was just giddy for a minute, is all."

Which she knew it wasn't all, and her snort said so; but, "My fault," she said. "They told me not to overdo you. Luke could've waited, he's on tape; I didn't have to haul you all that way up."

"Not to fret," I said. "I'm glad to have seen the flat."

She looked at me as though she didn't like the way I'd said that; and quite right too. But she didn't challenge, and I didn't explain.

The two of them helped me up, and saw me watchfully down the stairs and over to the car. Sue unlocked the passenger door for me, then pushed hard down on my shoulders as I sat, to be sure I ducked low enough and my head went in cleanly. I leaned cautiously back, looking for a way to lean that didn't hurt, closed my eyes against recurrent dizziness and barely heard the conversation outside:

"You going to be okay with him the other end, then, Suzie?"

"Yes, of course I am. All those nurses, they'll be queueing up to get their hands on him. God knows why, mind, he's a sorry piece of meat just now . . ."

"Yeah, well. You take care of him, you hear?"

"Why should I?"

"He's the only piece of meat in your fridge just now, pet."

My eyes opened then, without much intent on my part, just in time to see Lee jog-trotting back to his post, before someone could steal the club and all its contents. Sue walked around the bonnet and got in the driver's side, settled herself and checked me over with a glance, had I done my seat belt up? Was I going to puke?

Yes and no, if those were really the questions, if I wasn't just fantasising meanings to apply to the expressions on her face. But I had a question too, and she wasn't getting away with this one left unasked.

"*Suzie?*" I said.

"Yeah? So what?"

"So who calls you Suzie?"

"Everyone."

"You told me Sue."

"Everyone but you. Don't know why, you just wouldn't. I nearly blew you out over it, that first night," smiling as she remembered. "Nearly told you to stuff it, if you wouldn't use my name the way I liked it."

"Why didn't you? You thought I was a creep anyway, you said so."

A sideways glance, a hesitation; finally, "Not by then, I didn't. You interested me, you seemed so screwed up and helpless, and that's always attractive; and— oh, fuck it, Jonty, I wanted to get inside your shorts, all right? I'm kinky for long tall white boys, the rest was just a bonus. I didn't care if you called me by a name I hated."

"Do you?"

"Do me a favour. Sue Chu? Of course I hate it. It's the only reason I married you. I sort of got to like Sue, from you; like a pet name you could use in public, yeah? So I had to change the other half somehow, and Sue Marks was the best on offer . . ."

All this time she was driving, nipping neatly through the city; which prompted one more sneaky question from me, "Are you a local, then, you know this place so well?"

"Sure am. Born and bred."

Which meant she hadn't married me for my passport, nor I her to share it in an excess of generosity. Bugger. Another fine theory out of the tinted window . . .

"We forgot Dolphus," I said suddenly, stricken.

Her eyes moved sharply to me, to the mirror, to the road; she pulled in to the kerb and said, "Do you want to go back?"

And would have done, no question, if I'd said yes.

"No," I said. "Not now. Doesn't matter."

"Sure?"

"Yes."

"I'll look after him," she said, doubting my assurance. "I do. Women and teddy bears first, if there's a fire. And I'll bring him tomorrow, early. Promise. Okay?"

"Okay. Thanks . . ."

At the hospital she walked me to my room, supervised my undressing and presented me with the threatened pyjamas, from a carrier bag she'd brought in from the car. Black silk they were, and tying with soft cords, no buttons: more like the *gi*, karate kit, than Marks and Spencer's best. Also they had Chinese dragons embroidered on the back and legs, which made me giggle and feel foolish. But they felt cool and delightful on my sore skin, slitheringly luxurious slipping between clean sheets, and well deserving of the kiss she claimed.

"Listen, about tonight," she said then, "would it be all right if I didn't come? I always used to see my parents, Thursdays, and I'd really like to go tonight. It gives Mum a break . . ."

"And you want to tell them how I'm doing, yes?"

"Well, why not? You're their son-in-law, they've been worried."

"I don't mind," I said truthfully. "Of course I don't. Why would I? I'm knackered anyway, I'll probably just sleep."

"Okay, then. Good. I'll be in tomorrow, early as they let me . . ."

And she kissed me again, and went away; and I lay quietly, drifting towards dozing, shuffling realities in my head until a nurse looked in to check that I was back. I'd opened my eyes at the sound of the door's opening, so she gave me a message to ponder: told me that Vernon Deverill had come calling while I was out, and would return this evening.

• FOUR •

CHARIOT OF FIRE

When he came I was ready for him, or as ready as I could be with my head so full of holes, drained empty of everything I needed.

At any rate I was sitting up in bed and wearing the black pyjamas, glad of the warning and glad of the gift, not to be taken at a double disadvantage. I didn't know the man (or at least what was left of me didn't know the man, my old and seemingly-reduced, though hitherto satisfactory, self), but everything I'd heard about him said that Deverill would be rapid to exploit any advantage he could see, even among his friends. And whatever Sue said – and whatever money he'd been spending on me, for whatever reason – no way could I see myself ever being counted in the number, the small number of Vernon Deverill's friends.

The nurse wouldn't let me out of bed again, even just to sit in my clothes in a chair by the window; and truth to tell I was half glad of the prohibition, because my body definitely didn't want to move. But pyjamas were at least better than a hospital robe, and forewarned was one hell of a lot better than being surprised, as I would have been if Sue hadn't taken me out that afternoon. He'd have caught

me napping, and God only knew what mess I'd have found
myself in thereafter.

God only knew what mess I was in already; or maybe
God and Vernon Deverill shared that particular secret
between them.

Maybe I could find out, if I was clever tonight.

Trouble was, I didn't feel clever. I felt stupid and hurt,
exhausted and unprepared and no way ready, not big enough
for this; and it seemed as though I waited in that tense and
useless state for hours before there were footsteps in the
corridor, someone opening the door, big male figures filing
through.

Deverill, a minder and a lackey, as best as I could tag
them; and even the lackey looked hard, despite his spectacles
and briefcase. I wouldn't want to tangle with any one of
them, even at my fittest and with all the protection of a
courtroom around us. The three of them crowding my bed
was pretty much the last thing that I wanted right now.

That I didn't even know why they were there made it
worse, but not appreciably. It couldn't possibly have got
appreciably worse.

"Jonty. How are you?" Big heavy voice for a big heavy
man, and not just metaphorically: Deverill was a burly
six-footer with cropped grey hair and fleshy features, the
smell of cigars on his clothes and the smell of power all
about him. Not much of his weight was fat, I thought; in
a rumble, no way would this man stand back and let his
minders sort it out.

I just shrugged, in answer to his question. Insofar as I
had a strategy for this, I meant to say as little as possible.
The less I told them, I thought, the more I'd learn.

Maybe.

"Totalled that nice motor I bought you, yes?"

Score one to me. I'd guessed this already, that he'd paid
for that impossible, that ridiculous car; but now I knew.

"Seems so," I said. "Sorry."

He grunted, and moved over to the table by the window, where all the bouquets stood in their ranks of vases. "One of these from me, is it?"

"The big one," I said, winning another grunt from him, this one approving. He fingered the flowers proprietorially, and I thought yes, that was absolutely right behaviour for this man, in this situation. He'd paid for the car, he'd paid for the flowers, they were his.

He was paying for me, I remembered bleakly; and why the hell had I ever let that happen? I didn't want to be in thrall to this man . . .

The lackey had come to the far side of my bed, where he could stand in the corner, out of everyone's way; the minder had taken a position classically by the door, wearing his suit about as easily as professional footballers wore theirs, I thought, looking totally misdressed. Briefly, I wondered if he had a gun concealed under the jacket. Then my eyes met his and I saw him grin, I saw him wink at me.

Christ. Neither did I want to be on winking terms with one of Deverill's bully-boys. A client of mine, a hard and dangerous man in his own right, had once crossed Deverill on a deal; smuggling drugs, I'd heard, when he wasn't supposed to. The following night a tip-off had brought the police to a bonded warehouse, where they found the alarm disabled, a sealed door jemmied open and my client unconscious, trapped beneath the tines of a fork-lift truck with cases of brandy tumbled all about him. No fingerprints anywhere other than his own, though the set-up was deliberately ridiculous, not intended to be taken seriously. He had multiple internal injuries, besides what harm the fork-lift had done to his ribs; and he wouldn't say a word, to the police or to me. No one doubted Deverill's involvement. Chances were he'd been there himself, his own boot doing a share of the damage, he was known not to delegate what seemed to him important; but he wouldn't have been alone, and he didn't keep a private army, only a small team of loyal hard men. Not unlikely then that this cheerful winker, this seeming buddy of mine had been there also.

"Vern." That was him now, showing me another aspect of his work: glancing quickly away from me and interrupting his boss's private train of thought, unfolding his arms to make a little sideways gesture with his hand.

Deverill had a wide vocabulary of grunts. This one presumably was an acknowledgement, *good, you're doing your job, lad*, because he stepped immediately away from the window, coming all the way around to the near side of my bed. Paranoia or just common sense, not to make a target of himself? I couldn't say, I didn't know how much actual danger he lived in. There were many people, surely, who'd be glad to see him dead; but most of them wouldn't be out there tracking him with a twelve-bore, nor hiring professional assassins. I assumed. On the other hand, it would only take one . . .

Yes. Knowing what I knew of Vernon Deverill – and that was only the common knowledge, little enough compared to what there must be to know, a thin stream flowing from a lake – I thought perhaps that if I were he, I wouldn't stand framed in too many lighted windows either.

"Well now," he said, turning suddenly to me and striking his hands together, "I don't suppose you'll have anything new to tell me, will you, Jonty?"

And though he tried to sound bullish, I thought there was something urgent and unhappy in his voice, *I don't suppose you will, but please surprise me* . . .

Almost a disappointment to me, that I couldn't; but at the same time a major relief that he'd phrased the question that way, that I could respond, "No. I'm sorry, not a thing. Not yet."

"No. Well, I hadn't expected . . . You said it would

take time. And I suppose this'll hold you up longer,
yes?"

"I'm afraid that's inevitable," I agreed, fighting not to grin
at my own private subtext there, all the extra meaning that
he hadn't cottoned on to yet. And might very well not, on
this visit at least: so long as he didn't question the staff here
about my condition, or didn't find them forthcoming . . .

He nodded, frustrated but accepting. "Don't rush things,
on my behalf or Lindsey's. Take your time. He's got all
the time we need," bitterly, cryptically. "We can keep him
where he is a long time yet. So get well first, before you
jump back into this. Understood?"

"Yes, sir," I said without irony, surprising myself as he
had just surprised me. I hadn't expected such a seemingly-
genuine solicitude from Deverill; that was not his reputation
with his employees, and it seemed that he was employing
me, though for what I still had barely a notion.

He needed me, I guessed, he must need me badly; and
his next words seemed to confirm that.

"Anything you want," he said, "the money's there. You
know that, don't you?"

"Yes," I said, and no lie that. If he'd paid already for a
smart car and private treatment, then demonstrably Vernon
Deverill's purse-strings were open to me, his wealth was
mine to call on. Which was a deeply uncomfortable position
for me, though I did my best to hide it.

"Good, then." Another grunt that seemed to say the
conversation was over, or his part in it; and it was picked
up smoothly by the lackey on my left, asking if there was
anything I needed or needed doing right now, anything I
couldn't manage from my hospital bed?

I shook my head, hoping he'd read a simple message: that
Deverill wasn't the only one who found it hard to delegate,
that what I had to do I'd do myself, as soon as I was fit.

"Fair enough," he said, and his voice too was friendly,

as the minder's wink had been, confirming my status as
one of the family, part of the team. And oh, I didn't like
that one bit, and I wanted to resign, but my need to know
wouldn't let me.

"There's been some more interest in the press," he went
on, balancing his briefcase on the edge of my bed, flicking
up the latches and lifting the lid. "Only in the extradition,
they've not made any connections beyond that, but I thought
you'd be interested to see it."

"Yes, right. Thanks . . ." I was interested in anything that
could give me clues without yielding up my ignorance as
a hostage to fortune. I was too vulnerable just now to take
any chances with a man like Vernon Deverill.

Four photocopied sheets came out of the briefcase; at the
angle the man held it, I couldn't see anything else that was
in there, though I did try. My need against his training, the
echo no doubt of his master's voice, *don't flash my secrets
around*; that time he won, but there'd be other chances, I
reckoned. Accepted by these men, maybe even welcomed,
what access I couldn't claim I could try to steal.

Which might be, very likely was what underlay all this.
Doing some job for Deverill, though I knew not what, I
could penetrate his innermost circles and learn more than
any outsider would have a chance at. I could be a spy, a
fifth column, an undercover agent digging for victory . . .

But why in the world would I want to? I wasn't CID or
a private investigator, I was a solicitor with an established
practice and no ambition to look beyond that, very content
with what I was doing. Why change that?

Because something or someone else had changed it for
me, obviously. I'd been reacting, perhaps, to a change forced
upon me; and Sue was right in the frame there, as the only
known agent of change in my recent life. Though she'd at
least given me the impression that she knew little of my
work and nothing of my connection with Deverill beyond

the fact that it existed and she didn't like it, none of that was necessarily true. Maybe she was the undercover spy here, exploiting my memory loss now as she might have exploited an infatuation earlier, feeding me disinformation to have me up and dancing to her tune . . .

What tune that might be, I didn't know and couldn't guess; nor who would be paying her to pipe it. There were no reasons that I could see, nothing was reasonable; wheels turned within wheels, and all perspectives were awry. I felt as though I were living in an Escher engraving, where impossible relationships appeared true and things sat side by side that could never have shared the same space.

But Escher only works, he only gets away with it because people are content to play to his own rules, the accepted conventions of pictorial art. Our eyes are lazy, and hence easily deceived; there's less work in labelling a paradox than there is in unravelling it.

And this was not a print to be admired for its technical ingenuity or its psychological acuity, this was my life. If one perspective could show me nothing but paradox and incongruity, I was in no position simply to throw my arms up in wonder or surrender or despair. I had to analyse and explore, to shift my own position and examine other people's until I found another perspective, from where things would fall into place and make sense. It had to exist somewhere, I was sure of that. I might be floundering, even in danger of foundering at the moment, but there must be solid ground out there if I could only discover it. People no less than particles have distinct patterns of behaviour. Nothing is truly random or chaotic, it only ever seems that way because we lack information or insight, or we're trying to force what facts we know into a false interpretation.

If I'd been playing detective for or against Deverill – or both? – then I could do the same on my own account.

Though it would be my own recent life, my own forgotten motives that I needed above all to detect . . .

I took the stapled sheets with a nod of thanks, perhaps my first material clue; and was glancing through them, trying to look intelligent under Deverill's assessing eyes, when the minder took two or three quick paces, across the room to the window. Something was odd there, that took me a moment to figure: it had been darkening outside as it ought this time of night, this time of year, but the minder was moving into light, seemingly, brighter than the rest of us.

"Jesus!" he yelled, staring. "Get out, Vern! Out *now!*"

Vern, I thought, must have taken a course, How To Be Protected. By the time I'd turned my head to find him, he was already at the door and yanking it open. No hesitation, no questions asked.

Not so the lackey on my left, who was fumbling to close his briefcase before his feet dared move. Graduate of a different course, perhaps, How To Protect Vern's Secrets.

Not so me, either. I didn't want to linger, though I didn't understand; but my body simply wasn't up to speed here. *Out of bed*, my head was crying; *wait* was the message that came back from my legs.

Crisis-time: and like Luke coming out of his tree, I could respond only in slow motion, and what had been a maximum benefit to him was disastrous to me.

Would have been disastrous, if I'd been left alone. If the minder had been doing his job, looking after his principal.

He was fast in his head and fast on his feet both, he had time to dive out of there and save himself to save Deverill later, from whatever threat came next. He might even have had time to hustle his colleague the lackey out of the room, and save them both. But his head snapped round and he saw me struggling, too weak even to throw the bedclothes back with any decision; and he made his own decision in that moment, and with one bound he was by my bed.

Not reaching to lift me out, no time for that. Though I couldn't see what was coming, I could see its light burning beyond the window, throwing strange shadows. *Get the fuck out of here* I wanted to say, I wanted to be a hero, but before I could find the voice for it he'd gripped the bed-frame below my line of sight and was heaving massively. The bed tilted beneath me, toppled, went smashing onto its side; and I fell out, of course, and the mattress fell heavily on top of me. And then a greater weight, a bonecrushing thud on top of the mattress on top of me, and I thought that was probably the minder vaulting over the top for what little protection a hospital bed-frame could offer him – unless he was laying his own body there as another barrier to protect me, and what the hell were his priorities, why me? – against the room-shaking rumble and crash of what came then through the window and through the wall.

The room did more than shake, the room came down. I was blanketed in darkness and stupid with shock, half-crushed and fighting to squeeze air into my lungs against the weight atop me, but even so I could still put names to some of what I heard and felt around me.

The snapping, sliding, thundering sounds were the ceiling and the roof above, I thought: above no more, but beams, bricks, tiles and gutters all slipping down to join us.

The sudden blow against my side and the brief inhuman screaming, that was the buckling of the bed-turned-safety-cage doing its new job, taking heavy punishment that would otherwise have come slamming unhindered into me.

The implosive *whuff!* that followed, the sound that sucked – yes, indeed. I knew what that was also, I had a name for that, and I was starting to scrabble under my mattress, trying to dig a way out through lino and solid concrete when much of the weight was lifted off my back, and then the rest of it as my unknown friend, my minder who I didn't have a name for yanked the mattress up and joined me behind its temporary shelter.

The air was full of dust and filth and first fingers of smoke, reaching around the mattress; but he held it across his back and shoulders, and I could see a path through rubble to where clean light still shone, beyond the twisted doorway. Then I couldn't see it so clearly because a figure stood there, a man bellowing, naming the three of us, "Dean? Jonty? Oliver, can you hear me?"

And that was Deverill, probably seeing nothing through the muck and the murk and the flaring light; and not one of us tried to answer him. I was too busy breathing, and trying to crawl; his minder, my new friend, my new hero Dean or possibly Oliver was too busy grunting encouragement as he inched along beside me, above me, between me and the catastrophe, hanging over me with the mattress spread like protective wings, like a shield; and the other in the room, the lackey Oliver or possibly Dean, he was too busy screaming.

I crawled across broken brick and splintered wood, blundering towards the light until at last I was grabbed at, I was seized and dragged out into the corridor, and Dean or Oliver came after. They tried to haul me immediately away, but I fought their hands off for a second, with more strength than I'd found to save myself; and I turned to look back into the room, just a moment I had to do that before someone stepped between it and me; and I saw a fiery hell in there, I saw a crumpled lorry parked in my bedroom and ablaze.

And I saw Oliver, unless he was Dean, trapped in his corner and dancing, a figure sewn entirely of flame.

He wasn't screaming any more, but I think I screamed for him. I'm not certain; they gave me an injection and took me away, and things were very muddled in my head for a while after.

I woke up or came round in another room, another part of the hospital; by the light that found its way around and between and through the curtains, it was also the beginning of another day.

There was a policewoman sitting beside my bed. Protecting me or waiting for me, I couldn't tell which. Both at once, perhaps; but when she saw that I was awake, she put her head outside the door and spoke to someone in the corridor.

A senior officer came at her summoning, a man whose name and rank I forgot as soon as he mentioned them, because I was too busy looking to listen. He smelled of smoke and wet ash, he'd had a wash but his clothes were rank with it; and he looked achingly, up-all-night-with-a-bad-job weary.

He asked politely if I felt up to answering a few questions; behind him, the nurse Simon pulled faces at me, *say no if you feel like it, I'll get a doctor in to back you up . . .*

But I wanted rid of this, all I wanted was escape and that clearly wouldn't be allowed until the questions had been asked and answered. So I shrugged an acceptance and he started in, with the WPC staying as note-taker and Simon fading out with more unspoken messages, *just buzz if you need me, I'll come and scare them away.*

Questions, questions. I told him everything I thought he'd need to know, about what happened last night; then he made me tell him again, everything I could remember. Nothing changed the bones of it, though: that Vernon Deverill had stood recklessly exposed in a lighted window; that his minder – Dean, not Oliver – had warned him away, and at the time I'd wondered how much risk there was, whether his ego actually stood in more danger than his physical self if he went unwarned, unguarded; that I was answered a minute later, when a truck came crashing through the window, right where he'd been standing.

That I didn't think it a coincidence, no, not at all.

The policeman nodded, scratched his nose, finally admitted that I might possibly be right about that. The truck had been legitimately parked on hospital grounds; it belonged to a contractor working on the new wing, and he'd been in the habit of leaving it on site for the last few weeks. Indeed, he had definitely left it at the top of the slope that ran down towards my former room. But he maintained that he had left it in reverse gear and with the handbrake full on, no chance of its running away; and there were other factors, the policeman said, that suggested it had been deliberately aimed at my window.

"Such as?" I asked.

"Well, the contractor didn't leave the lights on, for a start. Says he didn't, at any rate, and why would he? But someone steering that truck down the hill in the dark, got to bump it up over the kerb and then hit one window out of a dozen, he might well want the lights on, yes?"

I nodded, remembering. "They were on, for sure. Everything looked strange . . ."

"Right. And Dean thinks he saw someone jumping free, a couple of seconds before it hit. As soon as they were sure it wouldn't swerve off line, I guess. Whoever did that was brave, mind, though he was stupid with it."

"Why brave? It wasn't going that fast, surely?" A flat-bed truck wouldn't have picked up much speed, rolling down a fairly gentle hill with no engine. Wouldn't need speed, momentum would be plenty to smash it through a window wall.

"Petrol," he said. "We're not certain yet, the labs are still checking, but we think the whole cab was soaked in petrol. That fire was too fierce, and too far forward. The diesel tank wasn't actually ruptured in the crash, there must have been another accelerant. So this guy's been splashing petrol all over, his own clothes would've been wet with it and the cab would've been full of fumes, and he turns the truck's lights on? Stupid. One spark from the electrics and ka-boom, the wrong guy gets fried."

The wrong guy had got fried anyway, though I didn't want to remind him: it was the lackey Oliver got caught in the inferno, not Deverill.

"Is Dean all right?"

"He's fine. Well, minor burns on his arms; that mattress was on fire before he got you out. But that's what saved your life, that mattress. He's a quick-thinking lad, yon Dean."

"Yes." Saved my life, saved his boss's; and was probably feeling bitter over Oliver, thinking himself a failure for not getting us all out and the briefcase too . . .

Briefcase. On the table by my bed were some crumpled, dirty sheets of paper; the policeman saw my eyes find them, and said, "You had that in your hand, when they pulled you out. Held so tight you didn't let go until they'd jabbed you, the doctor says."

I shrugged. "Must've been instinct, it's not that important."

"No," he agreed. "We checked. Just a report from a Sunday paper. What's your connection with Lindsey Nolan, Mr Marks?"

"Christ knows," I said, heartfelt and honest. "I don't even know what my connection is with Vernon Deverill. Ask the doctors; I can't remember a bloody thing."

"Mmm, they said that. Nor about the accident that put you in here in the first place, I understand?"

"That's right. Why?"

"Well, our colleagues in Penrith need to put in a report on that, and there are no witnesses that they can find, so they were hoping you could throw some light on what happened. But more than that, I'm curious myself now. This makes two apparent accidents in a week, either one of which might have killed you; and we're fairly certain that

the second was a deliberate attempt at murder, so naturally
that raises questions about the first, do you see?"

Oh, I did, I did see very clearly; but, "That would mean
I was the target last night? Not Deverill?"

"That's right."

"No, that's nonsense. It must be. Why would anyone want
to kill me?"

"We don't know, Mr Marks. That's another question I
wanted to ask you, actually. Work as a solicitor, you're
going to make enemies, but does anyone particular come
to mind just now? Had any threats, perhaps?"

"No, none. Not that I remember," added quickly, as I
remembered how much I'd forgotten. "But I don't know
what's happened to me since January. If you, if you ask
at my office, they might be able to tell you . . ."

He looked at me a little oddly, said, "We tried that, but
they weren't very helpful. Nothing they knew about, they
said; but it not being your office any more, and legal matters
being privileged information, there wasn't much they were
prepared to tell us. We should take a look at your new
employer, they said."

"Wait a minute. Not my office . . . ?"

"You left," he said, "at the end of January. Very suddenly,
and without notice. Hasn't anyone told you that?"

No. No one had told me that. Another mystery, another
question; another significant danger to life as I knew it, as
I used to live it and wanted to again. My new employer
presumably was Deverill; which was probably – properly –
death, as far as finding another job was concerned . . .

Right now, though, being unemployable hereafter was if
not the least, certainly a minor among my many worries. And
nothing much I could do about it anyway, from a hospital
bed. Phone up and apologise, perhaps? Promise to do better,
try harder, sweat my little socks off for the company's good,
if they'd only take me back?

I didn't think so. I didn't generally do things without a reason; if I'd done weird things, logically there ought to be weird reasons for them. Weird, but valid. I wasn't saying sorry for anything, until I knew why I'd done it in the first place.

Well, maybe one thing. No more than that; but one thing I thought no motive could excuse.

Meanwhile, if you want to know the time, ask a policeman. So I did that, and he told me: for a wonder it was good and early yet, barely seven in the morning, and so much for its being always later than you think. I had a dose of Rip van Winkle's jet-lag, not tuned in to the season yet, seeing April light through the curtains and timing it for a January dawn.

I grunted, and shifted uncomfortably on the bed; *mirabile dictu*, the policeman took the hint. He left me his card, "I'll keep in touch with the hospital in any case, keep tabs on your progress, but call me if you think of anything useful. Anything at all. And tell the staff at once if you see anyone hanging around . . ."

I nodded, promised, waited till he went away. And then waited just a minute longer, and in came Simon, as I'd expected.

"How was it, then? Third degree?"

"Nah, no more than second."

"Well, that's all right, then, you can take another question. What would you like first this morning, a cup of tea or a wash?"

I grimaced. "Simon, tell me something."

"Sure, if I can. What?"

"What am I doing here?"

Just for a moment, he was utterly still; then, "Don't say you've forgotten? Not since yesterday?"

"No, of course not. I had a car smash, I know that. But that was, what, six days ago now. What I want to know is, why am I still in hospital? Do I need to be here?"

"Well, let's see, now. You were in a coma for three days . . ."

"Sure. I'm out of it now."

"You took a terrible crack on the head . . ."

" . . .Which has been scanned and X-rayed and poked about every which way you know, and there's nothing wrong with it."

"Except that you've lost your memory."

"Which I am not going to recover lying here, am I? There's no treatment for that, you can't give me a memory-pill and hey presto?"

"No, I suppose not. What are you saying, Jonty?"

"I want out."

"Oh, come on. I saw you when you came back yesterday afternoon, you were dead on your feet."

"That's just bruises and weakness, nothing major. My first time out of bed. I don't need to convalesce in hospital, I can do it just as well outside; and I'd rather."

"Why?"

Many reasons; but, "I don't like being beholden to Vernon Deverill," I said, "And I especially don't like being a sitting target for anyone who's got a grudge against the man. I bet there's still a policeman on this corridor, isn't there?"

"Well, not a policeman, no. Private security bloke, working for Mr Deverill, I think . . ."

"Right." And the window opened on an inner court, no access: safe enough, they must have thought, or they wouldn't have brought me here. Or left me alone. "I'd rather go somewhere I don't need protecting."

Simon sucked air worriedly through his teeth, and said, "You can't go without seeing the doctor."

"Bullshit. Of course I can."

"You haven't even been checked over properly after last

night," as he scanned the notes at the foot of my bed. "Honestly, Jonty, you can't just walk out of here . . ."

"Honestly, Simon, I can. I'm going to. Are you going to help, or what?"

In the end, he helped. He still fussed, but he disappeared for five minutes and came back with a trolley: breakfast on top, clothes on the lower shelf. Not mine, of course – or not those that Sue had said were mine, the sensuous stuff of yesterday. Those were all gone in the ruin of my former room. What was in the drawer had been salvaged, though, they'd put the fire out pretty quickly, Simon said, before it got through the wood; so my keys and purse and other things were sitting on a tray beside my bed, smelling of chemicals and char but otherwise okay.

Simon wouldn't say where these new clothes had come from, whether he'd raided doctors' lockers or the morgue; but he'd found jeans that fitted well enough, a loose sweatshirt and some deck shoes I could squeeze into if I didn't bother with socks. A tattered denim jacket to go over the top and a baseball cap to protect my abused head a little; I'd be fine, I assured him. Looked like a nice day out there, and I didn't have far to go.

Where was I going? I was going home, of course. As soon as I'd eaten and had a proper bath. The fire had left its tang on me also.

What about the security man in the corridor? He couldn't stop me any more than Simon could, he didn't have the right; but just to be sure he didn't try I had a little ruse in mind, if Simon was prepared to help me further . . .

Which he was, bless him. A policeman might have been a different matter, but Simon wasn't worried about private muscle. He took me to the bathroom in a wheelchair, in my pyjamas and a dressing-gown; and the crop-haired ape in uniform with *Scimitar Security* shoulder-flashes didn't bat an eyelid as we passed. I clearly wasn't fit to go anywhere under my own steam; I was under the aegis of hospital staff; and he had his orders and another room besides mine to keep an eye on, because Dean had been kept in overnight, Simon had told me, and his room was just across the corridor from me.

As soon as the bathroom door had closed behind us, I was levering myself carefully up onto my feet; clothes are okay as a cushion, but the deck shoes were not so comfortable under my arse. Besides, I wanted to prove – to myself and to Simon, in case either one of us suffered a change of heart – that I could stand up for myself.

Could, and did: stiff and sore for certain, but nothing worse than that, that I could feel. No pain worth hospitalising, at any rate. And the ache in my head had subsided also, the residue no worse than a hangover, and I could surely live with that. So we peeled off the pressure bandage that swathed my skull and found that whatever piece of mangled metal had come into contact with my head, it had torn the scalp every which way. The greater shock was finding wide tracks of my floppy blond hair shaved down to stubble, where the doctors had put seams of ugly black stitching.

While the bath was running I persuaded Simon to show off his barbering skills again, trimming what was left of my hair to a kind of chopped velvet all over. It was an improvement, of sorts, though the stitches stood out more; I was going to be grateful for that cap. Then I shucked off dressing-gown and pyjamas, to stand buck naked in front of the full-length mirror. The bruises looked better than ever, fading to browns and yellows around the edges now while their hearts were still purple and black; sunset glories I carried on my skin. But another night's rest had eased them, so that they looked far worse than they felt. I was more concerned with the dressings on my arms and legs and what might lie beneath them, what secret damage I'd taken.

But it was six days now since the accident, and I'd always healed fast; and again nothing felt too bad, bending and stretching. I started to pick at sticking-plaster, wincing as it lived up to its name; behind me, Simon chuckled.

"Get in the bath, Jonty. They'll come a lot easier after you've soaked them."

True enough. I subsided, into a few inches of water at the sort of temperature you wash a baby in; and snarled and sat up again, to turn the hot tap full on.

Lay back in currents of heat, my eyes closed and my mind drifting in the steam, my skin stinging and my muscles relaxing and my throat sighing and moaning in gentle pleasure despite Simon's laughter.

Never had any bath been so necessary, or felt so good; never had any man been more reluctant to move than I was then.

But it had to be, I didn't have the time to waste. I sat up long before I was ready to do that, and soaped myself all over to show again how much improved I was since yesterday; soaped my head also as there was no point using shampoo, but I worked up as much lather as I could with fingers that dug like cruel nails into a scalp still far too tender to be treated like this, only to show that I could.

Do so much to myself, I thought, and I could surely take anything the world was going to do to me . . .

Then it was up and out of the water in a surge, splashing everything, the wheelchair and my new clothes and Simon included; and then that surge was reflected inside my head like a tidal suck, draining strength and will, leaving me giddy and weak and clutching at a grab-rail to keep from toppling over.

"Knackered now, aren't you?" I heard Simon's voice say distantly, echoing in my mind like in a tunnel, hollow and leading nowhere. But I could hear his grin too, though my eyes were too dizzy to see it; *you didn't fool me with all that visible energy* was what he was really saying. "It's okay, you just stood up too fast. You said it yourself, you're convalescent; you've got to go easy for a while. Don't rush your fences. Now hang on, while I do this . . ."

And then I yelled, as he ripped the first dressing off my arm; and no, soaking it hadn't noticeably helped at all. But my vision cleared, at least, and my mind stopped swirling. Nothing like a little superficial pain to focus you right there in your body, good and sharp.

Simon methodically stripped off every plaster and every pad of lint. He sucked his teeth over a couple of significant gashes, that were carrying stitches; those he put new dressings on, and told me to get them looked at in a few days' time. The remaining scabs and scrapes would heal better for some air, he said, and left them uncovered.

Bending over made my head spin again, so he dried my legs for me while I patted a towel gingerly at all the sore places I could reach. Then he helped me dress, and we argued cheerfully over the wheelchair until I put a stop to argument by opening the door and walking out of there.

Well, scuttling out of there. Sidling, perhaps. Peeking to see if the security guard was looking this way; seeing that he wasn't, and slipping as fast as I could manage, as quiet as I could manage down the corridor and out of his line of sight. Simon followed me, with the empty chair; he was grinning, I was praying.

There was a process to be gone through, he said, if I insisted on discharging myself; especially if I wouldn't even wait to discuss it with a doctor. Papers to be signed, he said. Please? he said; and I nodded, and let him guide me to an office behind reception.

He left me there, and went to phone a taxi. I sat, with a grunt of relief, and argued with the administrator until she produced my file. I signed a release form, told her where I was going, said no, I wasn't accompanied, but the taxi would take me straight there; and then I repeated this new method I'd discovered for resolving the irresolvable, I got up and walked out.

Simon was waiting, just outside the automatic doors. I joined him, stood for a moment soaking up the sunshine, and said, "I suppose you'd be outraged if I offered you a tip?"

"Damn right," he agreed. "I know exactly how much you've got in that wallet, and it wouldn't begin to cover it. Besides," when I didn't grin back, when I forced him to take me seriously, "I was just doing my job."

"No, you weren't. Smuggling patients out past Vernon Deverill's security guards is no part of your job, Simon."

"No, but I enjoyed that bit."

"It's not going to get you into trouble, is it?"

He shook his head positively. "I don't work for Mr Deverill."

"Even so, he's got a lot of clout . . ."

"So's my charge nurse. I'll be fine. Here's your taxi. Safe home, mate . . ." and he was gone.

Every road and alleyway within the hospital grounds was lined with parked cars; the main loop was slow with traffic as constant arrivals trawled for space. The taxi-driver grumbled under his breath when we came to a dead stop, queuing three behind a car that was heir-apparent to a place currently being slowly and carefully backed out of by an old Morris 1000. If I drove such a car, I thought, I too would be that careful; why take risks with a pocket heaven?

And why would someone who feels like that, I thought, *whose ideal is a car more than thirty years old already, why would such a person be driving – let alone crashing at speed – an MR2?*

At last the Moggy was out onto the roadway, given plenty of manoeuvring-room by us polite queuers; and in the brief pause where all was static, before its driver could select

a new gear and potter forward, a car came neatly out of
an alley-mouth where it had clearly been lurking, it drove
twenty metres the wrong way up this one-way loop and
nipped into the space the Moggy had vacated.

And it parked, and its driver got out and walked blithely
away while all of us in the queue were still manipulating
our startled jaws back into position; and I think, I hope that
any other day, any other driver I'd have been cheering for
the sheer nerve of it, once I got over my startlement.

Not this day, not this driver. I was sliding low as I could
get on that back seat, almost ducking my head below
window-level not to let Sue – no, Suzie, let her be Suzie –
spot me as she sauntered up to the hospital's main entrance,
her arms full of gifts and packages and Adolphus.

Not much money in my purse, just a fiver and small change;
but no matter for that, it was enough. Enough to get me
home, at least, and I wasn't looking any further.

Never would have done, probably, if my insouciant
mother had had her way with me, if her training had held.
This was how she'd always wanted me to live; it was the
way she lived herself, St Matthew her guiding preceptor,
though in her own translation: *Tomorrow? What's with
tomorrow? This is today, my son, and it won't last, so grab
it.* Unnatural parent, she cared not a jot for my career or my
safe, solid prospects or my comfortably-settled love life. If
I'd been visibly unhappy, I guess she might have worried;
as I wasn't – or hadn't been, any maternal visit these last ten
years – she'd cultivated blithe unconcern into an art form.
She might have failed utterly in her objective, if she'd really
meant to turn me out a carbon copy of her own disinterested
self, but that was necessarily not a problem. I could go to
hell in a handcart, so long as that was the way I'd chosen
to go; her philosophy couldn't point a finger at me.

During my teenage years, while she was burdening me

with freedoms I didn't want and I was rebelling as hard as I could manage, loading myself with chains, often and often she'd say, *There's only one rule in this family, darling: don't ever find yourself stranded, because I may not be able to come get you. Run and find out, go and have fun, any party you fancy anywhere in the world; but just you make sure you've got enough cash to get home with.*

With licence like that, was it any wonder I never took advantage?

Well, hardly ever.

I'd been a little prig, probably: a schoolboy with savings, a teenager who refused to be a tearaway, a student who studied and wouldn't ever play beyond his means.

And, of course, a solicitor who drove a Volvo about twenty years too soon . . .

Ah, what the hell. Too late for regrets. *Non, je ne regrette rien*, about the only one of my mother's precepts that really had taken with me, even if in a form she thought perversely twisted; and if my whole life thus far had been designed to make sure I never had cause to regret, I could at least do myself the courtesy of not changing the standard now. *Be safe, be certain* had always been my battle-cry, impetuosity the thing to fear, the stuff of later regrets . . .

And besides, here I was finally doing something my mother would wholeheartedly have approved of: coming home from some kind of a party a week late, with massive holes in my memory and just enough cash for the taxi-fare. Bingo. Must remember to tell her, whenever she surfaced next . . .

Ten minutes in the taxi, one side of town to the other: and these streets were second nature to me, every corner long since logged and charted. There was the pub, the *Beamish Boy*; there was the delicatessen, with its yellow paintwork and its inevitable student conclave just outside the door;

there the two rival corner-shops on adjacent corners, and here at last were the street and the door that meant home to me, and had done for as long as I wanted to remember.

I handed over the fiver, with my usual embarrassed mumble that meant *keep the change, if there is any*; I got out of the cab, and watched it drive away; I fished my old key-wallet out of the unfamiliar pocket of these unfamiliar jeans, and waited for my fingers to find the ones that would let me in.

And of course they didn't, because those keys weren't there.

I'd *known* that, damn it, I'd seen it in the hospital. 'Home is the place where, when you have to go there, they have to take you in' – but it was startlingly, frighteningly easy to find yourself homeless. Me, I'd just put my head down and run without thinking, to where instinct and history both said I'd find welcome and security; and here I was, and here was neither one of those, and I'd been a fool to expect them.

Still, you can't obliterate history, and affection's roots can run deep even when there's little to be seen on the surface. She didn't have to take me in, maybe, but she might yet choose to.

So I went to the door anyway, and knocked; and I'd been so hasty to run out of the hospital before Sue – Suzie, damn it, Suzie – turned up that I was still ahead of the day here, Carol hadn't left for work yet.

Carol opened the door, and saw me; and me, I saw the effort, the tremendous effort it was for her, not to slam that door in my face the moment she clocked who I was behind the scabs and the bruises.

"What the hell," she said, who never swore, "what the fucking *hell* do you want here?"

Shelter from the storm, but I couldn't ask that, she had to offer. "I want to talk," I said, with a helpless, hopeless gesture. "I've got to talk to you, Carol."

"What, now?" with an ostentatious glance at her watch, *some of us still go to work, Jonty.*

"Well, no, but . . . I didn't have anywhere else to go."

"Oh, really? What happened to your little ethnic friend?"

"I can't handle her at the moment, I need . . ."

"Frankly, Jonty," she said, "I don't give a damn what you need. You're not my problem any more. Your choice, if you remember, not mine. So now it's my turn to choose; and no, I don't want to talk to you, now or preferably ever. And no, you certainly can't come and wait the day out in here, if that's what you were suggesting. If you can't go back to the little wife, you can camp out on some park bench for all I care. Go and play wino in a doorway, at least you look the part. Been good for you, hasn't it, this big change thing? You really look like you've grown . . .

"But fuck off and do your growing somewhere else, not on my doorstep. I'm *not* going to talk to you, I'm not going to listen to you, even; and if you're still here by the time I leave for work, I'll call the police and get an injunction. Understood?"

And she didn't even wait for my nod of acceptance, *understood*, she just did what she'd so much wanted to do before, and slammed the door in my face.

· FIVE ·

RA-RA AVIS

Firm, but fair. If I believed what I'd been told – and it was surely impossible not to do that now, despite my soul's rejection – then I had to believe also what it implied, that I'd treated Carol appallingly.

I thought I'd seen her in every mood, but I'd never seen her as angry as this; and this was a couple of months after the fact, after the act, after I'd demonstrably left her. She didn't ordinarily stew, she didn't hold grudges any more than she used what she called cheap language. She'd see my leaving as a betrayal, of course, she'd have to; a betrayal that renewed itself with every day apart, just as what we'd had formerly had been renewed and strengthened – or so it had seemed, so we'd both affirmed – with every day together.

That must be why she was so embittered, that I'd made what seemed a waste and a deception out of all those long years of promises and trust. I'd taken the bulk of her adult life with me, when I left; and I had no way to give that back, no way to persuade her that she should believe memory rather than revelation, the way it had seemed to be rather than the way she saw it now.

That I was still nine-tenths in love with her, at least; that I was the reverse of her, that I valued what we'd lost all the more for having lost it; no, I wouldn't, couldn't have raised that with her even if she'd let me talk at all. I'd surrendered the right, although I couldn't remember when or how. Indisputable now, that my hands had packed and my feet had walked away from Carol. No matter that no shadow of my doing it remained to haunt me; the thing had been done and was I thought unforgivable.

Which was probably the only thing left that Carol and I could agree on . . .

Took me a minute, but I did walk dutifully away from her door. Though it had been my door too, my home, and only my intellect could believe now that it wasn't; my heart still yearned for its familiar comforts and hers also, strength of shoulder and softness of breast, tanglements of hair and her low voice like an echo of the sea, distant, potent.

But I did walk, and I'd have walked to the pub if it was open, though I barely had the cash to buy myself a pint, and what's one pint in a crisis?

Too early, though, by far. The *Boy*'s doors would be locked for hours yet. Even the off-licences weren't open, even if I'd wanted to follow Carol's recommendation and play wino in a doorway, which I didn't.

Instead I just carried on walking, blindly, heedlessly; and because I wasn't thinking, my feet fell into old long-established habits and carried me through the park and down the hill towards town.

And because I wasn't thinking, I didn't think *I can't do this, I'm in no condition, I can't walk forty minutes without a break*; but I'd not been going long before my body reminded me, and I'd not got halfway before I had to sit down because my legs simply wouldn't take me further.

But it had turned into a sunny morning, warmly spring; and my way to town led through parks and public gardens, so it was really no hardship to slump down onto a bench and lift my face to the restorative light. *Ten minutes*, I told myself firmly, *just ten minutes, and I'll get moving* . . .

Only that I had nowhere to move to, I had been moving without purpose and having stopped, I couldn't find the impetus to move again. It wasn't just the soreness of flesh barely healed and the weakness of muscles barely off a bed that held me static in the sun for longer, much longer than my ten minutes' allotment.

It's hard to tell time, with your eyes closed and all your body, mind, spirit disorganised. Half an hour at least I sat on that bench, or it might have been an hour, maybe more. And I might have, no, I would have sat there longer still if someone else hadn't been moved to move me.

Chance? Fate? Luke says there's no such thing, he says that accident and coincidence are only labels we apply to the more mysterious workings of the higher powers, benign or otherwise. He would say that, of course, but sometimes I feel impelled to believe him. Other times I find it hard enough to fit my head around Luke; his theology, his Manichaean puppet-master vision of all people as pawns in a multiplex game that as little resembles chess as chess does hopscotch becomes altogether too much for me, and I crash through into a comforting atheism where there is neither god nor devil to disturb the workings and imaginings of men.

Which is, of course, promptly etched to nothing by acid reality, the next time I consider Luke . . .

Of his own kindness, then, or else prodded by some power or principality of indeterminate intent, a man who had been seemingly catching up on the sports results two benches down – though I thought in honesty he'd just been absorbing sunlight as I was, practising photosynthesis for the next life – stood up, walked over and offered me his paper.

"Looks like you're settled for the day there, son," – he was American, of course; catch a Brit being so offhandedly open-handed with a stranger – "you might as well have the benefit of this, if you want it."

As cover, he meant, as he'd been using it himself; perhaps he meant as more literal cover, perhaps he was saying *get your head down, put this over your face and have a snooze*, if Americans talk about snoozing. Whatever, I took the paper with as good a smile as I could manage through my all-too-British startlement and a stammer of thanks, too late; he was five metres down the path already and didn't bother to look round to acknowledge it, only made a vague gesture with one hand to suggest that he had heard, but that his offer was too commonplace to merit even a token gratitude.

Well, now I really didn't have to move. Only a tabloid, but it could still take me an hour to read; and maybe some subconscious process would have made a decision for me by the time I reached the back-page cartoon, maybe I'd have figured out what to do or where to go . . .

I read the headline, a 40-point SLEAZE SENSATION ROCKS CABINET, then checked out the pictures on the front page: politicos scuttling down Downing St, gazing at their crabwise-shuffling feet to avoid catching the eye of the camera; and then, boxed off from that story, the picture of a great tree falling. And beside it a lesser headline, triple-stacked: COLBURNE VALLEY PROTESTORS: 'WE'LL BE BACK!'

Which was the gift, the sending, the forefinger of fate – or angel or devil, whatever, if it wasn't sheer coincidence or chance – nudging me when I seemed not to be quite on track.

What did I know from Colburne Valley? Fuck nothing except the one thing, I didn't even know where it was; but that didn't matter. I didn't have to go there. It was a trigger, that was all, gifted or sent or whatever, and it fired me like a slow bullet – a dumdum blond, call me, soft head and all

– from the tunnel of my depression as if it were the barrel of a long gun. No great speed, but a deal of distance . . .

Except of course that this bullet had to provide its own propellant. I was up on my feet already and moving as best I could, heading for town again as fast as my aching legs would carry me; but that was neither fast nor far, and nowhere near enough. And my Volvo was God alone knew where, but nowhere near me; and its substitute the MR2 must be a write-off, even if I had any sense of its possession, which I didn't; and there wasn't any way to get where I was going, other than by car. Well, there was, but not for me. A succession of buses I guess I could have managed, if I could only get money for the fares, but not the climb after. This current walking was almost too much, and this was downhill all the way.

Like so much else, I thought, smirking, loving the pun, *like my life, suddenly* . . . But that wasn't true, or not necessarily true. At least I had a target now, something to shoot at; and that brought its own focus by definition, I wasn't careering blindly any more.

More puns threatening there, more disturbing to me. If a man is a composite of his parts there were fundamentally two things that defined me, my career and Carol, and both of those were seemingly gone now.

So don't think about it now. One foot in front of the other, think about that, it's getting harder . . .

Which it was. I was sweating and breathing fast, driving against my body's reluctance and clamping my mind against its tendency to spin. Never mind my job or my love life, I focused by necessity on my feet.

Step by step, and all too aware of each one of them, I made my way into the city centre. Found where I was aiming for, stepped up from the street, pushed the glass door open; and even as I was walking in I was thinking this was maybe not such a bright idea.

I needed a car; I'd come to a car-hire company, first I
could think of. So far so good.

So here I was walking into this nice smart expensive
polished shopfront, asking to hire one of their nice smart
expensive polished vehicles; and me with my face all scabby
and unshaven today, the skin still puffy and yellow from
fading bruises and the sweat of effort like a sheen across
my brow, moving strangely because it was getting harder
and harder to drag the weight of my bones against the deep
weariness and the deeper hurt, looking in short like I'd been
living the life that Carol had recommended to me. Thank
God the boozers weren't open, or I'd have had the smell
of beer hanging over me like a garnish, just to make the
unlikely impossible; but even without that, I still must look
like a street-stricken wino in borrowed finery, because the
clothes on my back might be clean but they all too clearly
didn't fit well enough to be my own.

Too late to check now, though, too late to back away.
The clerk behind the counter was already watching me with
interest; and I might have lost everything that defined me
to myself but it seemed that I still had some pride, unless
it was sheer bloody stubbornness instead.

Whichever, I walked boldly in where no man of my
description had walked before . . .

Walked? Shuffled, more like. Waddled, maybe. My
legs wouldn't stride, and my bare feet in those deck
shoes conformed to someone else's bunions were already
beginning to blister. If I wanted to walk without wincing
– which I did, most definitely – then I had to go flat-
footed and with care, leaning at curious angles to shift
my weight.

All in all I was a procession in my own right, and
something of a sad one. I watched the clerk struggle with
a smirk that would rise despite his training, and felt a flush
of anger in response.

Good. Use it. Apologetic would be the worst thing, just now . . .

I leaned a little on the counter when at last I got there, glad of its good support after that long stretch on my feet, and this last couple of metres over carpet seemingly the longest; and fixed the clerk with my best version of a steely stare, and said, "I'd like to hire a car. Please."

"Yes, sir," swallowing his smile, but I thought maybe reserving a little pleasure for later, for when he turned me down. In fact, I thought I saw his nostrils flare as he set a form on the counter between us, and was doubly glad I hadn't had the chance of a drink. "Any particular type?"

"Doesn't matter. Nothing too small," I amended quickly, thinking that I might need to stretch out and sleep in it. "I'm going across country. Just me, no baggage or anything, but I'm not comfortable driving a little car . . ."

And I was talking too much already, explaining where I didn't need to, starting to plead almost; I bit down hard on my too-eager tongue, and was silent.

"Have you got your driver's licence with you, sir?"

Thank God, I had: one old habit not apparently broken in the recent upheavals. It was in the back of my purse, where I always kept it; and while I had the purse out, stained and strangely-smelling as it was, I thought I might as well produce my Access card as well, to add a little verisimilitude. *I may look rough just now, but at least I'm creditworthy . . .*

So I fished, and my fingers found plastic just where they ought to; but when I eased it out it wasn't my Access card at all. Wrong colour.

Gold colour . . .

American Express it was, when I looked more closely. And yes, definitely gold. Which required more disposable income and considerably more creditworthiness than I'd ever mustered yet; but there was my name embossed into the plastic, and there was my signature on the back when I turned it over to check, and I supposed that I should be getting used to this, but oh, it was hard . . .

When I looked up, the clerk was frowning as he watched me, and I could read his thoughts as clear as if they'd been written in mud baked under a hot sun: *that surprised you, didn't it, sir? Whose pocket did you lift the purse from, then, didn't they look like a gold-carder?*

But he didn't say anything yet, he must be saving it for later. He took the licence out of its plastic holder and checked it minutely, probably wishing they'd introduced photographs already so that he could prove immediately that it wasn't mine; then he grunted – in frustration, I thought, at finding no convictions, no penalty points – and asked if I'd ever had an accident.

I lied, of course. What was I going to say, *yes, I'm fresh out of hospital, discharged myself early after I totalled my car last week, but I can't remember a thing about it*? No, I lied in my teeth and just hoped not to have another smash, because surely the insurance wouldn't cover me after I'd signed my name to a false declaration.

Another grunt, and I wasn't at all sure that he'd believed me; but I suppose he didn't have any right of interrogation, he just had to take my dishonest word for it. So we filled in some of the form, and then he ran the card – *my* card? – through the machine for authorisation, and I knew, I just knew he was expecting the little screen to flash a warning at him, *Card Stolen! Alert Police!*

But obviously it didn't, and neither did it have any problems with the amount it was going to cost me to hire an Orion for a week. The disappointment on his face was manifest, he couldn't hide it. There was nothing left for him now except to challenge my signature when I produced it; and he tried his best to do that, he spent a long time scrutinising it against the card, but in the end he had to give way.

Which in some respects was as much assurance to me as to him: if he who was trained and practised and trying so hard couldn't spot enough difference between two signatures to pick one as a forgery, then likely neither one was. Which meant that I really had signed that card and I really was gold Amex material suddenly; and it might all be mystery bordering on magic, but it was one more confirmation that I wasn't being conned here, I wasn't being set up. Whatever had changed in my life, I'd effected those changes myself; and what I could do once, I could work out now why I'd done it.

Sure I could, no sweat. None at all . . .

I took the keys that the clerk so reluctantly gave me, and walked out of there feeling surprisingly grateful. Every business had the right to turn down custom; his manager couldn't possibly have blamed him, the way I looked and acted, however solid my *bona fides* might appear. But he hadn't let prejudice rule him; he'd done his checks, I'd passed, he hired me a car. However much against his better judgement, he was letting me drive away in the company's property, and yes, I was properly grateful.

Next question, could I actually do it? Could I drive, was I in any condition?

Answer, yes and no. No, I wasn't in any condition; but yes, I could drive despite that.

Slowly, but I always drove slowly anyway, except apparently when flying MR2s off tight corners; uncomfortably, but I'd expected that; safely, so long as I stopped often to rest. I had to concentrate fiercely, the old days were gone when driving was easy and natural; and I couldn't concentrate for more than twenty minutes at a time, half an hour at the most. Any longer than that and my vision started to blur, I couldn't move my eyes left to right without a sharp pain inside my skull, my hands started to shake on

the wheel and my legs ached cruelly just from working
the pedals.

So I established a routine, designed to save me the
insurance money I wouldn't get if I drove off the road
from exhaustion; designed to save also my life, perhaps,
and others' with it. I watched the milometer religiously, and
took a ten-minute break every ten miles, tilting the seat as
far back as it would go, just lying still with my eyes closed
and trying to relax, neither to think nor anticipate.

At thirty miles I started looking for a tea shop, and found
one open in a village five miles further on. Same again after
another thirty, more or less; though by then I was into the
rugged, rolling moorland that was prelude to the Lakes, and
close enough not to want to stop. Made myself do it, though,
for the pleasure of a good hot cup of tea on a dry throat –
could be the last, was very likely to be the last for some time
now – and the good sense of it, not to break a habit that was
working, that had brought me most of the way across the
country without a dent or a scare.

I was hungry: hungry enough to slaver at the scones and
the coffee cake, with barely enough cash in my purse to
pay for an individual pot of tea. But hunger was good,
it was helping, keeping my mind sharp and giving a
physical focus to my body so that I thought less about
everything else that was wrong with me, all the damage I
was carrying.

Back in the car again, another twenty miles and now
this was known country, and that helped too. I wasn't
following a route-map in my head any more, signs and
numbers; I was spotting landmarks, turning left just after
the ruined barn and then looking for another unexpected
left, hidden back of a twisted tree that had exploded into
leaf since my last visit here, to hide the track even
better.

Picking clues from landscape, clues from memory – and

rejoicing that I could still do that, that some things in this grotesquely-altered world were still as I remembered them, as I had left them last – and always, always heading up.

Came a time, came a place where the track went up no further, where it petered into wheel-ruts and nothing amid the sheep tracks. There must be an ongoing right of way to the top, but it seemed that even Wainwright had never found it; so far as I knew this particular route featured in none of the guidebooks and was marked on no tourist trail. Even the farmers seldom came this way after their sheep any more; the deep tracks of Land Rover tyres in mud were breaking down year on year as winters passed and they were not remade, as they crumbled through the droughts of summer and before the roots of tough grasses.

And here at the track's end a thin smoke was rising, straight and true like the trunk of a tree until the wind caught it and it eddied into confusion like a moorland tree in the spring's blur; and I turned off the engine and left the car right there, and all but ran a dozen eager, stumbling paces to the lip of the hollow.

This was it, my secret place, my refuge: a haven in my teenage years and a constant reassurance since, somewhere I kept in my head like a treasure. Not my home, never that by any definition, let alone Frost's; I was under no illusion here, I was only ever taken in on sufferance and I could get turned away at any time, licence revoked and *never come back, this place is closed to you.*

But it never had been, yet. I came when I needed to, and here I found what I needed. Here I found Luke, today as always, heating water in a billy over his small fire; and he smiled up at me and made a gesture of welcome, said, "Jonty, come down. I've been expecting you."

He always said that and as always I believed him, though

I'd come as always on impulse and without warning. Had no
way to warn him, indeed, there wasn't an address to send
a postcard to; and yet every time I came there was already
water heating and two mugs set out. Something cynical in
me always murmured that the water wasn't so hot yet, and
that it was easy enough to hear a car coming up the track,
working hard; but Luke would never work to set up a false
implication, just to impress. He wouldn't see the point.

Besides – if he cared, which he didn't – he was impressive
enough simply in himself, that spirit clothed in that flesh
which was called by his name. He stood up as I slithered
down the grassy slope into the hollow, he met me with a
hard hug at the foot; and I toppled into his arms like a child,
I clung like a child in despair, my eyes screwed tight shut
and my face buried in the loose cotton weave of his shirt.

Smoke and spices he smelled of, and not the first to do that
to me since I'd woken into this remade world; and I thought
maybe that was another reason why I'd started to believe
Suzie when she talked of impossible things. Not only that
she'd had photographs and known about Luke, but also that
she'd tasted like him, a little. In her case it was cigarette
smoke and Chinese spices, poor substitutes, but resonant in
combination; now here – at last – was the truth, the thing
itself, Luke's own golden skin that smelled of woodsmoke
superficially and beneath that the strange spicy otherness
that I privately called the tang of angels.

He pushed me away too soon, but that was Luke. Ice-chip
eyes surveyed me, glacier-green and seeing everything, but
only in black and white: admitting no compromise, no
shading.

"You've been hurt," he said, and his strong hands shifted
from my shoulders to my face, brushing feather-light over
scabs and bruising.

"Yes," I said, trying not to flinch, and failing.

"Come and sit down. Water's heating."

Water was; and when it seethed in the billy, when it spat hissing onto the hot stones that made Luke's hearth, he lifted it two-handed, bare-handed from the fire and poured into two chipped enamel mugs. I didn't blink, either at his immunity of flesh or else at being given nothing but near-boiling water to drink. I'd been here before.

Instead I sat slowly, wearily, awkwardly cross-legged on the grass, cradled the mug for the comfort of its heat in my knackered hands and let my eyes wander around the hollow. Every time I came things were different here, there were different things; and yet it always looked the same, it had only ever looked like a junkyard set in a quarry garden, metal scrap and mechanical parts rusting like nameless, neglected sculptures among plants and shrubs and even trees that surely shouldn't grow up here.

I was fifteen when I found it first, on a solitary adolescent hike; and Luke had been sitting over his fire and smiling up at me, and water had been heating.

I thought he was nineteen, then. I remember working it out practically on my fingers – *older than eighteen, for sure, but younger than twenty* – and feeling certain, feeling so cocky I didn't even need to ask.

Looking at him now, with another dozen years banked up behind me, I still thought he was nineteen; still thought that was exact. Full growth but no maturity, whip-fast reflexes and not an ounce more flesh than he could need or want; fire and hunger, passion and arrogance and the habit of instant judgement with no sense of perspective, no leniency.

And beauty, of course, he was the child of delight; and pain, of course, an extraordinary pain that faded as his perfect body aged, which meant not at all; and above and surrounding and engulfing all, the certainty that there was no forgiveness, that there could be no reconciliation in this world or any other.

And that also was pure nineteen-year-old thinking, and

not subject to debate. No, he never changed; and I loved him for it, and grieved for it, and depended on it, and that also would not and could not change.

He sucked unconcernedly at water that would have blistered my throat, and said, "Tell me about it."

What, you mean you don't know all about it already? But even a creature who could access infinity was presumably not omniscient, or Luke would never have found himself here, on this cold hill's side; and as he was now, no, of course he didn't know, how could he? He might have some sense of prescience for what affected him closely, but he had no all-seeing eye on the world's events.

Nor television nor radio, and he'd hardly be reading the papers every day.

So okay, I'd tell him. I would. But I'd come here to escape, I'd crossed the country in an effort to leave it all behind, not to bring it with me. So – looking to divert his mind without any real hope of it, just grabbing almost at random – I said, "That's a new caravan, isn't it?"

Whether he actually needed a caravan, I wasn't sure. I knew he could sit all night in the rain quite unperturbed; I thought he could nest in the open in the snow and not be cold. But even Luke's parsimony fractured occasionally. He always had a fire, though I could never reason any need for that or for his heating the water that he drank; and he'd always had a caravan up here, though he was rarely to be found inside it.

Once it was an ancient, nameless thing on blocks, painted institution-green, its door half hanging off and the roof not that secure. Then it was an Elddis, not new but neatly made, holding together against the weather and Luke's contemptuous mistreatment. Something must have happened to that, I thought; he wouldn't have changed without cause, and little less than a total disintegration would be cause enough.

But changed he had. Luke's new home was an Airstream

from America, a long gleaming silver bullet of a caravan, all aerodynamics and riveted aluminium, more plane than wagon except that it lacked the wings . . .

Ouch. Not a good thought, that, around Luke. I had no evidence that he could read my mind, but likewise no evidence that he couldn't.

"Yes," he said, dealing only with what I'd said aloud, thank God.

"How'd you get it up here? Friendly farmer?" The rough track would have been no problem, an Airstream could take any amount of banging about, but Luke had no way of towing one himself.

"No," he said, "I lifted it."

And didn't explain how – on his shoulders, like Atlas? Hanging from a rope while he flew above, like a helicopter carrying a tank? – and obviously didn't want to, for all my curiosity. It had taken me a while to learn, back when I was a curious and fascinated teenager, but he loathed talking about those talents and abilities that marked him out, what powers had come with him in his great transition.

So there we were, seemingly two young men facing each other across a quiet fire, and neither one of us keen to talk about what the other wanted; but he was Luke and I was Jonty, and so of course I talked about the loss of my natural world, so very much less than his.

Or started to, at least. Didn't get very far.

"I had a car smash," I said. "Apparently. I don't remember a thing about it; but that's not all that's gone, that's the least of it. I can't remember anything from the last couple of months, and I've done so much that's strange, but I don't know why. Listen," with a wry little chuckle, first time I'd managed to laugh about this or any of it, "I've even got married, Luke, would you believe it? Not to Carol, either . . ."

He nodded. "I know."

"Do you?" What, was he omniscient after all? "How?"

"You told me."

"You mean – you mean I've *been* here? *Recently?*" And, at his nod, "When? Exactly?"

"Six days ago," he said, exact enough for anybody.

I counted back in my head, then did it again on my fingers for confirmation. "Was I driving a green sports car?"

Luke just shrugged at that; I groaned, slapping the side of my own head in apology and then yelping at the stab of pain that rightly followed, and maybe there was more wrong with my memory than the doctors knew. Forgetting my bad head was stupid, but forgetting Luke's limitations was worse than stupid, it was offensive. To me, if not to him. I'd known him all my adult life and longer; and no, he wouldn't know the colour of the car. How could he?

But logic said yes, I had been driving a green sports car. Logic was blushing, in fact, logic was humiliated. Suzie had located the crash in Cumbria and I hadn't thought beyond that; there'd been so many questions some of them had to get away, and that one had finished up free and clear, totally overlooked. But it shouldn't have. It was no great mental leap from *Cumbria* to *Lakes*; and from Lakes to Luke was no leap at all, it was apple pie and Wensleydale, a natural connection in my head.

Put it plain: I'd driven over to see Luke, and then I'd crashed the car.

Afterwards . . .

"Luke," I said, "what did I *say?* What did I tell you?"

"You told me that you'd got married. In a church," added with sublime distaste, a curl of the lip that was part sneer and part physical revulsion, as at something rank and rotting.

I grunted. "What else?"

"That you were working for Vernon Deverill now."

"Yes? Doing what?"

"Trying to get a crooked accountant out of jail, you said."

"Right, I figured that. But did I say why? Or how?"

"No. I didn't ask."

No. He wouldn't have. "So what did I come over for, anything special?" There must have been a reason, I thought. Young man a few weeks married, ex-solicitor living it up on a villain's petty cash: whichever role counted for more, neither one fitted comfortably with my driving all this way to spend a day, just a single day with Luke.

"You asked me questions about the Leavenhall Bypass protest, and Scimitar Security."

"Shit. Did I? And I suppose I didn't tell you why?"

A smile, a shake of the head. Motives didn't interest Luke, it was only the thing done that mattered. Which left me little better off than I had been. I knew that the Leavenhall protest had happened, was happening still; and that Luke was involved, and that the bypass was going ahead regardless – which last actually didn't need saying, given what had gone before. Luke was involved in the protest, therefore the protest was failing. He had a demonic eye for lost causes, had Luke.

But why I should have been interested in a new road or the opposition to it, I couldn't imagine. Vernon Deverill had a connection, yes, he owned the company that was building the road, as well as the councillors who had given him the contract; but so what? There were few major projects in the region that didn't bear his fingerprints, somewhere along the line. And Scimitar Security rang several bells with me on a personal level, but none of them seemed to have a particularly relevant chime.

"Can you remember what I asked you? Exactly?"

"Yes."

Of course he could, I was only making noises in my confusion. Luke did this to me sometimes: just a few minutes in his company and I'd be working to assert my humanity, my fallibility. Asking questions when I already knew the answers, saying things twice although he'd heard the first time, that sort of thing. Making mistakes that in retrospect had to be deliberate, though only on some far-down level I couldn't consciously access. Telling him, maybe also telling myself that I really wouldn't want a memory etched in anodised steel, not a word or a moment ever to be lost.

I'd take dictation from him if he'd sit still that long, I'd write down every question I had asked him and his every response; but not today, I decided. Maybe not tomorrow, either.

"Your head hurts," he told me.

"No kidding." That slap on the skull I'd given myself had started a throbbing curse of a headache, which would likely build into a sweet little migraine ninety-odd miles from my stock of Migraleve.

If I still had any stock of Migraleve. If Suzie hadn't changed it all for a bagful of Chinese herbs . . .

Here and now, though, migraines were an anxiety but not a problem, Migraleve not actually an issue. What need chemicals with Luke at hand, Luke's hands to hold and help me?

He never fixed anything for good, mind, never for real. I still got migraines, and bronchitis in the winter, and arthritic pains in my hip whenever the weather turned wet, where I'd broken it as a kid. But right here and for now, Luke's touch would be better than any analgesic.

Would be, and was. He said, "Come here," and I said, "Would you?" when I already knew that he would; and I shifted round the fire to sit with my back to him like he was going to give me a massage, and instead his hands closed tight and hard around my head.

Closed, gripped, *squeezed*; and never mind what the doctors said, that I had no fracture in my skull. I swear I could feel all its separate pieces shifting, under that pressure. I wanted to scream, but had no breath to do it; best I could manage was a gasp and a whimper, too weak even to sob.

The squeezing was internal also. Not only my bones, my brain felt crushed between his fingers, like a sponge in a vice. My head would be a coconut, I thought, when he was finished, just a dry shell with no life in it; it would rattle and hiss when he shook it, a percussive instrument, because there'd be nothing inside but desiccated coconut.

But he only kept it up for a second or two, and amazingly I could still think when he lifted his hands away, my eyes once they had finished watering could still see; and when I shook my head now, it didn't hurt. When I slapped my forehead, that didn't hurt either. Bone-ache and brain-ache, both were gone. No migraine threatened now, I was just crazy-tired suddenly, my muscles sucked of strength and my bones of solidity.

I twisted my head round to smile at him, and even that much was major effort. "Thanks."

He nodded, didn't ask how I felt now or anything so unnecessary. He knew how I felt. His hands moved more lightly down my arms and over my chest and my crossed legs, and the bruises were not so sore and the healing cuts didn't itch so much any more.

Then, "Go and sleep," he said, "you will need to."

He was not wrong. I could barely manage the vertical without help, which he didn't offer; made it at last and staggered the dozen paces to the open Airstream door and had to grip the frame to keep myself upright there, for one last glance back at Luke.

He was looking into the fire, turned right away from me, not watching, not concerned. He'd done his part, and I was on my own again.

Fair enough.

*   *   *

Luke might have a new caravan to adorn his hollow – 'lifted'
he'd said, and I thought maybe that applied more ways than
one: I'd never seen him use money, and Airstreams came
expensive, especially this side of the pond – but once inside
there was only the stretch of it, only the added space to say
so. Otherwise it looked just the same as the last one, or the
one before.

The skin was intact, but nothing inside remained. The
interior had been gutted: walls and doors, furniture and
facilities all gone, all ripped out by a rough and untimely
hand before they were ready to go. There were scars to
affirm it, and holes uncouthly plugged with rags and plastic.

Never knew how big something really was, till it was
empty. This was *big*. And not at all cosy, not homelike
despite the rugs and blankets, the coats and curtains heaped
like an unruly sea across the floor. Luke's nesting material,
the only concession to comfort I'd ever known him make;
and oh, I was grateful for it that day. I kicked a pile into a
corner – at least insofar as an object cigar-shaped can have
corners, which is actually not a very great distance from not
at all – and tumbled down onto it. Worked the deck shoes
off my feet, tucked knees and elbows up nice and tight and
fœtal, and fell asleep in all my clothes and dirt.

Woke up sometime in the middle of the night, no watch so
I didn't know when. It was dark, that was all that mattered,
and I needed a piss quite urgently.

No toilet, of course, that was gone along with all the
bathroom fittings. I got to my feet and blundered to the
door, felt my way out and then stood on the step for a
minute, to let my eyes find some good in starlight.

In fact what they found was the glow of the fire, not dead
yet; and Luke's shadow sitting over it, just as I had left him,
and he still wasn't turning round to look although certainly
he would have heard me coming out.

I made my way along the side of the caravan and then behind, into an unlikely copse; emptied my bladder long and delightfully against a tree; then went straight back inside and straight to sleep again, not pausing even to wish Luke goodnight.

From the look of it, he wasn't having one anyway. Actually, I wasn't sure that he ever did. I thought maybe the nights were his bad time, his private Waterloo endlessly replaying. I'd certainly never seen him sleeping through one.

Me, barring that one brief break in it I slept sweeter than I had in the hospital, even, under their chemical blanket. Some added value in Luke's magic fingers, perhaps, or else in this little bubble of strange that he inhabited, the very air up here seeded with somnolence to keep mere mortals quiet.

Or else it was just that I was knackered and I needed sleep, and sleep was there for the taking and so I took it. Could've been that to keep the pragmatists happy, something that in my experience the world always tries to do, even against the intent of angels.

Personally, I believe in miracles. Very small-scale, very private little miracles like sleeping luxuriously late and then waking to find your body better than it ought to be, stiff and sore but not hurting. Like warm spring sunshine on the grass outside and the sky utterly blue above, very much against the weather forecast; fruit for breakfast and damper fresh-baked in the fire's embers and a wonderful lethargy in me, a total contentment in simply lying on the greensward and listening to birdsong, watching Luke with half an eye as he moved around the hollow, barely talking at all.

Certainly not asking questions, not even thinking of taking dictation.

That day and the next were my rest and recreation, while my

scabs peeled and my stubble grew and I didn't even itch, I just felt massively and marvellously settled in my body and in my head both, all questions put aside.

On the third day I rose again from the peaceful dead, and became human once more; and being human was plagued with anxiety and curiosity, itches impossible to scratch.

And I had the car, and Luke seemed utterly disinterested in what I did with my time; so I bumped slowly, gently down the track to the road below and drove to Penrith, where I interviewed a sergeant of police.

Who gave me two facts to play with, each of a deep and abiding strangeness.

The first was that I was wrong, completely one hundred per cent – or no, better, one hundred and eighty degrees – wrong in the assumption I'd made after Luke broke his little bombshell about my having been to see him that day. No, I wasn't on my way back to the city when I crashed. I'd been east of the Lakes, for sure, but travelling *west*. As if I'd driven halfway home and changed my mind, done a U-turn in the road and headed back to Luke's again.

"Any chance you could have forgotten something, sir? Something important enough to go all that way back for?"

I shrugged. There was always the chance, I supposed – hell, in this brave new world of mine, *anything* was possible: I was a married man with a deeply crooked buddy, wasn't I? – but it certainly wasn't likely. You didn't take things to Luke, to be remembered or forgotten.

"Anywhere else you might have been going, then?"

"Well, there's always my mother's house. Don't know if she'd have been there, but I've got keys." I'd had keys, at least – and checking my unreliable memory and then my pockets, yes, I still had keys. That much of my history I hadn't given away. And it wasn't impossible, actually: in crisis, I might have gone home to Mum. On a whim, even, late at night and heading in a different direction. It was the sort of behaviour she'd approve, that she'd always despaired of seeing in me: a handbrake turn on the highway, a race through the dark towards some unsentimental dream of shelter . . .

Then he told me the second piece of news he had, that changed the picture once again.

They'd found a witness, he said, a local lad on his way home after seeing his girlfriend safe; a little drunk, a little high, he said, but not enough to make him unreliable. It's how they knew for sure which way I'd been going, he said, this boy's report: no clues otherwise to tell them, no skid-marks on the tarmac or buckled and broken barriers. I couldn't have braked at all, he said, and the manufacturers needed to look at the aerodynamics again, no car should fly so high, whatever speed it was doing . . .

But this boy, he said, of course the boy stopped to stare as I'd driven past. A flash sports car on the road so late, what fifteen-year-old would not?

I was travelling fast, the boy had said, apparently, but not stupidly fast for such a road in darkness. Not flying-fast, not then.

So the boy had got a good look; and for all that he'd been looking at the bonnet and the spoiler and trying to spot if it had twin exhausts, he'd seen something else also that he'd mentioned to the police as a positive fact, absolutely no question in his mind.

He'd seen two heads in that car as it passed him, driver and passenger both.

Two men, he thought, though he wouldn't swear to that. Only a fleeting glimpse and no faces, a girl with short hair could've fooled him.

That was just two or three minutes from the smash, at the likely speed I'd been travelling. The boy hadn't heard the car stop at all, to let the passenger out, though he hadn't heard it crash either: only its roar fading and I guess the memories of his night out rising to replace it, till he forgot to listen any longer.

There must have been a stop, though, the sergeant said. The passenger must have debussed. They'd had another look at the wreckage, he said, and found it hard once more to believe that I'd survived at all, let alone come out of it with so little damage. Comparatively little, he insisted, when I murmured about ten weeks of my life lost. I could have been dead, he said; I should surely have been laid up for months, with many bones broken and all my innards tangled.

But what was sure, he said, was that no one – no matter how lucky – could have been in that smash and walked away and left me. They'd been checking bloodstains, he said, and those few they'd found on the passenger side were my own.

So, I must have stopped to let this other person out, somewhere not a mile from where I'd crashed. There was nothing there, no home, no habitation; which had them wondering about the accident again. Especially in the light of this report from the city, about an attack with a runaway truck, he said.

They were double-checking the brakes and the steering, he said, but there were no signs of tampering, or any mechanical problem.

Their best bet, he said, was that I'd had a row with my unknown passenger, and stopped the car to throw them out; and then driven off in high dudgeon and at high speed, and swerved to avoid some fluffy bunny or other obstruction in the road, and *whee!* blasted into Britain's controlled airspace without filing a flight plan. Which was an offence, he said jovially, but they wouldn't be pursuing me for it, they didn't think they could keep up.

Basically, I suppose he was saying *help!*; and I couldn't do that, all I could do was reply in kind, *sorry, not a clue, none of it makes any sense to me.*

So at last he let me go, once I'd signed a couple of forms and shrugged off his doubts and prognostications about the likelihood of a speedy insurance settlement. Reminded about money and the general worldly need for it, I went into the nearest bank to raise some cash on my gold card. No problems. God alone knew what my credit limit was these days, but clearly I hadn't reached it yet. Once back in the city, that was one more thing I'd have to sort out, I supposed; a serious talk with the manager at my own bank must be on the cards.

From the bank to the hospital, where I inveigled a young houseman into checking my stitches; as I'd anticipated, the wounds had closed well enough that he ended up taking them all out. From there to Smith's for a Dictaphone and a writing pad, spare tapes and batteries and a couple of coloured biros – starting a new job, I always liked to start clean, with gear dedicated to that job and that alone – and then I pigged out on steak and kidney pie and chips in a greasy spoon before I drove back to Luke. I never did notice it when I was there, when I was with him; but once out of his bubble, water and plant-life seemed suddenly desperately inadequate to sustain a man, and I was always ragingly hungry for meat.

• SIX •

AND THEN SHE HIT ME

He smelled it on my breath, of course, when I got back. Again I caught the full blast of his displeasure, contempt and revulsion in a single facial twist, but he didn't say a word. He wouldn't. If he'd been with me, he'd have snatched the pie from the plate or the fork from my mouth – he'd done both of those to me before, when I was younger – but he was always a creature of action, never words. He'd never really seen the point of words.

But I wanted words from him now. I wanted access to a certain address on his hard-storage silicon-chip many many megabytes of memory, so infinitely reliable, not like mine; I wanted all the data that he'd stored and I'd so carelessly lost.

"Just repeat it for me, Luke? Word for word, everything we said?"

"Why? It was just talk. I gave you the facts."

"There might be other facts," I said, "hidden in the actual words I used, clues I can pick up on now . . ." Or else in the way I'd said things, excited or cynical or sarcastic; but no use asking him to repeat tones of voice or other subtleties. I think he also heard in black and white.

He frowned over that, said nothing, was doubtless trying

to defeat me with silence the way he always used to. But I was older now, and more resistant.

"I was working for Vernon Deverill," I said. "Right. But I don't know why, and neither do you. Maybe there's something I said to you then, that I can use now to work out what was going on, why I'd get involved in something like that. Come on, Luke. Just read it out like a playscript, yeah? Won't take you that long." There would have been many pauses from me, many silences from him; even half a day's-worth of talking would compress into an hour or two of tape.

"I don't know what a playscript is," he said.

Right enough, he wouldn't. Nor did he have any curiosity, to learn. But I explained what I wanted, speaker and dialogue and no possibility of confusion; and he nodded and began, so crisp and fast that I missed the first dozen words because I didn't have the Dictaphone switched on yet.

"Me: Hullo, Jonty, I was waiting for you. You: Of course you were, you always are. Smartass. Me: Sit down and drink. You: No more now, thanks. Luke, you won't believe this, but I've got married . . ."

And so on, maybe half a day and half a night of talking; and yes, he did compress it into a couple of hours, and it was hard to get him to stop long enough for me to change tapes, and my hands were trembling by then so I nearly made a hash of it; and that was only with the strain of hearing him do this, I wasn't trying to make sense of the words any more. That would come later, with the transcript.

Except, right at the end, because it was the end my mind went back and unpicked the final few words from the continuous seam of Luke's recital. They were my own words, mostly: "'Bye, then, Luke. And thanks a lot, that's a real help. I'll tell you about it sometime, yeah? And I'll bring Sue over to meet you soon." And he'd said "No," and I'd said "Yes, I will," and I could just hear myself laughing as I said it, defying the angel. And then I'd said, "Tara, then," and that was that; and those were the last words I said to anyone in my whole mind, except of course for whatever I said to the mystery guy or possibly gal I picked up and drove in the wrong direction; and oh, it felt strange sitting there with that great hole torn in my memory, and trying to darn it with stitches taken from my own words that I had to hear from someone else, that I didn't remember saying and didn't understand.

No more R & R, though I did try. I spent another day with him, writing down all the taped conversation like a playscript: which was exactly how it felt, giving myself lines I had no memory of having said. Doing it in capitals and different colours, his lines in red and mine in green, for clarity; and then trying to compact all the information into a witness statement in my head.

Wishing for once that he'd been a normal human man, afflicted with normal human curiosity. Luke didn't ask questions, so all I could do was infer as much as possible from the questions I'd asked him, and the few facts I'd volunteered.

But the sun-time, the fun time was over. It rained all day, and the rain drummed like impatient fingers on the aluminium skin of the Airstream, and I couldn't relax. And I was straining my eyes trying to work in the gloom in there, no lights, not even a candle to help me; and I couldn't concentrate anyway, what with Luke either sitting out there by the sodden stones of his firepit while the rain ran off his hunched back to pool in his pockets or else coming inside streaming water and standing to drip dry in a corner, saying nothing, watching me.

I was on the verge of giving up, of leaving. I wanted to do that, I was abruptly hungry to move, to leave this drained bucolic idyll and relocate in some kind of active life again.

If I'd been Luke, or simply myself but as hard as Luke, sharing that one quality, it would have been easy: on my feet and out, into the car and off with no words, even, no farewells. He'd done that to me before.

I couldn't do it to him, though. Leaving Luke I'd always found next to impossible, until he explicitly told me to go. I should have been better at it by now, but this was one last late hangover from my teenage days, as if because Luke didn't change therefore neither could I; as if with him I would always be that difficult adolescent so clumsy in his timings, often hanging around long after a welcome was worn out simply because he didn't know how to say goodbye.

Acquired social skills shrivelled and died, in a place where they could expect little use and no respect. I sat with my tapes and my pad and pen, scowling in the gloom, wishing for just a little more strength of purpose, just enough to get me on my feet and my tongue moving. *Thanks, Luke, I'll be off now* – that would be ample. A perfect compromise: less than I felt that I owed him, but more than he would want or expect from me, my thanks no use to him and the information unnecessary.

So little, and yet I couldn't manage even that. I wanted out of there, sure, but my desire to leave just wasn't quite enough on its own with no target ahead of me, nothing to shoot at, nowhere to go.

I might have stayed another day, two days, overwhelmed by apathy; I might easily have stayed to the end of the week, until the hire car had to be returned. But there were suddenly figures moving through the rain as I lifted my eyes for the hundredth time to the smeared window. Kids they were to me, teens and early twenties: half a dozen of them in black and khaki with half-shaven heads or dreadlocks; thin beards or acne or facial tattoos; many piercings with silver through the ears, the eyebrows, the nose and lips and no doubt otherwhere I couldn't see.

They came single file down into the hollow, and straight to the Airstream door. Opened it without knocking and filed in, shedding jackets to the floor and squeezing water out of their hair, and Luke said, "I've been waiting for you," and as ever I believed him.

As did they, nodding and grunting and sitting in a group at his feet, almost, gazing up at him with something close to awe; and I remembered that so well, wasn't sure that I'd lost it yet.

But their glances at me were something other, sideways and suspicious, laden with questions: *who's he, Luke, what's he doing here? Do we need him, do we want him? Can we lose him?*

And they made it easy for me, they were the trigger to my latent charge: a second reason not to stay, beyond my own discomfort, they had me up and easy, collecting my stuff under one arm and, "Thanks a lot, Luke, you've been great. I'd better be off now, I've got to do something with all of this, it's no good just sitting here tailchasing in my head. I'll be back soon, though. Soon as I have some answers, I'll let you know. And I'll bring Suzie next time, okay?"

"No," he said, as I'd known he would; and I laughed, quite unforced, and made a gesture that meant, *yes I will, and you can lump it, mate*, and went out into the rain shielding my hard-worked written pages beneath my jacket as I dashed up the slope towards the car with never a look behind me.

Bumping down the track, feeling as though I were passing through a curtain, a veil of rain into another world, I thought perhaps I wasn't ready to leave shelter yet, though more than ready to leave Luke.

A few miles down the valley there was a village, with what might have been the last classic red phone-box left in England; and they obviously loved their phone-box, or someone among them did, because when I went in there was a clean square of carpet beneath my feet, a vase of fresh spring flowers on the shelf, directories clean and complete and a telephone unvandalised and working.

I phoned my mother; or at least I phoned my mother's house, one more building where I used to have the right of residence but which I couldn't possibly call home.

Surprise, she wasn't in. It was a machine that answered me, her changeable voice high and bright and artificially cheery: "Sorry, darlings, I simply can't be had at the moment. Leave a message if you want, so I know you've been thinking of me; but you know what I'm like, don't hang around waiting for a reply. If you need me, phone again . . ."

And then a long, long string of beeps, so many I thought maybe the tape would run out before her messages did; many friends, it seemed, wanted her to know their thoughts. Nothing new there, then.

At last the longer tone, dash not dot, and I could have added my ten penceworth; but what point? I had little enough to say, and she wasn't in any case there to hear. She might be anywhere; so many messages, she might have been away for weeks already; but that meant nothing. Sometimes she didn't come home for months on end.

Love you, Mum I could have said, but didn't. Never had.

I just listened to the silence for a moment, thinking of the tape going uselessly round and round, and then hung up nice and quiet, not to disturb it.

And didn't know what to do now, where to go; so I got into the car and drove without plan or purpose, and in the end old habit or some subconscious intent made the decision for me, because when I came to the first crucial junction I was already in the right-hand lane and indicating before I thought about it, and making that turn brought me round to face east, heading back to the city.

I let that stand, didn't fight it; but didn't hurry either. Again, on a more domestic scale, nowhere to go. Foxes have holes, the birds of the air have nests; but the son of my mother . . . ?

I could seek out a friend, I supposed, beg a bed for the night. But all my friends now were Carol's friends too, most had been her friends first, and I wasn't any too certain of my welcome. Nick Beatty would be all right, I thought; my best mate for many years, he'd been best man at the wedding, so I could depend on him; only the last I remembered, Nick had got himself a new girlfriend. Whether they were still together or not, either way that could be awkward. And he'd be full of questions, he'd want to talk all night, and I just wasn't up to that.

Better to gold-card it, I thought, at least for tonight. Find a hotel, somewhere big and concrete, comfortable and anonymous. Tomorrow I'd go to the bank and have a talk with someone, find out just what kind of credit stood behind the card, and just where it had come from. Go in to work too, talk to one of the senior partners: discover how I stood, in what bad odour with my former colleagues and employers, whether there was any chance of my being taken back on the strength. After some delay, perhaps, I could offer them that. Physically I might feel okay now, but a man with his recent memory missing hardly counted as well enough to work.

Which reminded me: one other thing I had to do, and the sooner the better. *Tomorrow*, my soul said, *do it tomorrow, with everything else*; but that was chicken-hearted. Good sense and good manners both said to do it tonight.

Which was maybe another reason why I didn't hurry back to town. Resolved on this, I'd still welcome any chance to put it off for another half an hour, another ten

minutes, anything at all that I could fit in between this and
that . . .

So I drove back across country and stopped to eat en route,
as much meat as a pub could provide and a single cautious
pint to wash it down; and picked a hotel in the city centre
with a car park underneath, parked and checked in, getting
a better room than I was paying for in exchange for a sight of
the card; and had a long shower and a careful shave before
I reluctantly dressed in those wrong-fitting, wrong-feeling
and now dirty clothes again.

And it was still only half past ten, and no way could I
persuade myself that it was too late tonight to do this. Try
though I might, though I did . . .

So I drank a complimentary miniature of cognac for
courage – not out of the balloon glass provided, just off
with the bottle top and glug-glug, straight down my throat
– and walked down four flights of stairs to the lobby, out
into the street, left and then right and hullo Chinatown.

All along the busy length of it, until at last I came to a
discreet door between two restaurants, a door surrounded by
brass business plaques and overlit by a transom, *Q's* brightly
shining from its dark glass embrasure.

And hesitated one last time, and was pushed past by a
handful of Chinese lads, arguing loudly and incomprehen-
sibly. At least, I assumed they were arguing; but given the
inherent tonality of the language, who could tell? Perhaps
they had to sound like that, heated and abrasive, just to say
what they wanted to say.

Suzie's brother, I remembered, had been dragged to death,
here we go round the mulberry city and you couldn't get
more heated and abraded than that; and I wondered why it
had happened, and I wondered how brave Suzie was being,
and how stupid. Whoever had done it, surely it had to be
because her brother had got across them in business; and
here she was carrying on her brother's business, and I didn't

know if she'd even considered that they might come next after her.

In their hands, of course, the lads ahead of me carried their snooker cues, cased like instruments and just as precious.

I let their hurry draw me in its wake; trudged up the stairs as they ran ahead, so that I had barely reached Mr Han the Herbalist before I heard the club doors crashing open, crashing closed some distance still above my head.

Between the two, between the opening and the closing I heard a burst of laughter. Quarrel or not, then, what I'd heard had not been fighting talk. *Just goes to show*, I thought, going on, going up. Even on your own known territory, appearances tend to deceive; only cross a border – physical or cultural, linguistic, whatever – and you can't trust your eyes to see straight nor your mind to interpret what they say they see. And the same, of course, for the other senses. Values shift, and reality shifts to accommodate them.

Here and now, my reality had undergone some shifts deeper than lingual. Epochal, almost. Walking in through the street door, I'd entered a world where I couldn't even understand myself.

Walked up, and up again; came to the club doors and hesitated, and went on further up. To go in there would only be another delaying tactic at heart, whatever its result.

And so to the top, the door to Suzie's flat, still labelled for dead Jack. I rang the bell, and waited; waited one minute, two, then tried again.

Tried knocking, in case the bell was *hors de combat*: first with knuckles, then with fists.

Nothing, no response; so that I did after all make my way back down to the club doors, and through them into the half-dark and the hard sounds of snooker, the soft voices and clinking, drinking noises of its players.

I went straight over to the bar, huffing with relief to see Lee behind it, as he had been when Suzie brought me

here. No doubt any other member of her staff would have
known me, as he had; but not I them, and I was sick tired
of having strangers claim me as friend, pupil, employee,
husband . . .

His moment of recognition came just a moment behind
mine; I saw him startle, saw his eyes move sideways in his
stiff head, and without looking round myself had my chief,
my only question answered. But I went on over to greet him
anyway; and while I was saying hullo he was sucking air
through his teeth, shaking his head, glancing that way again
and then back to me.

"Wouldn't like to be in your shoes, mate," he said. "If
you can walk and talk, you're in big, *big* trouble."

"Oh? Why's that?"

He didn't answer, or not directly: just jerked his head
expressively, and said, "She's over there."

I turned at last and saw her, slim shadow moving among
shadows, down the far end of the hall where no players
were. She was standing with her back to us, bending and
rising, picking balls out of pockets and setting them back in
place on one of the tables; I made my way slowly towards
her, hovering still for a few seconds when that way was
blocked by a player crouching low, taking all the aisle's
width to make his shot.

She was filling a wooden triangle with reds, still hadn't
looked around to see me; so I called out before I reached
her, "Suzie?" on a rising note.

And she stiffened, and had to put a hand down suddenly
to the baize surface of the table to catch herself, to hold
herself up, it seemed; and it took a second or two of no
movement from either one of us before she could turn her
head to find me.

Once her eyes had fixed me, once she was focused she
straightened and turned, to face me directly across a couple
of metres' distance. Cold and hostile she looked, holding

herself up on her toes with every muscle tight, ready to jitter backwards if I made any move to come closer; and this I hadn't expected, and struggled to understand.

"You," she said, and stopped. And tried again, forcing hard words through a tight throat, "You bastard, where the filthy fucking hell have you *been*?"

"I went to Luke," I said.

"You went to Luke. Brilliant. You didn't think to *tell* anyone, I suppose, or leave a note, or even phone, maybe, when you got there?"

"Luke hasn't got a phone . . ."

"There are phones," she said, and her voice was all breath and hiss now, she must be one of those people who only got quieter as they got angrier, "even in the bloody Lakes there must be phones. You could've made the effort. But you didn't want me to know, did you? You lied to the hospital, you said you'd be staying at Carol's when you signed out, they showed me the forms . . ."

"I did—"

"I even *phoned* Carol," she said, with a vicious twist to the word, "and she was horrible, she laughed when I said that I'd lost you. But she said you weren't there. So I tried your mother, I've tried and tried," *all those messages*, I thought, "but she's never there and she doesn't call back. I've been right through your sodding address book, and none of your friends could help; and yes, I did think of Luke, but no one could help there either, could they? They don't know where to find him, they said you're dead secretive about that, you keep him to yourself . . ."

Not so; Luke kept himself to himself, more like. Didn't want visitors, didn't want to make friends or influence people except in the very limited range of his concerns. He'd taken me into his circle, yes, but always refused to let me expand it further.

"Suzie," I said, "I didn't lie to anyone. I did go to Carol's, because that still felt like home; and when she turned me away, Luke was just a spur-of-the-moment thing, when I couldn't think of anywhere else to go."

"You're not *supposed* to go anywhere else," she said, her voice cracking suddenly, "you're supposed to come here. This is home, I told you that, I showed you . . ."

Home is where the hurt is, I thought, hearing it in her and seeing it now, underlying that dissolving anger; but I couldn't help her there, I couldn't give her anything but truth. "Doesn't work that way," I said, soft as I could manage. "You must know that. Home's not an intellectual concept, it's a feeling thing; and you can't have feelings for a place you can't remember. I can't, at any rate."

She made a vague, hopeless gesture at that, and tried to come back strong again too late, having given herself too much away. "Okay, you didn't have to come to me. But you didn't have to run away from me, either . . ."

"It wasn't you," I said, trying to reassure. "It was just everything; and that bloody truck the worst of it, watching someone die, I couldn't hack it."

"You should've—" *You should've come to me*, I think she was going to say in defiance of what she'd said last, *good hugs a speciality*; but she bit it back, remembering; and tried to change dance in mid-step, "You still could've phoned, you must've known I'd worry, I've been *frantic* . . ."

Yes; and I'd been not thinking about her at all. Fleeing the city, I'd fled all that the city implied, until the need to know had drawn me back tonight.

"I'm sorry," I said, knowing it inadequate, only hoping she never found out just how disproportionate we'd been these last few days, she and I. "Luke has a way of taking things over, so you can't see much outside of him; and it's all been such a muddle in my head, I don't think I could have talked to you anyway. Couldn't have talked to anyone, really."

"You talked to Luke," she complained; and I hid a grin, thinking that this much at least I could manage. Simple jealousy of Luke had always been a common factor, uniting all my girlfriends.

"Not really. You don't talk to Luke, not that way. There's no point, he wouldn't be interested."

She grunted, not entirely believing me, I thought, only letting it go; and then, coming round onto a different tack so hard that I wanted to duck for fear of some metaphorical boom cracking into my skull, she said, "So what are you doing now, then, what are you doing here? What did you come back for?"

Not for me, she was saying, facing the truth with a fierce honesty, *not if you could go away so easily, with never a second thought or a look behind.*

And she was right, of course, and I couldn't deny it, she deserved as good as she gave me; so I said, "Don't worry, I won't get under your feet. I've got a room in a hotel. It's only that I really need my computer, I didn't like to let myself in without telling you, but . . ."

And then she hit me.

It was a sweet clunking forehand slap, delivered with power and genuine feeling, if no great precision. She caught me half on the cheekbone and half on the ear, and the shock as much as the force of it sent me reeling back against the table behind me, clutching at its rim for support as my legs failed momentarily.

After the shock, the stinging pain; I shook my head hard against that and a ringing dizziness, and the first thing I heard as my hearing came back on-line was the sound of applause from the other end of the hall.

First thing I saw as my vision cleared was Suzie, seeming more than a little awestruck at what she'd achieved. Looking past her I saw a static picture, every player in the place standing stock-still, staring; only beyond them, behind the bar was there any movement, and that was Lee still clapping slowly, with a broad grin on his face.

"You just don't get it, do you?" Suzie whispered, fighting it seemed to stay angry, to hold on to that amid a turmoil of other emotions; and there at least I could agree with her wholeheartedly. No, I didn't get it at all; and the clarity of anger would be a boon right now for me as well as her, only that I couldn't manage it. I ought to, I thought, being made a public target; but it wasn't there, I didn't have it in me.

"You vanish for days," she went on, "for all I knew you could've lost your memory again, you could've been really ill if the doctors had missed something, you could've been dying with a brain haemorrhage in some hospital the other end of the country, and them not having a clue who you were; and then you turn up out of the blue and you want to just pick up your computer and *go* again? Stay in a *hotel*, and not *get under my feet* . . . ?"

Her fingers twitched at her sides, like she wanted to hit me again; but I lifted a hand to rub vaguely at my tingling ear, and her face changed as she came a rapid step closer.

"Oh God, you're okay, aren't you? I haven't . . . ?"

Despite everything, my mouth twitched into a smile, on the side that wasn't sore. "No, you haven't given me a brain haemorrhage, I'm not going to drop down and die."

She snorted. "Too bad, you deserve to. And I was just beginning to fancy widowhood, all that insurance money, I could have had a party . . ."

She'd done this before, talked up a storm in self-defence; I ignored it. What was harder to ignore was the cool touch of her hand displacing mine, stroking the stubble on my temple and the smoothness of my cheek, trying to take away now what pain or shame she'd put there.

Not meaning to, only reacting and not thinking at all, I reached up and gripped her wrist, to take her hand away.

For a moment she went entirely rigid, and her eyes were blank; then she smiled tightly and turned her hand inside my loosening grasp, so that her fingers linked with mine. A quick tug and she was away up the aisle between the tables, and I could go with her hand in hand or I could stand and fight, pull free; but everyone was watching still, grinning or still giggling most of them, and I wouldn't feed their greed for entertainment. Save it for when we were private . . .

So I let her tow me all the way through the club and out of the double doors, with no more than a wave of her hand at Lee in passing, *keep an eye on things, I'm taking this errant man upstairs*. Which she did, and there at least I could slip my hand free of hers, because it's both difficult and foolish to hold hands on a flight of stairs too narrow to climb two abreast; and at the top she was busy with keys and didn't have a hand free to recapture mine even if she'd wanted to.

I followed her in at the beckoning jerk of her head, and she led me silently all through the flat to the big empty bedroom; and turned to confront me there, gestured at the futon, rolled out now and made up ready for the night, and said, "You can go where you like, you can do what you like; but as long as you're in this city, Jonathan Marks, this is where you sleep, right? This is yours, you bought it, you can sodding well sleep on it . . ."

And there were tears leaking down her face suddenly, though she dashed at them with an angry hand, and I didn't know what to do.

Fell back on the helpless male thing, a half-hearted pace forward and an open-handed gesture she wouldn't see because she'd turned her back now, a muttered meaningless phrase, "Look, Suzie, it'll be okay . . ."

And then she turned again, all the way round as if she'd only meant to do a three-sixty in the first place, and her cheeks might be wet still but her eyes not, they were glaring.

"And what's with this 'Suzie' stuff, all of a sudden? Sue to you, I said, I always have been."

"That's why," I said, with an inward sigh, *here we go again*. "If it was only me called you Sue before, if it was something special between us, then it's better for both of us if I don't do it now. It'd be like me taking over someone else's name for you, it's invested with too much that I don't share any more . . ."

"I do," she said.

"I know. But I can't pretend, love, I can't be the Jonty you married when I don't remember the first thing about him."

"Then don't call me 'love'," she said. "Bastard."

But she said it entirely without heat, with a neutral gaze; I tried to meet that with one of my own.

"Suzie, then?"

"Suzie." She nodded, and we could have shaken hands on it, we were that formal for a moment. Until she scowled, and said, "But you're still a bastard, and I hate you for it. Come on, I'll show you where your toothbrush is, and where we keep the towels. I suppose you don't remember?"

Of course I didn't remember; and she didn't actually mean that anyway, she didn't make the first hint of a movement. Just stood there looking at me, daring me to defy her; and all I could do was prevaricate. "I've booked a room already, at the Palace. It's too late to cancel that, they'll charge me anyway."

"So pay anyway. Or charge it to Deverill, that's better. That's what you usually do."

"Is it?"

Even I could hear how my voice sharpened at that; she gazed at me thoughtfully, then nodded. "Yeah. Every time you buy me dinner. You're dead tight, you."

I twitched a smile at her. "Well, maybe. But I don't want to do that tonight. Or at all, until I know why he's prepared to pay my bills for me." And then, going on quickly as her face clamped, "But all right, I won't go back to the hotel tonight. I'll sleep on the sofa, or something."

"You'll sleep here," she said, her finger stabbing down once more at the futon. And reading my face as easily as I was reading hers – but she'd had more practice, after all, weeks and weeks of it, unless I was benefiting from experience I couldn't consciously remember – she added, "There's a spare bed in the other room. I'll use that."

"No, I will."

"You'll sodding well do what you're told, for once. This is king-size, so are you. The other one's little, so am I. It's just physics, or geography, or whatever. I don't fit in here, without you."

She'd been using it, I thought, none the less; but I was tired of arguing, happy to lose. At my shrug of submission she beamed broadly, took my elbow, steered me towards the door. "Come on, then. Towels and toothbrush, yes? And I'll show you where your clothes are, too. I mean, for God's sake, where did you get this stuff? What is it, the jumble-sale leftovers that Oxfam wouldn't take? You look better underneath, mind. Hundred per cent better than last time. Luke must be good for you. But God, I was scared when you ran away. Don't you do that, right? Don't you *dare* do that again. Whatever happens, we can sort it out . . ."

We were nearly at the bathroom door by now, and it was incredibly hard to stop walking, to resist the constant flow of her words and her intent.

"Hang on," I said. "I should phone the hotel, at least, if I'm not going to sleep there . . ."

"Why?" she demanded.

I shrugged. "Maybe they won't charge me full rate, if I cancel now. Maybe they like to know how many guests they've got in the building, in case there's a fire. Or maybe it's just a matter of courtesy, but I won't feel comfortable, else."

She snorted. "Didn't phone me when you bunked off, did you? Didn't show me any courtesy. But go on, if you want to. If you must."

And she waited, and so did I, because I still felt like a stranger here, I couldn't go searching while she watched; and it took her a second before she grunted in frustrated understanding and said, "Just round the corner there, on the floor. By the hi-fi."

"Thanks."

It was a cordless phone, silently recharging. I picked it up, found the hotel's number on the key-card they'd given me at reception, and dialled.

A woman answered after a couple of rings; I said, "Oh, hullo. My name's Jonathan Marks, I checked in with you this evening . . ."

"Oh yes, Mr Marks. Thank you for calling. I'll just put you straight through to the manager."

"No, wait, there's no need for—"

"He asked me to, Mr Marks. As soon as you called, he said."

He was expecting a call? Weird. Spooky. I hadn't been expecting to make one. But I didn't have time to puzzle it through, because he was on the line almost immediately.

"Mr Marks? Michael Hobden, I'm the duty manager tonight."

"Right, hullo. Look, I just called to say I won't be coming back . . ."

"No, that's fine, sir. I quite understand, and I do apologise for this. It certainly appears as though one of our staff tipped off the press; at the moment our guests are having to run a gauntlet of reporters outside the door, which is intolerable for all of us, but clearly you're the party most injured. There'll be no charge for the room, of course. If you'd like to give me a number where we can reach you, then whoever's on duty can let you know when the coast is clear for you to come and collect your car, or make arrangements for someone else to pick it up; but I'm afraid that'll be tomorrow morning at the earliest. I'm afraid they know your room number, so they'll probably have your car tagged as well, and I don't think they'll be going away tonight."

"Oh. Yes, a number, of course. Hang on . . ."

I had to yell for Suzie, and ask her; the number wasn't on the phone. He vowed without any prompting to keep it confidential, and then he apologised again and brought the conversation to a tidy and diplomatic end. I put the phone down, stared at it for a bit, then turned to find her watching me curiously.

"Suzie? Why would the press be chasing me?"

"Oh. Yes, of course they would. Hold on . . ."

She disappeared, came back a minute later with a bundle of papers. One she discarded on a sofa, the other two she passed to me without comment.

I hadn't been headline news, apparently, though it was only a local paper; but front page at least, I'd been, and for two days running. The first time was a report on the truck and the fire and Oliver's death, naturally, and Deverill's narrow escape; I was in there as a subsidiary, an also-survived, but they had me down as 'Mr Deverill's lawyer, recovering from a road traffic accident', which was interesting. Deverill had many lawyers, but not one of them was me.

The second paper, the next day's edition, had me again front page, and second only to a nursery sex-abuse scandal where the protagonist was coincidentally one of my own clients. This time, at least I was the focus of the story: THE LAWYER VANISHES, the catch-line ran, *Missing-Memory Man Goes Walkabout.*

I scanned the story swiftly, grimaced, glanced at Suzie. "The police too, huh?"

"Afraid so. Maybe you should tell them that you're here, yes? Before they come looking? They don't find you at the hotel, they're going to come back. I bet most of those messages are them already, press or police," nodding towards the answering machine, where a blinking counter told of a dozen calls waiting.

"Back? You mean they've been already?"

"*Everybody's* been. I made a list. Two lists: phone calls, and personal visits. You can look at them in the morning. Not now." *Tonight's for us*, unspoken but very much there in her body language, half diktat and half appeal. *Please*?

To me that was as much a threat as the press, the police and the sensation-seekers combined; but – hell, I'm slow, but I get there in the end. She'd been through shit, this girl who seemed to love me, and that was substantially my own fault. I owed her one night at least, on her own terms.

"Can you turn the phone off?"

"Sure can." Her fingers moved on the handset, and, "There," with another of those huge smiles, far too large for her fine-featured face to encompass.

"And not answer the door?"

"Better than that, I can lock the fire door at the bottom of the stairs. They won't get up further than the club."

"What if there's a fire?"

"We'll get into the bath together, turn the shower on, and if they don't rescue us in time we'll be soup by morning," but she didn't look at all distressed by the idea. Content to die with me, she was, this girl, at least in fun; and I wouldn't, couldn't even call her by a pet name or anything approximating to it, and I didn't see how we were ever going to bridge this gulf between us.

She ran off down the stairs, jingling keys; I went to look at the paper she'd kept but hadn't shown me. Found myself reading the top story this time, about a body discovered, a man burned to death in a stolen van. For a moment, I didn't see the connection; but the report went on to imply – simply by admitting that the police had refused to confirm it – that this dead man was being sought at the time of his death two days ago, for questioning with regard to the burning truck that had killed Oliver, had so nearly killed Deverill and Dean and me.

Reading between the lines, then, presuming that the reporter and the police both had good information, this guy had tried to assassinate someone, Deverill or me; he had failed; and now he was dead himself, in a way that horribly echoed his bungled attempt. Locked into the van, he'd been, no accident. Which made it an execution. For trying, or for failing? I couldn't say, couldn't guess, even: didn't have enough information. I just heard Suzie coming back up the stairs, and put the paper down quickly where she'd left it. If she didn't want to talk about that tonight, then emphatically neither did I.

I didn't recognise the toothbrush that she showed me, on a quick where-to-find-things tour of what she called my property: not the splayed, broken-bristled old thing, Boots' finest, that I'd been using in defiance of my dentist for a year or more. She'd thrown that out, she said, the morning after I moved in. She'd taken me shopping, she said; and hence this sleek and streamlined designer object that felt strange in the hand and would surely feel stranger in the mouth, though doubtless it slayed plaque at fifty paces.

Must have been some shopping trip, that, and too bad I didn't remember it: you spend so much money all at once, you should have it logged for life. The toothbrush was nothing, but the futon she told me I'd bought, I'd insisted on; she'd been sleeping till then in her brother's bed, and we'd needed shelter from her ghosts, I'd said. Apparently.

Privately, I doubted it had been quite like that; I'd never slept on a futon in my life and would never have thought to try. More likely I'd said, *we need a new bed*, and left it to her to choose. But if she chose to remember it otherwise, I was in no position to argue.

And then she took me into the second bedroom where I found ghosts of my own – books that had been mine since university, folders from the office, sheets and sheets of A4 covered with my scratchy hand – and she threw open a wardrobe to show me where my clothes were, and that must have been some shopping trip indeed, because I knew none of them.

Okay. I could be almost blasé about this now; unfamiliarity was becoming commonplace. But it was strange none the less, trying to imagine the state of mind I must have been in, to have done this. Losing the bed of a dead brother-in-law, yes, that was more than reasonable, that was right; but to have left or thrown away everything, *everything* I used to wear seemed so extreme, it was one more thing that I simply couldn't connect with, on any level.

I didn't ask, but I must have made some questioning, doubtful noise, or else my face was asking for me. Suzie chuckled, stroked my cropped hair and said, "Carol assassinated all your old clothes. Went at them with pinking-shears, then sent them round here in a taxi, in boxes, in bits . . ."

Very thorough, she must have been. Not only my old, despised court clothes were gone, displaced by smart Italian suits; not only my shabby muckabout jeans and my faded check shirts and my sensible M & S underwear, all missing, with designer denims in lieu and silk shirts, socks, boxer shorts and black mini-briefs that looked like they probably cost an extraordinary amount per square cotton centimetre; but every belt and every pair of boots, every tie and every set of cuff links that had been mine had been replaced. This was another man's wardrobe I was confronting here, picked with another man's dress-sense, unless Suzie had made all the choices and our relationship had been so lopsided that I couldn't once say no.

It had all been bought with another man's money, also: there was thousands of pounds'-worth of clothing on those hangers and in those drawers.

Deverill presumably had done the paying, directly or otherwise; why he should do so I still didn't understand. Why I should let him was another question and becoming more urgent by the hour. *Tomorrow*, I tried to soothe myself, *tomorrow, we'll turn detective in the morning . . .*

"Do us both a favour, get changed," Suzie said. "Those things are smelly. What are you like underneath?"

"Had a shower before I came."

"Good. Are you hungry?"

"No."

"Have you *eaten?*"

"Yes," I said, infinitely patient.

"Okay, then. Find something to wear and come through. If you want your kimono, it's on the back of the bedroom door. And it's twice the size of mine, so you can't get muddled . . ."

And then she was discreetly gone, leaving me to raid at will. But I was too tired to play dressing-up games with those smart suits; and in all honesty, once I'd shucked off the second-hand stuff I'd been wearing all week I really didn't want to get properly dressed again, however new and clean the clothes.

So I picked up on Suzie's suggestion, only surprised that she hadn't made a command out of it, *wear this and this, come on, hurry up, or shall I stay to strip you?*

I pulled on a pair of boxer shorts, suppressing a grunt of pleasure at the feel of good silk settling against my skin; and then I scuttled shyly down the passage to the big front bedroom, where there were indeed two kimonos on hangers on the back of the door. The larger one was underneath, grey and pink, silk again but a completely different grade, heavyweight and protective for all that it was fraying a little at the hems. You couldn't call this second-hand, though certainly it had been worn before; the only proper word was antique.

It hung to my ankles when I slipped it on, wrapping me around in reassurance. I tied the belt, resisted the siren call of the nearest mirror, and went barefoot through into the living-room. In this flat, on that floor, splinters were hardly a concern.

Suzie had made Chinese tea again, there was a steaming pot on the coffee-table and cups with; but there was also a bottle of Macallan and a couple of glasses.

So happens that Macallan is my favourite drinking whisky. I did not think this coincidence or a lucky guess, I was well past that now.

She gave me an approving smile, and patted the cushion beside her on the sofa; smile changed to scowl when I sat instead on the floor opposite, with the table between us.

"Jesus, don't do me any favours, will you, Jonty?"

"I'm here," I said.

"Big deal." But that was only a mutter with her eyes averted, betraying her seeming intent: because for her it *was* a big deal, that was clear, simply to have me safe back again. For all that she had only the least part of me, the physical body she'd married but not at all the man inside; and for all that even that much wasn't cooperating, the body wasn't sitting where it was told and doing what she wanted. She'd settle for this grotesquely difficult situation sooner than what had gone before, the total loss of me.

Which was another marker to help me plot how deeply I'd entangled her in whatever mesh I'd been making, those few short missing weeks. My heart ached for her, vulnerable and helpless as she seemed, beneath the bluster: caught like some innocent, blundering fly, I thought she was, in a web of confusions and deceit. I wanted to help her, I wanted to peel sticky threads from her wings and set her free; but I didn't even know what the deceits were, let alone who had set them or what they were for. All I was contributing here was more confusion.

Could've been me, I thought, deceiving her for some cruel cause of my own; or vice versa, perhaps she was the deceiver and doing it still, doing it even now to keep me muddled . . .

"Okay," I said, taking tea when she passed it to me but reaching for the whisky also, pouring a slug into one glass and then into the other when I glanced the question and had her nod in response. "Answer some questions for me?"

"Yes," she said. No hesitation, no equivocation in her: total exposure offered if I wanted it, if I could think of the right questions to ask, and no, surely this girl was not deceiving me.

"That first night," I said slowly, watching her face, looking for signals. "I hung around the takeaway, asked you to go for a drink; you brought me here. Yes?"

"To the club, yes."

"You wanted to get into my shorts, you said. Did you manage it?"

A hint of a smile, and, "Not that first night, but I could've done. You were up for it, I reckoned. Easier then than it is now," glaring at me over her cup, putting it down to light a cigarette, blowing an aggressive cloud of smoke at me. If we'd been on the beach, she'd have kicked sand in my face.

I just shrugged. "So what did we talk about? What did I say?"

"Not much, in the end. All tongue-tied you were, like you were suddenly ten years younger and this was your first date ever. It was sweet, really. Weird too, mind, being with a stranger who wouldn't talk to me. But Lee was there to keep an eye out, and there were friends of mine on the tables too, so I wasn't worried."

"What did we do, then? If I wouldn't talk?"

"Well, I talked. For a bit. But I still wasn't getting much out of you, so we ended up playing snooker. What else would we do?"

"I don't play snooker," I said.

"You didn't use to. You do now, a bit. When I can get you in there." She grinned then, and said, "You're not exactly a natural talent, but you say you enjoy it." And then she stopped, seemed to listen to herself, shook her head bemusedly. "This is so strange. Telling you what you like to do . . ."

"Stranger hearing it," I said. "But all right, we played snooker. Anything else?"

"Not much. You went off about two o'clock, I think, said you really had to get back. At the time I thought you just needed sleep, you looked terrible: pale and jittery, like you'd been overdosing on work and caffeine for weeks. But I guess there was some guilt in there too, because of Carol."

"I hadn't told you about Carol?"

She shook her head. "Not that night. No. And I didn't ask. Didn't want to know. Why spoil something that might be nice, before it even happened? I'm a terrible slut, me. Used to be. That's why you wanted to marry me, you said, to stop me sleeping around . . ."

Did it work? I wanted to ask, meanly; but I thought it might get me slapped again, so I sipped Macallan, savoured its rich sherry flavour and then the bite that comes after, and asked a different question.

"What next, then? Did you chase me?"

"No, you looked like you could live without the pressure, so I let you go. Didn't ask for a number or anything. Your choice, if you came back. Actually, I thought probably you wouldn't: just one more bizarre night, I thought it was, and I've had a few of those," she said, with all the wise experience of twenty-four. "But you turned up again. At the club, the next night. You still looked haunted; but you'd shaved, and you smelled nice, and I don't think you'd eaten all day, so I took you down to Uncle Tang's and fed you. We had lobster, because you said you didn't mind getting messy but you couldn't use chopsticks. That's when you told me about Carol."

And that memory required a meditative pause, a sip of whisky, a sip of tea, a drag or two on the cigarette; and then, "So I said what are you panting after me for, then? And you said you hated yourself but you couldn't help it. If I'd been a nice girl, I suppose I would've sent you home right then. But I'm not, so I didn't," added unnecessarily.

"After that it became a sort of regular thing, you'd come to the club for an hour or two every night. To wind down, you said, but it never looked like that, you went off as fretted as you'd come. So one night I brought you up here instead of letting you go. Carol would be asleep, you said, but you phoned anyway, and left a message on your answering machine so she wouldn't be too panicked in the morning; and then I took you to bed."

A reminiscent smile from her, that I only wished I could match. It wasn't only motives and understanding that I'd lost here, there was simple experience too; and yes, I hated myself for it, but yes, I pined for the loss of that one. Didn't ask for a description, though. Instead, I put a new spin on an old classic. "So how was it for you? How were you feeling about it, I mean? I guess I was fixated, but were you just thinking of it as a one-night stand, or were we starting an affair, or what?"

"You weren't fixated," she told me sternly. "You were in love. You said that. And me – I don't know. Not then. I liked you, I fancied you, you interested me. That was about it, at the start. I didn't fall in love with you until I met your mother."

"Oh, Christ." I should have known, I should have guessed

she'd have been in there somewhere, stirring away with her
fiddling-stick. She'd have to be.

That did me in, for asking questions. I wasn't interro-
gating anyone about my mother, for fear of what answers
might come back at me. I drank tea and whisky and watched
Suzie smoke, and she seemed content to smoke and drink
and watch me in return.

Slowly my body remembered how late it was, how weary
tomorrow would be; and when I'd yawned for the third time
in five minutes, and was shifting awkwardly in search of a
more comfortable way for my bones to sit within my flesh,
Suzie said, "Go to bed, then, why don't you? If you're that
knackered?"

I ran a hand down over my face, felt just sheepish enough
to tell her. "I guess I was waiting for permission."

"Not from me. This is your home, you live here. Do what
you like. I'm going to have a bath."

I cleaned my teeth and went to bed, wishing her no more
than a brief, awkward goodnight and closing as many doors
as there were between us.

No pyjamas, only cool cotton and silk against my skin, the
lightness of a feather duvet over my back and the unfamiliar
firmness of a futon beneath me. I stretched across its width,
and lay on my belly thinking that even with Dolphus on
guard beside me – brought home again from the hospital
and back in what was clearly his regular place, and *thank
you, Suzie* – I'd still never sleep.

And did sleep, swiftly and easily; and then was startled
awake again sometime in the dark, by the sharp sound of
a door clicking open.

Took me a second to get a grip, to remember where and
therefore who I was. That done, though, it wasn't hard to
identify bare feet padding on bare boards.

More sounds, silk on skin: or silk off skin, rather, another kimono falling to the floor. And then a hint of a shift in the futon's frame, as another lighter weight came onto it; and ever the gentleman, I stopped pretending to sleep and slithered a little way across, to make room.

Didn't roll over, though. Lay with my back to her, not so much of a gentleman after all; but I was still getting more messages than I wanted, learning more than I needed to know. Every fractional hesitation in her body as she slipped under the duvet, every tight little breath told me stuff I didn't want to hear.

And then – *two fingers to hesitancy*, and much more what I would have expected from her – she wrapped her arms tight around me and was saying it all aloud, mumbling into my shoulder blade so that I picked it up by bone induction mostly, as her lips traced the shapes of the words against my skin.

"I'm sorry, I can't do it, I can't sleep through there with you in here, I can't bear it. I've missed you so much, I've been so scared; and I don't care if you're not who I think you are. You look like him and you smell like him and you feel like him, your voice sounds right, everything's right for me except what you say, so don't say anything, right?" A hand came up to touch my lips to silence, the fingers lingered like a kiss. "You don't have to talk, I'll do all the talking. Just don't, don't throw me out of bed . . ."

Well, I'd never done that to a girl yet; and I'd slept with some I didn't pretend to love, though not for a long time now. The problem I had was with the agenda that got into bed alongside Suzie. She had too much invested here, and I nowhere near enough. That imbalance was perilous to both of us, I thought.

So no, I didn't throw her out of bed and no, obedient to instructions I didn't speak; but no, neither did I turn within the circle of her arms to make a gift to her, my body as playground, reassurance, another definition of home.

Nearly she took it anyway, her hands sliding down now, over chest and stomach and further down; but they found the waistband of those boxer shorts that I was wearing still and stopped at the elastic, sensitive to messages.

"Oh, you bastard," breathed into my ear on half a chuckle, half a sob. "What is this, a last line of defence?"

I just grunted, trying to make it non-committal though I guess she took it for a 'yes'. At any rate, the fingers of both her hands slid in under the waistband but paused politely at their first touch of pubic hair, making a V together like an arrow-head directed at my groin, dangerous, threatening, too damn close. And when I made no move, either to encourage or repel, she sighed against my spine and left them there, nestling a little closer so that her neat naked body touched me at all the points it could.

Now truly sleep was impossible. For her also, I thought: she wasn't talking any more and only her skin moved in little involuntary twitches against mine, but I didn't believe she was sleeping. We lay there with nothing to share beyond the moment and its pain, and even our pain was individual, each of us suffered alone and she far more than I; and at the last, when I guess she couldn't bear it any longer, she inched cautiously away from me and turned her back, coiled up on the far side of the futon and tried not to touch me at all.

After a couple of minutes I thought I heard her crying, as quietly as she could manage; but I was trapped by my own pretence, and could offer her nothing of comfort. I lay still, and waited till that wanton sleep came back.

SEVEN

C'EST LA VILLE, C'EST LA GARE

Suzie was gone when I woke again, some time gone. Strong sunlight lay like a bar across her pillow, squeezing its way in between the curtains, but the sheet that side was cool.

Not I was cool: hot and sticky under the duvet, bladder-full, I unpeeled myself from the futon's unexpected comfort and blundered in my boxer shorts all through the flat towards the bathroom.

Suzie watched me from the kitchen door, chewing on an apple. Grinning behind it, I thought, at my ungainly, uncool hurry; but only her hand offered me a greeting, and that was subdued. A half-wave with no flourishes, uncertainty to match my own.

Knowing she was out there, sure she'd be waiting with some ambush I couldn't predict or prepare against, I took longer than I might have done. After a piss I tested out her power shower with the jet as hard and hot as I could stand it, pounding against the back of my neck to blast my bones awake. I cleaned my teeth and then I shaved with care, not to give any bloody hostages to unkind fortune, or to Suzie Chu Marks; and in her bathroom cabinet I found my own brand of aftershave, in among other men's toiletries I neither knew nor used. Not her brother's, surely; I was getting on top of this game now, guessing good, I thought. I guessed they'd turn out to be mine: gifts from her or else the choices of that unknown, that stranger, the Jonty Marks she'd married and I'd mislaid.

Clean and dried and sharply scented, my mind no longer sodden stupid after a hard sleep, I finally felt ready to face her; so I unbolted the bathroom door and walked out to find a steaming cafetière on the table with a mug beside it and a saucer full of pills and capsules.

She was back in the kitchen doorway again, dressed in a loose silk shirt and leggings, cradling a cup in her hands and leaning oh-so-casually against the jamb, knowing precisely the picture that she made. She offered me a small smile and said, "Drink. Eat."

"Not my idea of breakfast," I said, prodding a finger at the pills, sliding them around in their saucer. "What are they?"

"Multivitamins, ginseng, guarana. Good for you. And lots of vitamin C. We'll go down to Uncle Han's later, see what he says; but these'll do for now."

I said, "Linus Pauling died, you know. Death on the high C's," trying to turn that smile of hers more real; but then I swallowed every one of those damn pills, washing each one down with a gulp of coffee. Continental high-roast, blisteringly hot and mind-blisteringly strong: my bean and just the way I like it. Nothing changed there, at least. This was a different message, *I know you inside out*.

I sat down for a second mug, and after a bit let my head topple back, my eyes close. Foolish man, dangerous action: she read 'vulnerable' and zoomed straight in there. Her fingers closed on my shoulders and worked them a little, somewhere indecisively between massage and caress; then they did a little shiatsu on my neck and skull, and she said, "I knew I should've chucked that aftershave. Now I'm going to have to convert you all over again. Nice smell, nasty smell – it's like training a dog. I'm patient, though, I'm the soul of patience. You can keep it on for today, if it makes you feel at home. Go get dressed, and I'll fix you breakfast. What do you want?"

"What have you got?"

"Everything. Cornies, muesli, Fruit 'n' Fibre; toast and marmalade, toast and honey; Woodall's, of course, and free-range eggs to go with . . ."

"What's Woodall's?"

Her hands were still, fractionally; then, "You told me about Woodall's. Best bacon in the known universe, you said it was to die for. And I said only if you were a pig, and you snogged me. First time of snogging, that was . . ."

Never mind the snogging, there was something there that took me a frowning moment to pin down. Timing, that's what it was. I'd never heard of Woodall's bacon; and if I'd introduced it to her regardless of that, then I must have met it myself somewhere in the time between my last active memories – late January – and the time I'd first snogged Suzie . . .

So do mind the snogging, mind it much. "Don't remember the date, do you?"

"I've got a diary," she said. "And don't *laugh*," clipping me over the back of the head right where I'd had the stitches and still had no hair to act as a cushion so that it really did hurt, though I didn't actually need to yelp so loudly, I just liked to see her anxious.

She wouldn't let me read it, but her diary fixed the date. February fifteenth: "That's right," she said, "I remember. A day too late for Valentine's, I was dead pissed off about that. No romance, that's your problem. One of your problems."

Least of my bloody problems, I thought it was just then. I was still trying to work things out on my fingers. "So somewhere in that fortnight or so, someone else must have introduced me to this stuff. Is it really that good?"

"It's brilliant," she said. "But you could've bought it in a shop."

"Maybe." If I'd been changing lifestyle already, determinedly spending money I'd never had before – then maybe. But I didn't think I'd have spent it on posh bacon, even so. Not without prompting. Never a priority in my life.

"But so what, anyway?" Suzie demanded. "So someone else told you how good Woodall's was, where does that get us?"

I wasn't sure myself, how to answer that; or not until I did it, at any rate. Suzie was good for me, seemingly: making me say things aloud, making concrete and usable what otherwise would have stayed unstated, nebulously in my head. "Because it wasn't any of the people I know," I said slowly. "This is a marker, or it looks like one from here. It's not important in itself, but it's the earliest thing we know about so far, that I don't recognise. If we can find out or figure out who it was that gave it to me, then that really might be important . . ."

"Deverill," she said. "Nothing but the best for Vernon. And I bet he's an eggs and bacon man, breakfast every day."

"Likely he is," I agreed, thinking of the weight of him, and the symbolism inherent in what he was. Real crooks don't eat muesli. "Why would I be having breakfast with Vernon Deverill?"

She shrugged. "I wouldn't know, would I? It was before my time. Since we've been together, you've had breakfast with me. But you were buddy-buddy with him all through. That could've started with a power breakfast, he probably does deals right from the time he wakes up. He probably does deals in his *bath* . . ."

Which was clearly heresy, and the outrage of it nothing to do with his presumptive nakedness. Bathtimes must be sacred in this flat; and breakfasts too, maybe, which was maybe why she was so demonstrably not having breakfast with me today? Trying to emulate me at last, to keep some distance here, not to waken more echoes that she couldn't bear to hear?

"You could always phone and ask him," she went on. "He's probably waiting to hear from you anyway, wondering why you haven't called. He'll reckon you owe him one. It was his bodyguard saved your bacon, remember; so go on, give him a ring and ask him about his."

She tried a smile there for self-applause, but it was a poor imitation of her usual. I thought she must be thinking about the circumstances, the truck and the fire; and no, Suzie couldn't easily joke about that. Neither could I, having seen the consequences, a man burning like a candle.

But I thought Vernon Deverill would know very well why I hadn't phoned him. He clearly hadn't known the extent of my amnesia when he came to see me, but he'd have found out by now, surely. He'd have copies of all the doctors' notes, I imagined. A man hard to say no to, he would be potentially a very useful friend . . .

Which was presumably why I'd been cultivating him so assiduously, even to the extent of working for him, and letting him make me gifts; and why he'd want to use me was one question, and why I'd let him was another, and I urgently needed answers to both.

In the second bedroom, what Suzie called my study, I opened the wardrobe to confront what Suzie called my clothes, though I still had no sense of ownership. Choosing was impossible; I just pulled out jeans and a sweatshirt at random, underwear and a soft pair of shoes and never mind the names on all the labels, they fitted fine and that was good enough.

Back in the main room, Suzie was pleased to approve; then, "Breakfast?" she reminded me.

Breakfast didn't seem half so important as getting a few

of those questions answered; I wasn't even curious to try
the bacon. Not this morning. Too much on my mind to
be concerned with my stomach. I'd have missed breakfast
altogether, except that I thought I'd not be allowed to and I
couldn't be bothered to fight.

"I'll just get myself some cereal," I said, moving purpose-
fully towards the kitchen to kill any ambition in her to do
it for me. Self-reliant I had to be, or she'd be pushing me
more and more into the role of partner, where she wanted
me, where I felt like a trespasser or a kidnap victim, both.

"Okay." For a wonder, she didn't even follow me through
to point out the proper cupboards – though on second
thoughts maybe it wasn't such a wonder after all. No fool,
Suzie; she'd recognise my need for space, and just now at
least was generous enough to allow it. "Tell you what," she
called after me, "I'll nip down the shop, get a local paper.
See what they're saying about you this time."

"Don't bother on my account," I said.

"I'm not," she said, and laughed, and was gone.

And was back too soon, far too soon, before I'd poured milk
onto cornflakes: back frowning and disturbed and looking
to me, giving me an equal share in her trouble and by
implication an equal voice in her response.

"What is it?" I asked, as soon as I saw her chewing on a
thumbnail and not bursting with whatever news it was had
brought her straight upstairs again.

"Someone's been messing with the fire door," she said.
"Trying to jemmy it open, I think. I had trouble getting it
unlocked, and it's usually dead smooth; so I had a look when
it was open, and the wood's all scratched and gouged around
the whatchamacallit, the plate thing."

I took a second to assimilate that while she stood quiet
and watched me, dark eyes all unreadable; then I said,
"What about the street door, did you check that?" Back to

the questions again, but practical ones first; I was tired of
asking who and why, and getting no replies.

She shook her head. "No point. The club's open till
four o'clock, remember, they could just walk in. And they
must've thought they could walk right up to the flat, only
I'd locked the fire door; and they wouldn't be able to do
much with the club right there, people coming in and out,
they've just had a quick go and gone away. But it's *scary*,
Jonty. It wouldn't have been the papers, you're not that big
a story; and I just keep remembering Jacky, and what they
did to him . . ."

Nothing in the world to say that this was the same people
who had killed her brother. I told her so, but she only shook
her head, that kind of useless reassurance not at all what she
wanted from me; so I gave her something of what she did
want, God help me, what else could I do?

Actually I hardly did anything that she could have seen, I
made only the slightest movement. It was in my mind that
the greater shift occurred, from denial to reluctant invitation.
All my *keep your distance* wariness came down, because I
kicked it down; that was what she saw or sensed, and she
came to me in a hurry and a hug, and it wasn't only training
or duty in me that hugged her back.

Short and slender, she fitted easily, familiarly against me,
her head nestled into my shoulder and neatly under my chin.
Compared to Carol it was like hugging a boy, almost, all
bones and tension and no prominent padding; except that
there was no more of a boy's awkwardness in her, hugging
a man, than there was a stranger's. Only I felt strange and
awkward, and that only for a moment. Guilty lasted longer
– why her when it should have been, used to be Carol? –
but even guilt wasn't strong enough to have me draw back
or push her away.

Her choice, when to move; and she made that choice
sooner than I wanted her to, in all honesty. One last

tentacular squeeze, and her arms uncurled themselves from my ribs; her head lifted and tilted, till she could look at me; her hands sat lightly against my chest for a moment, then slid up over shoulders and neck to cup my cheeks; and then she kissed me.

Stood on tiptoe to do it, and still had to stretch; and my hands were helping, gripping her waist and lifting almost, supporting certainly, without my brain having anything to say in the matter.

It was a kiss stillborn, though, a kiss that failed, a clash of agendas with no common purpose. Stale and unprofitable it was, stumbling and uncertain; and again it was she who moved to break it, wriggling free of me and stepping back.

"Thanks," she said, avoiding my eyes as if she were awkwardly thanking a stranger for a too-personal service rendered. Which she was, perhaps; but only from my perspective. I think I blushed, a little.

"What now, then?" I asked, trying to bump us quickly over onto an easier track. When in doubt, dodge the issue; it's a native human reaction. She had her way, a stream of words meant often to hide whatever she might be feeling; I had mine. I'd sooner be doing than talking.

"Police, I suppose," she said, shrugging. "They'll be no help, but doing things properly – it's a promise I had to make to Jacky, before he ever let me work at the club. No short cuts, nothing unofficial."

Smart lad, her Jacky, if he could keep her acting responsibly even now. I offered him silent, respectful applause while she switched the phone on, first time since last night, and looked to me: "What's the number for the police? I don't want to go 999, they wouldn't love us if we tried to pass this off as an emergency . . ."

I took a breath to tell her – one number served the whole city, and I must have dialled it a thousand times, the years I'd been working here – but before I could name even a single digit, the phone rang in her hand.

She quirked an eyebrow at me, pressed a button, said, "Yes? Hullo?" and listened; grunted; quirked again, and passed the phone to me. "It's the hotel," she said, deflated by anticlimax.

Me, too. Calls in dramatic circumstances should have dramatic content, even if the drama's only a matter of timing. I said hullo, and could hear the uninterest in my own voice; presumably this was the call they'd promised me, to say the coast was clear and I could go and collect my hire car unpestered.

So much for presumption. Not the same man I'd spoken to last night, but the same anxious discomfort in his voice as he said, "Mr Marks? I've been trying to reach you all morning . . ."

"We had the phone switched off," I said, without a trace of apology. "What can I do for you?"

"Something rather strange has happened, Mr Marks. I understand from my colleague Mr Hobden that you did not in fact occupy the room that was allocated to you last night?"

"Well, only for an hour or so. I had a shower and a drink . . ." And were they going to charge me for it after all? House policy, perhaps, overriding the earlier decisions of a night manager?

"But you left no luggage in the room, is that right, Mr Marks?"

"Yes, that's right." None to leave; but already I was getting an inkling of where this was leading, and hairs were rising on the back of my neck. I lay no faith in coincidence.

"I'm glad of that, at least," he said. "You see, the room was broken into sometime during the night. There's no damage that we can find, except that the lock was forced; but it was turned over very thoroughly, and if there had been any property of yours in the room, I'm afraid it would be gone now."

"No, nothing," I confirmed. "Have you told the police?"

"Yes, of course. They're here now, as a matter of fact, and they'd like a word with you, I think . . ."

"Uh-huh. Put them on, would you?"

Only a uniform constable, for a busted hotel door; but after I'd spoken to her she invited us to stay where we were, to await a visit, and no surprise that it wasn't she who came visiting.

Who it was, it was the same plain-clothes and presumably quite senior detective who'd talked to me in the hospital, whose name nor rank I could remember.

Luckily, though, "Detective Chief Inspector Dale," he said as Suzie opened the door to him, as I lurked a little distance behind her.

"Hullo," she said neutrally. And then, "It's only a jemmied door, do we need a Detective Chief Inspector?"

"Nothing but the best," he said, his voice all affability as he stepped into the room with a young suit at his heels, some DCI-in-training, no doubt. "But I talked to your husband once before, Mrs Marks, at the hospital that morning, and it saves time if we don't have to cover the same ground twice . . ."

First policeman I ever heard of who didn't want to cover the same ground twice and three times and a dozen times more; but I nodded when he caught my eye, and shook his hand when he held it out to me, even gave him something of a smile when he said, "You're looking better than you were, lad, last time I saw you."

"I expect I am," I said. "I wasn't at my best."

"No. Any memory come back, then? Doctors told me it might . . ."

"Nothing. Sorry."

"Aye, well. It might yet; and you'll let us know, yes? If it does?"

"Yes, of course," though I thought I was probably lying. I no longer hoped to recover anything from those lost weeks;

but if I did, I thought, I'd want to keep it to myself awhile. At least until I had it sorted, the old world and the new held in some kind of equilibrium in my head.

"Good lad. Now," moving smartly on against my incipient resentment, *don't you patronise me*, "let's see if you can remember this, shall we? Are you by any chance any relation to Mrs Elspeth Marks of Eskdale, Cumbria?"

The way he asked it, he already knew; but my heart was sinking none the less. *Oh Ellie, God, what are you up to now?* Most of my troubles, adolescent or adult, had started something like this.

Still, I'd never denied it yet and wasn't about to start. "She's my mother," I said warily, wearily, whatever.

"She sure is," Suzie put in from behind me, and how could she be so cheerful about it? Naïvety, that was how, that was the only explanation: sheer inexperience of her new role as daughter-in-law to the Lady of the Lakes.

"Mmm," he said. I noticed his little Klingon was in the corner now, taking discreet notes. "It's a pity you didn't tell me that before, don't you think?"

"Is it? Why?"

"Because it would have answered one of my other questions, wouldn't it?"

He waited, I gave in. "Would it? Which one's that, then?"

"What your connection was with Lindsey Nolan, of course."

I tried, but I couldn't find any 'of course' there, any connection at all. Two people, two different universes so far as I knew.

"Give up," I said. "How do they fit together, then, my mum and Deverill's bent accountant?"

"How do any man and any woman fit together?" he snapped back, and I thought he was just being a policeman, couldn't walk a conversation past an innuendo without picking it up and playing with it. I gave him nothing for it, no smile nor grunt nor grimace; and after a moment I think he believed me, or at least pretended to. "She's one of his known acquaintances," he said.

"'Known acquaintances'? What does that mean?"

"In this context, it means she was his mistress. I'm sorry," as if that news had somehow power to hurt.

"Lover," I said, automatically correcting. "Not mistress. My mother was never anyone's mistress," though plenty of men's lovers she had been, and a different woman for each of them, to my judgemental eye. "But – Christ, Lindsey *Nolan* . . . ?"

"Uh-huh. Did you really not know?"

"I really didn't know." And was still trying to take it in, to make it fit somewhere between what I knew of my mother and what I knew of the runaway accountant, currently languishing in a Spanish jail.

Didn't compute, really. Must be something I didn't know, I thought; about one or other of them at least, maybe about both.

But that was hardly news. My mother was all mystery to me, always had been.

"Since when?" I asked. "And how long for?"

"Since the middle of last year, that we know of; and she still would be, I suppose, if he hadn't done a runner. She'd be visiting him in Durham nick."

"No."

"No what?"

Actually the word had been out there in the big wide world, making its own way before I'd thought to say it, let alone stop it. Still, too late now, and I had this habit of honesty. "No, she'd have been long gone before you picked him up. She'd have choked him off, petered him out, packed her bags and left. My mother has an instinct, she can smell trouble coming and she always, *always* gets out in time, before the shit starts flying." Always. That was an article of faith with me, and the world would shake the day I was betrayed in this. Unless that was another aspect of my new world, of course, that the old had shaken itself to pieces and I'd been rebuilding in a universe where my mother didn't have the nose for a hard rain coming or the sense to seek shelter before it fell.

"Oh, yes? So why are we looking for her, then?"

"Because you've been misinformed. Obviously. Last year's lover, maybe, but she'll know nothing to interest you, one sniff and she's gone . . ." Then it caught up with me, the full sense of what he'd said. I gazed at him for confirmation, saw it in his tension; and, "You don't know where she is either, do you?"

"Either?" he repeated.

"I don't have a clue," I told him, to his transparent and intense frustration. "She's not at home, you'll know that; and when she's not home, she moves around. Sometimes she gets in touch, usually not; only if she wants me. And if she's wanted me any time since January, I wouldn't know. Would I?"

"Doesn't it worry you?" he challenged me. "That she's disappeared?"

"We're not close," I said levelly, and let him read what he liked into that. My anxieties were my own affair, not for sharing.

"Mrs Marks?" He turned past me to Suzie, and I was suddenly stricken with doubt, holding my breath to hear my mother betrayed. "Do you know where your mother-in-law is just now?"

"Sorry," she said, "haven't a clue," and her voice was all Oriental inscrutability, and neither DCI Dale nor I had any notion if that were true or not.

So he was back to me again, and, "Well, never mind. She'll turn up. Meanwhile, she's definitely a connection; and you may not be close, but you'd get involved, wouldn't you? To protect your own mother?"

Yes, of course I would, but he wasn't listening. "She won't *be* involved," I said, "she won't need protecting. Involvement doesn't happen to my mother."

"Unh." Another grunt, and then, "So let's see if we can work out what your involvement is, eh? Why don't you tell me everything you can, about what Nolan was up to?"

"I only know what I read in the papers," I protested.

"Wrong. You only think you know what you read in the papers. Actually, you know a whole lot more than that. That's what Vernon Deverill's employing you for, havn't you twigged that yet? You're his secret weapon, to get his money-man out of jail."

Out of a jail in Madrid, and fat chance of that; what did I know of Spanish law? Still, some things I couldn't argue with, and this was one: that Vernon Deverill had given me a lot of money – and *why so much?* was a question that still needed answering, that this kind of mission didn't resolve at all – and that it was something to do with Nolan, which meant it had to be something to do with getting him out of jail and off the hook.

"So come on," Dale said, "talk me through it. Lindsey Nolan. Who is he, what's he done, where is he now and what's he waiting for?"

If he was a friend of my mother's, then even this much was treachery, or would be in another kind of family; but would she immolate herself for me? Would she hell. I said, "He's an accountant. Deverill's right-hand man, or used to be: Deverill made things happen, he brought the money in, Nolan squirrelled it away. Half a dozen laundry schemes, tax shelters, *very* smart investments that had the SIB looking at them good and close for any sniff of insider trading, and all they ever found was a massive stink and no evidence at all.

"He was bloody good at his job, and he should've stuck

to it. Deverill would've looked after him where he needed looking after, which was anywhere in the big wide world outside his job. But Nolan got greedy, or ambitious, or whatever; he wanted to be someone on his own account, maybe, not living forever in our Vernon's pocket; so he went a little bit freelance, didn't he, working evenings and weekends for himself.

"He sat on the board of a big local charity, Deverill encourages public virtue; and because of who he was, they made him treasurer. And he played all his old games on this new money, and by the time anyone noticed he had a neat little half-million or so sitting in his own bank and earning interest when it should've been out there on the streets and doing good.

"Someone tipped him off, that he was blown; so he jumped on a plane to Spain before you lot could catch up with him. He got picked up over there, though, and at the moment he's sitting in a cell fighting extradition, yes? He was, at any rate, the last I remember."

"Still is," Dale confirmed. "But that was very neat, son, a nice little summary. You had that ready."

And actually that was how it had felt in my mouth, in my head: like a tidy package waiting to be accessed, and not for the first time. Which made it the first access to any of my missing mind. Not the facts, I'd had all those from before, I remembered reading them, hearing them, seeing them on telly; but their collation into that handy couple of hundred words, I couldn't have done that without practice.

But there was nothing else I could call to mind, no further facts, try as I might at Dale's urging; and no, I was sure, my mother had never mentioned Nolan to me. But then, had I spoken to my mother in the last six months, nine months, year? That I wasn't sure of, couldn't swear to one way or the other. Very Pinteresque, my mother and myself; many pregnant pauses. Long, *long* silences a speciality.

"All right," he said at last, reluctantly and far too late. "Let that go, for the moment. Whatever's in your head, we can't get at it. But you must have files, yes? You've been working on this, working on something, at least—"

"For Deverill," I said, finishing his sentence. "You suppose he'd let me put anything significant on paper? Come on, be reasonable."

"Well, you're not one of his regulars, are you? You're not practised at his game, I thought maybe you'd do things your own way."

It was a point I granted him, grudgingly. I said I'd look, but I wasn't hopeful. Actually what I wanted to look at was the computer; there if anywhere, I thought. But I wasn't going to plug that in and boot it up while he was here. If I even admitted its existence, I thought he was in a mood to take it away; and I wasn't having that. He could take what I gave him, when I chose to give, and nothing more.

"So let's look at what happened last night," he said, deprived of anything else to look at. "There's the place you were thought to be, the hotel; and there's the place you actually were, which is here; and burglars have had a crack at both. That's not a coincidence, Jonty."

"No," I agreed.

"So what were they after?"

"Well, me, presumably."

"What for?"

I didn't know. He knew I didn't know; this was getting us nowhere, and Suzie's mask was about ready to crack. I saw her rub a finger across her lips, the most nerves she'd shown so far in public.

"Put it this way," I said. "We're assuming that for some unknown reason, Vernon Deverill has hired me to help get Nolan out of prison, yes?"

"Aye."

"So who'd be most keen to frustrate that?"

"You tell me," he said; so I did.

"You would. You lot. You've had him arrested and banged up, presumably you want him to stay that way. If I was you, Detective Chief Inspector Dale, I'd be asking questions around your own team. Okay?"

Clearly not okay, not by a long chalk, though Suzie was practically cheering. A point for us, and it was nice to be unequivocally on the same side for once.

He tried to wring some other suggestion from me and failed utterly, for the very good reason that I had no other suggestion to make. The unknown me might have been able to help him further, but not I. I think, no, I'm sure that he thought I was stalling or stonewalling, being stroppy and uncooperative; but in the end he gave in with a shoddy grace. He tried me with the man dead in the van, but I couldn't help him there either, I'd never heard the name. At last he left, though he promised to return. "And you keep in touch, Jonty," he said. "Anything happens, anything occurs to you, your memory comes back, anything, you let me know. Understood?"

Oh, yes. Well understood, officer; and thanks for calling round; and farewell.

And with the door closed against his returning, Suzie and I stood looking at each other, waiting perhaps for a bright or brilliant move, a suggestion, a solution; and the phone saved us from our own failures and each other's. We both moved for it, but I was closer; I almost had my hand on it before I checked, *her flat, her phone*, and glanced at her for permission.

And got it with an irritable wave of the hand, *it's your flat too, how often do I need to tell you?*

And picked the phone up, heavy in my hand, and felt no presentiment at all; and said, "Hullo?", expecting only to hear the voice of a stranger asking for Suzie; and heard instead the voice of my mother running like silver, creaking like wood in the wind and coming with such delicious timing that surely I should have known, it could have been no one else. DCI Dale wouldn't be down to street-level yet, and here was his most-wanted mother coming through to her son beautifully behind his back.

"Darling," she said. "Is it safe, can I come out yet, can I go home? I'm bored with all this hiding."

"God almighty, Ellie . . ." I needed a sofa, right there and ready to drop into; and there wasn't one, and I wasn't up to the walk across the room. Not when there was wall at my back strong enough to slide down, floor beneath me strong enough to hold me once I'd slid.

"Oh, is that *her?* I don't believe it," from Suzie, "is she all right, where is she?"

And from my mother into the other ear, "That sweet wife of yours hasn't improved your language any, swearing at your mother," which was deeply rich coming from her. And also suggested some sort of collusion, some idea of common cause between her and Suzie, which I didn't much like. An uncomfortable pairing that would be, even outside of crisis.

But meanwhile we were in crisis, we were deeply in the shit and someone was heaving bricks at us; no time for stray anxieties, *my too-well-known mother and my unknown wife, what dark games might they be playing, these dangerous women, at what might they play in the future?*

"Mother, where are you? Where've you *been?*"

"I've been keeping my head down," and I rather thought that was genuine surprise in her voice, and I was genuinely surprised to hear it. "Like you told me to, darling. Only I was bored, and I thought one little trip to town wouldn't hurt, if no one knew I was coming. I'm at the station."

"You're *what?*" But the shrieked question was redundant, because she'd told me already; and doubly so because her response was inaudible, drowned by a bellowing tannoy. Had to be the station for sure, and let's hope Dale nor anyone else had put a tap on the telephone. "Why didn't you— no, never mind." *Why didn't you tell me you were coming?* – but I'd asked my mother that a dozen times in my life, and the question had never made any sense to her. Why spoil the surprise? Darling? Instead, "Did you know the police are looking for you?"

"No," she said thoughtfully, I thought truthfully. "You didn't tell me about the *police*, darling."

But there was no responding question from her, no *Why would they be doing that?* I chewed my lip, feeling fretful and uncertain; then said, "Look, listen. Stay where you are, okay? I'll come down . . ."

"Right you are. You'll know where to find me," she said cheerfully, and hung up.

When I left, a minute later and in a rush, it was no surprise to find Suzie pounding down the stairs beside me. I'd almost expected that; almost counted on it, indeed.

Even so, honour required a challenge. "You don't have to come, she's my mother."

"She's my mother-in-law. And you're foul to her. I think she's great," stretching up to fit her own baseball cap onto my head. Two birds, one stone: cover the bad haircut and the tracery of red-and-purple scars, advertise her club. And remind me that she was looking out for my interests, where I was forgetting all about them in my urgency. *Three* birds . . .

Crashing out of the street door and into the street, "You never had to live with her," the automatic defence, used so often before when friends had met my mother. But then, a thought that seemed to follow naturally from what her words implied, "So *do* you know where she's been, or what she's been doing? If you get on that well?" Maybe my wife talked to my mother, I was thinking, where I did not. Except that apparently I did, apparently I'd told her to get the hell out for a while; so maybe my wife had been privy to that conversation, or the thoughts and fears that lay behind it.

"Nah," she said, holding me up a second while she took cigarettes from her pocket, stood still to light one. "If I'd known where she was, I'd have known where to find her, wouldn't I? When I was looking for you, you bastard?"

"Oh. Yes. But," part two, "do you know why she'd have gone away, did I tell you that? Why I'd have told her to?"

"No. Did you? Maybe you knew the cops were after her."

Maybe that was it, though it didn't feel right; and then I remembered, *You didn't tell me about the* police, *darling*, and that was what didn't feel right about it.

"Something else," I said. "Not the cops, she didn't know about them."

"So ask her," Suzie suggested. "Find out what she does know about."

I just grunted. I would do that, of course I would, but already I was not expecting too much joy from an interrogation of my mother. Tried that before, too often; failed too badly, also too often.

We shouldn't have stood still so long. There was a banging of car doors and a hurry of feet, and suddenly more people to ask us questions. These were the press, frustrated from their vigil last night, determined to get answers today: where had I been, what did I remember, how much had I lost? How did I know Vernon Deverill, why was I working for him, what could I tell them about the fire-truck?

Luckily I'd had some recent practice with reporters, and national ones at that, so much tougher. A few months ago – no, more than a few, better than half a year it must be now – a young client of mine had died of other people's carelessness. Poor little Marlon Thomas, violent, confused, inadequate: and now dead with it, dead at seventeen and his death a matter for questions in Parliament and front-page headlines on every paper in the kingdom, a lead story for all the media. And he was my client and I had to be his voice as best I could, and in public because it would never go to court, no one was ever going to be charged with the rank negligence they were guilty of . . .

So I'd had my taste of dealing with the press, and learned the knack of it. How to say what you want despite the questions they ask, how never to say more than you need. I told them enough to satisfy their editors, if barely; then I pushed through the scrum with Suzie all jabbing elbows and scowls at my side, and rather to my surprise they let us go.

I glanced down and sideways, to where Suzie was swinging healthily along keeping easy pace with me and smoking as she went; and I said, "Do you have to do that?"

She knew what I meant, and for some reason she looked delighted. "Yes," she said unequivocally. Then she took the cigarette from her mouth, hawked deep in her throat and spat a neat ball of phlegm into the gutter.

"Oh, for God's sake . . ."

But she was laughing up at me, her head cocked on one side and her eyes alight. "Just checking," she said, slipping an arm through mine and hugging herself against my shoulder as we walked. "Finding the bits of you that haven't changed a bit. Actually I stopped spitting, after you blew a gasket in the street one time. What is a gasket?"

"Something you blow," I said distractedly, and barely registered her snort, her nudging elbow, *fnaar fnaar and who's a dirty boy, then?* There was only a short walk from here to the station, and my mother was waiting at the other end of it; I wanted to be ready to meet her.

Couldn't meet the situation, didn't know enough; but I'd had a lifetime of coming face to face with my mother, and that always called for preparation, mental alertness, on your blocks and balanced and fit to run.

Didn't help much to have Suzie on my arm, or shouldn't be helping: enough of an unknown quantity on her own account, team her up with my mother and this was a triangle balanced on its point, on my frail shoulders, and I doubted I could bear the weight of it. So why was I not exactly glad, perhaps, but not at all sorry to have her there?

Because you're chicken, my private voices murmured. *Because your mother scares you at the best of times, when nothing in the world is going on that touches you or her; and this is not that, not by the longest of chalks; and any dilution is better than the pure spirit unadulterated. Sooner a cocktail than a straight shot, every time . . .*

Fair enough. Good analysis. I chanced another glance down at Suzie, who was still puffing on her cigarette and not in the least at the pace that I was setting, was even tugging at me a little, trying to hurry me faster; and this was something new to me, even those friends who enjoyed my mother not tending to scamper quite so eagerly as this towards a new revelation of her. Carol had always dragged her feet, lingered, tried to delay.

With, always, my own full connivance.

Today we went swiftly through the sights and smells of this one-street Chinatown, then cut through an old Georgian square, across a busy road and down a back lane. Steel-shuttered storefronts and graffiti'd walls, a couple of pubs and a casino; and so out into width and light and traffic, and the railway station like a palace the other side of the parade and my mother somewhere inside it, waiting for us no doubt like a queen.

The chair she sat in, like a burnished throne, screeched on the tiles as she leapt up, drawing all eyes to us.

"She'll be in the bar," I'd said; and she was, of course

she was. *The only civilised place to wait, dear*, and the availability of alcohol taking second place – of course – to the general aura of civilisation. A close second, perhaps, but nevertheless and genuinely second. Sometimes I'd even found her without a glass on the table, waiting with nothing but her cigarettes for company.

Today she had a drink, a real drink. She was apparently celebrating her reappearance with a brandy and soda and I supposed we could be grateful for the soda, her concession to the clock, still reading a distance short of midday.

And she might have had more than one already despite the early hour, because her chair skidded across the floor and her cigarette missed the ashtray and her voice hit the roof as she saw us.

"*Darlings!* How wonderful – but you, Jonty, let me look at you, what have you been doing with yourself? This can't be honeymooner's pallor, surely, not still? And I hate the hat. You've had all your hair cut off, haven't you? Who are you pretending to be?"

Jonty Marks, married man and associate of villains. I didn't say that, but I came very close to saying something acid, some reminder that I'd been sick and she hadn't come to see me. And caught myself just in time, remembering that she'd apparently been in hiding and apparently on my own instructions. She might have been anywhere in the country, a long way out of our local media's reach; likely she didn't even know about the car smash or the amnesia, let alone anything that underlay or derived from them.

She hugged me, fragrant and light in my arms though her hands gripped tightly; and then she moved on to Suzie, and I found the space to be surprised at that little premature stirring of bitterness in me, that she hadn't come to the hospital. Even without the excuse, I wouldn't have expected her. Why be bitter, at something so utterly in character?

I'd thought myself immune to any harm now. And was seemingly wrong. *Wrong again, Jonty.*

My mother, the curse of my rational years, all the years since I'd hit double figures: I watched her embrace my wife, and wondered what more damage she could do me, how much more to expect.

"Sit, sit," she said. "Have a drink, let's talk. How's he been, my stupid son, has he been a good husband, Sue love?"

"No," Suzie said confidently, publicly, nothing confidential about this information, "he's been crap. I'm giving up on him, the moment I find anything better. But listen, Ellie, we need to talk to you; and not here. There's all sorts of stuff been going on, and some of it's nasty. The police really are looking for you, you know. So I think we should just go straight back to the flat, yes?"

And somehow she had my mother out of there, very quickly and with no fuss at all; and five minutes later we were climbing the stairs again, single file and me bringing up the rear and not having said a word, Suzie had done it all; and I thought that maybe there could be advantages to being married to this girl, and the obvious nudge-nudge attractions perhaps the least of them.

Stupidly, I was expecting Suzie to play hostess for my mother, to show her all around the flat; but of course Ellie had been here before, she was more at home than I was. Or seemed so, at least; and I who'd known her twenty-seven years could never tell what with my mother was seeming and what was real, so I just treated everything as real and showed no surprise if it inverted.

She tossed her straw bag onto the nearest sofa, ran a hand through her hair – dark curls hinting towards grey, worn short and loose this year, apparently, barely collar-length: cut for the wedding, perhaps, a new hairstyle to greet a new daughter? – and said, "So what's with this police stuff, then? Bad enough that I should be hounded from my home by big business and its corruptions; now it's the police?"

"Seems so," I said. "What big business, what are you mixed up with?"

She stared at me, took a breath; and Suzie dived in there quick, grabbed my mother's breathing-space and used it. I'd never seen the trick done better, rarely seen it done at all. My mother's no politician, but she's picked up some of their less admirable habits, and bulldozing a conversation is one she's particularly fond of. She breathes in the middle of sentences once she's going, gives no one any chance to interrupt.

"Look," Suzie said, interrupting as if to the manner born, and she should have been my mother's child, not I, "you both need to listen to each other, you've both got stories we need to hear," and that was clever, that 'we', slipping herself into both teams at once, "so you might as well sit down and get comfy. I'll make some tea, but I want to hear too, don't start without me . . ."

"Coffee," my mother said, settling herself neatly beside her bag, feet together and hands folded in her lap as my grandmother must have taught her. Great if you're a little old lady in tweeds, as my grandmother had been; doesn't look so well in a rangy woman who carries half a century's history mapped on her face and body but seems fit still for the other half to come.

"Coffee, right. Sorry, I forgot." My mother doesn't drink tea: too insipid, too traditional, too colonial, whatever. "Jonty?"

"Bring us a beer," I said, sprawling on the other sofa.

No response to. that, beyond a moment's stillness; she didn't so much as frown or glare or give me any other sign of her undoubted disapproval, *sun's a long way short of the yard-arm, boy, do you want to grow up like your mother?* But when she did bring me a beer, an Oranjeboom in its bottle as

I like it and ice-cold from the fridge, she brought an ashtray also and laid it on the floor where clearly she intended to smoke right beneath my nose, and I was fairly sure this was punishment. And no doubt condign, for surely I deserved this and worse, far worse: whatever the motives were that underlay what I'd done – whatever it actually was that I had done – finding myself subsequently or consequently married to a fire-breathing, tobacco-tasting Anglo-Chinese beauty who could actually talk to my mother seemed like the least of my deserts.

Hard on myself always, however rightly so, I was ordinarily hard on my mother also; but I was not ordinarily in my mother's company. Confronted with her reality rather than only the shadows of her that lurked malevolently in my mind, it was hard now as it often was to reconcile image and substance, and particularly hard to be hard on her as I wanted, as I needed to be, as she in her turn deserved. *Come on, then, mother: tell us about your fancy-man the embezzler, the man who stole from charities and ran away to Spain. Tell me why you never told me, tell me how involved you were and where you've been hiding out since . . .*

"Come on, then," I said, and didn't even call her 'mother' though I knew she hated it, though I felt like doing it all day long. "Tell us how you are."

"The same as ever," she said robustly, "why should I change? Because you did, finally? You've seen the light, boy, I've been bathing in it, God knows how long. Shove that ashtray over."

"I've changed how?"

She snorted. "Look around you. Look what you've got here, look what you're doing, compared to what you were. A milksop you've been all your life, and now this; and never was a mother better pleased, I can tell you. Ashtray, please."

Obediently, I pushed the ashtray across the carpet. "I mean

how did it happen, though? From your perspective? How much have you seen or heard of me recently, what do you know?"

"He's serious," Suzie said, appearing round the corner from the kitchen, kettle in hand, clearly and quite rightly not after all trusting us to wait. "He's lost his memory, Ellie, crashed the car and can't remember a thing."

"Crashed the *car?*" For a moment she was wondrously still, squinting at me through her smoke. "Are you all right, Jonty?"

"He's fine," Suzie said, answering for me when I showed no signs of answering for myself. Too busy drinking it in, me, this moment of traditionally maternal concern from my most untraditional, unmaternal and ordinarily unconcerned parent. "Had a nasty bang on the head, but that's all."

"Ah. Hence the haircut."

"Hence the haircut," Suzie confirmed maliciously, twitching the cap off my head to show her the full horror now we were private, just a cosy family threesome. "But it's as well he looks like a weirdo, he's been acting like one. Can't even remember me, thank you very much, he thinks he's still shacked up with that Carol."

"Oh, God." The cry of outrage, of despair; and then, typically, the percipient question after. "Does he want to be?"

"Christ knows. Ask him."

No good asking me, ladies, I don't know what the fuck I want any more. But I wanted them to stop talking about me like this, at least to my face; that much I knew.

"Will you two leave it out?" I demanded. Quickly, before one or the other – most likely my mother – could actually ask that impossible question. "We've got more important things." And hearing myself say that and flinching a little, and then pressing on regardless over the top of Suzie's muttered, "Oh, thanks a bunch, big fella, love you too," and my mother's strident challenge, "Like what?"

"Like where you've been and why," I insisted. "Like what I've been doing, and why; and how come we're both suddenly standing up to our chins in shit, and people are lobbing rocks; and what we're going to do about it," though the notion of combining forces with my mother was enough to give me the screaming abdabs. I'd almost sooner hand her to the police and myself to Vernon Deverill to be his plaything. Almost.

"Hold your breath," my mother advised, "close your eyes and start swimming."

"Yes," from Suzie, her voice much amused, "but which direction?"

"Away from the rocks, darling. Obviously."

Times like that, information is a great flotation aid. "Tell us," Suzie said; and,

"What, have you got amnesia too?" my mother said to her.

"Nah, but he's dead secretive, him. Never tells me anything."

Which was seemingly true and curiously telling, though I'd never tell her that I found it so.

She sat at my mother's feet now instead of mine, to share the ashtray; and maybe that was all it was, pure practicality, but it felt like a declaration, them against me, and that felt like punishment again.

And then, at last, my mother told her story.

In brief, almost in a sentence, and to my great confusion.

"You came to me," she said, her cigarette stabbing in my direction, "and told me to get the hell out, dig a hole and pull the earth down on top of me, go somewhere nobody could find me or my life wasn't worth a small packet of dry roasted peanuts, you said."

"Yes, but why? Surely I must have told you why?"

"Because of Suzie," she said, or I heard her say, or I thought so.

• EIGHT •

LUNCHING WITH THE ENEMY

And she saw or heard Suzie's bewilderment, my own, in grunts and glances and shrugs; and for a second she wasn't with us, as we were not with her.

And then she cottoned to what we'd heard, and sighed, and said, "Not *Sue*, you stupid boy," as though the misunderstanding were entirely my fault. "Ess you ess eye," she spelled slowly, patiently, to her idiot child. "SUSI. It's an acronym."

"What for?"

"God knows. You told me. I forget. Security firm, though. After Lindsey, you said, and they might come after me. What it stands for, who cares?"

Brilliant. Some weird organisation was threatening her life, apparently – my own hectic imagination was thinking SPECTRE or SMERSH, cheap Sixties Bond-substitutes, sinister foreigners in distinctive clothing – and she couldn't remember who they were.

But sitting below her, Suzie had gone very still, while the smoke rose like drawn silk from her cigarette with never a waver from the vertical line; and when I tried to catch her eye, to share this most unfunny of jokes, I saw instead how she was staring at nothing at all, and how her skin had paled from its normal indescribable colour to something indescribable and sick.

"Hey, Suzie? What's up?"

My voice, it seemed, called her back from wherever she had gone, though not quickly. She turned her head to find me, though her gaze was still unfocused; and she said, "I know who they are."

"Yeah? Come on, then. Who?"

She shook her head at that, said only, "I can show you."

And stood up, and walked to the door like a zombie, no life or grace in her, only purpose; and there turned to look back at us both, and snapped, "Are you fucking coming, then, or what?"

No, it's just the way I'm sitting. But there was a tremor in her voice and a terrible tension in her fingers, where they had closed around the handle of the door; and this was not the time to be stupid. Not the time to comfort either, to utter inanities or ask unnecessary questions. I went to her, my mother followed me and we all trooped down the stairs again.

For once even my mother didn't talk, she could find that much sensitivity. And Suzie, who tried so hard to hide sometimes under a run of words: Suzie was achingly, shiveringly silent, and I didn't know if this was anger or fear or what, or where the hell she was taking us.

We went in the car; *too far to walk, then, or she'd have been storming, working this off on the pavement and dragging us all but unheeded at her sparking heels . . .* Which deduction was about the limit of my acuity, and no, I really wasn't cut out for detective work, my mind didn't see round corners.

Certainly it didn't see this coming, where Suzie was driving us.

*   *   *

Actually it wasn't that far, the other side of town but still
within the city limits; Suzie could have stormed it in less
than a quarter of an hour, even pulling us in her wake. Might
have felt better for the doing of it, also. That was my own
experience, at least, that hard walking could grind down the
hardest of feelings.

But she wasn't thinking of herself, wasn't looking for
therapy here or was just in too much of a hurry for us to
see this. And when we got there, when we saw, when she
told us – yes, then I could understand the rush in her, though
no more than she could I understand the story.

She drove us to a compound, and a church.

The compound was wide, and its fence was high: steel
mesh topped with three ranks of razor-wire coils, angled
out. Notices warned of guard dogs, and for once I didn't
disbelieve them.

Inside the compound were some one-storey brick buildings, petrol and diesel pumps sheltered under a canopy, a
couple of Portakabins and half a dozen vehicles with spaces
for a dozen more. The company name and logo was on the
wall of one building, on the sides of each cabin and each
vehicle, on a sign raised in one corner of the compound
where it could be seen easily from the road; barring one
or two light vans, the vehicles were armoured trucks; and
the name of the company was Scimitar Security.

The logo had a great curved sword crossing a shield, and
on the shield were the letters SUSI.

That much I could see even through the Mini's dark-tinted
glass; when Suzie wound her window down, I could lean
across her and read the small print that ran all along the
bottom of the sign.

*Scimitar Security is a division of Scimitar Universal
Securities, International.*

Scimitar Security was also, I remembered, the company

Vernon Deverill had used to protect his interests, viz and
to wit his bodyguard Dean and his rogue solicitor wild card
me when we were in hospital after the fire-truck, before I'd
wangled my escape to Luke; and also and again Scimitar
Security was the company Luke had talked about, protecting
the Leavenhall Bypass construction site and other projects
under protest, all of them Deverill's developments.

Two occurrences, one coincidence I could cope with;
Scimitar was a big player in the security business, and
not just locally. Not so strange to come across them twice,
especially if Vernon Deverill was involved in both events.

This was number three, though, and seemed to link Suzie
to my mother and myself in a way that had nothing to do with
a marriage: and then there was my own previous experience
of Scimitar, when young Marlon had died; and this web
was too tangled, had too many threads to be coincidental
any more.

A hundred metres down the road, right next to the compound
stood the church.

Stood in its own compound now, and not a graveyard:
pretty much in a building site, indeed. The low stone wall
that used to separate it from the road lay in a line of rubble,
replaced by a high mesh fence. Where once perhaps dead
people had been planted against a hoped-for resurrection,
the land between fence and church proper was all churned
mud, softstanding for a Portakabin and some heavy plant,
a JCB and a little earthmover, a giant generator closed off
against the possibility of weather.

Just inside the fence, another sign: *This site acquired for
Scimitar Securities, a SUSI company. Caution! Demolition
in progress – Parents keep your children out!*

And Suzie drew up there also and held us sitting in the
car, held us looking; and after a cold, hard while I said
gently, "Come on, then. What's the story?"

"This was my brother's next project," she said, and you could hear, I could hear and maybe even my ridiculous mother could hear how difficult these words were for her, how sharp their shapes in her mouth, how she bled to speak them. "He was bored with the club, once it was up and running. He was going to give it to me anyway, to look after. Manager and junior partner, he said. And him, he was going to buy this place and do it out the same way. It wouldn't be the same, it's not our community over here, but there's no snooker club either, this side of town. And he was going to have a gym here too, he thought it was big enough; and aerobics classes, Weight Watchers, the works. He was full of it, really excited and bubbling with ideas, like he hadn't been since the flat was finished . . ."

And she was full of it too, the precipitation of undissolved grief mingling with dark suspicion, her brother and my mother, all too much and I hadn't even told her about me yet, where I'd had a SUSI guard standing over me in hospital; nor about Marlon; nor yet about Luke's encounters with Scimitar at the roads protests. If the video of his tree-tumbling stunt showed the security firm's badge anywhere, I didn't remember and Suzie, I thought, hadn't noticed.

No need to tell her right now. She'd been guttingly open with us, but I didn't have to reciprocate. First time for everything, I guess, and that was the first time I'd felt even fleetingly grateful to be amnesiac. Suzie wouldn't expect me to know anything; even now it was my mother she wanted to interrogate, not me.

"He warned you, you said," and she twisted round in her seat, the better to stare my mother down. If anyone could, I thought, Suzie could; but I didn't really believe it even of her, I didn't expect to see it now. "So what did he say, exactly? How much did he tell you?"

"Oh, he told me enough, dear. He said that these people could be after me, probably were; and he said they were killers and I couldn't possibly fight them, so I should run and hide somewhere they wouldn't think to look. And if I ever saw a van or a uniform with Scimitar or SUSI on the side, that was them and they'd found me. They might come in plain clothes, he said, so I shouldn't trust any strangers, just in case; but if they came in uniform, I could be absolutely rock-solid sure."

"Okay. Okay," Suzie kicking hard, rising brilliantly through the clouds and not saying a word, not saying *no one warned Jacky, how come you got lucky and he didn't, why didn't someone, Jonty, anyone warn my poor bloody brother?* "Why, though? You must have asked him why."

"Because of Lindsey," she said. "Because whatever it was that man was mixed up in that had made him run, they thought I was mixed up in it too."

And she shrugged, *can you believe that?*, at the ignorance of these people; and I almost smiled at the gesture, so very much my mother. Of course she wasn't mixed up in someone else's twisted manipulations, she had far too good a sense of self-preservation. Besides, she'd doubtless have been too deeply tangled in her own, much too busy to bother.

Suzie was nodding, following the logic, not knowing my mother well enough to see that there was no logic there; and I thought probably her next question would be tangential, *so why were you hanging out with that man?* or something like it. So I interrupted in the moment of her silence, earning myself a glare that I could feel, although I wasn't even looking in her direction.

"Wait a minute," I said, "that makes no sense at all."

Only to us, my mother's smug smile said; and again Suzie drew breath to speak, probably to disagree with me; and again I snatched the moment for myself, before their misunderstandings dragged us away from what I wanted to say, from what seemed to me imperative and urgent.

"Lindsey Nolan was defrauding a charity," I said, "to

coin himself a bit of petty cash. What's a security firm's interest in that? I doubt they were making donations, and they certainly wouldn't be employed to protect the charity's funds. Why would they be the least bit concerned? Let alone threatening to murder his girlfriend, after he'd skipped the country?"

Suzie grunted, seemed reluctantly to concede that as a fair point, and glanced at my mother for an explanation.

And got another of those patented shrugs, and "How should I know?" said my elegant, eloquent parent.

"Didn't you *ask?*" demanded my wife, disbelieving. "I mean, Jonty must have known something, or he wouldn't have known to warn you . . ."

"Of course I asked. But does he trust his mother, with information vital to her health and wellbeing? He does not."

Meeting a brick wall there, Suzie tried the other tack, the what-were-you-doing-hanging-out-with-Nolan-anyway line of enquiry; and this time, as I could have forewarned her, the wall wasn't brick but breezeblock. This time it wasn't that my mother didn't know the answers, only that she was under no circumstances going to divulge them. Suzie battered, she had persistence on her side if nothing else; but my mother had a long life's-worth of acquired skill in guile and evasion, and no slip of a girl was going to break that down.

At last Suzie seemed not to accept defeat, not that, but simply to recognise that if she was going to carry on banging her irresistible head against my mother's liquid, changeable immovability – which certainly she was – then there must be more comfortable places and ways to do it than twisted around in a Mini. So she turned to face forward, with a cold glower at me *en passant*, set the car in motion and took us slowly back towards the flat.

I don't know if she was looking in her mirror more often

than usual, perhaps to watch her brother's dream or else this first faint hint of his enemy retreating and retreating at our rear; but after a couple of minutes she was surely looking in her mirror more often than even a paranoid learner would. Then she started taking wrong turnings, taking us away from the flat and towards nowhere in particular, so far as I could tell.

Easy enough to guess what was happening, but I asked anyway.

"What's up, Suzie?"

"We're being followed. Big black limo, see it? Couple back?"

My turn to twist in my seat; and yes, I saw it. Classic baddie transport, blacked-out windows and all.

But then, our windows were blacked out also; *let's not jump to conclusions, folks. Family.*

I said that, or some part of it. Took it on faith that she was right, that they were following; but, "Let's not jump to conclusions, they may not be malign . . ."

"Oh, what? Do me a favour! My brother's dead, your mum's been living in hiding, someone tried to explode you with a burning truck; and now someone's trailing us and giving off very bad vibes indeed, and you want to give them the benefit of the doubt, do you, Jonty?"

Actually, right then I wanted to hug her; just one of those impulses you get sometimes. But she was driving fast round some tight corners in traffic, and it didn't seem the moment, somehow. Besides, she was right. Jumping to a conclusion here was the only safe, the only sensible thing to do.

And that only the first jump in what could prove to be a triple or a whole series. The next, I thought, was obvious; time to leap without looking. "I'll jump out," I said. "At the lights," added quickly, not to let them think I thought myself a hero, to fall and roll in the road at speed.

"The fuck you will," Suzie snarled. "Fucking hero," and

all my good work gone to waste. "Who says they're after you, anyway?"

"Only one way to find out. And I'm *not* being a hero. Forget the movies; anyone on foot in a city can get away from a car. It's easy."

"Suppose they get out of the car?"

"Then I'll grab hold of the nearest policeman and cry sanctuary. That's what you do, too; if they keep coming after you, just drive to the police station. Promise?"

"Why don't we all drive there, right now?"

"Because we're too much in the dark here," though I was improvising this, I hadn't thought it out in the slightest. Maybe I did have a touch of the hero in me after all; unless it was only adrenalin pumping through my system, *fight or flee* and going tamely to the police not on the list there, not a biological option. Or else it was the biological male in me, wanting to protect my womenfolk. All sorts of reasons there seemed to be, if not the one I told her. "If we split up, they have to do one thing or the other, come after you or come after me; and at least that tells us something."

She didn't look convinced, but I wasn't offering her a veto on this one and the gods were against her anyway, there were traffic lights just ahead turning red with a lovely sense of timing.

"See you back at the flat, okay? And if it's you they want, don't be stupid, right?"

"Tell it to yourself," she muttered, "don't tell it to me."

"Yeah, yeah. See you. 'Bye, Ellie . . ." And altogether heroically I stepped out into the road as soon as Suzie had nosed reluctantly to a stop, slammed the door behind me and was off, picking a way through the traffic and then sprinting across a car park, my mind already plotting a route that was all footpaths and alleys, no chance for a car to track me.

Far end of the car park and halfway up a grassy bank, I looked behind, quick as a flick; and yes, there was someone coming after. Had the car stopped or gone on, had they divided as we had divided, were there enough of them to do that, had I gained no advantage at all for myself or my family?

Couldn't tell, couldn't see, didn't have time; whoever was chasing me was coming fast. Fit and hard he looked, what brief time I had him in my eyeline. So I jerked my head to the front again, and ran.

Up and down the grassy slope, in and out the alleys: I ran and he followed, and at last, unintentionally, here we were in Chinatown, or lurking just behind it. Slippery cobbles and the smell of rotting cabbage, no sunlight; the old city wall on the one side and the backs of restaurants on the other, above them the backs of clubs and other businesses; and above one of them was the flat. I was more or less leading him straight to my mother, straight to Suzie, handing over hostages with a fixed and stupid smile . . .

Perhaps I'd have stopped then, regardless; perhaps I'd have gone with him to any fate he chose, only to keep them safe. I didn't need to choose, though, because it was him who stopped, just long enough to bellow at me.

"Jonty! For Christ's sake, mate . . ."

At that – and with the comfort of distance, I was still keeping thirty or forty metres ahead – I looked back, saw him not running and let myself not run any longer. Stood gasping, shaking, hugely overdrawn on oxygen; and now that I was looking, not seeing only an enemy chasing, I could see who that enemy was.

Hard to think of him as an enemy, when I'd only met him the once and that time he'd saved my life.

So I stood still, not going even halfway to meet him as he came but not running now, how possibly, how the hell could I run?

Besides, fit and hard he undoubtedly was, and I wasn't. He'd have caught me, soon or sooner. Better to give myself over now, try not to make it look too much like defeat or surrender.

"Dean. Hi . . ."

"What the fuck are you running for?" Bastard wasn't even breathing hard. "What've you done? Apart from pissing Vernon off?"

I shook my head. "Nothing, as far as I know," though that of course was not far, not far at all. I could have done murder and not known it. "Only someone's after us, and . . ." And running away had seemed like a pretty good idea, at the time; now, of course, I felt nothing but stupid, cowardly, ridiculous.

"Yeah," Dean said. "Vernon's after you."

I shook my head. "Someone else." *Someone worse*. "Whoever sent that truck through the hospital wall, most likely. Unless it was you broke into my hotel room last night, and then came round the flat and tried there?"

"Not me. No one else of Vernon's, either. I'd know. Do you want protection?"

Yes, I did want protection; but not, I thought, from Vernon. Last time, it had come in a uniform with *Scimitar* on the shoulder-flashes; and somehow, in retrospect, that didn't make me feel any too protected.

So a quick change of subject, nice and clear: "How are your arms?" I asked, remembering that he'd been burned badly enough to be kept in hospital overnight.

"My arms are fine," he said, "all new and shiny, pink as a baby's arse. Do you want protection?"

Bastard. No, I said, thanks very much all the same; and he said, "Well, see what Vernon thinks."

"*No*, Dean. It's my choice, not his." My life, and I was only just starting to get a grip, and that only on a couple of corners; I wouldn't willingly cede any fraction of that little control to someone else.

"Maybe. Okay," lifting his hands in mock surrender as I

glared at him, "I won't ask him. I swear. But if you change your mind, just say. We can fix you up. Not a problem."

And then one of those strong hands – and yes, there was new smooth pink skin across his knuckles, clearly to be seen now that I was looking – reached out to grip my elbow, light and easy as a loose noose, and he said, "Come on, then, Jonty. You're invited for lunch. We'll have to run for the bus now, you've lost us a lift and believe me, you don't want us to be late . . ."

And I went, of course, how not? Still painfully aware how close we were to Suzie and my mother, I'd have gone anywhere, I think, with anyone. Going off for lunch with Dean seemed like a pretty good option, in the circumstances. Even with Vernon Deverill for host.

Dean had been joking, it seemed, about running for the bus; no trouble for him, but now that I'd stopped I couldn't have run anywhere to save my life or my mother's. Or my wife's, come to that.

He'd been joking altogether about the bus, as it turned out. We walked slow and steady to the wall's end, and if he kept his hand under my elbow all the way no doubt it was only there as a support, he'd seen how blown I was; and there was the bus station, right enough, but there was a taxi-rank also and we took a cab.

Deverill lived out of town, and no surprise there, I'd expected nothing else. A drive of four or five miles brought us to a pair of wrought-iron gates, watched over by a closed-circuit camera on a vandalproof pylon. Contrary to orthodoxy, form doesn't have to follow function; the gates at least were beautiful.

Clever, too. At a word from Dean the taxi-driver just drove straight at them, and they swung silently open for us, while the camera turned its head to watch.

Deverill's driveway added maybe another mile to the journey, winding narrowly through mature woods and then running straight across sheep-pastures – lush and level as a lawn, these, so different from the sheep-scattered hills of yesterday, not Luke country at all – and a mediaeval bridge so narrow that pedestrians had needed passing-places even when they built it, little niches of shelter in the stone.

And then, at last, there was the house.

A big square Georgian statement, *we've got money*, a couple of centuries later it should have been National Trust, it had that look about it; and that it wasn't, that it was still a private house in the '90s only renewed and underscored that original statement. *Some of us have still got money, and we're quite willing to flaunt it*, that house said to me today.

Just a couple of cars parked in the forecourt, one the same darkened limo that had trailed us through town, the other a Jag in vibrant red. Some other guest for lunch, perhaps? Or Vernon's private car, for when he didn't want to travel in chauffeured splendour?

Whichever, it didn't matter. If another guest, then our difference in status became all too apparent, all too quickly; Dean directed the taxi around to the back of the house, through a stone arch into what must have been the stableyard, what was now clearly parking for staff. A dozen cars here, none of them quite new and none of them at all grand; and once he'd paid off the taxi, even Dean had to sound a buzzer to get us in through the reinforced door, for all that the cameras had watched our arrival and knew exactly who we were.

This part of the house had been altered past any recognition, almost past bearing; narrow corridors and small offices, computers everywhere, strip lighting and fire doors and not a glimpse, not the least ghost of how it used to be. Cruelty to eloquent buildings, this was. Deverill clearly believed in bringing his work home with him. But Dean hustled me along with no more than a nod to any of the people we passed, and he took me through one last heavy door and into an utterly different world.

Here was the hallway, rising three stories above us; and there ahead was the front door, a massive job in oak and iron and another reminder of my comparative rank here. We'd driven all round the house and walked back through it, only because I didn't have clout enough to rate the front door, or Dean didn't think that I did.

Marble columns in the hall here, original floorboards worn and warped with age, glowing dark with polish. Dean marched me across them, tapped at a closed door half again as high and as wide as standard, and pushed it open without waiting for a reply.

His head gestured me through first. I walked in obediently and was vaguely conscious of his closing the door again behind us and then staying there, standing probably with his back to it and his legs no doubt apart and his arms I imagined folded like any cheap cliché of a watchful guard in a situation of uncertainty, not knowing whether his companion is prisoner or guest. He'd saved my life, I thought, and taken burns himself to do it, because it was his job to do that, at that time; things had changed somewhat, and might change more. If they changed enough, I thought, Dean might take my life with no more hesitation.

Ach, don't be morbid, Jonty Marks. Get a grip, will you? He's not Mafia, even if he likes to pretend he is. And whatever reason could he have to want to kill you, or Deverill to want you dead?

More questions, real or not; and I had no answers to those either. Fine. *Let them go, worry when you need to.*

Right now I had enough to worry about, in the way Vernon Deverill was looking but not striding across this

wide room to greet me, very much not holding his hand
out to a luncheon-guest in welcome.

The room had Regency paper on the walls, that might
even have been original; it had watercolours and oils that
certainly were. I rather thought the furniture was also, or
some of it. A table and a sideboard particularly might have
been made two hundred years ago to stand just there, and
not have been moved since.

The leather-covered chairs around the fireplace were not
so old, though old enough for sure, cracked and worn and
comfortable-looking. One of them held a woman in her
fifties, who held a glass in her hand and gazed at me across
the top of it, assessing, quite unforthcoming.

If that was a habit, it was catching. Deverill's one hand
also held a glass, while his other fiddled in his jacket pocket;
and his face was as revealing as the windows of his limo as
he gazed at me all down the length of a sizeable Bokhara
rug, and said, "I don't think you were entirely straight with
me, son, last time we spoke."

"Be fair, Mr Deverill," I said, respectful but not presump-
tuous, not 'Vernon' now. "Would you have been? In the
circumstances?"

"What circumstances are those, then?"

Sometimes, with some people, bullets are very much for
biting. "I was sore, I was scared, I was very confused; and
in my business, in this region, you're pretty much public
enemy number one, Mr Deverill. What am I supposed to
do, suddenly open my heart to someone whose agenda I
can't understand, whose motives I have every reason to
distrust?"

"A man in that position," he said slowly, thoughtfully,
not at all challenging my definition of his own position,
"I'd have said you'd be glad to trust someone."

Yes, but not you. And not Suzie either; I'd run to Luke.
Old bonds grip most tightly. But Deverill actually sounded

disappointed in me, let down that I hadn't chosen him. I almost wanted to say sorry. Maybe I was being manipulated here – *again*, my most private voice murmured – but I thought that this was genuine, that there was something of a frustrated paterfamilias in him that sought the trust as well as the respect of those he let into his circle. Big on loyalty, I thought he'd be; murder on betrayal.

"I needed time to think," I said, grabbing a catch-all defence, weak in the face of hurt. "If I'd told you straight out, 'I'm sorry, Mr Deverill, I can't remember you or the job I'm doing for you,' you'd have given me no time at all, would you? You'd have told me to keep it that way, and found someone else to do the work. I just had to stall you for a while, until I could find out what was going on."

He grunted. "So why did you run out on me, then? Why the vanishing-act?"

If his ego was that big, that he saw my disappearance only in terms of himself, I had no problem with pandering to it. "You'd have been coming back next day, I figured, and I couldn't have fooled you twice. You'd have talked to the doctors by then, you'd know about the amnesia. And I don't like hospitals anyway, I wanted to be up and doing, trying to make sense of things. Besides, someone had told me by then that you were paying for the room, and I really didn't want to be beholden to you any more than I was already."

"My man saved your life," he said neutrally.

"I know. I've not forgotten that."

"Glad there's something, then. How much else is there?"

"I'm sorry?"

"What do you know, about my business?"

I glanced at his other guest, the woman who sat listening, absorbing everything, I thought, and giving nothing at all; and he said, "Don't be coy, boy. No secrets between us."

"Fair enough, if you say so; but may I know who we're sharing your secrets with?"

"What? Don't be . . . Oh." His head turned between us, his gaze went to her and back to me; and he said, "You don't remember?"

"I'm sorry. No."

"Well, then. For the second time of asking, this is my ex-wife, Dorothy."

Typical of him, I thought fleetingly, that definition: again, he'd see everyone only in relation to himself. Or in ex-relation . . .

And it seemed that her mind tracked mine, because she rose to her feet, held her hand out, and said, "Dorothy Tuck. I use my own name now."

She would, I thought. Her handshake was firm and determined, and so was her voice, and I thought neither one was deceptive. The only surprise was that Deverill could or would still deal with her on this basis, one-to-one and no secrets between them; he was a man I would have expected to cut himself off from his failures.

She sat again, and looked at me expectantly. Fair enough, I thought. In the circumstances, it was up to me to open.

"All I know," I said, "is that you hired me to do a job for you, which is something to do with finding out why Lindsey Nolan pinched all that money and ran off to Spain."

"He didn't," Deverill said. "He was set up. He's too damn clever to be that clumsy."

"Okay, whatever. The other thing I know," being brutally, dangerously honest here, the only way to play it, "is that you've been paying me far too much, whatever the job entails. And you're not famous for your open-handedness or for being an easy mark to rip off, so there's some hidden agenda here that I don't understand. I also don't understand why you picked me for the job, whatever the job actually is; and I certainly don't understand why I ever said yes, why I quit my old firm to work for you."

"You offered," he said. "All this was your idea, none of it came from me."

Oh, God. That meant we really were in the shit. "Tell me about it?" I suggested.

"Sit down, first. Have a drink," and a gesture of his fingers, *abracadabra*, turned Dean from bodyguard to waiter. A minute later I had a heavy gin in my hand – no consultation there, no *what would you like, Jonty?*; it seemed that Deverill drank gin at lunchtime, and therefore so did his guests – and I was sitting, he was standing, starting to pace.

"You approached me," he said. "Right out of the blue, I'd never heard of you. You phoned my people, said you needed to talk to me about matters that should be of concern to me. I thought that sounded like some kind of blackmail threat, but I had you checked out, and everyone said you were just this dead straight lawyer; so I said I'd meet you. Are you sure you don't—?"

"I'm sure," I said. "Truly. Means nothing to me."

"All right. But it feels . . ."

"I know," I said. "Believe me, it's pretty weird from my side too."

He grunted, getting his head – with an effort, I thought – briefly around someone else's point of view; and then, moving swiftly on, "So we met, and *you* told *me* what I was sure of anyway, that Lindsey had been set up. But you knew it for a fact, you said, though you couldn't prove it yet; and you thought you could get the proof, proof positive, you said, only to do that you needed my help. You had to look corrupt, you said, or you'd never get near them."

"Hence the money?"

He nodded. "Hence the money. And you gave up your job, and spent a lot of time just being seen with me. That's what convinced me, I suppose, more than anything: that you did set out to wreck your own career, very publicly. You had to be serious then, unless you had a *very* fancy con job in your head."

He was not wrong there. Very serious indeed, I must have been. But why, about what? *To save my mother's life* was the only possible answer. I'd told her she was in danger; presumably I was trying to protect her in some way I couldn't currently fathom.

Would I do that? Would I lay down everything I had, everything I'd worked for and everything I valued in my own life, because that way I might just manage to preserve Ellie's?

Well, yes. Put it like that, I would; and apparently I had, though it felt very strange to think it.

I must have been looking pretty strange also, the minute or so that I sat there, that the silence lasted. At any rate they were both watching me by the time I dragged my eyeballs back into focus again, and both seeming pretty amused.

"Have a drink," he said. "Might help."

"Uh, I've got one . . ."

"I know, but you're not using it. Drink," and he demonstrated, taking a swig of his own; and yes, I did that too, I imitated him. And yes, it did help, briefly. Fizz and tang, gin and lemon achingly cold from the clinking ice; and a lump of ice slid into my mouth as I drank again, and I sucked on that until it was nothing, and that helped too.

"So how much more did I tell you, Mr Deverill?"

"Bugger all," he said.

"But if I was spending all that time with you, and you were giving me all that money . . ."

He shrugged. "You said I had to trust you. You wouldn't tell me anything, not until you could prove it. Dot said you were taking me for a ride, but . . ."

"Not necessarily that," she said. "I was right, though, wasn't I? You should have insisted on being told. You've lost it now, both of you. Unless that's one thing you *can* remember, Jonty? Who you were stalking, I mean?"

I shook my head, slowly. "Sorry," I said, shifting from truth to deception, not quite lying in my teeth but as near as dammit. "That's all gone, too."

"Oh, for God's sake!" Deverill snapped his fingers for another drink, handed his glass to Dean without looking round, too busy he was glowering at me. "You must have been keeping notes, though, something, you must have *something* to tell us who? Or you told young Sue, maybe, she'd know?"

"I don't think so. If there are any notes, I haven't found them; and Suzie hasn't said anything, except how secretive I was," and still was now, juggling too many secrets in my head and already finding it hard to remember who knew what. If there were notes, I knew where they'd be; but I wasn't going to say in this company, any more than I was going to mention SUSI. Lots more I wanted to find out first, before I'd even consider laying any cards on the table. Many people I wanted to speak to; and among them Lindsey Nolan, only that he was in a Spanish jail and likely to remain there a while longer.

Right now, I thought I'd better speak to someone else.

"Can I phone the flat? Just to let Suzie know where I am?" *And my mother*, but I wasn't sure if they'd clicked that she'd been the other passenger in the Mini, and if not I certainly wasn't going to tell them. I'd apparently told her to keep her head down; I'd bloody sit on it if I had to, if there was no other way to be certain that she would.

"Yes, of course." Another click of the fingers, and Dean appeared at my side with a cordless phone in his hand, the suspicion of a wink trembling around his right eye.

"How did you find me this morning, anyway," I asked casually, "have you been watching the flat or what?"

Deverill laughed. "Not since last night. I called them

off, once you turned up. If you'd been doing a runner, you wouldn't have come back, would you? I was sending Dean to fetch you over tonight, no hurry; but we saw your wife's car in the street, and it seemed like a good time to get things straight. Nothing but coincidence, that's all."

Which he'd acted on instantly: a warning there, I thought.

And then I gazed at the phone in my hand, and thought again; and finally had to say, "Um, I'm sorry, but does anyone know my number?"

Suzie took some calming down, even after I told her who'd been trailing us. She'd developed a major antipathy to the man already; she'd been frightened on the road and bitterly resented that now; and though she certainly wouldn't admit it to me I thought she was uneasy in the flat today, with those scratch-marks around the lock as reminders and only my mother for company.

"Come home, Jonty." Three or four times she said that, with different emphasis in response to my different excuses. And at last, "If you've done your business, come on *home*. What do you want to eat with them for? Come and eat with us. You don't even remember my cooking . . ."

True, I didn't; but, "Better not," I said.

"God, you're such a wimp! Just tell 'em: say, 'Look, I don't like you. Maybe I work for you but that doesn't mean I have to have lunch with you, and my wife and my mother are waiting at home, so take me back, please.' That's all, it's easy. Or call a cab, you've got the phone in your hand. Harry Wong'll come get you, I'll give you his number, can you remember it long enough to dial?"

"No, stop," I said, laughing now. "I don't," *careful, they're listening*, "I can't see me doing that, somehow, can you? Truly? You would, maybe. Not me. You look after, look after Elle-même," hoping that neither of my auditors would quite catch that, or work it out if they did, "and I'll be along soon. Is the club open?"

"It will be by now, yes. Lee's looking after it. Why?"

"If you're worried, lock the fire door and ask him to watch out for anyone trying to come up."

"I'm not scared," she said fiercely, as I'd been sure she would; untruthfully, I thought. "I'm not locking myself in like some cowering bloody rabbit in a hutch . . ."

"Okay," I said equably. "It's your choice. But I'll tell you this, lover, I'm scared for you. So take care, yes? Don't answer the door without the chain on."

"Yes sir, no sir. Don't give me orders."

"Hey," I said.

"What?"

"Did you promise to obey me? When we got married, I mean? I bet you did. Church wedding, and all. To keep your parents happy. I bet you didn't change a word of the service, did you . . . ?"

By then, I was talking into empty space; she'd blown a loud raspberry down the phone, and hung up on me.

Dean was at my elbow again. I swapped the phone for a replenished glass of gin, and did it grinning.

"One more question, Mr Deverill. This may sound foolish, but I do have a reason. What kind of bacon do you eat for breakfast?"

"Woodall's," he said instantly. "Best in the country. Why?"

"Just narrowing things down a bit," I said vaguely. Actually, just checking on the score: it didn't after all tell me anything I didn't know already, but that was one for Suzie, she'd called it exactly.

Two for Suzie, because she was right, I didn't want to eat with these people. I thought I ought to stay for lunch, though, regardless. I might learn something.

No doubt they were thinking the same, thinking me vulnerable where in fact I was only ignorant. There was so little that they could learn from me that they might possibly want to know, I felt smugly safe and unconcerned.

Until, through in the dining-room and following my host's example, picking up the cutlet bones in my fingers to suck off the last shreds of meat, I happened to glance out of the window into the stableyard.

Happened to see a four-square van roll slowly past and out of sight.

White it was, with a logo writ large across the side.

Scimitar Security, it said.

· NINE ·

STILL LIFE WITH RAVEN

There must, I suppose, have been a pudding; but add that to the list, the many lists of things I can't remember.

There must I suppose have been conversation, ditto; I may even have made a contribution to it, ditto ditto.

Perhaps I was overdoing the shocked-and-stunned effect; perhaps I should have been better prepared. I knew, after all, that Deverill worked with SUSI, that Scimitar was his security of choice; and I'd seen earlier that he worked largely from home, that the heart of his organisation was here. No surprise, then, or it shouldn't have been, to see a Scimitar van making a collection or a delivery, or both. Important papers, money – anyone working as close as he did to the fringes of the law would work significantly in cash, and need significant amounts of it – anything crucial to the running of his various businesses might have been carried to and fro under professional guard, and quite reasonably so. No need for this touch of chill under my collar, the hand of fate exhibiting its exceedingly poor circulation; no need even to react, let alone overreact the way I undoubtedly was. I knew that, I told myself that even as I did it.

But it was only a couple of hours since my mother and Suzie between them had named the bad guys in this story, since I'd found that name threaded deeper and further through the weave than even they knew. And now here they were, or some troops of theirs, right outside the house and probably inside by now, just a corridor's length away from me; and it was no great wonder if my cutlery skittered on the china, as my mind skittered from blind fear, *this is a trap and they've come for me*, to wannabe detective, *I must find out who's driving that van and what they're doing here.*

And back, and to and fro like a hot potato tossed from hand to hand, and each hand blistering.

Uncertain and afraid, of course I did nothing, neither started asking questions nor made a desperate bid for freedom; and so happened neither was necessary, because Dean – my good friend Dean, who winked at me and saved my life and so forth – came in and did good work again, gave me an answer and an opportunity.

Came in and went to Deverill, spoke to him but didn't whisper, didn't bother to hide what was happening.

"They've brought that girl," he said. "The one who was so fancy with the bulldozer?"

Deverill glanced at his watch, and nodded: a man whose empire ticked its heartbeat on his wrist, and clearly kept excellent time.

"I'll come now," he said. Touched his napkin to his lips and rose from the table, with a gesture to me, *stay there*, as I shifted uneasily. "Finish your coffee, Jonty. More in the pot, if you want it. Talk to Dot, keep her company. I've some business to see to, but I'll be back."

I didn't much want to talk to Dot, I wanted to go with him; but lacking the chance of that, at least there was one question I could ask, anyone would ask in the circumstances.

"What bulldozer, Mrs – uh, Ms Tuck? Do you know what they're talking about?"

"Mrs Tuck," she said comfortably. "I'm too old to go Msing," with the air of someone who had made the same pun many times before, and still enjoyed the opportunity. I gave her the smile she was looking for, she chuckled, and then she said, "Yes, of course I know. No secrets from me, Vernon told you that. And this was no secret anyway, it was particularly public and embarrassing."

"What was it?"

"Do you know – I'm sorry, do you *remember* – about the Leavenhall Bypass, all the fuss there was?"

I nodded. That had begun before Christmas, long before the first rip in my sense of continuity, and had been very much in my bailiwick: I'd defended a couple of students charged under the Criminal Justice Act, landed lucky with some sympathetic magistrates, and got them off in defiance of the evidence. That was early days in the protest, but Luke had been involved later; so yes, I was well up to speed there. Or thought I was.

Didn't know about the bulldozer, though. That must have come later, after the first trees were felled, falling itself into the pit of my absent memory and not the sort of detail Luke would have thought to tell me about.

"There was excellent security on site, of course," Mrs Tuck told me. "The protestors had been encamped there for months, everyone knew the dangers of sabotage. There was a double fence topped with razor wire, there were dogs, there were guards on constant patrol twenty-four hours a day. All the vehicles, all the plant was immobilised every night as a matter of routine.

"What no one thought of, what no one recognised as a danger was that the protestors might import plant of their own. One night, this girl drove up in a bulldozer she'd stolen from council roadworks five miles away. She'd locked herself into the cab, and the men on duty simply had no way to get at her, without taking considerable risks with their own lives. They couldn't even power up the plant that was there, and drive it to safety; as a matter of course, the keys and various internal components were not kept on-site. For security, you understand?"

I nodded. I understood, and my heart sang. Basically, what she was telling me was that Vernon and all his money, all his hired muscle had been taken to the cleaners, by some radicalised slip of a girl.

"She tore the site apart," Mrs Tuck said. "She destroyed the guards' own vehicles first, so that when they finally decided to go for help, they had to go on foot. Communications had already been severed; she'd knocked down a few telegraph poles en route, and their mobile phones didn't work in the valley. Out of range of any transmitter, or else they were in a radio shadow, I forget.

"At any rate, by the time the police arrived, the site had been totally wrecked. She'd destroyed the fence, smashed all the Portakabins and overturned or otherwise damaged most of the plant. Also, of course, by then all the other protestors had come to join the party; they were busy tearing apart whatever she'd left in one piece.

"And the girl herself was gone. Her bulldozer was the only vehicle left viable, but it didn't carry a single fingerprint; they'd wiped every square inch of it, to be certain.

"That didn't help her in the end, though," added with a touch of satisfaction. "It's taken a long time, and cost Vernon a considerable amount of money; but they've found her at last, and brought her in."

Brought her in for what? I didn't ask; I only walked to the big bay window, hoping to see for myself.

And saw, and saw far more than ever I'd hoped or dreamed to see.

Out of the angle of the bay, I could see the van parked in the furthest corner of the yard, nose to the wall. Dean and Deverill stood a few metres away, relaxed and easy, talking to a couple of men in Scimitar uniforms: the drivers, presumably. The bringers-in.

One of the men moved eventually, going to the rear door of the van and unlocking it, working the big bar handle and folding the door back flat against its hinges.

Inside, I could see a narrow corridor that seemed to be walled with doors like a public toilet, divided into separate cubicles. Only one use I knew for such a design, which was to transport prisoners to court or around the country: the police had them, so did all the major security firms who'd bid for contracts in the great free-for-all, the open and competitive market that had been declared in the prison supply service. The sight of it brought my mind back to the other context in which I knew the name of Scimitar: my only memory of the company from before my accident, but a significant one in my life.

Little Marlon Thomas, famously deceased, putting his name and mine in all the papers: *Dead drunk* had been their favourite line. Nothing too surprising in that, teenagers will drink more than they can handle, especially hard-seeming street kids like Marlon. The inquest verdict had been death due to lack of care, on account of its happening when he'd just been sent down for armed robbery and he really shouldn't have been able to get his hands on a litre bottle of vodka, but again he was hardly the first to manage that.

No, what made Marlon's death stick so particularly in the memory, what had made it such a good story for the media was that it had happened, he had died between court and prison, on a forty-minute drive.

Locked in a cubicle in the back of a van he'd been, all alone with his bottle; and he was the first juvenile to die that way, under the charge of a private firm.

The firm, of course, had been Scimitar Security; very possibly this was the very same van he'd died in, now apparently on private hire to Deverill.

*   *   *

The man climbed up inside, and I couldn't see him for a minute. No one else was trying to; they stood heads together, talking, betraying no interest at all.

Then there was a shadow moving inside the van, a figure, two figures coming forward; and a girl stood blinking in the doorway, with the man behind her.

She was half-turning, one foot reaching down to find the stirrup that would make a step to help her to ground, when he pushed her and she fell.

She fell hard, with a yelp of shock that I could see but not hear through the double glazing, that I could see cut off when she hit the ground. Actually, I think perhaps I'd yelped myself, and cut it off equally abruptly.

It was only a drop of three or four feet, and she shouldn't have landed so awkwardly on one shoulder; but she rolled and writhed, and I saw how her hands were held behind her back, in a tie or more likely in cuffs. *Kidnapping and assault*, I thought, *so far*; and I wondered if Deverill knew what he was doing, that he was handing a propaganda weapon to his opponents.

Then I stopped wondering anything so stupid, remembering who this man was and certain at least of that one thing, that he knew exactly what he was doing.

Right now, he still wasn't paying any attention. He stood with his back to the girl, giving instructions to Dean that seemed from his gestures to be about some other matter entirely; the man in the van stood still also, framed in the doorway, a threatening shadow but no more, no worse than that; and the girl lay for a moment to gather her strength, and then struggled up onto her knees.

I wanted to applaud; and then suddenly I wanted to shout, I wanted to get out there and tell them to leave her alone, I wanted to take her home.

I *knew* this girl.

*   *   *

At least, for a moment I thought I knew her, the first true sight of her I had with her face in sunlight. She was young, of course, very early twenties, young enough that I could comfortably think of her as a girl; her hair was dark and strange, shaved at the sides and long at the back, narrow plaits interwoven with ravens' feathers and held together in a ponytail that fell to her waist; her nose and ears and eyebrows were pierced with silver rings. It was a face, a look, that seen once you don't easily forget, and I could understand how Deverill's men had tracked her down with no name or address to work from, only a description from a hectic situation in the dark.

Then at last my inefficient, my lackadaisical memory placed her where I had seen her: not in sunlight, no, but in hard wind and cold shadows, in the sound of rain drumming on aluminium, in Luke's Airstream over in the Lakes' airstream. So no, I didn't know her after all, we'd only been briefly in the same place, she arriving and I leaving, she helping me to leave by that arrival; and even so I still felt responsible somehow, I still wanted to dash out there and save her. She was too young to face Deverill in his anger . . .

Never old enough for that, a weary cynicism, the voice in the back of my head; and no, I didn't move. Not scared, perhaps, not entirely that; only wise, perhaps, not to involve myself with something that in reality I knew I couldn't change. Gestures are futile, and common sense has always been one of my strengths.

But I stood and watched, I felt I owed her that at least, a witness for the world.

I watched, but Deverill not, he hardly gave a glance in her direction after his first, the glance and the jerk of the head that sent Dean over to attend to her. Seen it all before, I suppose; or else that was part of the punishment, being rendered so insignificant that the man she had so offended couldn't be bothered even to watch his retribution enacted on her body.

I watched, but Mrs Tuck not either: "I don't care for that sort of thing," she said, when I'd muttered or hissed or gasped something that must have sounded to her like an invitation, *for God's sake, have you seen what they're doing to that kid?* "Vernon says that it's necessary, but I don't believe that it needs an audience."

Whether that was directly aimed at me, I wasn't certain; but if so, it missed its mark. I didn't feel like an audience at all, I felt like a participant, a conspirator, very much a part of the drama for all that I only stood and watched. Maybe that's universal at such times, maybe that's just what happens: but I thought it was all being acted out for my benefit, I felt so complicit. I thought that if I wasn't there, this wouldn't be happening.

This wouldn't be happening to her . . .

First thing Dean did, he snapped his fingers towards the guy in the van – *learned that from Deverill,* I thought, *very much his master's man* – and asked for something, or demanded it rather, that's what his body language said: *this is my speciality, I'm in charge here now.*

And he got what he wanted, something small and silvery glittering in the air as the man threw it, as Dean's hand snatched it from its arc.

Dean bent over the girl then, and she flinched away, frightened already: beaten up already, I guess, I thought I could see bruises. But he gripped her arm to hold her, then slid his grip down to her wrist, turning her away from him to see what he was doing; and I could see also then, and all he was doing was taking the handcuffs off her with the key he'd just claimed, and maybe this wouldn't be so bad after all . . .

I guess that's what the girl thought also, I saw her turn her face up to find him, looking for mercy, perhaps, looking for hope. Not seeing or else forgetting, as I was trying to forget, how much he was his master's man under his master's indifferent eyes.

I almost didn't see his arm swing, it moved so fast as he lashed her across the mouth with steel, those handcuffs an improvised knuckleduster; but I saw her fall back from the impact, and I saw him kick her in the ribs and stomach; and when he stood back for a moment, when she pushed herself up onto her hands and knees I saw blood running on her face, dripping onto the tarmac.

Brave girl, stupid girl, even now she seemed to think she could make a fight of it, she could or should resist. She tossed her head to send a spatter of red across Dean's clean white shirt, where he had taken his jacket off to his work; and she somehow dragged herself up onto her feet and stood swaying, frowning, trying to focus. Trying to stare him down, I suppose, trying to defy him.

Neither her bravery nor her defiance touched Dean, I suppose he only saw her stupidity. One quick pace forward he took, and he kicked her knee with the side of his shoe. Just an office shoe, black and shiny, he wasn't wearing boots for the better kicking of captives; but her leg twisted abruptly against the joint, and she fell again with a useless flailing of arms, that couldn't stop her landing sickeningly on her face.

"Come away," Mrs Tuck said behind me, motherly, concerned. "This isn't for you."

But it was, my guilty soul said it was entirely for me; certainly I couldn't turn and walk away, however much I wanted to. I needed to know; or she needed me to know, or I thought she did, she would if she knew I was watching.

*　　*　　*

Dean's feet rolled her around the hardstanding for a while, he kicked and she rolled and he kicked again. When she stopped rolling, he stopped kicking. He stood for a moment looking at her stillness, then he went into one of the outbuildings, the former stables that were garages and storehouses now by the look of them. After a minute he came back with a bucket of water in his hand and something else slung across his shoulder, a length of cord or cable.

I was expecting him simply to chuck the water over her, a cold wake-up call from her dreams of agony, back to the real thing again; but no, he stood over her and tipped almost delicately, and the water flowed in a hard spattering stream into her face. Washing the blood away, *how kind*, and filling her mouth and nose; giving her a choice, *kindness personified*, that she could choke or drown.

And had to wake to make it: so she woke and choked, her slight body arching with the effort; and turned her face out of the stream, so that then Dean did simply fling the rest of the bucketful across her, soaking and chilling and making her buck again with the shock of it.

He tossed the bucket aside, bent over and seized her by the hair, by that long decorated ponytail; and he dragged her across the tarmac, and she lay slackly in her pain, in his grasp, and not fighting him at all any more.

He hauled her back to the van, pulling the handcuffs from his pocket, where he had stowed them. With those he fastened her wrists to the van's rear bumper, so that she lay face-down and her upper body dangling, just off the ground. *Just like Jacky Chu*, I thought, though the thought sounded quiet and distant in my head, not attention-grabbing. Nothing in the world could have grabbed my attention from this, nothing could shout loud enough to get through.

Dean gripped the fabric of the collarless, sleeveless shirt the girl was wearing, tugged a little to test it and then jerked once, twice and a third time, ripping it roughly down all its seams and tossing the remnants aside.

Half-naked she was now, but there seemed to be nothing directly sexual in that, though no doubt the added humiliation counted for something. Mostly this was for efficacy, I thought; because Dean took the coil from his shoulder then, unwound it – electrical cable it should be, bright orange and heavy as it was, and trying to hold its curves – and swung it through the air for practice, lashed the tarmac a time or two, then doubled it over and lashed her exposed shoulders instead.

She lifted her hanging head and screamed, silent to me this side of the window, and I thought maybe silent to them out there as well, silent even to Dean beside her; I thought maybe she didn't have the breath to scream with, for all that she had the pain that made it necessary.

Me, I didn't have the eyes to watch any more. Still present in my skull they were and not blurring, not weeping; but not making sense to me now, images without meaning. I turned away from those, fought to focus on the room, the woman in the room, the large handbag on the small table beside the woman in the room.

"Er," I said, "there wouldn't by any chance be a phone in that bag, would there?"

Phones by the dozen, of course, elsewhere in the house: but none in here, or none that I could see, and I was suddenly urgent about this, I wanted it done now.

Wonderful woman, she proved to be all that I hoped she'd be. "Yes, there is," she said, and produced it; switched it on for me and passed it over.

My fingers were punching buttons already, a number so familiar I never stopped to think; and when a breathy, familiar voice answered at the second ring, I just said what I'd said many times before, "Dulce, it's Jonty. Come and rescue me . . ."

"Don't we always?" she demanded, chuckling. "Where are you?"

And that was where I ground to a halt, because I didn't know, except in a general sense. And the voice of doom was whispering in the back of my head, *they'll never come this far out of town, forgot that, didn't you? Taxis don't like driving miles to pick up a fare . . .*

But these particular taxis I'd been using since I was a student in the city, I thought they'd come if I could only tell them how to find me; and when I asked Mrs Tuck if she could give me directions, she just beckoned imperiously for the phone.

Once she'd got it, she gave Dulcie neat and clear instructions; and when she'd finished I bade her farewell, said nice to have met you and like that, and found my way back to the hall and then defiantly out of the front door, to sit on stone steps in sunshine – balanced, it seemed to me, as this adventure had been, between the dark weight of Deverill's limo on the one side and the crisp, smooth efficiency of what must surely be Mrs Tuck's Jag on the other – and wait for someone to come and take me away from here.

When the taxi came, it was Dulcie's daughter Tina behind the wheel.

Originally, she'd been trained to spell Dulcie at the switchboard; like any family business, what had been right for the parents was seen as right for the kids also. But when she hit twenty-five, she rebelled; she wanted to drive like her brothers, and if they didn't give her a car she'd go and find another firm that would.

So she got her car, and started picking me up from parties instead of chatting me up on the phone. She flirted as her mother did, because it was good for business, as her father and her uncles and her brothers no doubt flirted professionally with their regular women clients, as they talked sport and local crime with me; and she drove probably better than they did, knowing that not me but the better half of her fares would be watching with a macho and cynical eye; and I knew just what protection she carried in the car and where she kept it, because she'd asked my advice about what was legal and what she'd need to hide. Sensible woman, our Tina.

Today I thought I just might need some of that protection myself, because she was turning the car neatly around on the gravel forecourt when the big front door opened behind me, and out came Dean.

Bouncing on his toes, he was, like a fit man looking forward to a little trouble; and he said, "Running out on us, Jonty?" like a man expecting the answer no, like he was expecting me to say *no, no, just taking a little air, Dean, a little post-prandial stroll* when the evidence was right there in front of us to call me a coward and a liar.

I looked at him, this grinning, winking buddy of mine, this lifesaver; and I said, "How the hell are you going to stop her talking?"

Dean laughed. "Come on, get with it. We know where to find her, we know where to find her boyfriend and her family; you think she's going to talk? Believe me, by the time we've finished with her she won't say a bloody word."

What, they hadn't even *finished* yet? God almighty . . .

"She'll talk to her friends," I said. "Not the police, but . . ." *Luke*, I thought, *she'll talk to Luke. She'll tell him everything.* People did, if they could only get him to listen.

"By the time we're finished," Dean said again, "she won't have any friends."

"Why, what do you mean?"

"She's going to be a good girl," he said, "she's going to

do exactly what we tell her to. They always do; and I'll be watching her anyway, making sure."

"What, then? What are you going to make her do?"

"I'm taking her back to Leavenhall," he said, "soon as she's learned to speak nicely to Vern and obey his orders. They're starting work on stage two of the bypass soon, so her friends are moving back there, they've got some more trees to protect.

"And what that bitch is going to do," he said, "is drive a bulldozer again, we've found her a big one; and first she's going to drive a nice path through all those trees, and then she's going to trash her mates' camp, the way she trashed our compound. And they're going to see her doing it, up there in the cab, all on her own. And I don't think they'll be talking to her after that, not after she's been a traitor and a tree-killer . . ."

That was clever, it was nasty, it was life-destroying; but it was better I thought than what I'd been most afraid of, better than the girl being beaten to death. Slightly, very slightly easier to live with, though I guessed I wouldn't be sweet on myself for a long time after this. Running out I was indeed, but on her rather than on them; and Dean knew without asking, no need to warn or to threaten, I wasn't running to the police any more than I had run to her rescue. They knew where to find me also, they knew where to find my wife . . .

No, I'd been wrong, Dean hadn't been looking for or anticipating any trouble when he'd come lightly down the stairs to intercept me. He knew I'd make none. This, I thought, was only a reminder; they had their eyes on me, I was on the payroll and I couldn't even sneak away without their knowing it, even when their gaze was seemingly turned entirely the other way from me.

He said goodbye, nice and friendly, my buddy Dean; and

I muttered something, I imagine, and got into Tina's taxi feeling craven and disgusting, wondering how much more they'd do to that poor girl before she was persuaded to speak nicely to Vernon Deverill.

They'd not had to do much to me, seemingly, to achieve the same effect. Not had to do anything at all: I'd gone to him of my own free will, to ruin my life under his aegis. To lay my hard-won reputation in his untender hands, deliberately to see it damaged or destroyed; and all for some unlikely undercover plot, to rescue my mother from the deadly consequences of her own folly . . .

I supposed dimly that that was praiseworthy. It didn't seem convincing, to me who knew myself too well; but it didn't need to convince. No story in which my mother played a leading role was ever going to be strong on conviction, looked at in normal human quotidian terms.

But whatever the complexities of her situation and my response to it, there was this one undeniable, irredeemable fact: that because of my involvement I had ended up here today, watching a girl being beaten senseless and listening to their plans for her future devastation; and I had done nothing to help her, nor would I hereafter, and all the logical persuasions I could muster couldn't touch the shame in me, nor the humiliation, nor the sense of something irretrievably lost.

Bright girl, Tina didn't try to talk beyond a cheerful hullo; one unresponsive grunt from me, and she let me stew in silence.

Not till we were well back within the city limits did I even lift my eyes from my restless hands, dry-washing like Pilate, just as uselessly. Gazing out of the window with a mortifying despair, I watched familiar landmarks pass and still took a minute, two minutes to realise where we were, and where we were going.

"Not this way, Tina."

"Not? Oh, sorry, I thought you wanted home . . ."

I did, but not the one she knew, the one she'd always brought me to before. Too heartsick to be bothered with explanations, I just asked her to take me to Chinatown.

Paid her off outside the flat, making her take a tenner for simplicity's sake while she was still trying to work out sums on her fingers, how much the meter was overcharging me for her unwitting detour; and climbed the stairs like Christian, greatly burdened and utterly alone; and let myself in with keys that still looked strange to my eyes and felt strange in my fingers, and found wife and mother playing house together, not a game I could play at all with either one of them.

Actually, they were making up the bed in the study for my mother to sleep on. Suzie broke off briefly to hug me, of course, and to ask how I was, how it had been, what had happened; and I lied, of course, I hugged her back and told her it was fine, I was fine, we'd just had a talk and hardly learned a thing from each other that was new. And my mother looked at me sharply, many years more experienced in hearing my lies; and then she hailed Suzie back to the bed-making. Clean sheets Suzie was insisting on, like a dutiful daughter-in-law; and the duvet didn't suit my mother, she liked the weight of proper English blankets over her while she slept. *When she can't have the weight of a man*, some cynical or dispossessed adult male had muttered to me once, in an aside I was barely old enough to understand. Blankets apparently were located on the top shelf of the airing cupboard, which meant dragging a chair through to the bathroom for standing on; but no thanks, they didn't need my height for help, they could manage fine between them . . .

So I left them to it, and never made a try to tell them

truly what I'd seen and done that day. I picked up the leather
shoulder-bag from its place beside the sideboard and carried
it through to the bedroom; pushed the door shut against the
murmur and trill of female voices, unlatched the bag and
took out the neat black box that had been my favourite toy
and my favourite resource both, the last couple of years
at work.

Cables, plug, find the nearest socket, switch on here,
switch on there; lift the lid, watch it through all its internal
checks and balances; and I sat on the bed with my computer
humming quietly on my lap, and watched even this safest
of havens do things I would never, never have asked it to
do in my original incarnation.

Me, I was a DOS man through and through, I hated the
mouse-and-icon mentality with a passion: lowest-common-
denominator computing I thought it was, computing for the
illiterate. I didn't read picture-books any more, and I didn't
see why I should be expected to drag a picture of a file
onto a picture of a waste-paper basket if I wanted to delete
something.

My computer, my well-trained computer should have
taken me through DOS and straight into Lexis, favourite
software of all solicitors; that's what I'd had it set up to do,
and that was certainly what it had done last time I used it.

Last time I remembered using it.

This time, it danced through DOS and into Windows, and
left me there with a little arrow to move around the screen
and lots of pretty pictures to point it at.

Took me a couple of minutes just to figure out how
to get out of that and back to DOS, I was that ignorant
of Windows: deliberately dinosaur, friends and colleagues
had called me, and maybe they were right but that was how
I liked it.

Once comfortably on home territory, at the DOS prompt
where I liked to be, I started exploring the system to see

what else had changed; and it only took ten seconds to find the big one.

Lexis was gone. Everyone used Lexis; I'd been using it in one form or another since before I graduated; the company would have ground to a halt without it. Already I felt totally stranded: all my cases, all my notes were gone . . .

And rightly so. Took me a moment to remember, but I didn't work for Hesketh & Jones any more, I'd resigned. If for anyone, I worked for Vernon Deverill, though I thought that maybe after today my resignation would be heading in that direction also, if it wasn't already inherent in my walking out.

The computer had been a company machine; I was lucky that they'd let me keep it, and they would certainly have been right to insist that I deleted all client information from it before I left. Perhaps they'd done that themselves, to be certain. That the program itself was gone seemed a little above-and-beyond, though perfectly proper in a legal sense: it had been a copy from their master disks, and clearly not my property. In any case, if I wasn't a solicitor any more, what need solicitous software?

Perhaps that explained the unwelcome presence of Windows, that I was just trying to plug a hole, playing with other systems until finally I found something I had a use for. A computer wasn't a lot of use to me without a job: I'd never been much of a one for games. And I'd have had time on my hands, I guessed, if I'd been playing playboy. Even with a new marriage on my hands also, I would probably have had time enough to try to break myself to an unwelcome government, the philosophy that seemed set to rule computing for the foreseeable future.

Or perhaps it was Suzie's goading, her refusing to accept my dinosaur tendencies in any part of my life, even those where she didn't noticeably have a role—

Or did she? I started scanning the directories for anything unfamiliar, for evidence that she had infested this most private corner. She'd said I wouldn't let her near it, but that wouldn't stop her proselytising. I found plenty of software I didn't recognise, all of it Windows-related: that was fair, whichever way you looked at it. If I was experimenting of my own free will, I'd do it properly; if this was Suzie's influence, she'd dump the lot on me all at once, and tell me to chew faster if I complained.

Before I found anything that could be called evidence, though, anything that sang directly of Suzie, I found something more arresting, something that froze me boneless.

I found a file called SUSI.DOC.

Sitting in a directory all alone, it was, announcing its own importance; and the directory was called WORK, so it all stood out, it was very much there to be found. *Poor security*, my cautious mind scolded my absent personality, *what the hell were you thinking of?* Two attempts at a burglary there had been, hotel room and here; and if it hadn't been worse than that, if it wasn't my blood they were after, they might very well have been after this.

With a .DOC suffix, it surely had to be an ordinary word-processing file, though I was a .TXT man myself. I looked for my regular writing package, WordPerfect, and found that gone also; looked for any other; and in the end had to guess or remember or work out how to get back into Windows before I could run the only one I could find, Word for Windows.

Spitting and cursing, *they call this thing user-friendly?*, I felt my way into the program with a series of ill-educated guesses, and asked it to open the file SUSI.DOC.

In return, it asked me for a password.

'Enter Password for file C:\WORK\SUSI.DOC', it said; and of course I couldn't, because I didn't have a clue what I'd used. Not such bad security after all, if it was secure even from me.

I felt a slow and useless rage building in me, like when I've gone a long way to visit a particular shop or gallery or whatever, and find it closed in normal hours because it's a half-day on Wednesday or the owner's daughter has her school concert that afternoon, or else it's a bank holiday and Sunday rules apply. It's just frustration, at being even temporarily denied access to something that I think ought to be open to me; but it manifests itself as anger at whoever made the rules, whoever thinks that Wednesday half-days or legislated Sunday hours make any kind of sense in the late twentieth century, or whoever schedules school concerts in the middle of the working day.

That day, of course, I could only be angry at myself. I'd set the file up with a stupid password, after all. Almost certainly, I had. Not my normal practice, but nothing about this was normal, and no doubt I'd have felt it safer that way; and not, of course, expected or anticipated or in any sense even considered the possibility of losing months of memory, and the password a small but maybe crucial fraction of that loss . . .

Ignorance is not and never has been an excuse; ignorance of the future is still ignorance. I was working up a fine if silent head of steam, cursing myself and loathing myself, when Suzie demonstrated her innate sense of appalling timing by walking unexpectedly in on me.

"Knock, will you?" I spat at her over my shoulder.

"Fucked if I will," she replied equably. "This is my room too."

"Then I'll go in the other room," and I was childishly on my feet already, closing the computer and stooping to unplug it.

"You can't, your mum's in there. Settling in for the duration, by the look of her; like hell she only came up for the day. You sit down," and her hands were on my shoulders, pressing obedience into my flesh, and somehow I had no resistance to her, "and tell me what you're in such a grouch about?"

Almost, I told her; beautiful and anxious and demanding, sitting beside me and smelling of musk and apples, she invited confession without even knowing what she did. That lack of resistance in me was more than physical; like a man on scopolamine I wanted to talk, I needed to talk. And like a man on scopolamine all I could do was jerk my thoughts from one track to another, not to control the flow of words but only to redirect it, to try and do no harm.

"I didn't tell you, did I? When I was, when I was working on all this, you said I worked a lot in the other room and in private, you said I wouldn't talk to you about what I was doing but I've put a bloody password on the file and of course I can't remember it, so I was wondering maybe did I give it to you? As a back-up, sort of thing?"

Actually I wasn't wondering that at all: if I'd told her nothing that must have been security also, on the principle that what she didn't know she couldn't blab. I wouldn't have breached that security by giving her access to everything she didn't know. But it was something to say, it was safe, and I had to say something.

She shook her head. "No, you never told me. Can't you crack it?"

"I don't know how."

"Oh, come on, I thought you were such a whizz at computers? Even the kids can crack computer passwords, in the movies . . ."

"I'm not a kid in a movie," but nor was I angry any more, only drained and weary and stymied once again.

"Well, work it out, then," she said.

"How? Have you got any idea how many combinations

there could be? Letters and numbers both, I don't know the program but I bet you can use numbers . . ."

"Yeah, but it's a password, right? You'll have used a word. And, I mean, it was *you*, Jonty, know what I mean? Even if you can't remember it, you've still got the same mind that thought of it, haven't you? So you can think of it again. Take you a few tries, maybe, but you should be able to work it out . . ."

For a second I only sat and looked at her, so close: narrow pointed face, black almond eyes, chopped hair with an olive-black sheen, skin of extraordinary hue. And then I kissed her, and her lips were soft and surprised, then laughing under mine for the moment before she pushed me away.

"What?" she demanded, serious now, if serious meant cocking her head to one side and squinting up at me with half a frown threatening between her eyes.

"I don't know if that was brilliant or stupid," I said, "but I'll go with brilliant for now, until it fails. So thank you."

She snorted. "Until you fail, you mean. Don't go blaming me, if you're not smart enough to outguess yourself."

She brought me a cup of coffee, and left me to it. I was distantly aware of her voice and my mother's rising suddenly into bursts of laughter, loud enough to come at me through the wall, or else down the passageway and through two closed doors between; but I wasn't trying to listen, barely even wondered what could possibly be funny on such a day, at such a desperate time.

It wasn't only the logic of the idea I had to thank Suzie for, it was the engrossing nature of it, the obsessive focus it could lend me. Staring at the computer screen, at the winking cursor that demanded a password I didn't know, I could cease to stare in my head at an abused and nameless stranger, and at myself stood in a window watching, doing nothing but clinically or cynically marking every blow, every added pain. Blinding myself to the world, I could block out my ghosts, for a while.

So. Classic password mentality, for young men with no experience of using passwords: this much at least I knew, I had read about. Men like me, we tended to use names, as being easier to remember; more than that, they tended to be names that meant something to us. Parents, siblings, first or current lovers; heroes from real life or fiction, Kevin Keegan or Judge Dredd; erotic masturbatory dream-partners, Demi Moore or Michelle Pfeiffer or Antonio Banderas.

Carol I typed, and *Carol Carter*, just to get them out of the way, out of my mind, as I had apparently put Carol herself out of my mind or else simply out of the way. Then, a little more seriously, *Elspeth* and *Elspeth Marks*, and *Ellie* of that ilk: it was my mother's story, after all, far more than it was mine. All the machine told me each time was that the password was incorrect, and it could not open the document.

More seriously still, really buckling down to it now, I tried *Suzie* and all the variants I could think of, *Suzie Chu, Suzie Marks, Suzie Chu Marks*; and then remembered that I hadn't called her that, that I'd refused to for reasons that seemed pretty good to me now, and ran the gamut again with *Sue* to replace *Suzie*.

Still nothing, only the flat denial; and my fingers were getting quite fast at this and my mind was sniffing around it like an eager dog, loving the challenge. I tried faces from the past, early girlfriends, my closest teenage mates; I tried my birthday, my mother's, Carol's; I yelled for Suzie, asked when was hers, tried that. No soap, but she lingered, so I asked for the date when we'd met. Sentimental as a kitten, she didn't need to check in her diary, even; but it had no result, any way that I could think to write it. Nor

did the date of our first kiss, though Suzie prompted me
to try it.

"Well, it wouldn't, would it?" I murmured, stretching,
giving my fingers a rest. "This is my mind we're trying
to second-guess here, not yours. Practical, not slushy. Ow!
Jesus, mind the machine . . . !"

I'd only said it to get a rise out of her, and I'd got that and
more; but there was a genuine point there, that I noticed and
accepted once I'd fought her off and sent her flouncing back
to Ellie. There really wasn't any point tracking the events
or moments that she remembered or valued, even if they'd
been shared; what would have resonated with me was all
that counted, and I'd never been much susceptible to dates
or anniversaries. Or any form of numbers, come to that. I
was a words man, always had been.

Heroes, who were my heroes? I didn't have any, not in
that sense. Not whose names I would alight on, looking for
an excuse-the-expression unforgettable mnemonic. Men I
admired, sure, and women too; but no idols, no mascots,
no obsessions. Except of course for Luke: but it would have
been *lèse-majesté* to have used his name in such a context,
he would have hated it and so I would never have used it.
I tried it anyway, I typed *Luke* just to be sure, and received
no reward beyond the confirmation that I was right, that I
hadn't changed so very much after all. I still knew what
was proper, what was owed to angels.

I wasn't always so wise. Once I'd thought of Luke as a
trophy, to be shown off. Sixteen and buzzing with it, first
girlfriend and desperate to impress: of course I'd taken her to
meet him, to be overwhelmed by magic, myth made flesh.

Julia, her name was. A small-town girl who liked discos
and glitter, she was not much impressed by the long bus-ride
and the longer slog uphill to Luke's hollow, less so by his
cool unwelcome and the chipped mug of hot water that was

all he had to offer. I hadn't warned her, not to spoil the wonder of him; it was too soon apparent that all she was wondering was how soon we could head back to civilisation. Recognising my mistake but too shy to admit it, never any good at leaving Luke even in the face of disaster, I sat as silent as the pair of them around his smoky fire until he got abruptly to his feet, said he was off walking.

My cue, my opportunity to rescue something from the day; but still I didn't take it. I only scrambled up, puppy-eager to trail him around the bounds of his territory and ignoring the speaking glare Julia shot at me, *get us out of this* . . .

Stupid with the hungers of youth, I guess I was praying for a miracle, for him to give us a glimpse of his true nature.

That at least I got, an early revelation that men should be careful what they pray for.

He led us tramping over the hill and into a wooded valley, while she followed sulking at my back, refusing to take my hand even down the muddy slides between the trees. Flocks of birds fled us, screaming. At the bottom the path ran parallel to a fence closing off a great tract of land that must have had a gamekeeper to patrol it, because the barbs on the wire were decorated with the desiccating corpses of his hunting.

Weasels and crows I knew, other predators I was less certain of naming in the mess of ripped fur or feather, exposed bone; but last in the long line was a raven, today's kill by the look of it, fresh blood on its broken chest and its wings splayed out in a grisly crucifixion.

Luke stood a long time, looking at that dead bird. I heard muttering behind me, and looked round to see Julia making faces, *this is horrid, this is disgusting, I'm bored and fed up and I want to go home*. All I could give her was a shrug, *I don't know the way home from here, we'll have to stick with him for a while yet*.

Then her face changed, no more messages for me; she was staring past me and the wire was vibrating beside me, and there was the rustle of long-dead creatures falling apart, falling away. I twisted around and saw Luke tugging and tearing, yanking the raven savagely from the barbs, doing more damage and I couldn't see the point.

Until he lifted the body to his mouth and breathed on it, spat on it, licked its dusty spattered feathers, the dark-edged holes in its flesh. Distantly I was aware of Julia retching, and it sounded real, a reaction not a comment; but all my focus was on Luke, on his hands where they were not cradling but clutching the bird, almost crushing it, threatening more damage still.

Its wings hung outside his clenched hands, moving as his fingers moved. He had its dead head in his mouth now, working it between tongue and teeth; and its wings moved, scratching at the air, but his fingers were entirely still.

He held it away from his face, and its head was glistening, running wet, and its eyes were dull with death yet its beak opened and it shrieked at him.

Julia shrieked too, and clutched at me.

Luke opened his locked hands and the bird, I suppose, flew. It fumbled into the air, at least, slow and mechanical-seeming, a travesty of life. Not skill or nature that kept it aloft, not the effort of its muscles or its feathers' spread. This was vile, and Luke felt that as we did: his face said so, shifting from detachment to something too complex for me to read, a cocktail perhaps of grief and anger and despair. This was the best that he could do, and it was pathetic, cruel, heart-rivingly sad.

We watched the bird-thing he had made blundering its way between the trees, catching on twigs and creepers and leaving feathers wherever it got caught; and I wondered how many more of these there were in the woods, how many dead creatures that still crawled or slithered or hacked at the wind with dishevelled, rotting wings.

Luke had turned and run then, off and away; and when he was gone, when the sounds of his going had faded to nothing, I'd taken Julia's unresisting hand and we'd made our way along the path and along the road it led us to, until we found a village with a bus stop and an eventual journey home.

I'd taken Luke no visitors since, though apparently I'd promised to take Suzie. Twice, now. And I'd talked about him as little as I had to and boasted not at all, not made a hero of him; and if not of him, then of whom?

Lacking true heroes, I played instead with any names I could drag easily from my memory, be they good teachers from school or college, authors and bands whose work I'd loved or hated, athletes or artists or famous lawgivers from Solon to Judge Jeffries to Lord Denning; but I had to look back to my adolescence for most of them, and over that distance none seemed to stand out more than the others, and it was no surprise that none produced what I was looking for, none was the key to unlock all my so-carefully-guarded secrets.

Fantasy figures, then? Again I was looking back ten years or more; I pictured my room as it had been then, all the pin-ups and posters on the walls; the bands I'd tried already, but I named as many of the women as I could and tried them all, and failed with them all.

And again was not surprised, because this didn't feel any more right than using Suzie's notions of what mattered most. It was me who'd set this up, a radically-altered me but me none the less; and I wouldn't have scouted a long-abandoned past for a brief but crucial phrase, I'd have used something current. Something relevant, either to my life or to the project . . .

Chinatown? No. *MR2*? No. Nor *Deverill* nor *Vernon* nor *Vern*, *Dean* nor *Leavenhall* nor – of course – *Scimitar* nor *SUSI*. *Nolan* I tried, and *Lindsey Nolan* and *Spain* and *Spanish Jail* and *Spanish Gaol*, and had no joy of them.

Passwords, books I'd loved; suddenly two paths of memory crossed, and threw me a new idea. In *The Lord of the Rings*, even the wiser-than-wise Gandalf had been stymied by this exact same problem, though the solution had been staring him in the face; he'd been caught by a pun, or else a bad translation. What he'd read as an invitation, 'Speak, friend, and enter' had really been an instruction, 'Say "Friend" and enter'. And I loved cleverness, I loved puns, and I loved that moment as much as any in literature . . .

So I tried *Friend*, and I tried *Mellon* which was Elvish for 'friend' and actually the word that Gandalf used to get them in; and neither one worked and I was furious with myself, my former self for not having thought of that, it would have been such a neat solution.

I was still stabbing that keyboard with sweaty fingertips, wearing my prints away, when Suzie came back; and no, she didn't knock this time either, nor would I have expected her to. It was the door's banging open that dragged my eyes up from the screen; she stood framed, akimbo, imperative.

"Come and eat," she said.

"In a minute." I was hopelessly pursuing some desperate strand of thought, the names of my regular, favourite or most recent clients: expecting nothing, getting nothing, unable to stop.

"No, not in a minute. Right now." And she swiftly bent and unplugged the computer's lead; which made no difference at all, it switched automatically to battery power. I thought probably she knew that, because she didn't so much as grunt her disappointment, let alone try to wrest the machine from my grasp, which would most likely have been her next move if she were serious. She was only making a point, not genuinely trying to cut me off mid-word.

Point made, she nevertheless hammered it hard home. "I've been entertaining Ellie all afternoon," she said. "Your turn now, she's your mother."

"Thought you liked her?"

"I do; but there are limits. These are they," in a phrase stolen indirectly from Ellie, directly from me.

My mouth twitched into a reluctant smile; she beckoned me with a flick of her head, and I put the computer down on the futon, switched it off and stood up with an effort, went to join this awkward, unexpected family at dinner.

Suzie had cooked Chinese, and the table was laid only with chopsticks and soupspoons and bowls.

"Can I have a knife and fork?" I pleaded, sitting where she told me.

"No."

"I can't use these," picking up the chopsticks to prove it.

"Yes, you can. I taught you."

"I've forgotten."

"So I'll teach you again."

"It's an impossible task. Dozens have failed before you. I'm cack-handed."

"I know. But I did it before. You got pretty good, in the end. For a cack-handed white boy, I mean. Do it once, I can do it again."

So she did it again, and it was too easy. Just a minute of uncertain fumbling, a single crack of her knuckles on my unprotected skull when I dropped a stick and offered that as proof, "See? Told you I couldn't do it, you're wasting your time," and then suddenly I understood, or my fingers did. I reached for a prawn and the sticks found it, gripped it, lifted it; almost dropped it deliberately, at the smug told-you-so expression on her face; but carried it to my mouth in generosity, chewed and swallowed. Hot and juicy and sharp with flavour, it stirred an appetite I didn't know I had; soon I was snatching food into my bowl without thinking about it, scooping rice urgently into my mouth, altogether too much at home with these alien instruments.

"You must be a good teacher," said my mother, expertly clicking her own chopsticks like a crab its claws. "Heaven knows I tried, but I never got anywhere with him."

That, I thought, could be the reason I'd never managed to learn before: that my mother had been the first to try to teach me, that my body had rebelled as much as my mind. As my body seemed now to be remembering lessons that my mind could not, demonstrating an acquired skill though the acquisition was lost to me.

Suzie looked so pleased with herself, was so patronisingly pleased with me I wanted to bite her.

Instead, I said, "Ellie?"

"What?"

"Tell us about Lindsey Nolan."

My deceptive mother turned her narrow, baleful glare onto me full force, said, "He's a man, an accountant, a crook. What can I tell you that you don't know?"

"For a start, you could tell us what was your interest in him."

"What he kept between his legs, of course," she said. "He was hung like a donkey."

Suzie choked; I didn't even blink. "No," I said.

"He was."

Past tense, she used, likely without even thinking about it. That was the only thing she was telling me here that I was ready to believe: that he was dead to her, that she had no ongoing interest. Trouble lifts its head, my mother departs the scene so thoroughly she'd probably swear herself she was never there at all.

"That's not what you were after," I said patiently.

"Listen, Jonty, I know children never like to think of their parents having a sex-life, but—"

"Mother," I said, "you can sleep with every thoroughbred racing animal in the Queen's stables, for all I care. Do it on Horse Guards, do it in daylight, I don't give a damn. Just don't lie to me, don't try to put me off, don't make yourself out to be more stupid or frivolous than you are. I think you must have told me once before, so try being honest with me twice in a row, why don't you? Tell me what the hell's been going on?"

And my deceitful, dishonest mother did just that: she came clean and told us both what her involvement was, in two simple, clear sentences, and why the hell couldn't she have done that hours earlier?

"I'm doing Vernon Deverill," she said, "for the *Journal*. Of course I wanted to sleep with his accountant, how not?"

Jonathan's Journal she called it, she named it after me though I never had a hand in its production, never contributed a word to its copy or a fact or a whisper of gossip to its proprietor. It sounded trivial, it sounded like a joke and she meant it to; but subscriptions cost a thousand pounds an issue, and she had dozens of subscribers. Every national newspaper was on the list and a good number of foreign papers also, along with every magazine which took a serious interest in current affairs; all the political parties, and not a few MPs on their own accounts; Ellie even claimed MI5 and the CIA among her readership, and I believed her.

Almost no one knew who researched, who wrote, who published and who reaped the substantial profits from *Jonathan's Journal*. That's why it carried the foolish name:

to offer no hostages to fortune, to give no useful clues to its authorship. Those few who did know – close friends, her bank manager, her accountant – thought that her louche lifestyle, her heedless amorality was only cover for the profoundly serious journalist she was at heart, whose every irregular issue stirred up scandal and controversy, exposing the bone of British corruption with dates and figures and names precisely documented, and a withering analysis of causes and motivations.

Myself who knew her better than anyone, I had always maintained that the profoundly serious journalist was another joke, an artificial creation, only cover to give some credibility to the chaotic, instinctive, selfish demon creature she seemed to be, that in fact she truly was.

Whichever way you read it, she lived two wholly separate lives: one forever superficial and demanding, the other drilling always to the core of things, ever questioning, ever wanting to know why. Again demanding, perhaps the only aspect her bifurcated personality could share between its divided parts.

"Heaven knows," she was saying, "he was the world's most boring man. In bed or out of it. But he kept a lot of secrets in his house, and he was careless about security."

Not like me, I thought bleakly, reminded. "Learn much, did you?"

"Plenty."

"Like, why he's in jail in Spain? Who set him up?"

"Not that, no. There was something big on his mind for a few weeks before he disappeared, but that's where he kept it, in his mind. It wasn't money, though. All that about him stashing cash for himself, that's nonsense. He was greedy, yes, but not that way. Information was his thing; when he got a sniff of something, he wouldn't let it go. Wouldn't talk about it either, though, and I couldn't find anything on paper. Even the note he left me when he vanished, that didn't tell

me anything except to go home and keep my head down.
I didn't do that, of course, I searched his house from top
to bottom first; but there was nothing there, I didn't find
a thing."

"How frustrating for you."

"Darling, you've no *idea* . . ."

That was stupid; of course I had a very good idea, and she
knew it, and she was trying to blanket herself in a distorting
image again, so that I wouldn't see her straight. Automatic
I thought that was, the defences developed over many years
cutting in because that was what they did, any time anyone
penetrated close to the heart of her.

I would have dug deeper, to be sure; there were many
questions I wanted to ask my mother, a great deal I needed to
know about Lindsey Nolan. But Suzie spoiled the moment,
saying, "I don't know how you can do that. Sleep with a man,
I mean, just to get something you want. If you don't want
him, I mean. It's like volunteering to be raped or something,
I just can't get my head around it . . ."

"Not at all," said my mother, slipping into slut-mode with
gratitude and grace. "It's a business transaction, is all; he
may not know it, but I do. I give him what he wants, I
take what I want. I'm a natural whore, I suppose, I'm very
good at it."

She's also very good at self-portraiture, she does it often,
and each separate portrait is a lie. "Come on, Ellie," I said,
for Suzie's sake. "Be straight with the girl. How often have
you done this, twice in twenty years? Or was there a third
time, was there one I didn't hear about? She does most of
her work in public records offices," I told Suzie directly,
"not in hotel rooms on her back. She's not that kind of
spy, she just wants you to think she is. Mostly, she sleeps
around just because she likes it."

My mother looked at me, pushed her bowl away and took
out a cigarette, blew a cloud of smoke across the table at me,

made it exceedingly obvious that we would learn no more from her tonight.

Neither from my computer, which no more than she was in a giving mood. I battled it for another hour after dinner, feeling that the whole endeavour was increasingly pointless, that I must have chosen some random sequence of letters or numbers or both for precisely this reason, to stop anyone who knew me – Suzie, perhaps? my mother, perhaps? – from working out the password and cracking the file open. Then I wasted another hour searching through papers in the spare bedroom, in case I'd written the sequence down; but the same logic applied. If I'd gone that far to keep my secrets safe, I wouldn't have left the key to them lying around where any snoop might find it.

Back in the living-room they were smoking and drinking tea and still talking about sex, trying to bridge a gulf that was philosophical, generational, impossible. To Ellie a tool, to Suzie still a revelation: no, they weren't going to come together anywhere on this one.

I sat and listened for a while, had nothing to say and couldn't settle; so I lied to Suzie, told her I was just going down to the club for half an hour, a drink and boys' talk with Lee, I said; and instead I went all the way down and out onto the street, into the evening clamour of a young city having a good time with itself.

There was a pub at the end of the street where I'd been drinking on and off for years, whenever I was meeting people for a meal this side of town. Even in the crush, they knew me: "Pint of Guinness, then, is it?"

"Please, yeah. And a smoke, and a box of matches . . ."

I found a seat, a high bar-stool in a dark corner; and I sat sipping slowly and sucking on a rare cigar, and decided that the advertising was all wrong: happiness was a foolish, an unapproachable ambition. Not to be wasted time on.

One more pint for luck, standing at the bar and watching carved wooden mechanical heads turn and gape above the mirrors, one of the landmarks on any pub-crawl in town but curiously fitting tonight, symbolic of something even if I couldn't understand the symbols. There thanks to a graceless God, I thought, sit Suzie and Ellie and I, and perhaps Deverill also: each of us only a staring doll, turning and working at the promptings of some machine unseen, operated by we none of us know whose hand . . .

Such thoughts in my head, and I wasn't even stoned: time I was in bed, I thought. In futon.

So I turned and went back to the flat, barely making it in time to intercept Suzie, who was on the point of coming down to the club to find me. She tugged the cap off my head and tossed it aside, ran her fingers gently over my soft fuzz and the lines of my scars, said, "Your mum's gone to bed."

A surprise, that, she was a nightbird, was Ellie; but I looked at Suzie looking at me from bare inches away, and a chill struck my heart. With Ellie in the spare bed, Suzie and I would be sharing again; and Suzie by the look of her meant business tonight. Which was perhaps why my mother had taken herself so conveniently, so unconvincingly out of the way. Perhaps they'd even talked about it, moving from abstract to specific, from sex in general to sex and Suzie and me. Neither one of them, I thought, would have had inhibitions about that. Ellie would have asked, and she would have been told . . .

"You should do the same," I said, "you look knackered."

"Yeah. You coming, then, or what?"

I shook my head: buying time, prepared to pay dearly for

it. "I'll just get the computer, and have another crack at it
out here."

"Jonty . . ."

"I've got to get into that file somehow," I said, entirely
reasonably, "and it needs to be soon. We can't go on
wallowing in ignorance."

"Well. Okay, then. But don't be long. You'll wreck your
eyes, staring at that thing all hours."

Not only my eyes but my mind also, all capacity for rational
thought. I was so sick of that message box, *Enter Password*
and the flashing cursor, it was turning physical; I thought
I might actually throw up if I sat with it for another hour.
But on the other hand another hour would maybe buy me
the night. Suzie would fall asleep waiting for me, and I
could crash out on the sofa, and we'd both be miserable and
stroppy as hell in the morning but at least I'd have made it
through unviolated, with the banner of my integrity snarled
into knots maybe but still flying, still flapping above my
head . . .

I could always pretend, of course. I could use the computer
as cover only and not even try to legitimise the excuse; I
could just leave it sitting on the table in front of me humming
and happy and telling lies, while I found something else to
do with my fingers.

Almost did it, too. I was casting around the room for
inspiration – something else to do with my eyes, that was,
and very welcome on its own account – when my gaze fell
on Suzie's cap, the logo almost glowing at me, blinking like
neon in my head.

I reached for the keyboard, my fingers stumbling with
certainty as they typed Q's.

*The password is incorrect. Word cannot open the docu-
ment.*

Okay, no trouble. *Jack Q's.*

The password is incorrect. Word cannot open the document.

Not a worry. I was only building up, creating a sense of climax, not to peak too soon. There was really no doubt at all in my mind; this was too beautiful, too clever, too appropriate to be anything other than the answer.

J'accuse, I typed; and of course I had accused, and this file was the list of accusations and the proof both at once, and everything was going to be all right now . . .

The password is incorrect. Word cannot open the document.

No. I couldn't believe it. This was too much, too cruel. I tried the same sequence again, in case I'd mistyped one of them, but I only got the same responses.

It had to be right, though. Surely it had to be right? Everything fitted, and I famously loved puns. Maybe the program was corrupt, maybe it was failing to recognise a true password . . .

Maybe I was floundering here, trying to blame a machine for my own shortcomings, my failure to think efficiently.

Try again. The pun was lovely, and it was relevant; I wouldn't have overlooked that. Could I have buried it one layer deeper, for security's sake? Given that the pun had been Suzie's own, and therefore accessible to her?

Hide a tree in a forest, a letter among other letters; bury a pun in another pun. I'd been, what, fourth form when we learned about Dreyfus and Zola and *J'accuse*; there'd been another boy two desks over from me, not a friend exactly but we had a love of words in common, we did crosswords together sometimes and created incredibly complex puns for each other's amusement.

And I remembered that history lesson well, how our eyes had been suddenly, irresistibly drawn to each other, how we'd snapped simultaneously, sniggering and choking, trying to swallow the howling laughter that seizes boys sometimes; how we'd only survived because the teacher had dropped a dry little joke of his own at just that point, and he of course assumed it was his wit that was convulsing us.

Grinning again at the memory, I leaned forward and typed that other boy's name:

Jack Hughes.

The password is incorrect. Word cannot open the document, and again I couldn't believe it. My reasoning seemed impeccable to me; I had nowhere to go from here, no more ideas, no hope.

I could take the file to a genuine computer whizz, I supposed, someone who would know how to crack uncrackable passwords. Some teenage genius with spots and adequacy problems, no doubt, whose contemptuous fingers would unriddle this in moments . . .

But I didn't know any, nor where to look to find them; and I was reluctant even to step outside the flat with the computer on my shoulder, in case anyone was watching. There were burglars out there who wanted something, after all; my money was on this.

Maybe I could copy the file onto a floppy, and take that? I didn't know if protected files would copy; I should find out. I should do that right now, top priority . . .

But I didn't, I only sat there staring at that uncooperative screen, utterly defeated; and every time I looked away from it all I saw was a girl in a stableyard being kicked unconscious and whipped awake while a man stood watching in a window. So I looked back at the screen again, better defeat than disgust. And then a figure caught my eye, moving beyond it; and that was Suzie come to fetch me to the futon.

"You've been ages," she said. "And you're not getting anywhere, are you?"

"No."

By then she was sitting beside me on the sofa, reaching to dig her thumbs into my shoulders. "Stiff as a board," she grunted. "Uncle Han's for you in the morning, you can't treat your body this way. Turn that thing off, have a shower, clean your teeth and come to bed."

No fight in me, I was all surrender. And when I'd done what she told me in the order that she said, I found her lying naked under the duvet and waiting for me, wide awake and intentional.

Most people do what they want to do; in a world without choices, you only do what you must. I shucked off the kimono and joined her, naked as she was and craven with doubt.

"Suzie . . ."

"It's all right," she said, "it is allowed. We're married, remember?"

Which was the problem, of course: that I didn't remember, that I was a monogamous man by instinct and still none of my physical loyalty lay with her, that it didn't seem all right at all and shouldn't have been allowed.

Only that she was there, all too much there suddenly. Warm and hungry, lithe and alien, exotic and unfamiliar; and God in my confusion I needed something to cling to, something tonight I needed that wasn't failure or fear or disgust. My hands closed on her slender shoulders, and not I think to push her away.

She may have been unsure herself, just for a moment, whether my touch meant yes or no, acceptance or its opposite. At any rate she grinned into my eyes, just at the moment that I touched her, and she said, "Besides, you know, we have done it before."

• TEN •

LUKE, BACK IN ANGER

Damn right we'd done it before, that was self-evident. These at least of my secrets she'd been made free of, she knew all the private touches that could chase my soul like silver in the light.

Briefly I felt at a tremendous disadvantage, unable to reciprocate, knowing nothing of her body beyond what was obvious, what was universal. But cooperative or competitive, whichever it was, that sense of inadequacy slipped away; I stopped feeling anything beyond her fingers and her mouth, sharp teeth and hair and hot slippery flesh and the mind-numbing generosity of her.

Generous once, at least, generous the first time. Then I was knackered, I wanted nothing but the comforts of sleep, though I was quite happy to sink into them with a friendly body pressed close and warm to mine. But not she was sleepy, she wanted more; I called her greedy, and she impugned my masculinity in a hissing whisper hard into my ear, and ultimately what the hell choice did I have?

At some point during that unhasty, exploratory, all but sleepless night, I remember her groaning on a giggle, saying she supposed she was going to have to train me all over again, and she'd had no idea before that men could grow up so ignorant. In response I kissed her breathless, and she had fine breath control; and the touch of Carol that came into my head then – *"Don't, Jonty, you know I don't like that. Like two oysters wrestling in a single shell. Gross. I like California kisses. Dry lips, no tongues, just sharing air . . ."* – was suddenly itself alien, and unwelcome, and not at all guilt-inducing.

I guess we did both of us sleep in the end, or doze at least in the dawnlight. Me, I remember being too weary to move, too brain-dead to talk any more; but those memories are chopped into fragments, so most likely I was dipping in and out, barely there at all. And I remember her breathing too slow, too sonorous for consciousness; I also remember her wide-eyed and watching me, though I don't remember the change, one to the other.

No clocks in that room, nothing to stir us or tell us that we ought to stir. I gazed at the light, I tracked the sun across the window, I felt no inclination to shift at all; at last it was Suzie who awoke us to the day and the day's demands. She stropped her cheek gently against my stubble, her hair tickled my nose and she said,

"Will you come and watch me have my shower?"

"I might," I said; and she led me by the hand from futon to kimonos and so decently through the flat, and thank God we were decent because my mother was sitting on the sofa where I had sat last night. She had my computer in her lap and was playing or working or snooping, whichever; and however glad I was of the kimonos they felt actually like no defence, no decency at all because her acidly satisfied gaze seemed to burn heedlessly through to the flesh and bones and bruises underneath, all the physical history of the night just gone.

I watched Suzie shower, too weary to feel the slightest desire now even in my head as she twisted and lathered and rinsed under a scalding jet. She looked almost a boy, with her small tight body and her cropped hair in the blurring steam; nothing boyish in what my skin remembered of her, though, this last twelve hours. Sometime, somehow I was going to have to deal with this, to find how I felt about what she'd done and how I'd responded. For the moment, though, what I felt most was grateful. She'd done it without knowing what it was that she did, perhaps, she'd done it for reasons of her own – *because she loves me*, a hard accusatory whisper in my head, as though her love were my fault and therefore certain to be betrayed – but she'd found me a way through the tangled thorns of my self-loathing. And if that way only led eventually to a deeper valley and a darker sky, what of it? Sufficient unto last night particularly were the evils thereof, and she'd got me through them. The next lot I didn't have to face till sunset came around again. For now, I'd sit with my face in the light and not worry.

Which was absolutely my mother's philosophy, and none of mine; but just then I felt it truly, which should have been enough in itself to throw me into a flat dizzy spin of panic. That it didn't, I could only put down to exhaustion . . .

Suzie stepped out of the shower, and I fetched her a towel. When I draped it around her shoulders she worked herself wordlessly like a cat against my hands; senseless to be shy or wary of her body now, so I dried her quickly, then shucked off the kimono for my own shower while she sat on the toilet seat still rubbing at her hair but watching me, her face unreadable to me through steam and water.

My turn to stand still and be dried off when I was done, though I flinched where she had not, earning a giggle and a gentler touch, and, "Hey, did I do that?"

"Well, I didn't do it myself. Will it scar?"

"You'll probably never play the euphonium again. What is a euphonium?"

"Big and brassy," where this wife I didn't remember choosing was a flute, I thought, slender and quicksilver, light and breathy and surprising. And I wanted to play on her again, and wasn't sure I'd ever let myself.

If the decision were ever left up to me . . .

My mother was still smug half an hour later, when we had come together to the table for breakfast. Suzie and I sipped tea and coffee respectively, clean and refreshed, haggard and unspeaking; Ellie seemed to regard this as some kind of personal triumph, unless she was simply amused by our youthful excess. Any minute now, I thought, she'd be offering unsolicited advice on how better to manage our sex-lives.

To forestall that, I said, "What were you doing on my computer, then, what are you up to?"

"An addendum," she said, "for the *Journal*. I'll send you a copy."

"That's the issue about Deverill?" And when she nodded, "You're not still going ahead with that, for God's sake?"

"Yes, of course I am. Why not?"

"Because it's had you in hiding for weeks, is why not. Because it's put you in fear for your *life* is why not . . ." *Because sometimes you appal me and always you madden me and you've never been any good at it nor really cared that much but you're still my mother, is why not . . .*

"I wouldn't say fear," she said. "It was you that was afraid. Touching in a son, but fortunately not catching. I've never killed an issue yet, and I don't intend to start with this one. If ever a man needed stripping naked in public, that man is Vernon Deverill. Besides, I don't believe it's Deverill who's been threatening my life. Do you?"

After yesterday? I opened my mouth to say yes, but then never gave the word a shape. Oh, he was capable of killing, I was sure of that, and exposure in *Jonathan's Journal* might do him enough damage to put him in a killing mood; but no, all the evidence said she was right, it wasn't him she should be scared of.

Not yet, at least, not till after she published. And she'd had other big fish killing-mad at her, but she'd always relied on anonymity for protection, and no one had ever broken through that to find her.

Thus far.

Her life, her choice; I wasn't easy with it, but what did that matter? To her, not a whit.

"Where've you been, anyway?" I demanded, abruptly shifting ground. "Where've you been hiding?"

"With friends," she said. "You told me not to tell you where."

"Can you go back?"

"Of course."

No 'of course' about it: not friends but self-immolating heroes in my book, if they were willing to put Ellie up, put up with Ellie for weeks at a stretch. Especially if they could pack her off one day and welcome her back the next, for another indeterminate stay . . .

"I think you should, then," I said. "This morning. Right now," as she glanced at her watch, as her mute comment pointed out that it was barely morning still, we'd been that late getting up.

"I've got a better idea," Suzie butted in suddenly. "If you've got your passport with you, Ellie . . . ?"

"My passport I've got," she said. "For what?"

My wife the wise woman, had my mother sussed. Always she had her passport with her, always her eyes on the distant horizon; and very little it needed to send her away. "I think you should go to Spain," Suzie said. "Mr Nolan'd like a visit, I'm sure, he won't be seeing anybody except the consul and his lawyers and anyone Deverill sends, he's probably dying for a friendly face out there. And you could ask him what he knows about SUSI. Whether it was them set him up, or what. As it's you, he'll tell you anything he knows, he'll be so glad to see you; and I bet he knows a lot. He's got to know something."

She was right, even my mother had to admit that. A minute's thought, a brisk nod, and, "Yes, I'll do that. Jonty, can you phone the airport while I pack? First plane to Madrid, please . . ."

"Hang on a minute," I said. "The police are looking for you, remember? There's not going to be a nationwide alert or anything, you're not that important," and oh, how I loved telling her that, "but Inspector Dale might have asked the local airport to keep an eye out for you. He'll be half expecting you to head to Spain, and I think he half suspects you're around here somewhere. Better if you drive down to Manchester or London and fly from there."

"No car, darling."

"Take the one I hired. It's a national firm, they're sure to have an office, whichever airport you go to. Hand it in there. You might have to pay a bit extra, but . . ."

"All right. Good. Has anyone got any cash? I'd rather not leave a trail behind me, if that nasty policeman's put a trace on my credit cards."

Cash on that scale I didn't have. The gold card would probably produce it; but before I could offer, Suzie went to the sideboard and rummaged among napery, coming back with a fat envelope. She glanced at me shamefaced as she handed it to my mother.

"I was holding out on you, Jonty. Private money, for emergencies . . ."

What, and I was supposed to be outraged? Apparently, yes; but in fact I only wanted to applaud the wisdom. So fast a marriage, of course she should take precautions. I hoped I'd had the sense to do the same; and I *must* go and see my bank manager, talk things through with him and learn what my financial situation actually was, how much of Deverill's generosity I had to hand and what other prospects he and I could find between us.

Actually, I thought, after yesterday, I'd rather like to pay Deverill all his money back, if only to send him the message that I was not the corrupt solicitor I'd been pretending to be, that actually he couldn't buy my silence. Though however I'd do that I wasn't at this time pretending to imagine. Even if I found another job – and there was a superfluity of solicitors in the system just now, too many for the market to bear, and here I was with my reputation in tatters of my own choosing – it looked like being the kind of debt I'd need a mortgage to repay. Suzie could do it, no doubt, with the club or the flat or both to offer as security; Suzie would do it, no doubt of that either, to buy her husband out of an intolerable situation; I wouldn't dream of allowing her, and that too was not subject to doubt.

So I sat there musing on Deverill and me and yesterday, and there was a brisk rapping on the door, and I unthinkingly let Suzie go to answer it. Worse, my mother had already checked the wad of notes in the envelope, slipped it into her handbag and was now on the other sofa and back on my computer again, typing something fast and two-fingered to get it down, she'd said, before it escaped her. No hint of self-preservation in her, no signs of her scuttling to the privacy of a bedroom; she just looked up distractedly to see who it was, with never a worry that whoever it was – Deverill, policeman, our wannabe burglars come back for a second try – would see her also, and might have come here precisely for that reason.

Suzie opened the door, and a woman's voice asked for me. I stood up, ever the gentleman, and here was yesterday walking into the flat: not Deverill, not Dean but Mrs Tuck. Smart two-piece, sensible shoes and a handbag, and had she come to handbag me?

To which the answer was yes, in a way. "Jonty," she said, with no preamble and no allowances for being overheard, "you left us very precipitately yesterday."

Suzie's eyes on me, silence from my mother's still fingers on my keyboard: what could I be but brave? Braver than yesterday . . . "Yes, well. I didn't like the postprandial entertainment." Lawyerly-brave, brave with words comfortably after the fact, and here came that disgust again like a resurgent tide of sickness. I could taste it in my mouth, feel it twist in my head, leaving me dizzy and weak and wanting to sit down.

She made a little gesture of distaste. "Neither did I. Not my idea of fun, but Vernon likes to make these little gestures. Preferably with witnesses, I don't know why. I expect it does something extraordinary to his ego; that seemed to be what powered him best when we were married, and I don't believe he's changed. But what I wanted to say, Jonty, I'm sure it's not necessary, but – well, I wouldn't like to think that what you saw yesterday would prejudice your relationship with Vernon. He's a hard man, but he's been very generous with you."

That much at least I was sure of, and the subtext was equally clear. This was my second warning: first Dean on the steps of Deverill's house, and now Mrs Tuck in my own home, or the closest approximation I had now.

"I'm very protective of my ex-husband," she went on, apparently not content to leave what was obvious unsaid. "Not that he stands much in need of my protection, you've seen how he looks after his own interests; but it's not a good idea to turn suddenly against those interests, that's the message. Am I getting through?"

"Entirely," I said.

"That's good. Not a wasted journey, then. And you'll carry on trying to find out whatever happened to poor Mr Nolan?"

"Oh, I will that," I said.

"Excellent." And then she gazed around her, and I'd hate to say that either one of them was outfaced, but Suzie suddenly interested herself in the documents she carried, and my mother ran a corrective eye across the computer screen.

And when Mrs Tuck said, "Mrs Marks?" they both of them startled, like two guilty things surprised. And I cursed silently in my head, for the information given away there in the jerk of my mother's head; and just as well we were getting her out of the country pronto. Her *Journal* might be secret still, though I might not have laid much money on it at that time; but she was a hostage to fortune, a hostage accessible to Deverill's hand so long as he knew where to find her. She and Suzie both now, if ever he felt the need to intimidate me.

Mrs Tuck smiled with the certainty of a job well done, and I wondered if this was what she'd come for: if all she'd really wanted – no, all *they'd* really wanted, she must surely be here with Deverill's blessing, if not on his instructions – was to confirm that the third party they'd seen in the car and now in the flat was indeed as they'd guessed her to be, my mother. And to make that confirmation public, to let me see that they knew now, which would get the message over very nicely, thank you.

Certainly Mrs Tuck had nothing of import to say to either Mrs Marks: she only said goodbye nicely and walked towards the door, at a speed nicely judged to give me just enough time to get there ahead and open it for her. Which of course I did; and behind me I heard my mother trying too late to cover herself, to make out that she was so totally absorbed in her work she'd barely noticed that we had a visitor.

"Jonty," she said loudly, aggressively and speaking as much to Mrs Tuck as to me, "does this so-smart machine of yours not even count my words for me?"

How would I know? I was as ignorant as she was, with the programs that machine ran now. And so I told her, once the door was safely closed and Mrs Tuck was gone; and then I asked her again what she was writing, what was so urgent that it had to be done now, when she was so urgent to be gone.

"Just notes, darling," she said, blithely copying whatever-it-was onto a floppy and slipping that into the shoulder-bag that lay at her feet, packed and ready to go. "Everything you've told me about Deverill, it's all grist to the mill. It's strange, how we've both been working on different sides of the same story. Don't you think it's strange? I think it's strange."

"Yes, Ellie, it's very strange. Are you ready to go?"

"You weren't very cooperative, though, the first time. When you came and told me to disappear. You won't remember, but you absolutely refused to tell me anything that time. Too dangerous, you said, and I should get out while the going was good and leave Deverill to people who understood him. Very domineering, you were. This has been much better," and she patted my cheek lightly as she stood up, fit reward to a son for moling for his mother.

Actually, I'd not told her that much this time either. Not a word about the girl beaten and abused in his stableyard, though I'd gathered that was pretty much standard practice, just his way of doing business. I could live with my shaming memory, just about, but I couldn't talk about it. That was one corroborative detail my mother's exposé would have to get by without. No doubt she'd have gleaned other stories on her own account. Pillow talk from Nolan, perhaps: I was sure she could be really turned on by whispers of brutality, if that kind of sadism-by-proxy response was what it took to get the information.

It seemed that she wasn't quite ready to go yet; she had nothing to read, she said, and she couldn't start a journey without a book. So she went back to the spare bedroom to raid my library, leaving the computer switched on and humming on the sofa. Prompted by her example, I fetched a disk from the bag it lived in, and discovered that indeed it was possible to copy a password-protected file. Read it I couldn't, but I could make as many copies as I liked.

Just one for now, because I had a cautious soul and I always, always made back-ups. I might make a batch later if it came to that and spread it around some computer-friendly friends, see if they could crack the code for me. Disk went into pocket, mother came out of bedroom with a double-handful of books, we all trooped down the stairs one more time. Being ultra-cautious, I had Suzie lock the fire door behind us.

Took Ellie to the hotel car park, gave her the keys and watched her drive away, and followed down all the ramps to the exit to make assurance doubly sure that she was gone; and then walked back to the flat to find a message for me on the answering machine.

A message from Carol, who had been so definite that she never wanted to see or speak to me again, who had threatened me with injunctions to be sure she never had to: a message saying come, come quickly, come now . . .

Well, what she actually *said*, she said, "Jonty, it's Carol. Luke's here, he's looking for you . . ."

And that was all. Her voice sort of died, there was a pause, she put the phone down; and that in itself, that hesitancy in the precise and punctilious Carol was enough to say *help*, to say *get over here right now, where the hell are you when I need you?* And Carol called for help so rarely, she would have to have been *in extremis* to do it at any time, let alone now when she was still so angry with me.

But then, Luke was enough to drive anyone to extremes. Yes, she'd need rescuing; and yes, I was sole candidate for that particular job.

"On my way," I said stupidly to the machine, not bothering to waste a minute by ringing Carol back. "Can I take the car, Suze?"

"No."

I was already holding my hand out for the keys; I drew it back slowly, scowling at her. "Why not? You heard, it's urgent . . ."

"Yeah. I'm coming too."

"Oh, what? It's not you he's looking for. What are you going to do, be sisterly and supportive with Carol? I don't think so . . ."

"I let you out of my sight," she said, "you go off and have adventures without me. You disappear for hours or days at a time, things happen to you you won't talk about," and I had a flash in my mind, a girl being methodically kicked around a stableyard, and I realised for the first time that she was seeing it too, or something like it, "and all I can do is worry," she went on. "And I won't *do* that any more, Jonty. I'm coming with. Besides, I want to meet Luke. Even if he doesn't want to meet me."

She had a point. And besides, I also had wanted her to meet Luke, I remembered threatening him with her when I left him last, as apparently I had also the time before.

"Come on, then," I said. "But can I drive? Please? I know the short cuts . . ."

"Is there that much hurry, then?"

"Oh, yes," I said.

Short cuts make long delays. I might know and use them all, but I didn't know the car. Nor did I fit it very well: I was too long in the leg or it was too short in the body, depending on whether you listened to Suzie or to me as we grouched on that hurried, awkward journey across town, as I kept missing gears and she kept wincing and every bone in her stiff and wary body kept saying what was undeniably true, that we'd have been quicker far going a slightly longer way with her at the wheel, comfortably in tune with her machine.

If the journey had been longer, perhaps I would have stopped, we would have swapped: perhaps. I don't think so, though. Not for reasons of male pride, though my *amour propre* certainly was offended, that I was making such a hash of this. I think I particularly needed to be at the wheel, to feel the responsibility laid firmly and irrevocably across my own shoulders as I brought my wife to the house I had shared with my lover. Though actually it seemed to me to be entirely the other way around. What I had had with Carol was a marriage, *pace* the Archbishop of Canterbury and the laws of the land; while Suzie felt at best to me like some new and casual fling, an erotic passion that went only skin-deep, bruise-deep, for all the bruises I had to show for it . . .

And if the journey had been longer, perhaps I would have lost some of the urgency en route, realising how very much I didn't want to do this. But there was no time for cold anticipation to break through the *hurry, hurry* heat of moving, of doing. I felt vaguely smug, like a knight-errant called to the aid of a lady who had spurned him before; but nothing more than that, nothing more honest, there simply wasn't the time.

Door-to-door I drove, and got out of the car still grumbling about the shape of it, how awkward the pedals and how stiff the gears. Suzie I think was no longer listening at all; she slipped her hand into mine as we stood there on the pavement, and it was that touch of chilly fingers that pulled me down, that rooted me in what was real: that I stood here hand in hand with the girl I'd left Carol for, and there was Carol opening the door already, must have been watching for us through the window . . .

And Carol didn't seem to notice, or if she noticed she didn't seem to care: which said a great deal about the current state of Carol's mind, and how she was coping with her house guest.

"Jonty, he's in the front. Will you, will you just take him away? Please?"

"Do my best," I said.

She held the door open, and we both stepped in; and no, she wasn't cutting Suzie dead, she wasn't trying to look straight through her because I saw their eyes meet and Carol's linger for a moment, and it was Suzie who looked away. There was even a vestigial curiosity in Carol, I thought, as if she remembered now that she'd been blazingly angry with me, and here was the cause of it all; but no sign of that anger now, against either one of us. We were here to do a job that she desperately needed doing, and for a little while she'd be nothing more than grateful.

What Carol called the front wasn't at the front of the house. It was a tag she had grown up with, to her it meant the living-room, the main social centre of the house, and it just so happened that in this house it was at the back. She wasn't going to change her language to suit a temporary geography; she'd changed mine instead. "What's important comes at the front," she used to say, "just think of it like that and never mind which way you're facing or where the street is."

That was the way it worked, why I'd always been happy to let her change my habits of speech or thought or whatever she wanted changed: because things made sense under her eye and within her philosophy, she could always find a reason. Nothing was ever unexplained. It had made life easy, to share it with someone so grounded in certainty.

Which was presumably why she was having so much trouble with Luke: because he was inexplicable, he didn't fit her world, he challenged the very ground she stood on. Literally, as well as metaphorically. She used to wave me off to see him, "Go on," she'd say, "go see your fallen angel"; but she never offered to come with, or asked to meet him. I guess in her heart she never believed in him for what he was, she only labelled me credulous and him some kind of romantic blond fakir. But today he was in her house, and even if he wasn't doing tricks he was so untouched by earth or any significant breath of humanity there could be no doubting now.

She stood back against the passage wall; I squeezed past and Suzie followed me, her fingers hooked into a belt-loop on my jeans, here where there was no space for holding hands. I didn't know if Carol noticed, or if it was done for Carol to notice, or if it was a genuinely nervous need to cling. All I hoped was that she wouldn't be difficult, that neither of them would get in the way. Managing Luke was never easy, even one-to-one and without distractions; and I was starting to feel nervous myself, only now starting to wonder what the hell he was actually doing here, why in the world he would have come.

Only once before had I ever seen Luke in a city, the time I'd brought him to this house. He'd wanted me to do it and I'd done it, though only because I was sure Carol would be away till he was gone. No consequences for me or for her, or not directly. The consequences for others had been appalling. Not my fault, not my responsibility, *not* mine to carry; but with me still none the less, and I had forebodings, premonitions that this time would be no better and very possibly worse.

And I felt Suzie's puzzled little tug as I walked past the doorway into what should be, what would be to her, what architecturally-speaking undoubtedly was the front room; and I ignored it, and pushed open the door ahead.

And God in heaven yes, there was Luke; but this was Luke as I had never seen him even on that other city trip, this was Luke all but shed of his skin. What lay beneath, his older and greater aspect burned through him, and he was wickedly hard to look upon.

Is it self-defence, I wonder, is it just a mental game of duck-and-cover when you come upon something momentous and your thoughts flick into a kind of random relevance, an oh-that-reminds-me mode?

I stood there with Luke filling my sight in his ice and steel rage, and what I thought was that this was the first time ever I'd come to him and there had not been water rising to the boil.

Nor did he say, "I've been expecting you," or anything like it. But of course we both knew that, he'd sent for me; and that was another first, though it was also the first time he'd had the means. Luke didn't use phones.

Ordinarily, he didn't use phones by proxy either; ordinarily he didn't have the need. Today transparently was not ordinary, and I was not nervous any longer. I was deep-down, dark shit scared.

I thought he didn't need the hiss and steam of water on a fire to greet me; I thought I could hear the hiss of blood or ichor or whatever it was that he had in his veins, ice turned liquid, perhaps, bitter and scalding. I thought I could see steam about his body, where ordinary mortal air met the reality of him and was burned or frozen or otherwise cruelly changed.

He was wearing white, which was new also, a change from his usual dull earth-colours: white jeans and trainers and a torn white T-shirt, and maybe there was meant to be a message in that, maybe he was robed in light as near as he could make it. But there was mud on the carpet where he had walked, mud cracked and drying on his trainers, mud and other stuff on his jeans, darker stains I didn't want to wonder about.

Suzie's hand had clenched itself tight around my belt; I could feel her breath on my neck, as she peered at him over my shoulder. Standing on tiptoe she must have been, to do that.

And me, I was reaching behind to detach her hand almost without thinking about it, to put my palm against her belly and press her gently backwards and away from danger even as I said, "Luke, what is it, what's up? What are you doing here?"

"I want you," he said, and his voice was hard like a rain is hard in the falling.

"Yes," I said, "but for what?"

"You have to show me Arlen Bank," he said, meaning *you have to take me there*. And his timing was beautiful, because this time yesterday I couldn't have done it, but now I could count the turnings in my head, I could pick it out on any map that marked it. Though maps were no use to Luke, of course, which was why he wanted me.

Arlen Bank was Vernon Deverill's house, where I'd had lunch and sparred with him and Mrs Tuck, and then watched something halfway to murder done on a girl whose name I didn't know.

Luke would know her name. She was on his list of visitors, of comrades in the struggle; by now, I thought, a day on – a day late – he would likely know what had happened to her. Which would likely be why he was here now and raging like ice on fire, and wanting to put himself on the list of Mr Deverill's visitors. Avenging angel was this face he wore; and oh, I was torn.

For her sake and for my own soul's ease, I wanted to be the most help I could to Luke today. It came too late, but not he alone was interested in vengeance.

I'd been here before, though, or close enough. Years ago, I had brought him to this house because he could find nothing on his own, and then I'd watched him go off with others on a mission of light; and the results of that haunted me as though my guilt were greatest. I wouldn't willingly see even Deverill exposed to the kind of damage that had been done that day, so how could I bring him Luke . . . ?

"How is she?" I asked, sure that he'd know who I meant and hopeful that his answer might give me some kind of clue, which way to jump. She'd been hurt past bearing, or past what I could bear; but she was tough inside, she'd have to be to survive the life she'd chosen. Maybe if he said she was okay, recovering, coming through, maybe then I could stand up to him and say no. First time in my life that would be, but there's a first time for everything . . .

"She's dead," he said.

Just that, two brief words and everything turned again. Gravity sucked harder, the poles shifted, not my world any more and I was dizzy with it. Not the wall that grabbed me, though, and stopped me sliding; that was Suzie, her arms tight about me and her body hard against mine, holding me up, keeping me here when my mind wanted to spin into a place where no light came.

"Who? What's he talking about, who's dead? Jonty, what *gives* with you two?"

Nothing much gave with us, in all honesty, and we gave little back; but this she was entitled to. Besides, I had a ghost to requite, and she was nearest.

"This girl I saw them working over yesterday, at Deverill's. They said they'd let her go . . ." But they hadn't, they'd worked her over and then killed her, regardless of Dean's intentions; unless he'd simply misjudged her strength and tagged her as tougher than she was. That could have been it, maybe she died under his ministrations without his intending her to . . .

But Luke was here, and they wouldn't have taken her all that way just to lose a body. So, "Where?" I demanded.

"Leavenhall."

And that made it worse, the worst possible, that meant they must have done everything that Dean intended and then killed her anyway. Or simply let her die, but that was the same thing. Her blood on their hands and very much on mine, her life I'd let slip through my fingers because I'd trusted my buddy, my lifesaving friend Dean to be cruel but true. I'd done what was easier, and so a girl was dead; and now I too was blazingly, killingly angry, and against Deverill because again that was easier than being killingly angry against myself.

"I'll take you to Arlen Bank," I said. "Let's go."

And tried to walk, and couldn't: not because my legs wouldn't carry me, fury was a great stiffener of weak joints, but because Suzie was still holding hard, holding me still.

"Why don't you just give him directions, Jonty?" *Or better yet have nothing to do with it*, her eyes were saying, but she didn't bother to put that into words. No one, not even Carol suggested the police.

"Directions?" I repeated vaguely, my mind slow to absorb and slower to find a response, clumsy suddenly with words. "Luke doesn't know his left from his right."

"I'm *serious*. I don't want you going with him, whatever's happened, I don't want you getting involved . . ."

"So am I serious," I said. "He can't tell left from right, he can't read maps, he can't read anything at all. His mind doesn't work that way. It's no good just telling him, he has to be taken places. And I am involved. I said, I was there, I saw what they were doing; and now she's dead," and how much more involved could you possibly be?

"Okay," Suzie said then, "but I'm coming too. You're not going off on your own. I'll drive."

"No." That was Luke, not me; and it wasn't her he was saying no to, it was the driving. The being driven.

"He doesn't go in cars," I explained, oddly anxious that she shouldn't take offence. "Not if he can help it. Or in buses or trains or any kind of transport."

"How the hell did he get here, then?" Carol demanded,

in a mutter from behind us. "It's a long bloody walk from the Lakes . . ."

And he couldn't have set off before yesterday evening, at the earliest: time enough for Dean and whoever else to finish with the girl at Arlen Bank, put her back in the van and drive fifty-odd miles to Leavenhall, put her through her paces there and then kill her. And that last they would have done in private, in the dark most likely; and then someone would have to find the body, however casual they'd been about disposal . . . No, chances were he hadn't left till midnight at the earliest.

But yes, he'd have walked it. Or run if he'd felt that he had to, if there was that much urgency on him. Luke hates to fly.

I shrugged, unwilling to put all or any of that into words. But Suzie seemed to have been reading my thoughts on my face. She glanced once at the mud on Luke's jeans and on his trainers, and grunted; then she looked down at her own feet, and sighed.

Soft black desert boots, lacing to the ankles: eminently practical, no excuse at all. And if she let me go alone, off to adventures unknown without her, she'd be forsworn. My turn now, to be reading her secrets on her face; she wasn't going to let that happen.

"Let's go," she said, as I had said before her; which left me nothing to say but goodbye to Carol.

And "I'm sorry," I managed that too, as Luke pushed past her on his way to the door. And it wasn't for the rudeness of my asocial friend that I was apologising, or not that alone; nor only for that and for the greater intrusion, a part of my life thrusting once more and very much uninvited into hers. So much I had to say sorry for, to a woman who'd refused to listen. At least she seemed to be listening now. At any rate she nodded slightly, a gesture of thanks or acceptance or at least something less than the contemptuous rage of our last meeting. That was the best she could manage, beyond following us down the passage to be sure the door was closed good and hard behind us; but for now, I thought it was enough.

Out in the street, both Luke and Suzie stood waiting for me to point the way. Luckily, we didn't have to go by the main roads; there was a back path, past some allotments and through a tunnel under a railway embankment, that would take us out of town and roughly in the right direction. Luke must have come here along the A-roads, the way that I had brought him, the only way that he would know, but I didn't fancy such a walk myself. Leading Luke through a crowd, or on roads with heavy traffic, sounded to me like a definition of a slow walk through hell.

Down to the dead end of the street, then, and here was the footpath; and talking of hell, here also was Shaitan the cat, sitting black and neat and erect in a tussock of grass. Shaitan my cat, Shaitan Carol's cat, it just depended what perspective you took, how you cut it. Obviously Carol had custody; and with so much else gone from my life, so many other and greater losses, I'd hardly given him a thought. But I was glad to see him now, even in passing; and I crouched down and held my hand out to him and sucked air gently through my teeth, making the little chirruping sounds he always came to.

And he arched his back and hissed, and all his fur was standing up as if he were only a cartoon cat and nothing real; and not I his eyes were fixed on as one paw felt for safer earth behind him, as he backed slowly along the fence. Not I but Luke, of course Luke, though I felt bitterly to blame because I had brought Luke here.

Luke stood stock-still, as Suzie did behind him; only Shaitan was moving, creeping blindly backwards until a fractional gap under the fence gave him a hole he could

squirm through. Then he was away, sprinting through the
cabbages, terror clothed in flesh; and that was much as Carol
had reacted, much as most people and all animals did. Off
her own territory, I thought, not in her own house Carol also
would have run, or at least got the hell away from Luke as
fast as she could manage.

For a fraction, it seemed to me that Luke looked utterly
bereft, standing there watching where the cat had fled from
him. And I thought perhaps that was why he loved trees so
much, because they didn't run, because they couldn't.

Then I reminded myself that this was anthropomorphism
at its stupidest, trying to ascribe normal human emotions to
Luke. After all, I'd never run from him, I was one of the
few who felt his magnetism the other way, who felt drawn
and not repulsed; and not for years had I made the mistake
of ever thinking that Luke loved me.

And indeed Luke stalked on now along the path ahead of
us, and there was only bright anger in his face and in his
carriage, reminding me what he was here for: that a girl had
died, was dead, and she also had been one of his few, his
crazy few, his band of siblings. She more so than me, even:
I might have been there first, but I'd never been one with
the tree-lovers, I couldn't work up the passion. And Luke
I guessed was here for justice or vengeance or whatever he
wanted to call it, to call that crime home to its originator;
and I'd give him all the help he needed in that good cause,
and maybe he did love us after all, or why would he be so
passionate about this?

Walking with Luke was like walking with a determined dog,
not at all a social activity. So long as the route was obvious
he ploughed ahead, sometimes far ahead, never a thought
for companionship or conversation; as soon as there was a
question over which way to go, he would stand and wait to
be told.

I'd known him wait patiently, serenely almost, though Luke was never truly serene; today he waited furiously, pale and tense and enraged apparently by our slowness. I took to pointing the way as soon as I was sure myself, so as not to face too nearly the glare of his glacier eyes.

Suzie and I weren't strolling, we weren't dawdling, this was a serious march for us as much as for Luke. Even so he left us a distance behind him, again and again; which left her free to grip my arm and talk to me as we walked.

Or to ask questions, rather, to demand to know. "Why did he go to Carol, then, if he wanted you?"

"Didn't know where to find me," I said. "Obviously."

"It's not obvious."

"Isn't it?"

"No. The way you talk about him, he knows everything."

"No. I told you already, he doesn't know his way about, places he hasn't been. He has a different kind of spatial awareness," *he used to dwell in the heavens*, "he can't get around on the ground, and he hates to fly." She didn't look persuaded; I tried a different way. "Take the wings off a bumble-bee, it'll never get back to the hive. Luke's like that. No navigational skills in two dimensions," and God only knew how many dimensions Luke had lost, "he doesn't see the world that way."

"He found Carol all right."

"He's been there before."

"How come?"

"I took him." The confession earned me nothing but an anticipatory silence, *well? Go on, then, I'm waiting*. Took me a minute, because I didn't like to think back to that night, it was a memory I could very happily have lost; but in the end she won. If you could call it winning, if the prize was something that anyone could want. She won the story, first time ever I'd told it to anyone but Carol.

"It was years ago," I said, "we'd just bought the place, me and Carol, and I think that level of commitment had us both scared shitless. At any rate, we were fighting all the time, over stupid things, the way we never did; and we had a week's holiday booked that we'd been going to spend playing house together. Nesting, you know? But we couldn't, we'd have killed each other; so she went to stay with her parents for a few days, and I went to see Luke . . ."

Young I'd been, young and grown-up both at once, car keys and house keys and so much worry in my pockets; what I needed most was a spell of total dispossession, nothing at all in my pockets or on my mind.

So I camped with Luke, drank water and ate what he picked from the hedgerows, leaves and fungi and fruits; and after a couple of days there was an old Beetle came bumping up the track, and half a dozen kids squeezed out of it, younger even than me.

But I was too young then, not wise enough to leave. So I stayed and listened to them talking horror to Luke, talking vivisection. They were students, it seemed, nice ordinary middle-class kids who smoked dope and took acid and didn't eat meat because that was the culture they'd found when they came to college, that's what their new friends did and so they did it also.

How they'd come to this, how they were friends of Luke's I couldn't gather and didn't ask. It didn't matter. Somewhere, sometime they'd met, the kids had met whatever criteria Luke used and had been admitted to his circle; and today they were all abuzz with outrage and conspicuous virtue.

None of them would do such work, they said, but a friend of a friend of theirs was a technician in the animal labs at the university's medical school. Unbearable stories they heard from him, they said, unimaginable cruelty . . .

Luke listened, nodded at the stumble-tongued examples they gave, and I thought how foolish they were, how young, not to realise that Luke had seen more cruelty than ever man could imagine. But then they came to the point of all this, they said the labs' cages were full just now with a new term starting and they wanted to raid, they said, they wanted to smash and to rescue.

But it had to be tonight, they said, terrible things were scheduled for the morning – *because we're worked up for it now*, I thought they meant, *and we'll lose our nerve by morning* – and they wanted Luke to lead them. Someone with experience, they said.

God knows what they were thinking, or why Luke said yes. Perhaps they thought that rules of wysiwyg applied, that all they were getting was a young drop-out who lived apart from unacceptable men and did as little harm as he could to the world around him. Perhaps Luke even thought he could do that for them, he could keep his nature caged within the weak containment of his skin. He learned to do it later, after all, for the tree-protestors and almost for the cameras, falling with only that slightest hint of flight. Perhaps this evening was to be a trial run, where Luke would touch the lives of men again and pray – no, *hope* that all they felt was the touch of another man.

At any rate, they did ask and he did say yes; and then the only trouble was how to get Luke from his caravan to the lab, because there wasn't time for him to walk or run it.

Luke hates cars with a passion, but even worse than cars he hates to fly.

No room for him in their ramshackle Beetle, even if he'd been prepared to squash, if they'd been prepared to squash with him. Everyone in the caravan was looking at me now, and what the hell else could I do? I'd taken enough from him over the years in escape and shelter, never had the chance before to give anything in return.

"I'll drive you," I said. Had to go back sometime, after all; better to spend a day or two in the house alone, before Carol came home and we started fighting again.

So I'd had Luke in my car, a once-and-only experience that was, and definitely not for sharing. He rode in the back for the extra space, and spent the entire journey with the window wound full down and his face pressed into the wind like a travel-sick dog; but it wasn't the wind, I thought, that made the car so cold despite the heater on full all the way. It wasn't the road, I thought, that made it judder so, that had the steering wheel wrench against my hands and almost had us flying off at the bumps and the humpback bridges.

Some kind of hell-drive that was, with me never feeling quite in control of the car; and going faster than I wanted, stopping harder, however lightly I touched my foot to the pedals. I wanted to tell him to behave, to sit still and leave the driving to me; but every glance in the mirror only showed me his face turned out into the air and his eyes tight shut, not to see the steel box he rode in. He wasn't doing this, or not consciously. Things happened around Luke, that was all, and I was learning something new today, how machinery reacted to his proximity.

Never had the chance before, never seen him get near to so much as a battery shaver. He had old broken engines rusting in his garden of trees behind the caravan, but they weren't there to work.

Still, we survived. We made it to the house, though I made it swearing privately that never would I drive Luke anywhere again. I'd given the kids my address as a place to meet, and as well that I had; they were meant to be following right behind my car, with the address only as a precaution, but they arrived fifteen minutes later than we did, eyeing me askance even as they murmured how brave I was to drive so hard on such a road, they wouldn't like to try it . . .

For *brave* read *stupid*, I understood, and shrugged and said nothing about it. Settled them in the front room with Luke, insofar as it was ever possible to settle Luke within walls; made them coffees and left them to it. They had plans to make and hours to kill, and they were welcome to use my front room for those purposes, in Carol's absence; but I wanted no closer role than that. Smashing labs wasn't my business, I wasn't even sure how much I sympathised.

"All I wanted was my house to myself," I said to Suzie, stumping along the footpath with Luke ranging ahead of us, not necessarily out of earshot – I didn't know how far his ears could reach, I'd never learned his physical limitations and wasn't sure that he had – but at least far enough for this to feel possible if not comfortable, talking about him in his company. "I couldn't have coped with Carol or anyone then, I needed to get my head straight; and I couldn't do it without privacy. I wanted them gone, but I could only wait for that, I couldn't throw them out. I'd invited them, after all . . ."

"So what happened?"

I just waited, was what happened. I waited for hours. They went off about midnight; I took a last cup of tea to bed with me, thinking that was it, no more rads for me, no revolutions. No Luke for a while either, they'd take him home or he'd find his own way, not my problem.

And I lay there in bed with my cup of tea and the radio on, wondering what they were doing, how it was all going; and an hour later I was still wide awake, not even trying to sleep, and the tea was cold and I hadn't heard a word of what I thought I was listening to, and I was still trying to picture things a mile away like a movie in my head, trying to give myself psychic dreams wide awake. God knows why, they were all strangers to me bar Luke, and I didn't need to worry about him; but I was worried.

And then there was a great knocking on the door downstairs, a pounding that went on and on like whoever

it was didn't know about stopping, they'd never got that
far. I rolled out of bed and fumbled into my bathrobe, and
half the street must have been awake by then and all of
them hating me because you do that, you always blame the
neighbour for his visitors.

And I'd just got out onto the landing when the knocking
did stop, finally; but I'd only taken two steps towards the
stairs when there was a different kind of knocking, right
behind me.

I twisted round, and I was sweating cold suddenly,
stinking with it; and worse when I saw who was knocking,
where he was. I think I screamed a little, maybe.

It was Luke, and he was outside the landing window,
knocking on the glass; and all I could see was his face
against the night, and he looked like he'd been lifted entire
from some cheap back-to-basics horror movie.

"His hair, his face, he was all running with blood," I
said to Suzie, and shivered again in the sunlight as I
remembered, as I had shivered that night when I opened
the door to him.

• ELEVEN •

ANGELUS EX MACHINA

The decision to let him in, I don't remember; but it must have been made in the face of simple logic, in the face of blood. *If I don't open the door*, I must have thought, *he'll only come in through the window* . . .

Don't remember the decision, don't remember taking the stairs in a sprint in the dark, though I daresay that I did, I must have done. What I do remember is standing cold in the doorway, shivering for better reasons than my bathrobe being all I had against the night. I remember looking out, then stepping into the street and looking up. I remember seeing Luke standing on the little slate pentroof we had like a canopy above the door; being there, to be sure, he was right outside the landing window and not flying at all, not hanging like some bloody movie monster in the too-supportive air.

He stepped off the roof and came down, you couldn't say that he jumped. And when his bare feet were on the pavement beside mine – too long a time they took, too slow they were – he said, "Come with me, Jonty."

I could see now how the blood ran off him, how it soaked his clothes and pooled between his feet. Not his blood, I was certain, though it looked black and terrible in the sodium lights.

Why? was the question, *why should I when I don't want to, when I don't know what the hell you've done and all I can see are the consequences, all I can see is the blood?* But *why?* was too much to manage, with my body racked with shudders and my mind spindizzy with the stink of blood and Luke and danger. I knew what he'd say, anyway. *Because I want you*, he'd say, and nothing more. He'd never say *need*.

So all I asked was, "Where?"

"The laboratory."

Of course, the laboratory. Where else?

"Let me get some clothes," I said, stalling, hoping he'd see it as some faint gesture of defiance.

"Hurry," he said; and I did that, I hurried. Defiance only runs so far. Me, I ran into the house, dressed fumblingly with fingers that were deathly cold and stumbled back down dark stairs into a street that seemed darker, as if Luke had barred all the lamps from working now. There were still shadows, so there must I suppose have been light; but I couldn't see it or use it.

Luke didn't speak again, he only turned and started running himself, not looking back, trusting me to follow. Assuming I could keep up. I did that, though barely; but I thought this hurry in him was almost as frightening as the blood that had drenched him, that he was leaving behind as black bare footprints on the paving-slabs: those I could see, and him, and nothing else.

He led and I followed, though I knew a quicker way than the one he took; and at last I couldn't run any more, I blundered into a massive wrought-iron gate and just clung, watching him; and when he was far enough away my sight came back, and I realised we were there anyway. This was the gate to the old university campus, and there was the medical school just ahead. The labs, I'd gathered from the kids' conversation, were in the modern block jutting out on the right; and to be sure, the foyer of that block blazed with light. Too much light there seemed to be, a beacon against the night, *hey, look at me!* I couldn't understand why it hadn't attracted attention already, burning alone like that, drawing the eye, surely asking questions . . .

There was the light, and there was Luke outlined against it, a silhouette of dark but flaming at the edges; and now, at the door, it seemed that he turned to find me and found me gone.

But took only a moment to see or sense me, there in the gate's twisted shadow. His arm beckoned, and I went to him. Slowly now, not hurrying in any sense at all, and cravenly afraid.

Again he didn't speak, he only led me inside through high glass doors that stood open but seemed bent out of true, so that they never would close properly again even if you had the strength to drag them against broken hinges and force them into their distorted steel frames. The kids had spoken of sledgehammers to smash the doors, but Luke had found a better way.

I wondered why there weren't alarms shrieking against the silence of the campus at night, why the place wasn't lit in strobing blue and swarming with police; but then all the lights flickered above Luke as he passed, one of the neon tubes imploded in a shower of glass that he seemed not to notice at all, and I remembered how even the most unsubtle machinery in my car had been affected by his presence. What chance the sophistication of a contemporary alarm, against a spirit or a field or an atmosphere so discordant it could disturb the engineering in a Volvo?

But I still wanted to know why no one had noticed the lights. Didn't they have security at the university? In the med school particularly, at a time when animal-rights activists were raiding and bombing like proper little terrorists?

There was blood in here also, tracks on the tiled floor and a little smeared across the glass of the doors.

Not all the tracks looked human. There were bare feet marked out, Luke's for sure, and prints of many shoes leaving; but there were paw-prints also, and a couple of unstraight lines as if some bloodied thing had been dragged on a string to leave a snake's path behind it.

Could've been snakes, of course, I thought. Bleeding snakes.

Did they keep snakes in medical labs? I didn't know, nor why they would have been bleeding.

Nor why anything had bled that night, only that there was too much, way too much blood. The foyer stank of it, and that was only the foyer. There was nothing there that bled.

Correction. Something scrabbled in a corner as I walked behind Luke; my whole body jerked, and I was cold again despite the sweat on me as my head twisted round to see.

It was a rabbit, only a rabbit. White once, a pink-eyed cutie of a little lab rabbit; not white now. Not cute. Smeared with blood and filth it was, and its hind legs didn't work. It must have clawed itself into the corner there on its front paws only, and its blood-soaked belly had left another of those drag-trails along the wall.

And now it stared, it glared at us, pink eyes shot red; and it yickered with long yellow teeth, and it screamed high and gasping, and it looked and acted entirely mad.

Must have been the pain, I thought, driving it loco. Someone said once, there's nothing so frightening as a mad sheep; but believe me, mad rabbit runs it pretty close. Anything shy and docile, I guess, turns scary when it turns.

I was scared, at any rate. I wasn't going anywhere near the thing, even to put it out of its lunacy.

Luke neither, he fixed his eyes forward and marched along the corridor, and me I was like a dog in his wake, tail between my legs and whining softly in the back of my throat. I'd have been dragging hard at the leash, if he'd had one.

He did have one, only that it wasn't material. Every step I took into that building, I didn't want to go one more; every step I took I followed with another, only because he was there ahead of me. And he'd come for me, he needed me although he wouldn't say it; and that was a first, and I owed him.

But God, I paid that night. I followed him, I dogged his heels like a good boy; and he led me along the corridor, along the tracks of blood to where more doors stood open and stairs and blood ran down into light.

A basement, of course a basement. Where else would a torture chamber be, where else keep your horror?

Down we went, two wide white tiled flights down; and not only blood on the stairs, there were animals here too. Dead animals, or as dead as makes no difference. Rabbits and rats and a cat I saw, and looked away from; and wondered what the hell more there was to see, what kind of hell it was that Luke had led me to. I could hear it, or something of it, unhuman screams and moaning, but the sounds shaped no pictures in my mind.

I was quickly answered, though, as we came to the foot of the second flight. Laboratories and store-rooms made this hell, and a long room like a corridor lined with cages. Pain and fear there must always have been down here, blood and death also, that was what it had been made for; but nothing on this scale, never before so much blood all at once, so terribly much death.

Most of the cages stood open and empty, and most of their former occupants lay dead on the floor there, or else in the labs or the doorways. Some kind of killing frenzy must have taken them; I saw a rabbit with its guts scratched out, but its teeth still embedded in the throat of the cat that had gutted it. I saw rats in tangles, four or five knotted together in a single murderous tie, impossible to say which had killed which. There were mice and guinea-pigs also, all the pets of my childhood, all dreadfully dead and all by each other's teeth and claws.

Luke, I thought desperately, *what have you done here, and why in God's name have you brought me here to see it?*

He beckoned me from a doorway, and I went to him, and then I thought I knew; because this was a seminar-room or some such, a table and many chairs, and there were no dead animals in here.

A hell of a mess and two dead men, but no animals.

Lots of blood.

The dead men were in uniform; or half out of it rather, half stripped, their clothes as ripped and shredded as their bodies. For a moment I thought they'd been policemen; then I saw a shoulder-flash unstained, and thought not. Security guards looked more likely. Ex-policemen, perhaps, or ex-army: heavy men, the pair of them, or had been. Discipline gone to self-indulgence, muscle gone to flab.

Everything gone now, gone to teeth and claws and tearing, and for a moment I thought the rabbits and the rats had killed them too.

Stupid, I thought. And not in accord with what I saw, what the room said.

The room, it seemed, was of the opinion that they had killed each other.

The table was upturned, the chairs were scattered and tipped; the two men lay in the centre of the room, in the arena created by the havoc round the edges, and they still had their hands on each other. I didn't go close, to see if their fingernails had been torn by all that tearing, if their teeth were stained with biting. Not my job, not my problem.

"Luke," I said, "how," I said, "why did they ever . . . ?"

"They went mad," he said. "Like the animals." His voice

was calm, neutral, unattached: *not my problem*, it seemed to be saying. And if that was so, if that described his attitude, then again the question came, why had he brought me here? Not to see it, that for sure, and for sure not to report it; nor I presumed to clean up, to cover up, to make it look like nothing had happened here . . .

"Where are the kids?" I asked dully.

"Gone."

Well, no blame to them for that; they'd planned a raid, not a nightmare. Not a visit to hell. And of course they hadn't tried to clean up, any more than I would; I only hoped they hadn't left fingerprints behind them. Later, though, I wondered a little; when he said 'They went mad', did Luke actually mean the security guards? Or did he mean the kids? Maybe the kids it was had gone mad, maybe they'd done the ripping and chewing when the guards disturbed them. Maybe they had cleaned up a little, at least to the point of making a half-hearted attempt at misdirection.

In that case, I really did hope they hadn't left fingerprints behind them; but all that came later. For now I stood with my eyes fixed on those bodies, first I'd ever seen and worse than anything I'd ever imagined seeing; and into the silence I dropped the only question left, the one that had been stirring all this time.

"Luke, why did you want me here?"

"You have to help them."

"They're past my help, mate. I'm sorry, but . . ." I still wasn't going any closer, but sometimes you don't need to feel for a pulse or auscultate for a heartbeat. Sometimes even a rookie can tell. Particularly when a head has been twisted entirely the wrong way on a neck or when a chest has been opened manually, when that rookie can look at a mess of wet red organs and *see* that the heart's not beating . . .

"The animals," Luke said; and now there was some emotion in his voice, now he sounded heart-wracked, with the weight of a world's grief on his shoulders. "I can't help them, and someone must."

"Why can't you?"

"Look," he said, and walked just a little way into the room full of cages, where he'd let me go alone before.

The sounds in there doubled and trebled instantly, manic screaming and shrieks, and some were pain and some were not. I saw a rabbit in a still-closed cage roll on its back and bite at its own belly; I heard thumps and rattles, the sounds of bodies throwing themselves about, but I was only watching that one rabbit, watching its fur stain darkly as it bit.

"You see?" Luke said. "It's the madness. They are mad of me."

Sweet way to put it, but he was right. Just his shadow in the doorway was enough.

"What do you want me to do?"

"Free them. Care for them . . ."

"We should phone the police, Luke, there are dead *men* through there . . ."

"You can do nothing for them," and again his voice spoke of his disinterest, his utter lack of concern. "And the police would cage again here, those that they did not kill. You must help the animals."

"Oh, for the love of God, Luke . . ."

He flinched at that, and I wanted him to. Laboratory animals, rats and rabbits set against men and seen as superior, more worthy, certainly more deserving of his time and mine. I had no sympathy; but it was only Luke, it was all Luke and as before I couldn't say no.

I did what I could, with fingers that trembled as they unlatched cages and separated the dead from the living. If anyone came, if anyone caught us down here – caught me, at least; they wouldn't catch Luke unless he were willing, no, determined to be caught – with the blood and stink on my hands and the knowledge that I had, I'd be lucky to get away without a murder charge.

But I set free every animal that could still run, and sent Luke to stand in an empty store-room out of the way, to give them a swift run up the stairs to freedom if they chose to take it. With him not in line of sight, I was free also to despatch a few of the more cruelly injured, snapping necks with that tricky little twist of the hands that you learn growing up in the country.

Thinking myself all done, I called him out again and said, "Let's get the fuck away from here, can we?"

"There are more," he said. "At the far end, and through the door."

"Well, the door's locked." I'd tried it, to be sure. "Nothing I can do about that." And he couldn't go down to open that locked door for me, because there were still a dozen small animals between it and us, free but clinging to their cages none the less, and he would kill them if he tried to walk that way.

For answer he jerked a fire extinguisher off the wall, balanced it for a moment in his hand, and then threw.

Old-fashioned it was to look at, for all that this was such a modern lab: big and red and heavy, seriously heavy. I could barely have lifted it one-handed, never have balanced it on my palm, never in a million years of trying have thrown it much further than its own length away from me.

Luke threw it, what, twenty-five metres? Thirty?

With one easy motion of his arm he threw it, and it burned through the air as though it too had a memory of wings long lost; all down that corridor of cages it flew, and it struck the door neatly beside the lock, and smashed it open.

"Let them out," Luke said quietly. "Please?"

And for that 'please' I went, I ran all those metres down to the broken door and through, and found a pen littered with shredded paper, and two mad sheep inside it.

God knows what had been done to them, those sheep. Each had a shaved area on the neck, and a black box on a collar, and wires going from the box into the skin. Whether it was that which had made them mad, or the fever that Luke brought, I couldn't say then and still can't; but they glared at me red-eyed, and they showed their teeth and wanted at me, no doubting that.

Given the choice, given any kind of choice I'd have left them safely penned. Choice I didn't have, though. I gestured to Luke, *get the hell back out of the way, these things are mean and I want them safely past you, not turning and coming back*, and as soon as he was out of sight I stood the fire extinguisher on end and unlatched the gate of the pen. I swung it wide open, to stand as a barrier between the sheep and me, and then I punched the button on top of the extinguisher. A jet of water spurted out of the hose; I grabbed it and aimed it through the mesh, straight into the face of the first sheep as it lunged at me, massive teeth snarling the wire.

It choked and turned aside, saw the empty corridor and charged off. I hoisted the extinguisher under my arm and directed the jet at the other sheep, herding it out of the pen and after its companion. No way to turn the flow of water off; I just dropped the extinguisher, slammed the gate and got out of there. With any luck sheep could climb stairs, even mad sheep could find their way out, to what I didn't know and didn't care.

Didn't care where Luke had gone either, or what he would do now. I just walked cautiously down the corridor and up the stairs myself, ears straining for any scutter of hooves on tile, any sound of threat.

Nothing in the corridor above, nothing in the foyer; the rabbit in its corner was still now, dead I hoped, I didn't go to check.

Outside and no signs, no sounds of movement. I took a

breath and started for home, my feet wanting to run and my mind saying *no, take it steady, try at least to look innocent and uninvolved in anything*.

Started for home and got not very far at all, barely fifty metres before I did hear something.

Not the sound of a sheep, the sound of a kitten: a faint mewing, coming from under a bush as the best path home led me through shrubbery towards the road. I checked, all my nerves brittle, my eyes jerking and my mind screaming *mad cat, beware!*

It wasn't mad, only afraid, or seemed so; and not afraid of me. It came crawling on its belly from the shadows, a black kitten too small to be alone in the night, and what could I do? I picked it up and cradled it, felt its mewing change to a mute purr, a slight vibration under its skin; and I tucked it into my jacket, pulled the zip up to give it comfort, and carried it home.

And so, when Carol came back from her parents, Shaitan was there with me to welcome her; and he made the difference, he was a buffer to set against our uncertainties, a small dependent life for whose sake we had to make this work . . .

That was the story I gave to Suzie as we walked that day, though I didn't tell it all, only as much as she needed. Or as much as I could bear, perhaps. I'd never told anyone but Carol before, and Carol couldn't have taken even what detail I gave Suzie. Wouldn't have wanted it.

The grip of Suzie's hand in mine was all for me, though, whatever comfort she could give; and her eyes watched me sideways, suspiciously, clocking I think that I was leaving some things out. Wanting it all, she was, or seeming so. I guess, when you've seen your brother appallingly killed, the deaths of strangers and animals are no great matter; knowing your partner's secrets matters more. Perhaps.

She didn't dig, though, or not into the messy stuff I'd left out. All she said was, "I remember this. There was lots about it on the telly, big story for a couple of days, yes?"

"Yeah, it was. National news. Once they'd had a look at the bodies, they decided those two guys probably hadn't killed each other," which was when I started thinking again about the kids, and what a frenzy could do to them, and what responsibility I carried by saying nothing. "The inquest brought in a verdict of unlawful killing, but no one ever got arrested. Some of the papers had big theories about black-magic cults, or some drug the scientists were experimenting with, that turned cute little bunnies into killers; but I know the university's animal-rights groups did get investigated pretty hard. I think the only reason the kids got away with it was that they weren't an organised group, they didn't belong to anything, they were just a bunch of friends who happened to throw up this one big idea . . ."

And were unlucky enough to know Luke, foolish enough to take him along . . .

Suzie grunted, thought about it for a minute, then, "So what are we saying here, Luke drives people crazy as well as animals? He hasn't driven you crazy. Or me. Though I don't think I like him much."

Well, that wasn't a surprise. Luke didn't go out of his way to be liked. Didn't go out of his way for any reason. "Just depends, I suppose," I said, thinking on my feet, trying to find a logical explanation for something that didn't actually seem to operate in a logical universe. "The wrong people in the wrong place, perhaps. I mean, you saw how Carol was, just with having him in the house there. Animals are okay if they can run away, it's when they're caged or trapped; and the same with people, I think. If they feel caged or trapped. He's got this aura, and I guess some people just can't take it at that intensity . . ." It hadn't been a lot of fun for me, driving cross-country in a car with him; and I was inured, I'd thought I was immune.

Another grunt, and she swung my arm vigorously in time with her pacing. "Well, don't you get into any lifts with him," she said, doing a mind-reading act, doing it well.

"Promise," I said lightly, earning myself a scowl.

"I *mean* it, Jonty. He's, he's not *safe*."

No. Safe he certainly wasn't, though I'd never seen him lift a finger to harm a living thing.

"I've known him a long time, love," I said, which was true; and, "I can handle Luke," which blatantly wasn't.

She snorted disbelievingly, *you think you're immune?* And she had both hands tight on my arm now to say that if I wouldn't be careful on my own account she'd be careful for me, she'd keep me close.

Which was fair enough, I supposed. She'd married me, after all. And I'd married her. She was entitled . . .

"What happens when we get there?" she asked, after a little while walking in silence. "I mean, he's going to have a confrontation with Deverill, I suppose, but what about us? Do we go in with him, or just hang around, or what?"

"I don't know," I admitted. I hadn't thought it out that far. "We'll just see what happens, I guess. What Luke does, what he wants. We don't have to wait, he can find his own way back." The same way we'd come, inevitably; that was the only route he'd know. "Could be a wasted journey anyway, Deverill may not be there."

"He should've phoned first," she said. I just laughed. There wasn't a phone in the city would work for Luke, even if he'd thought to use one.

Talking passes the time; time passes, and you get there in the end. We walked, we talked; we mostly followed Luke, who spoke not a word to us; and eventually we came to a village and found the right road out of it, so that five minutes later we stood outside Deverill's impressive gates, impressively closed to us.

Suzie and I stood, at least. Luke of course had ranged ahead, seeing nothing to say that his quarry lived here. The name was there, carved into the stone gateposts on either side of the drive, but he wouldn't see that.

So I stood still and waited until he looked back from the next corner, and then I beckoned and he came running.

"This is Arlen Bank?" he demanded.

"This is Arlen Bank," I confirmed, looking to see if either one of the posts held a buzzer or an intercom, any way to communicate with the people inside.

"Good," Luke said, and he swarmed up one of those gates in nothing flat, a handhold and a foothold and another hand and he was standing ten foot above us, standing on tiptoe on top of the gate and staring into the grounds beyond.

Look out, Luke, you'll fall – but that wasn't funny, would never under any circumstances have been funny, and I'd never under any circumstances say it. Besides, he had a perfect balance; I'd seen him do harder, madder things than this, and never give a hint of falling.

Turned out that the intercom unit was on the pylon beside the gates; turned out that we didn't need to use it. The camera atop the pylon was whining softly, seeking us out, zooming in; I waved at it, a vague and stupid gesture, and wondered if I needed now to buzz them anyway, and tell them who we were. By the time I'd decided that etiquette said yes I did, it was again too late; there was a car bumping over the grass inside the gates, a serious-looking 4 x 4 in too much of a hurry to divert onto the tarmac'd drive.

Probably Luke had broken some kind of security beam, I thought, in climbing onto the gate. It was just too quick otherwise, to have spotted us here and got a vehicle this far in response.

The car stopped and Dean jumped out, looking pretty

serious himself. It'd be okay once he saw me, I thought, or at least it would be better; I wasn't sure how far my writ ran, either as colleague or life-savee, but I thought I could argue us as far as an interview with Deverill.

But of course Dean wasn't looking at me at all, he was only looking at Luke, where he stood so high against the sky; and so far as I could tell from the back of his head in silhouette, Luke was only looking at Dean.

And then he wasn't only looking at all, he was jumping down, even as Dean yelled, "What the hell do you think you're doing up there, shit-for-brains? Go on, get the fuck out of here . . . !"

But Luke got down on Dean's side of the gates, he floated down and landed on the balls of his feet as lightly as any lad from the Kirov or the Royal Ballet, and even I couldn't tell if that was just his natural grace or something more.

He came to ground maybe five metres in front of Dean; and five metres quickly became three and two and one, because Dean went charging like a bull, or like a hard efficient bulldog angered by an affront to his master, and there wasn't time for me to shout more than his name as a warning to him even if he would ever have paused to listen.

He charged in, thinking that this would be easy: *some kid playing games*, he was thinking, no doubt, *some cocky nineteen-year-old fancies a dance on the grass . . .*

If Luke had really been nineteen, no doubt that's what he would have got, just a Dean's Excuse-me and the bum's rush after, with more than grass-stains on his skin to show for it. But I didn't think you could count Luke's true age, not in years, not in any human scale; and you certainly couldn't count his looks. Pretty enough to tumble, he looked, and far too pretty to brawl.

So Dean went charging in, quite likely smiling inside, looking forward to this; and when he came up for air he

was smiling right up front, smiling wider than ever he'd
smiled before.

He was smiling because Luke had torn open both his
cheeks, and all the flesh was flapping loose and happy.

It had been so quick, I had to play it through my head
again. Child of my times, I needed the slo-mo action replay
before I could quite believe it. Dean likewise, I thought: at
least he stood there staring, doing nothing more, while his
mouth gaped wider far than it was meant to and the blood
ran freely over his jaw and fell like rain on his T-shirt.

He had been charging, then, and Luke had lifted his
hands, that was all, to catch Dean's head between them;
and then suddenly Dean hadn't been charging any more,
he'd been standing rock-still, all his strength and momentum
nothing against Luke's solidity. Hitherto-irresistible force
meets truly immovable object, and that's what happens, I
suppose. Nice to know, after all this time.

What happens, to be precise, is that object sticks its
thumbs into force's mouth, one on either side, and tears
the flesh like damp cardboard until the rips reach almost
from ear to ear . . .

Suzie gasped and ran forward – brave girl, stupid girl –
while I was still rooted with shock. She ran to one of the
gates and tried to pull it open, then tried to shake it off its
hinges while it moved no more than I did, than Dean did,
than Luke.

Then Luke did move again, and so did I. I sprinted up
to where Suzie was trying to climb the gate now as Luke
had, clinging to the wrought-iron risers with both hands as
she fitted her soft boots into decorative whorls and frets. I
grabbed her round the waist and pulled her down again, held
her hard against my body as she struggled, as she fought to
be free; distantly I was aware of her sobbing foully, "Let
me *go*, you fucking bastard, for Christ's sake let me help

him if you won't, you shitting coward," and so on and on in a relentless monotone while her eyes and mine were riveted to the mad circus beyond the bars of the gate.

Luke held Dean around the neck now, with his other hand clamped in his hair; and as we watched he pulled, he peeled Dean's scalp away from his skull as swift and easy as peeling a satsuma. There was a wet, choking sound from Dean, closest he could get to a scream perhaps with his throat full of blood. So much blood there was, it was soaking Luke's filthy whites also; but he wasn't near done yet, it seemed. This wasn't enough. His clawed hand let go of what it held, let the mess hang from Dean's neck, a slack wet flap of dripping skin and hair; and then it gripped Dean's T-shirt and yanked once, ripped it from him like a sodden rag and tossed it aside.

The same for his jeans, the same single tug to tear riveted denim into shapeless nothing, and then Dean was naked but for underwear and shoes. Luke sank his nails into a blood-streaked shoulder and tore skin from flesh and bone just as easily. Baby-pink skin, that was, freshly regrown from the burns Dean had taken saving me; and his body might just as well have saved itself the effort of regrowth. Might as well have saved itself the effort of saving me, come to that, wouldn't be in this mess now if I'd burned up like Oliver . . .

Suzie gasped, and her breathy cursing died to a mutter, to a moan. She stood trembling now within the circle of my arms, so that I could let her go and climb the gate myself, knowing myself as useless as she would have been if I'd not prevented her from trying; what could either of us do against Luke? No argument would touch him, no pitiful muscle would hinder him for a moment from what he chose to do.

Knowing that, I climbed anyway, watching my hands and feet now, not watching Luke. Maybe that was why I climbed: to have something else to look at, to focus on.

But I wasn't totally focused, because the lightest touch on my ankle stopped me dead. I looked down and saw Suzie stretching up, to hold me. Mostly what I saw was her eyes, huge and dark in a face turned pale and sick, slicked with sweat. She couldn't say *don't leave me*, not with her conscience and mine both screaming *go! go!*; but those desperate eyes said it for her, and they did more than her hand did, to keep me still on that side of the gates.

I was at the top now, more or less, one elbow hooked over. When I looked across I saw Luke dragging Dean towards the nearest tree, still with that arm around his neck and the other hand still tearing strips of skin. Dean wasn't resisting but he was conscious yet, I could see his feet stumbling in the grass although Luke must have held most of his weight now, his legs surely wouldn't do it.

I don't know trees, but this was something tall and sparse, more trunk than branches: spruce or fir, my mind wanted to claim against my ignorance. Whatever, it was way too high and unladderlike for mortal man to get up without climbing irons. But Luke just kicked his trainers off, slung Dean over his shoulder and started up it, clinging with fingers and setting his toes in the bark as if there were rungs to hold him.

Up and up he went, maybe forty feet up before he found a branch to hold him; and me, I just clung to the gate and watched him until Suzie tugged at my trousers, more imperative now, *come on down, there's no point even pretending any more . . .*

So I jumped down beside her, and we clung together instead; and we only watched – no sound, no movement, in me at least no feeling left at all – while Luke set Dean in the groin where branch met trunk, and skinned him.

I could see too well despite the distance, despite the height. I could see with a rare clarity, as if my eyes had a zoom feature suddenly, and a finer focus. Good country

air, perhaps; or perhaps it was this also that made Luke
stand out in crowds or solo on hillsides, that he walked all
the time in a different kind of light.

I didn't think of looking away. I wanted to cover Suzie's
eyes, to stop her seeing as I was seeing, but I had no right
to make that choice for her; and she chose as I did, or was
compelled as I was. At any rate, we watched together as
Luke methodically flayed my friend Dean, peeling his skin
from him like wet tissue paper, length by length.

Too late – knowing it was too late, knowing it would
always have been too late but doing it anyway just for the
gesture, just to have something done – I did briefly fight off
that sapping paralysis of watching, long enough to trot over
to the security pylon and jab the buzzer, jab and jab until
surely I must have alerted someone on the other end of the
intercom. I didn't wait to talk to them, though. Their camera
would tell them better than I could, what was happening to
their buddy. Me, I went straight back to Suzie. Wrapped my
arms around her with a whispered "Sorry" into her hair –
*sorry I left you even for a moment, sorry I abandoned you
to stand and be a witness here alone* – and stood with her
again, the two of us witnesses and very much alone but for
each other.

Dean had saved my life in hospital, but not I saved his, I had
no way to do it. You'd have needed a helicopter, to come at
Luke in that tree; you'd have needed a squad of Marines to
tackle Luke anywhere, and I wasn't sure a squad could do
the job.

Suzie and I, we did what we could, we bore witness; and
when it was over or all but, when Dean was dead or dead
enough – looking dead at least, looking like a side of meat
even to my unwantedly-good sight, looking reduced that far
from human – it took only the slightest movement in her,
the first hint of a turn to turn me too. We turned away

without discussion, without thought; I put my arm around her shoulders and felt her shaking, pressed her close against my side so that she could feel my shaking too.

We walked down into the village and found a phone-box; I shoved a coin in the slot and phoned Dulcie.

"Come and rescue us," I said. "We're at Arlen Bank Side – that's the village, not the house where I was before. We'll be in," I peered through the window, squinted to read through dirty glass, "in the Lord Hurlington. Come soon."

"On our way," Dulcie said, no hesitation. "How many of you?"

"Just two. Me and my wife," I said.

Dulcie came herself at that momentous news; presumably she wanted to congratulate me personally, and commiserate with Carol. When she stepped out of the taxi to find me at an outside table negotiating brandy down the neck of the diminutive and still-shaking Chinese girl perched on my knee, her face should have been saved for a better occasion. I was in no state myself to enjoy it.

I gave her the briefest possible introduction, "Dulce, this is my wife, Suzie Chu Marks," because Dulcie was a long-time friend and she deserved that much; and being a long-time friend she didn't ask for more, she didn't ask anything at all. Reading something of the situation in our faces, she just mothered us gently into the cab and drove off.

This time, halfway back to the city, I remembered to tell her the address had changed. "Take us to Chinatown, I'll show you where . . ."

Nothing more than a nod of the head to that, but the back of her neck was eloquent: *I want the full story*, it was saying, *when you're ready to tell me*.

Our eyes met briefly in the driving-mirror, and I guess mine were making promises, but they were probably lying.

I wasn't sure I'd ever get to learn or remember the whole story myself, and parts of it I was sure I'd never want to tell. Even to long-time friends.

Suzie spent the whole journey huddled tight against me and I thought I understood, I thought the numbing shock of what we'd seen was all. God knew, it was enough. But she lifted her face from my shirt just once, as we came in sight of the flat; and she whispered, "He looked, he looked just like Jacky did, when they took me to see him in the morgue . . ."

Nothing I could say to that, I only held her closer and touched my lips to her forehead, tasting cold salt bitter sweat; but inside I was cursing. Cursing myself, for forgetting that. I should have covered her eyes after all, or turned her away from the sight of it. Would have done, if I'd only thought.

Out of the car, and I paid Dulcie with another mute meeting of eyes if not minds; then my arm around Suzie's frail-seeming shoulders and we went up those stairs like Siamese twins, joined at the heart in horror.

At the last landing before our private stairs, we found the wrong door closed, the wrong door open. The club was locked up, when it should have been open for business; but the fire door stood ajar.

"Didn't we lock this?" I thought we had, but I was ready to blame my slipshod memory again, if she said no.

"Yes," she said. "Look . . ."

And her hand was trembling again as she showed me where the wood was split and torn in the frame, where the door had been smashed open.

"Jonty . . ."

I licked my lips, where they were suddenly too dry to bear; and when I could find my voice at all I whispered, "You stay here."

"No."

"Suzie, whoever did this, if they're still up there . . ."

"If they're still up there, two of us is better than one. I

said, no more adventures without me," though she looked a
long way, a very long way from adventurous. "And anyway,
Lee should be here, he should be in the club and he's not.
And he's my friend, nearest thing to a brother I've got now.
I'm coming up."

"He's probably gone for the police," I said.

"Don't be stupid. He'd have phoned them, wouldn't he?
I'm coming up."

And she was too, she did. It was as much as I could do to
make her walk behind me. Or tiptoe, rather, as I soft-shoed
it as quietly as I knew how.

The flat door also had been broken open, though it was
pushed to now. I hesitated, almost lifted a hand to knock; but
then I laid that hand flat against the wood, and shoved gently.
It swung in, and there was the room as I was expecting now,
as I was dreading to see it: chaos and disaster, papers strewn
everywhere.

Blood on the papers, blood on the carpet too, and I hadn't
been expecting that.

The door a little wider, and I could see one of the sofas;
and fuck! yes, there was someone in the flat, and I had a
moment of frozen panic before Suzie made some kind of
hard, anxious noise in her throat and pushed past me.

Then I could see through the runnels of dried blood that had
matted his hair and masked his face, I could see what Suzie
had seen faster, something of Lee beneath. I ran across in her
wake, my feet skidding unheedingly on letters and magazines,
bank statements and God knew what important documents.

His eyes were closed, his breathing irregular and rasping;
he had the phone in his hand, and the butt end of a broken
snooker cue at his feet. Suzie's quick fingers were at his
throat, feeling for a pulse, I guessed. I picked up the
phone, ready to call an ambulance and then the police;
but she said, "No. Run down to Uncle Han's, get him.
Hurry, Jonty . . . !"

My reaction, her reaction: not the time to argue, which was wiser. Lee was her friend more than mine, and of her culture; that made it her call. I dropped the phone on the sofa and hurried, taking each flight of stairs in three or four reckless bounds till I came down onto the first-floor landing, and to the door that hid Mr Han the Herbalist. Suzie had been threatening me with this man's doctoring ever since she brought me here from hospital, our little trip out; so far I'd dodged or avoided or postponed, one way or another. My body, my call. I thought. She obviously didn't . . .

Whatever. *Please ring buzzer and wait*, the sign said, but that day I just crashed through the door. Small reception-room, a few chairs, all of them occupied; the clientèle was mixed, from elderly Chinese to young Western.

There was a middle-aged Chinese woman sitting behind a desk; she looked up, started to smile, said, "Jonty. We've been expecting you." Then, registering my urgency, "What's wrong?"

"It's Lee. He's in our flat, he's been attacked. Suzie said to fetch Mr Han . . ." Doctor Han? I didn't know. I was back to that again, strangers knowing me too well while I was totally at sea with them.

"Yes. Of course. One moment." Unflustered but very focused now, every movement precise and necessary, she stood up and rapped firmly on a door behind her, then pushed it immediately open and went through. I heard conversation, tonal, guttural, incomprehensible; and thought, *Doctor, will I ever speak Cantonese again?* Because that was my tutor lying hurt upstairs and very likely for my sake, injured because of me. My tutor and friend, apparently. And my wife's near-brother, and in a hell of a mess: and all because I couldn't remember what was important, and I was too stupid to figure it out in retrospect . . .

* * *

Suzie's Uncle Han was probably no blood relation – I hoped!
Bad genes in the family pool somewhere if I were wrong,
because God, but he was ugly – but he came running like
a father at her demand, sprinting bow-legged up the stairs
faster than I could keep up with. By the time I reached
the doorway in his wake he was already kneeling on
the sofa beside Lee, his battered leather medicine-bag
was open on the floor and he was dabbing something
onto Lee's scalp with one hand and peeling back eyelids
with the other, muttering through buck teeth as he dabbed
and peeled.

"Suzie," I said, "he needs a hospital."

She just glanced at me, one brief glare, *shut the hell up,
what do you know?* and turned back to Han again.

"I do know," I said mildly, as if she'd spoken that aloud.
"I've had my own experience, remember? Head wounds can
be dangerous. He needs X-rays, maybe a scan . . ."

She grunted, glared again, but this time did at least
condescend to put it to Han, in a rapid singsong; the
language sounded less harsh somehow, when she spoke it.

He replied in half a dozen hard, chopped syllables; she
blushed, and reached for the phone. Didn't offer me a
translation, but I could provide my own: *What, you mean
you haven't called an ambulance yet? For God's sake, girl,
I can give him first aid, but he needs a proper check-up, you
of all people shouldn't need telling that . . .*

Before she could dial, though, even three easy digits, Lee
stirred and groaned and opened his eyes; and I saw her hand
freeze on the number-pad, I saw her choose not to use it, not
just yet.

"Lee?" she said, and a few words of Cantonese; and when
he didn't respond to that, beyond moving his eyes slowly
to find her, she put the phone down and tried him again in
English. "How are you feeling, Lee?"

A little pause, as if he were feeling himself out from the

inside, checking; and then, "Fuck," he said, and tried a smile. Didn't look good, but it worked well; I saw the tension leave Suzie's shoulders in a rush.

"All right. Just sit still. Uncle Han's here, he'll sort you out."

Then they switched to Cantonese again, Han asking questions, I guess, and Lee responding weakly. Han reached into his bag and came up with a handful of dried leaves which he sorted into Suzie's cupped palms, a little of this and a little of that. She took them into the kitchen; me, I wanted to seize this hiatus, to seize the phone and make the call myself, get the guy the attention I thought he needed. But I felt displaced, no part of this, isolated by language and culture both; so I only stood there in the doorway, neither in nor out, hoping that Lee could tolerate a little delay.

My thumb played with the brass plate below the bell, tracing the engraved lettering, *Jack Chu*. Perhaps we should get it replaced, *Suzie and Jonty Marks* it should read instead, there was something morbid about keeping it this way; but again that had to come from her, when she was ready.

Jack Chu. Jacky, she always called him. I wondered if he'd actually been Jack, even, or if his birth certificate said John . . .

And my thumb was still then on the plaque, as my mind kicked off on a tangent; and I took one pace into the room and looked around, and in all the chaos I couldn't see my computer anywhere.

This wasn't the time to say so, obviously, though it was burning suddenly on my tongue. Suzie came back from the kitchen with one of her fine porcelain cups, something in it steaming and aromatic; she held it to Lee's lips, ignoring his unfocused efforts to take it for himself. As he sipped, she spoke to me without looking round: "Jonty, be useful. Bring a flannel from the bathroom. Wet and warm, not hot . . ."

I fetched her a flannel and a bowl of water, earning myself

a vague smile for reward. When Lee had drunk his tea or medicine, whichever it was – both, presumably – and had had his face washed, the worst of the blood rinsed away, I interrupted another three-way conversation in Cantonese. Trying to be useful indeed, to drag their minds back to the one thing I was certain of. I picked the phone up off the floor and said, "Suzie. Ambulance?"

"Oh. Yes, I suppose. Hang on, though. Lee? Jonty wants you to go to hospital. So does Uncle Han, I guess. Just to be safe. Okay?"

I wouldn't have given him the choice, myself; but he didn't really make it anyway, he only shrugged and let us decide us for him. I was already punching buttons on the phone when Suzie said, "It'll mean the police too, Jonty."

My turn to shrug. I was no great fan of the police even in my last life, working with them every day; right now they were after my mother and I wasn't fond of them at all – *and besides, you've seen a murder done today and not reported it; that makes you an accessory, that makes you a fool* – but let them come. We'd need to report the burglary anyway, to claim on the insurance.

The ambulance service was experimenting with some kind of triage; when I got through to them, I had to explain that a young lad had been attacked, that he had a head wound and had been pretty much unconscious for a time, didn't know how long. That would bring us prime service, a team of paramedics on the run; it would also, I knew, bring the police without my having to call them.

Hanging up, looking round at where Lee sat pale and stained on the sofa with his attendants on either side and the steaming cup in his hand now, one small battle won, I thought probably he shouldn't be drinking anything till the doctors had seen him. Nor sitting up, probably, and certainly not trying to talk. Not being interrogated . . .

"Lee," I said hesitantly, "what happened? Can you tell

us?" *Can you remember?* I think I meant, anxiety at least as high as curiosity or anger.

"There isn't much," he said. His voice was thin and reedy, and I got a scowl from Suzie for asking, even as she stroked his damp hair on the side he hadn't been hit. I heard her murmur, "You don't have to," but I think Lee heard the same as I did, the underlying message, *do if you can.*

"There was no one in the club," he said slowly, frowning, working the story out from his jangled memories. "I was just tidying up a bit, when I heard this great bang from the landing. So I looked round and I could see two men, doing the fire door with a sledgehammer. They hadn't bothered to close the club door or anything, they weren't worried. They went up to your flat," which sounded odd where I'd have said *they came up here*, till it dawned on me that probably he didn't know quite where he was yet, and definitely I wanted that ambulance, and as soon as possible, "so I locked the club quick and followed them up," he said.

"Wait a minute." This was Suzie, trying to get her head around it. "Two men with a sledgehammer, and you followed them up? On your own?"

"Just burglars," he said. "Burglars usually run. Oh, and I took something with me. I broke one of your cues, Suze." And then he giggled at the way that sounded, while she shook her head, *so what? I don't give a damn*, and I thought that the heavy end of a snooker cue could make a lethal club, if only he'd been the type to use it. "But they didn't run," he went on, unnecessarily. "They must've heard me coming, I made sure of that, I went up dead loud; and they were ready, they grabbed me as I came in. Beat me up a bit, I suppose. And they asked me something," he said, frowning to remember. "Oh, yes. They asked me where the old woman was. That's what they said, the old woman. I thought you'd love that, Suze . . ."

They hadn't meant Suzie, obviously; but I saved it up

in any case, I just knew how much my mother would hate it.

"So what did they hit you with, to knock you out?" I asked, thinking that it couldn't have been the sledge or he wouldn't be talking, most likely wouldn't be breathing any too well or too much longer.

"Did they hit me, is that what happened? I don't remember that . . ."

Suzie glanced at me, suddenly fretful; I gave her the best smile I could, and, "Nothing to worry about. No one ever remembers being hit," which was an exaggeration, but true enough. Even so, I was glad to hear a siren in the street below, to see the square shape of one of the new US-style city ambulances nose to a halt outside.

"I remember sitting here, after," he said. "I don't remember waking up, but sitting here, yes. Looking. All this mess they made. And picking up the phone, I remember that. Thinking I should call somebody. Did I do that, is that why you're all here?"

"No," Suzie said gently. "You just went back to sleep for a bit. And no wonder, with that bad head. Be quiet now, here come the people to take you to hospital . . ."

The paramedics were tougher far on him than I'd been, tougher on everyone. No question of Lee's walking down all those stairs, even with willing support on either side to hold him up, even though he swore that he could do it. They brought a stretcher and strapped him down, against accidents of gravity or his own stubbornness or both. Sooner them than me, I thought, watching them carry him out.

Mr Han left immediately behind them, heading back to his surgery no doubt, and Suzie after him: "I'll follow the ambulance," she said, "stay with Lee. He's got no family here, someone should be there for him. I'll phone you later."

"Sure, fine. I'll be here." Couldn't go out, actually, with all the doors bust open. "You go, I'll see to everything . . ."

Left alone, I thought I ought to prioritise: check for what was missing, what was damaged. Phone the insurance company – only I'd have to find the policy first, find out who we were insured with. Which meant clearing up all those papers, going through them, getting them sorted . . .

Instead I walked to the window to watch as they drove away, the big white ambulance and the little black Mini; and there moving into the space they left was a police car. Suzie was getting the best of this deal, I thought. By a long way.

Just a couple of lads in uniform, though, this time at least. One of them I knew slightly, from his having arrested a few of my previous clients. That made it easy: a burglary interrupted, a guy knocked on the head – possibly with his own snooker cue, that's it on the carpet there, no, no one's touched it since we found him – and no more story than that, nothing to stand out. That might buy us a little peace, though I didn't think it would save us in the end. I thought either a computer or some officious little paper-processor would register our names or the address, and pass the report up onto DCI Dale's desk; and then I thought he'd be round again with more questions. Who did we think had broken in? What did we think they were after? Why didn't we call him immediately, why did we tell the uniforms we thought it was a casual break-in when this was the second time in as many days, when did we last see my mother . . . ?

But that was for later, and with luck not any time today. Today I showed the lads around, they asked what was missing, I said a portable computer but not much else that I could see. Presumably they'd panicked after Lee came up, I said, grabbed what was instantly accessible and ran. They gave me a crime number for the insurance and a phone number for a 24-hour locksmith to fix the doors, said to let them know if I turned up anything else, and went away.

I scooped the living-room papers into a single pile in the middle of the carpet for later sorting, and went through to the spare bedroom, where the mess was worse: not just individual papers but whole files had been strewn around in there. Assuming as I had to that they'd been looking for something specific – a folder labelled 'SUSI', perhaps? – I could only hope they'd had no more joy than I had, in finding it. Okay, they had the computer now; but I still had a copy of the SUSI file, and thank God for my cautious soul and my ingrained habit of making back-ups. They had as much information now as I did – if they could crack my password – but at least I hadn't lost it.

Making vague gestures towards tidying up, I stacked folders on every available flat surface; and doing that, I found a box of computer disks. Flicking through them for curiosity's sake, I discovered master-disks for all the software I'd had installed on the computer. *All* the software . . .

I stood there with those disks in my hand, wondering how easily I could get hold of another machine, whether I had any friends left who'd give me access to theirs . . .

Another discovery, though, gave me another option. Next to the box of disks, a box of keys, usefully labelled: Q's, it said, written in thick felt pen on the lid. I took the keys and the disks, checked that I still had the SUSI disk in my pocket, and went downstairs to the club. If I left the doors open, I'd be able to see anyone coming, and I might not be there long. It just depended.

Lee had left all the lights on, I found, as I unlocked the doors and went inside. And of course he'd left the computer on also; the screen glowed quietly behind the bar, showing that none of the tables was in use. If it was a dedicated machine, wired up only to calculate table-use and charges, then I was sunk. But if I could make it exit that program and run another, maybe I'd be in business.

I slipped behind the bar, resisted the temptation of a quick slug of whisky to concentrate my mind, and examined the machine. A floppy disk drive it had, and the manufacturer's name was familiar; I could be in luck here.

And was. A tentative touch on a couple of likely keys produced a menu, including instructions on how to exit the program. I followed that, and found myself happily at a DOS prompt. I fed in the first Windows disk, typed *a: setup* and punched the air in triumph as the disk whirred and the machine got down to work.

And poured myself that whisky after all, due reward for a smart idea . . .

Twenty minutes later, I had *Word* up and running. I asked it to load the SUSI file from my floppy; it asked me for the password in exchange.

Not by nature a praying man, I offered up a quick prayer anyway, and typed in the full, the proper baptismal name of my old schoolmate. Not Jack at all; if I was right, I'd buried this pun one stage deeper yet. Musing on Suzie's brother's name had given me the key to this one. I thought, I hoped.

John Hughes, I typed, and pressed 'Enter'; and never mind how confident I was feeling, I still gasped aloud with relief or surprise or wonder, I still had half a mind to applaud myself for genius unsung as the screen filled with words.

• TWELVE •

J'ACCUSE

I stood because there was no seat behind the bar, stood and read my own words – no doubt of that, I recognised the style – and was amazed.

And frightened, and appalled, and full of doubt and puzzlement.

Item: the screen said, because I always did like to itemise, to make lists, to have things neat and orderly and arranged and without Lexis I would have been thrown back on my own resources, *Marlon Thomas is alive*.

I wanted to argue with it, with me; with the world, even, to say that this was bullshit. But, *I saw him with his mother, getting on a country bus*, the screen said, and how could I disbelieve myself? I'd known Marlon well, and his mother also; and in an unreliable world, twenty-twenty vision was a blessing. My eyes I never questioned.

But – *alive?* Marlon Thomas was dead and cremated. I knew, I'd been there. Seen the coffin go . . .

Seen the coffin, but not seen the corpse. And looking back now at that scene, that day, it did seem that Marlon's family perhaps hadn't been so heartbroken as they'd wanted the rest of us to believe. His mother's constant access

to her handkerchief, his sister's sidelong glances at the
policemen present which at the time I'd thought just
teenage bravado . . . Yes, sure, you could read that scene
another way. You could call it all fake, all bad acting that
no one thought to see through because it was a funeral,
for God's sake, we were burying a seventeen-year-old
boy and you didn't question, no one was going to stand
there and weigh this against that to find them wanting in
credible grief.

After the funeral, I remembered, the family had dropped
from sight. I'd gone round a couple of weeks later, ostensibly
to return some papers we'd been holding but truthfully just
to see how they were coping; and I'd found their council
house boarded up and awaiting its next tenant, none of the
neighbours knowing where they'd gone.

Fair enough, I'd thought at the time. A son dies in custody,
perhaps a total change of environment is the best solution.
They'd turn up sometime, I'd thought, somewhere; people
usually did.

Living people, at least. Dead people, not usually; but this
one had.

I followed the bus, I'd written, *to Carlisle, but I lost them
there. I didn't want to get too close, because they'd know the
car and they must have been watching for a tail. Even the
other side of the country they can't have felt safe, though it
was pure fluke that I saw them. I'd been shopping for herbs
for Carol, and I just happened to drive through Middleton.*

*Item: Marlon's grandmother lives in a home in Middleton.
A sentimental journey, perhaps? 'It's risky but you'll want
to see your gran, she'll want to see you, just to be sure.
Worth the chance, once. No one's going to see you anyway,
you're dead.'*

Only he wasn't dead enough, apparently; I had seen him,
what, three months after the funeral, and that was too soon
to persuade myself that he was just a look-alike. Seemed

like I'd had no doubts at all. If I had, they'd never made it onto the file. Only the certain sighting was there, and the obvious conclusions.

Item: When they buried Marlon, there must have been a body in the box. A body in the right condition at post-mortem, with a likely cause of death.

If I remembered rightly – which I did, absolutely – cause of death had been suffocation, following aspiration of his own vomit when unconscious through drink.

Scimitar had taken a lot of bad press, but they'd kept their contract, ferrying prisoners to and fro. That had surprised no one, I thought, despite the shock-horror stories and the ranting editorials; the policy was too new to be reversed, and whatever the official enquiry concluded the government wasn't likely to revoke a contract on the basis of one mistake.

Which presumably had been a significant factor in Scimitar's calculations, what made the job worth while. 'We'll take some stick, but we'll get off with it in the end,' they must have said to each other before they said yes to Mrs Thomas, or whoever it was who'd approached them with a proposition.

Even so, it was hard for me to see why they'd accepted. Money, of course – Marlon had raided a string of building societies, he'd got away with over a hundred grand and almost none of it had been recovered – but Scimitar's major contracts would be worth millions, and any security firm trades largely on image. Taking a serious dent in that image, even for a pay-off in the high fives, didn't seem such a good move to me.

Still, they'd done it. They must have done, this scam wouldn't work else. With them on the team, it was almost easy. Leave the court building with Marlon aboard; then at some remote spot en route pull up next to another vehicle,

and do a quick swap. Boy out, body in. Marlon goes off free
and clear; the van doesn't even finish its journey to the nick.
The guards drive straight to the nearest hospital, say they
heard noises, checked, found him apparently unconscious
and this bottle with him, doctor . . .

They identify him, and so of course does the grieving
mother. If they need fingerprints for official confirmation,
it's in their hands to collect them, so that's easy done; they
do it once there in the morgue, under the doctors' eyes for
witness, then they tear that set up later and get another from
Marlon.

The difficulty, of course, would be the body. Not a
look-alike, necessarily, but they'd need a kid of the right
age and like enough, so that no one at the hospital would
question it when the papers printed photos of the dead
boy. And he'd need to be freshly dead and convincingly
so, vomit-choked throat and his blood full of alcohol, no
significant signs of other damage . . .

Not impossible, but this at least was not easy. I wondered
if Mrs Thomas knew anyone who could supply it, who
could pick a kid off the street and kill him reliably and to
specification; or if Scimitar had perhaps taken that also upon
themselves. They'd have the organisation, after all. They'd
named, traced and collected one protestor out of a colony,
they could certainly find a shaven-headed and muscular lad
for body-double duties. There were enough around.

And from what I knew, had heard and had guessed already
about them, Scimitar had the ruthlessness also. Weak on
motive, maybe, but the rest was there.

Things were falling into place a little, questions were
starting to be answered. I'd uncovered a scam that must
have included a murder; not enough evidence to go to the
police with it, but no real wonder if I'd wanted to investigate
a little on my own account.

It still didn't tie in with Nolan, though, or my mother; nor with Luke and his trees; nor with Suzie and her brother's terrible death.

I turned back to the computer, and paged up to read the next screenful of my notes.

Item: Vernon Deverill's work-crews don't speak English. They live in camps like navvies, don't mix with the locals, don't visit the pubs. There are Scimitar guards on the camp gates, to keep the men inside and visitors out.

That seemed odd, but I didn't immediately understand the implications. And of course I hadn't spelled them out, when I'd written these notes. Why would I need to? I knew why facts were relevant, and I wasn't the world's fastest typist; I wasn't going to explain things to myself. Alas . . .

There was a sudden burst of conversation on the stairs, voices and laughter; I glanced around, and saw a bunch of lads in the doorway. Cues in hand.

"I'm sorry," I said quickly, "the club's closed tonight."

"Oh? Why's that, then?"

"Lee's sick."

"Where's Suzie?"

They weren't aggressive, exactly, just disappointed at having their evening spoiled. I gave them a smile, and, "Suzie's busy. I'm her husband," added before they could ask.

"Yeah, we know that. Seen you here with her. Lucky man," from one of them. "Can't you turn a table on for us?"

"Sorry. I'll be locking up in a minute."

Grunts and mutters, but they went away like good lads. I thought maybe I should put a notice on the door and lock myself in; but I didn't think I'd be here long. And it was better for trade, probably, to apologise and explain in person if anyone else did come along. Last thing I wanted was to see Suzie's business hurt.

*   *   *

If Deverill was using foreign workers, and keeping them penned in, chances were their papers weren't in order. Illegal immigrants, most likely: cheap labour, no union troubles, no insurance payments and he could skimp on Health and Safety practice, except when the inspectors came around. Though inspectors, of course, could be bribed, as could their bosses. That was Deverill's real area of expertise in any case, knowing who was vulnerable and who could be made amenable, where a little money could exert a lot of influence.

If anyone did get hurt, they could be whisked away from the site as quietly as they'd been whisked in; and what better way to whisk them in and out, than in a security van? No windows, to say who or how many it carried. Invisible transport that was, for any number of men.

That would be how they came into the country, too. The 'I' in SUSI stood for *International*; doubtless their vans ferried to and fro across the Channel every day. So long as the paperwork stood up, no customs officer would expect to search such a vehicle.

The only real surprise was that my mind hadn't tracked this way before. I hadn't had the details, okay; but the opportunities were so obvious suddenly, with hindsight. A bent security firm must be a priceless asset, to its owners and to any bent company that employed it.

Though it would need to be bent all the way, right up to the very top . . .

Item: Vernon Deverill set up Scimitar Securities in the mid-eighties, shortly after he married Dorothy Tuck. It may have been her idea; she was on the board from its inception, and took an active role in running the company. And when they divorced in '91, she took SS as settlement in full, though she could have screwed him for a lot more.

Since it passed into her sole ownership, SS became SUS

became SUSI in quick succession. It's raised its profile enormously, landed several juicy contracts – govt and private sector both – and made a small fortune for Dorothy. No question, it's her baby.

Oh, fuck.

Item: Lindsey Nolan is a computer buff. He's not just Deverill's chief accountant, he's the techno adviser also; he set up all the systems that launder Deverill's dirty money. He also approves and supplies finance for everything. Which means he knows all Deverill's most dangerous secrets, which is why Deverill is so keen to get him out of jail.

And also to find out who put him there; because Deverill is right, Nolan is far too good at hiding things to get caught in so obvious a scam. If he was ripping off a charity – which he might, he might well, he presumably has no conscience or he couldn't do the job that he does – he'd at least do it clever, not stupid. He's a clever man.

Item: My mother is a stupid, stupid woman. She was tumbling Nolan before he did a runner, but only because she's writing up Deverill for the Journal. *She never asked him about SUSI.*

Well, no. Why should she have?

I was trying to figure that out, trying to second-guess myself, when I heard someone else on the stairs. No voices this time, just one person in a hurry.

I looked round, ready to turn them away with a smile and another apology; but it was Suzie who appeared at a run, already turning for the last flight up to the flat before she registered the open door and the lights. Suzie who checked abruptly, who stared in and saw me.

I went around the bar to meet her halfway, and for a moment I thought she was going to hit me again.

"Jonty . . ." No violence this time after all, but she gripped my shirt in both fists and there was a break in her voice, almost tears in her eyes as she said, "What are you doing here? I've been ringing and ringing and you didn't answer, I was *scared*, I thought they'd come back . . ."

So I found myself apologising after all, though I'd done nothing to apologise for. I hugged her close, because she so obviously needed that, and said, "I'm sorry, love, I didn't think. I found the keys, and I wanted the computer. How's Lee?"

"He's going to be okay," she muttered. "I wouldn't have left him, only I phoned my mum when I couldn't get you and she came, she's with him now. She'll take him home when they let her, feed him chicken soup and fuss him to death, he'll be fine . . ."

She pushed me onto a bar-stool and climbed into my lap, no weight at all; and yes, her cheek was definitely wet where she was rubbing it against my shoulder, and I had the taste of her spiky hair in my mouth as I said, "I thought chicken soup was just a Jewish thing."

"Nah, chicken soup's universal. What are you *doing* down here?"

"Learning things," I said. "I cracked that password."

"Oh. Good. What things?"

Too much to explain, it felt like, but I'd never get away with that. "Deverill's ex-wife," I said. "She owns Scimitar." It was too confusing, to say SUSI.

"Christ. Where did you get that from?"

I couldn't tell her, the file didn't say. But, "Public records, probably. It wouldn't be a secret."

She just grunted, then slipped off my knee and went to look at the computer screen. Me, I stayed where I was, thinking how ironic it was. There was Vernon Deverill, hiring me to find out what had happened to Lindsey Nolan but having no secrets from his ex; and there was me playing private investigator, having apparently already uncovered or deduced some connection between Nolan and susi that I must have thought significant, and I couldn't tell him because I'd known it would get straight back to her. The pawn pinned, the spy ultimately compromised . . .

"Hey," Suzie said softly.

"What?"

"This. *Item:*" she read aloud. "*Jack Chu was buying a property that overlooked* susi's *compound;* susi *wanted it, but the property was a church and the Church Commissioners preferred to sell to a project that would use the building rather than demolish it. So Jack Chu won; and Jack Chu is dead.* What does that mean?"

"I don't know," I said quickly, though I was suddenly afraid that I did. "I guess I was just putting in everything I could find out about Scimitar. Just making lists, that's all. It might only be a coincidence."

Nothing but silence to that; she didn't think so, any more than I had. Any more than I did now.

Then, "There's something else," she said slowly. "The evening paper today, I was reading it in the hospital while they did their tests on Lee," and she had it with her, pulled it out of her jacket pocket now, rolled into a tight cylinder.

"What?"

"You'd better look . . ."

She laid it out on the bar between us, turned it round so that I could read it, held the edges flat for me.

Not the headline story, but the second lead: GIRL DIES IN FALL, it read.

The body of a young woman was discovered this morning, in woods near the Leavenhall Bypass development. First indications are that she died of massive internal injuries, after apparently falling from a tree. The police have not

*yet named the woman, and they said they couldn't be sure
yet that her death was an accident; her body shows other
injuries inflicted before the fall. They are appealing for
witnesses.*

*Leavenhall has been the focus of continued protest against
the road-building programme. An unconfirmed report says
that the dead woman had been an active member of the
protest group.*

We looked at each other across the bar-top there, and now
it was me that wanted the mute reassurance of a hug. She
didn't give me that, though; instead she gave me words, the
same words that were in my own head that I didn't want
said out loud.

"Luke," she said. "It was Luke, wasn't it? They let her go,
like you said they would, and it was Luke who killed her."

"We don't know that," I said weakly, "we can't be sure."
But I was horribly afraid that we could. Trees were Luke
all over, we'd seen already today how he liked to tree his
victims. And that made better sense than the alternative, that
Dean had killed her after all. At least, if you could look at
the world through Luke's cold eyes, it made sense. She was
a tree-killer, therefore he killed her. But before she died –
as he dragged her up the tree, perhaps, as she desperately
pleaded for her life – she would have said, '*Not me, it wasn't
me, they made me do it. It was that man, that Dean. They
took me to this place, Arlen Bank it was called, and they
did, they did such things to me, Luke, I couldn't help it, I'd
have done anything to make them stop* . . .

But nothing stopped Luke. He took her up the tree, and
dropped her down; and then he came looking for Arlen Bank,
for Dean. And I took him there, and I brought them together;
I even yelled out Dean's name, to give Luke the identifi-
cation he needed; and how much responsibility, how many
deaths could one man carry on inadequate shoulders . . . ?

*   *   *

The item about Suzie's brother was the last on the file. Put it all together, it seemed little enough to have cost Vernon Deverill so much money. A slim collection of hints and implications, and none of them backed up with any semblance of proof. Not so much use after all, not at all what I'd been hoping for. Without the disciplines of the office, where paperwork was essential, I must have been falling back on old habits from school and college: starting a project with brilliant intentions but very quickly losing track, starting to keep information in my so-trustworthy head to save the effort of typing it all up, knowing my ever-dependable memory would never let me down . . .

"Come upstairs?" Suzie said. "Please?"

"Two minutes, love."

Two minutes was all it took to leave another copy of the SUSI file on the computer's hard disk, hidden behind another name and another password, and then to delete all the other software I'd installed. Call me paranoid, but if they came back one more time I wanted as much protection as I could manage, for what little information that file held. Could be that it would fall to someone else to follow it up, in the long run; I pictured myself whispering instructions on my death-bed, where to find the first clues that would lead to a trail of murder and corruption, starring myself as only the latest corpse . . .

What the hell, I'd seldom had the chance to be paranoid before; now here it was, and I intended to enjoy it.

Not much fun to be had up in the flat, in the mess with Suzie. We phoned for the locksmith and while we were waiting, as we trudged around making vague efforts to sort the mess, she looked up from where she was trying to sponge blood off the carpet and said, "What's it all *about*, then, Jonty? Have you figured it out yet?"

Not *did the computer tell you*, please note. I loved that girl, just then.

"I guess," I said. "Sort of. Mrs Tuck runs SUSI, and she's using it as cover for a whole series of scams. I came across one of them by chance, because it involved a client of mine; and I think either your brother spotted another when he was in the church one day, or they were just afraid that he might. The kind of club he was planning, he'd be open all hours; and the way that place overlooked their compound, anything they were doing there, they were going to be seriously restricted . . ."

She went very still for a minute. Then, "You mean that's why he died? They killed him just because he might see something, sometime in the future?"

"Or because they'd have to stop doing some things, just in case he did. I'm only guessing," I added, trying to temporise; but I'd always hated dishonesty, and I couldn't keep it up now. "I think that's it, though. That or something like it. I think that's the sort of people they are. They tried to buy the place out from under him, but when that didn't work they just wiped him out."

Her head was bowed that so I couldn't see her face, but her voice was thick and almost unrecognisable as she said, "They could, they could just have shot him or something. Couldn't they? They didn't need to, to do what they did . . ."

No, they didn't need to do that. And I was only guessing again as I said, "I think that was for misdirection, love. Being so extreme, it couldn't possibly have been anything to do with a business deal going bad, now could it? It had the police looking for Triads, remember . . ."

She seemed to nod, a little. Then she scrubbed a little, and I didn't say a word about how scrubbing that hard would only work the stain further into the carpet, not lift it out at all; and then she said, "What about Nolan, then? And your mum?"

"I don't know." Still didn't know, despite the hints I'd thrown myself. Talking through what I did know, though, "Nolan computerised all Deverill's businesses. That's on the file. Which presumably means that he computerised Scimitar, before Deverill gave it to Mrs Tuck in the divorce."

"Did he?" Suzie hadn't read back that far in the file; hadn't read anything, most likely, except the bit where her brother's name had caught her eye.

"Yeah, he did. So, Nolan knew SUSI's computer system; and Mum said he hated to let things go. And he'd be dying to know how well Mrs Tuck was actually doing with the company, or maybe how she was managing to do so well with something that had been pretty minor when they let it go. She'd have changed all the passwords first thing if she had any sense, but I bet you he still had a way in. He built the system, after all; and computer nerds are like that, they leave themselves secret ways in and out as a matter of course, almost. Just to prove to themselves how clever they are."

"Uh-huh?" She glanced up at me, and I blushed. Stupidly. Passwords were very different, passwords were necessary protection and nothing more . . .

"So say Nolan takes a sly butcher's at SUSI's accounts," I went on quickly, still thinking on my feet, extemporising but liking the sound of it, "and he finds, what, that they're making a lot more money than they should be?"

"Well, so what if they are?" Suzie challenged. "This man works for *Deverill*, for God's sake! He'd be pleased and proud, wouldn't he? That she'd learned her lessons so well?"

"Yeah, logically he would. And he's in no position to blackmail her . . ." Shit, and it had felt so right. Still did,

though, it just needed to go one level deeper. "Okay, it's
not the money. It's the way they're making the money, the
things they're doing to get it. Deverill's bent as a corkscrew,
and he's a hard man running a bastard organisation; but there
are things he wouldn't do, maybe. He wouldn't murder, to
make a deal work." Maybe.

"What about . . . oh. No," and she shook her head, and
I could read her mind exactly. *What about that girl?* she'd
been going to say; and *No, you're right, he didn't have her
killed, did he? That was your friend Luke did that.*

"He was going to let her go," I said softly, to let her
know how closely we were tracking, and also that I hadn't
forgotten. I wasn't running away from Luke, only putting
him aside to be confronted later. "And he wouldn't have
killed your brother; he'd have bought him off, or moved
his own business if necessary. And he wouldn't have killed
some kid at random just to get my client out, either."

"Sorry?"

I explained; she whistled softly. "Jesus. They do go for
it, don't they? Tell you what, if I was Nolan and I did know
something they didn't want me to know, I think maybe I'd
be quite glad to be in jail in Spain. At least it's safe."

"Yeah. I'm quite glad my mother's heading that way.
I don't suppose they'll put her in jail when she arrives –
more's the pity, it'd do her no end of good – but at least
she's out of the way for a while."

"They think she's still here," Suzie said. "Those men who
beat Lee up, they were looking for her."

"Her, and my computer." And they wanted my mother
for what Nolan might or might not have told her, though
according to her and my own notes, he hadn't told her a
thing about susi; and Mrs Tuck had seen my computer this
morning and sent her men to collect it and my mother both,
to find out how much we'd figured out or dug up between
us. If they cracked the password and read the file, then the

answer to that was probably too much; if they didn't, if they couldn't find out what I knew – well, I was pretty sure they'd murdered Jacky just in case, at a time when in fact he knew nothing at all . . .

Suzie was getting slowly to her feet, leaving bowl and cloth and bloodstain just where they were. Her eyes were fixed on mine, and again our minds were tracking each other's uncomfortably closely.

"Me working for Deverill protects us," I said slowly. "That's probably the only thing that does. If I get rubbed out now, he'll want to know why; and what I found out, a real PI could find out too. Enough of it, anyway. Enough to point the finger at her." So could my mother, of course, which was why I'd told her so little, except *get out now* . . .

"Maybe. But if we died in a car smash, say, and it all looked dead accidental, she could work on him, couldn't she? Tell him you'd just been ripping him off, you didn't really know a thing, there wasn't really a story at all. Or she could plant stuff, make it look like you were chasing a whole different story. She could do what she likes right now, he wouldn't know any better . . ."

"Come on, let's get out of here," just like my mother and never mind the locksmith or the flat or anything. Right now it was saving Suzie's life that counted, hers and my own and nothing more than that.

It felt a lot safer, simply to be in the car and moving. Me, I would have been content with that; but Suzie not, she had to go on asking questions.

"Where do you want to go?"

"I don't know. Nowhere."

"Unh?"

"Nowhere she'll think to look for us. Not your parents' house, not any of your friends or mine. She's probably got a list, all the places we like to hang around in."

"Can't we go to the takeaway? Dad'll be there, and he could use a hand, with Mum at the hospital."

"No, be real. That's about the fourth place they'll look."

"Dad's dead mean with a cleaver," she said, almost hopefully. "And we owe them one, for Lee."

"Suppose they come with guns?"

She grunted. "Well, where, then?"

"Just drive." I almost said *go round the ring road*, and stopped myself just in time. They'd taken her brother round the ring road.

With no place particular to head for, she started coming up with questions again instead. "How come you didn't tell Deverill about her?"

I don't know, I wasn't there. In a manner of speaking, at any rate. I could guess, though. Why not? Looked like guessing was all I'd ever do, about that missing time.

"She's his ex-wife," I said, "and his best friend too, as far as I can see. He trusts people exactly as far as he can buy them, and not a fraction further; but he trusts her. And what, I'm supposed to go waltzing in to this scary guy who doesn't trust me an inch, and tell him that I can't prove a damn thing, I can't even offer him a convincing argument, but I know anyway that it's somehow because of her that his man Nolan is languishing in jail in Spain? I don't think so."

"Well, if you put it like that . . ."

"No other way to put it, girl. That's our ammunition, and it's so damp it's *oozing*. I guess I was playing for time, trying to find some proof that I could show him; and meanwhile pretending that I really didn't know anything. So long as that was what was coming back to her, I'd be safe, I suppose. She wouldn't want to bump me off without due cause, in case he got suspicious."

"Unh. Tell you what I hate most about all this?"

"What's that?"

"That you never told me what was going on. You

were playing for your bloody life, and you never said a word . . ."

Ah. I had a theory about that; but, "If I had done, that would've put you in danger too."

"Bullshit, Jonty. I was in danger anyway, just from being your wife. They wouldn't stop to find out what you'd told me and what you hadn't. Why bother? Two people die as cheaply as one."

"Okay, so maybe I was just a secretive bastard. How would I know? I don't remember."

She gave me a suspicious sideways glance, as if our thoughts were tracking one more time and she didn't like the direction one bit; but she let it go.

We were down by the river now, pubs and offices and new developments on the left, bollards and chains and water on the right. As safe as anywhere, I supposed; as deadly as anywhere. Suzie twitched the wheel, bumped us up onto broad flagstones and killed the engine.

"What?"

"I don't like driving in circles."

She got out, slammed the door, walked over to stand barely this side of the bollards and chains, her toes almost overhanging the edge. Too close; I followed her hastily, stood behind and put both my arms around her.

She twisted her head around and up, scowling. "What?"

"You be careful. If you fell . . ."

"Jonty, I'm not going to fall. Besides, so what if I did? I can swim."

"Not in there. That stuff'll poison you before you drown. And anyone can fall, if they stand too close to a drop." *Look at Luke.* "I mean, one touch of vertigo, and you're gone . . ."

"I don't *get* vertigo."

"Why take chances?"

"Jesus . . ."

She turned, inside the circle of my arms; looped her own
around my neck; pulled my head down and kissed me.

"Is this what it's going to be like?" she demanded.
"You being fussy and over-protective, all our goddamn
lives?"

I nodded. "Next car I buy's another Volvo."

"Over my dead body, mate."

"That's what I'm afraid of," this warm and supple body,
these too-fragile bones broken beyond repair. That was me
all over, all through: frantic to see them safe, all the people
I loved.

"You're not closeting me," she said. I thought perhaps
she meant 'cosseting', but I didn't like to say; besides, she
was kissing me at the time, and I couldn't have got my lips
around it.

Then, taking my hand and tugging me for a walk along
the quayside, "I still don't see how you got to Nolan. Or
how you got Deverill to cough up all that money, or why
you'd want him to, come to that . . ."

Me neither. "Because I had to look corrupt, I told him.
But I must've known that would get straight back to Mrs
Tuck. I wasn't fooling her, so—"

"Yes, you were," Suzie said suddenly. "That's exactly
what you were doing. If she knows that you're setting
yourself up to look like a corrupt lawyer so that some Mr
X will bite when you make your move, whatever that is,
then she knows you're off on some totally false trail and
not at all after her. Doesn't she?"

"Does she?"

"Sure she does. And that suits her fine, she's not going
to bother you as long as you're so obviously wrong about
everything . . ."

I shook my head; these were deep waters, deep and
muddy. Lies within lies, it was all so complicated; I turned
to look into the deep and muddy waters of the river, and

Suzie said, "That still doesn't explain what led you to Nolan in the first place, though."

"No. But look, I was after Scimitar, yes? I knew they'd sprung my client, and murdered some other kid to do it. It wouldn't have taken much for me to find out they were providing the security on Deverill's roads; and I already knew that Luke was involved in the protests over there. So I go to see Luke and his friends" – wrong word, maybe, even I wouldn't choose to call myself a friend of his, only that I'd never found a better – "and talk to them, spy on the compounds a bit, find out about the foreign work-gangs. And while I'm over that side of the country, of course, I go to see my mother."

"But she didn't know about SUS— about Scimitar. She didn't."

"No, I know. But I knew there was a connection between Deverill and Scimitar, and everyone knew about Deverill and Nolan. He'd been in the papers, remember, he was a big story and they'd all run features. So my mother tells me she's been working on Deverill, she tells me about her and Nolan because she's like that, she's always been very upfront with me about the stuff she gets up to, she used to love to shock me; and something clicks, something connects somewhere. Don't know what, but it doesn't matter right now. I realise that she's in danger if Mrs Tuck ever finds out about the *Journal* or simply decides that Nolan told her what he knew. So I tell her to cut and run, tell her just enough so she knows who to be scared of but no more, because if I told her any more she'd decide to investigate Mrs Tuck instead and likely get her throat cut; and then I'm on my way back to town when I have the accident."

That wasn't right, quite, I'd been heading the other way when I crashed; heading back to Luke, perhaps, to warn him too? No, Mrs Tuck's whole organisation was no danger to Luke, that was foolish. Something, though, something had turned me around and taken me back. Still, never mind that for now.

"So where do we go from here?" Suzie demanded.

I looked at her, she looked at me; she nodded first. Two minds on but a single track.

"Deverill," she said. "We've got to. Proof or no proof."

Luke or no Luke. Deverill wasn't likely to be in the mood to see us, with his main man tree'd and skinned, but I didn't want to remind her of that. Besides, she was right. One way or another, we had to make him see us.

He travels fastest who travels alone, maybe; but he travels a hell of a lot faster in a car than he does on foot, even if someone else is doing the driving. It had taken us an hour and a half the first time we went that way that day, following Luke to guide him. Second time, we'd pretty much done it in ten minutes. We were just coming up to the village when we saw the big limousine with the black windows coming from the other direction.

"Bingo," I said delightedly. "That's Deverill. Flash him hard, see if he'll stop. Give him a toot, too. Got to make him look, his driver might not know the car . . ."

Suzie flashed and tooted, and the limo slowed as we passed. I waved frantically over Suzie's head, uselessly, his windows as dark as ours; we stopped and scrambled into the road, and yes, the limo had stopped also and the driver was getting out. I didn't know him, but that was no surprise; Deverill ran a major operation, many staff. And he didn't have Dean any more, to drive him around . . .

Looked like a Dean-substitute, the driver, bigger and just as hard. He gazed at us entirely without expression, which was probably a better idea than the thin smile I was forcing, unconvincing even to me.

"The boss in the back there, yeah? This is urgent, I need to . . ."

I needed to talk less, apparently; he already had the back door open, and was gesturing me inside.

I bent over, peering in and already folding to let my body follow my gaze, so that I could sit and talk on a level with Deverill, tête-à-tête and eye to eye if we couldn't be mind to mind.

And by the time my mind registered what my eyes were giving it, my arse was already sinking into soft leather and I was halfway to helpless as Mrs Tuck smiled graciously at me from the far side of this plush and padded car.

Feet still on the tarmac outside: my legs stiffened to thrust me up and out of there, but of course it was too late for that. The driver had gone from my line of sight; I heard Suzie yelp, Mrs Tuck chuckle.

"Well now," she said softly. "I was just sending my boys to look for you, and here you are come to visit. Vernon will be glad."

The driver thrust Suzie into the front passenger seat, though she was spitting and kicking and trying to take his eyes out with a gouging thumb.

"Shut the fuck up and sit still," he warned her, equably enough, "or I'll hurt your bloke. Get it?"

"You try it, shitfuck, you lay a hand on him and I'll put your balls through a bloody mangle . . ."

But that was bravado and nothing more, and she knew it, he knew it, we all knew it. I was hostage against her good behaviour, as she was against my own. I suppose I could have forced a stand-off, one hostage against another: I was bigger, stronger and significantly younger than Mrs Tuck, I could have done her some serious damage.

But the driver was a harder bastard for sure than I could ever bring myself to be. He'd have done things to Suzie I couldn't bear to contemplate, let alone replicate, and he wouldn't so much care what I threatened in response. Suzie had been wife and lover and partner to me, all in these few short days of my reborn life; Mrs Tuck was only his employer. Why should he mind to hear her scream? It was his job, I suppose, to prevent it, but he did prevent it simply by its being nothing more than his job.

I did nothing, said nothing; after a minute Suzie subsided to sit in a matching silence, while the driver found a lane he could back into, to turn this long car and take us all to Arlen Bank where Deverill would be so glad to see us.

THIRTEEN

ONE MORE, LUKE,
AND I FORGET EVERYTHING

Cars follow character. I knew that but I'd forgotten it, I'd made unthinking assumptions. *Dean got out of the limo, Deverill was in the limo, therefore it was Deverill's limo.* Stupid bloody assumptions, and look where they'd got us now . . .

Cars follow character: it was, inevitably, Mrs Tuck's limo. There'd been only the two choices, parked out front at Arlen Bank when I'd been taken there for lunch, this and the Jag; and that was no choice at all, if I'd only been thinking and not assuming. Of *course* it was Mrs Tuck's limo. A statement necessarily louder than her ex-husband's, and distinctly different: Deverill would be happy to be alone in the Jag, where a limo really required a chauffeur.

The big gates opened noiselessly for us and we swept through, both Suzie and I glancing involuntarily to the tree where Dean's body had been hung. Not there now, of course, some long ladders must have been found from somewhere to bring it down. Nothing there at all now. I would dearly have loved to have seen a police car or two, some scene-of-crime officers in their white nylon overalls, all the signs of an official investigation; but *dream on, Jonty,*

Deverill wasn't going to follow that route. His man, his to avenge.

Up the long drive and this time not parking out front where Mrs Tuck's status allowed her. One word from her, her driver left the Jag standing solitary and took us around to the old stableyard at the back, where there were only a couple of other cars remaining. The company staff must have been sent home, only the hard men kept back in a crisis; and Mrs Tuck sent for, a wise and efficient voice in a crisis and as hard as any, with all her organisation to call on . . .

The limo stopped close by the door, and Deverill was already there, stepping outside with a couple of men at his back. He wouldn't have been expecting this, the limo returning so soon; typically he was coming to check it out himself.

If the driver would only follow basic training, get out to open the door for his employer, maybe Suzie could slide over into the driver's seat and hot us away from here, wheels spinning and gears crunching in a mad chase for freedom . . .

But of course the driver was trained better than that. He sat rooted, and Mrs Tuck managed her door all by her own sweet and ladylike self.

I didn't move, any more than the driver; neither did Suzie. Not from hope or expectation now, not because either one of us had any kind of plan left – my mind was tracking hers again, I was certain, and her mind was as numb and empty as my own – but only because sitting still was easier than moving. This was the event horizon, and nothing but a black hole waited outside the car; why hurry? Let it come, let it all come; but we could at least make it come to us.

"What's this, then?" That was Deverill, coming to meet her halfway: a move that probably bespoke their relationship, or he thought it did. Me, I thought they had a relationship seriously different from that, only I couldn't think how to show it to him.

"Prompt delivery," Mrs Tuck said, her voice redolent with satisfaction. "As promised. We found them on the way."

"On the way *here?*" Deverill didn't even stoop to peer into the car, he wouldn't give us that much acknowledgement.

"Presumably."

"Why?"

"I don't know, I haven't asked."

That, I thought, was my cue to move. I opened the limo door and stood up, gazed at Deverill across the car's wide roof and said, "Mr Deverill, I need to talk to you."

"Son, you need to do better than that. Not right now, though, I'm not ready for you yet. Lock him away," with a casual gesture to the men behind him. "And the girl, she's here too?" He glanced at Mrs Tuck, not into the car to see for himself. Getting a nod of confirmation, he turned back to his men. "Put her somewhere else, I don't want them together."

"Yes, sir. Er, where . . . ?"

"The Portakabin, for him. That's what it's here for. Bring her into the house."

"Hey, wait a minute! What the hell are you talking about? We've come to see you of our own choice here, we've got some information we think you need to know. You can't just lock us up like some high-handed mediaeval baron! Get real, Deverill, there are laws these days. False imprisonment, kidnap . . ."

"You get real, Jonty." His face was heavy, expressionless, terrifying. "This is the second time you've come here today. First time, you brought some psycho climber with you, killed my lad. His body's here still. You want to see it?"

No, I didn't want to see it, not at any closer quarters than I already had. I shook my head.

"No, right. But if I show it to the law, I don't think they're going to blame me for taking a few precautions, second time you come."

He had a case, maybe; but he wasn't serious. That 'if' was the only significant part of what he'd said. He wasn't going to show Dean's body to the law, that wasn't his style; nor would I be laying a complaint about my treatment. I'd either be too damn grateful for walking out of here alive, or else I wouldn't be walking anywhere, except maybe to paradise. Chasing after Dean.

Suzie opened her door, stood up slowly, reached to take my hand; and I knew it was futile, but it was engrained too deep in me to be resisted, *protect the ones you love.* I said, "At least let Suzie go, she's got nothing to do with Luke and she can't tell you anything more than I can . . ."

But before he could sneer and shake his head and say *I don't think so, Jonty. That valuable to you, makes her valuable to me also,* he was already too late. Suzie had made her pitch.

"No," she said, "don't you do that," she said, and I wasn't at all clear which of us she was talking to. "I'm here, and I'm staying here till we leave together."

"For God's sake, Suzie . . . !"

"Shut the fuck up, you," and that at least was definitely directed at me; like the dig of her nails into my palm, a biting reminder, *no adventures without me.*

"She stays," Deverill said, flat and final. Talking to his men, not to us. "But not with him. As I said."

They nodded, and moved towards us; and Mrs Tuck's driver made three big men, and I could feel the quiver under Suzie's skin that said she wasn't running unless I ran first, and it was all too late in any case. Neither one of us was likely to be fast or fit enough to make it out of the yard, let alone off the grounds and away.

So we stood there tamely, like classic victims, our

body-language rolling us over and showing our throats, saying *do what you will.*

Which – surprise! – they did, as they had always meant to. Mrs Tuck's driver took Suzie's elbow in one big hand, and would clearly have dragged her away if she hadn't gone with him under her own steam. One quick, frightened glance she gave me, *Jesus, Jonty, what have we got ourselves into here?* and then she went; and I watched her small figure all the way, in through the door and out of sight, and swore silently, bitterly to myself and at myself. I'd brought her into this; somehow, I had to get her out . . .

Me, I rated two companions on my walk directly to jail. A silent man on either side, strong hands on my arms to guide and hold me against any stupidity; and they took me the other way, across the yard and out under the arch.

I'd missed seeing it on the way in, my eyes and mind both too busy with other questions, but *Portakabin* Deverill had said and a Portakabin there was, newly set on the grass beside the drive. It was smarter than your average building-site cabin, decked out neatly in SUSI's white livery with navy trimmings, the *Scimitar* logo writ large along the side; and the small windows all had a framework of bars bolted across them. To keep intruders out, no doubt.

And of course to keep detainees within.

A steel-sided shoebox of a size for giants' shoes, inside I thought it had become a plaything for giants' children, *let's build a doll's house, with walls and doors and everything.* Where human children would have had only cardboard and glue to work with, these had used steel for the interior also, to make walls far stronger than the plasterboard divisions I was familiar with from clients' cabins; even the doors had metal frames, and I guessed metal mesh reinforcement under their hardboard skins. But still it was only a box lidded and divided, ultimately utilitarian, painted an uncompromising white. There was no furniture at all, which I suppose was adding to the impression of a toy-place, an environment filled with someone else's fantasies, my nightmares.

The outer door brought us into a corridor. The room on the left should have been an office but for its utter disuse, the door standing open and a fluorescent light-strip shining down on nothing. Half a dozen more doors in the long wall of the corridor: but it wasn't that long, there was barely room for half a dozen doors, and no space at all between them. That reminded me of something. A public toilet, yes, a row of cubicles with only one purpose and no need to waste valuable real estate with any more elbow-room than this; but something else also, something far more significant . . .

Something else that belonged to Scimitar, had their logo on its sides. Something designed by the same hands, most likely; and with the same intent, only a more mobile version that didn't need a truck and a crane to shift it. I remembered the glimpse I'd had into their escort van in the stableyard, before they'd brought the girl out of it. The same line of doors I'd seen then, except they'd been narrower, even more jealous of space.

So when they pulled the nearest door open and shoved me through it, it was no surprise to find myself in a chamber, a cubicle that could never have been meant for anything other than a cell.

Two paces long and one pace wide, a light recessed behind a grille in the ceiling, a high narrow letterbox of a window, barred outside the glass; nothing else to be seen in here, not even the hinges or the lock of the door. No eyehole in the door, no slot for passing meals in or waste products out. I supposed, if they were ever questioned, they could claim it simply as a store-cabin: *look, no facilities for keeping people, who's been making such a ridiculous claim? There aren't even any toilets, see . . .*

And there weren't, and I wished I hadn't thought of that; suddenly I wanted to piss, rather urgently.

Plain fear, I thought that was. I tried to crush it under a rising and legitimate anger; tried to feel outraged at what had overtaken us, that we who'd come here in all innocence had been imprisoned and threatened and separated. In truth, though, I couldn't manage anger, I understood Deverill too well for that. He had reason enough to do this, at least by his own dark lights. Dean had died, and he thought we were responsible; what more did he need?

Hell, we *were* responsible. I was, at least. Suzie had only come along for the walk, for the curiosity, for me; and oh, I was anxious for Suzie, didn't see how I could protect her. Truth wouldn't be adequate, he couldn't take his revenge on me and then let her go. I needed to turn his anger to another target, to Mrs Tuck, to show him something worse than the death of his man; and all I had was guesses, suspicions, allegations that I couldn't prove. Not enough.

Nothing I could do then except sit on the floor in that bleak and featureless cell, wrap my arms around my knees and stare through the slit window at the darkening sky; sort in my mind everything I knew or guessed or suspected, and find somewhere in that chaos the weapon that I needed. It was in my hands to save Suzie's life or to lose it, to grip it or to let it slip, and right now my hands were empty.

Mostly people do only what they want to do, however they justify it to themselves. Rarely, they find a stronger imperative: something to drive them further and deeper, till they will do all that they can bear to do, regardless of the cost. Discipline or hunger, fear or fury or greed: motives vary. So do consequences.

For me, I learned that day, the driving force was love.

I wish I could find comfort in that, but there is none. You do what you can bear to do, and nothing more.

How long did I spend in my cell, alone with myself? One hour at least, probably two and maybe more than two. It was full night outside before I heard footsteps and keys opening locks, before the door finally was pulled open.

I was on my feet by then and ready, if anyone ever is ready for nemesis.

It wasn't nemesis came through that door, nor was I ready for it.

For her.

I'd been expecting Deverill, come to interrogate; what I got instead was Mrs Tuck, come to ensure my silence.

She had the tool for that, after all, right there under the palm of her hand, convenient for any use she cared to put it to.

She stood in the corridor, her hulking driver behind her, and she looked at me weighingly, took my measure. Then she tossed the keys to him, said, "Wait outside," and stepped herself into my little cubicle, quite unconcerned it seemed at sharing such close quarters.

Quite rightly unconcerned.

"I need the toilet," I said, though it wasn't true any longer, something deeper than fear had dried me from the inside out. Nor was it part of some careful plan, only reflex. If they gave me the chance to escape, I'd hesitate too long before I took it.

"Too bad," she said. "Cross your legs," she said, "that's how we like to keep our guests. Makes it harder to run, you see." And she smiled, sweet little middle-aged woman showing her teeth.

"Have a lot of guests in here, do you?" The question again was pure bravado, me playing tough-guy detective still investigating up to the final bullet, but only because I thought it was expected of me. If not Mrs Tuck, then Suzie would surely expect it.

"Oh, a fair few. One way and another. We've been watching you, of course," she said, cutting abruptly to the chase. "Ever since you first came to Vernon, claiming to know something about Lindsey Nolan. Then, I thought you were a con-artist, though it didn't seem to fit your profile; now I'm not so sure. I think perhaps you were conning us both, weren't you? Telling Vernon nothing of any value, so that he would tell me, and I would think you were no risk?"

"I don't know," I said. "I don't remember."

"No, perhaps not. But I think you've been rediscovering, haven't you? Talking to your mother, among others."

"She doesn't know a thing," I said quickly, truthfully.

"Be sensible, Jonty. It wasn't passion that took her into Nolan's bed, the man's a frog. My sources tell me that your mother is something of an investigator on her own account: like mother like son, yes?"

Yes, damn it, though I hated to admit it. Had spent much of my life, indeed, trying to deny it or hide it or else run away from it . . .

Mrs Tuck must have had good sources, to learn anything about my mother's less visible life. But, "She wasn't interested in you," I said, still truthfully. "He never told her anything about you, and she didn't know to ask."

"Well. I think I'd like to hear that from her directly. Where is she?"

"Gone back to wherever she was hiding out before," I said, lying in my teeth. "No good asking either of us, I told her not to tell us. Oh, and she's got a copy of the file on disk, the one you pinched my computer for? Maybe I've been lying to you, maybe she does know by now. If she's read the file yet, she does." *It's too late to hush this up,*

I was telling her; and, *if we turn up dead, you'll have an avenging angel on your back, too loud to silence.*

"Mm. What's on the file, Jonty?"

"What, haven't you cracked the password yet?"

"Not yet, no. Have you?"

I debated inwardly, whether to give it to her. Once she'd read the file, she'd know how little I was certain of; but she'd also know that given that much to start with, any good investigative reporter would dig out everything there was to dig. And she clearly knew something at least of my mother's reputation.

Besides which, I had a lie to support; and if I played mysterious she might not believe even that I'd got into the file myself, let alone given it and its key to my mother.

"John Hughes," I said. "But don't ask me why, you have to work that out for yourself."

Not much sense of humour, in the glance she gave me then; but no blame to her for that. I wasn't feeling so much like laughing myself. Being defiant was only another way to pass a little more time, to slow down what was coming. Just a tad, perhaps, but every breath counted. I could measure out my life, I thought, in the number of breaths I had left, and no danger of losing count. I'd put the last one off, any way I could; but that again was just reflex. I had no expectation of a miracle for me. Best I dared hope for was miracles for other people, for my mother and Suzie; I could maybe bargain for those.

John Hughes. She jotted it down in a little notebook, showed it to me to confirm the spelling, put the notebook away with a satisfied *snap!* to the catch of her handbag; and then said, "The other thing I want from you, Jonty, is your assurance that you will say nothing to Vernon. About Lindsey Nolan, or anything else you have learned. Your problems with him are your own concern and none of mine; you're in his hands now, we were contracted only to supply you. But I need to know that you won't try to divert him, with stories about me and my business activities."

"And if I do?" I challenged.

"I have your wife," she said, "locked in a room in the main house. Vernon wants to talk to you, not to her." Which meant *no limits*, that didn't need spelling out. Suzie was hostage, against my good behaviour. No contest.

"No stories," I conceded immediately. "Though I can't see why you're worried. After what he did to that girl, right in front of me – I mean, what have you done that's going to bother him?"

I was only talking, counting breaths, putting off the bad time; I didn't really expect her to tell me. But she smiled again, and said, "Vernon has his own scruples. I don't share them."

"Murder?"

She made a little face, a little gesture, *comme çi comme ça*, that seemed to me to be saying yes and no, that and other things and that not the worst of them, not the big one. I thought perhaps I'd given something away there, shown her too much of my abiding ignorance. Too late to salvage that; my eye wandered around the cell and found again what I'd noticed earlier, patches of fresh white paint showing clearly on the grubby walls.

"What do you use this thing for, anyway?" I asked, hoping only to get her talking, to win back a little of what I'd lost. "Most security firms don't run to private detention facilities, they don't need them. Even if they were legal, they wouldn't need them."

"We don't operate on quite the same basis as most firms," she said, with a hint of smug.

"No, I'd twigged that. Keep that kid here, did you, before you killed him? The one whose body you swapped for Marlon Thomas?"

Her eyes widened slightly, all the reaction I needed. Point to me.

"He was a client of mine," I said conversationally, "did you know?"

"Yes, I knew that." Of course she would know that, I was only trying to misdirect her. Leave her wondering how I'd found out about Marlon, whether the boy had been in touch with me, or with anyone else who might have come back to me with the news. It was a fruitless game, but I did want to rock her certainties a little. "And yes," she went on against my expectation, "we did keep that other boy in here for a while, though the cabin was in our compound then. We brought it here this evening for Vernon's convenience."

"For us," I said, nodding. He'd want his prisoners where he could lay his hands on them any time, day or night; Deverill liked to witness his justice being meted out, in person. I'd seen that.

"For you," she confirmed, "and for that wild man you brought here. When we lay our hands on him. I've men out looking now. Who is he?"

I laughed. "Luke? He's not a wild man, he's an angel. Your men won't find him, he'll be long gone now."

"You could tell us where to find him."

"I could, but I won't." Not that I was concerned about Luke; even if they found him, they'd never hold him. Never come near to hurting him. I just needed to mark a boundary, to say *thus far and no further*. "How long did you keep that boy, then? Before you used him?" My mind was filled with pictures, a terrified kid crouched in here – in his own filth and stink, most likely, I doubted that they'd given him a pot to piss in – using perhaps his belt buckle or a rivet from his jeans to scratch his name in the paintwork, desperate to leave a mark before they took him away and put him down, before they came back with new paint to obliterate his traces . . .

"Oh, a few days. But we'd used him already," she said,

"before we brought him here. We already had a supply of boys; it was easy enough to find one who fitted the description."

She paused, looking at me with a half-smile, waiting for reaction; all I gave her was a shake of the head, *I don't understand*, but that it seemed was all she wanted. The smile grew, still more prim than generous, and utterly in contrast to the words it shaped itself around.

"We have an ongoing arrangement," she said, "with some clients who are fond of teenage children. Paedophiles, I suppose you'd call them. The clients are an informal grouping, and they're quite widely scattered across the country. We pick up suitable children, deliver them, move them around; often we hold them for a while in facilities like this. And when they're no longer wanted, of course, we dispose of them."

So many fresh-painted patches on the walls, so many obliterated names; I couldn't suppress a shudder. Carol and I had visited Belsen once; now, for the first time, I thought I'd found a place I could shrine beside that in my head, *nothing truly changes*. If I lived long enough to make a memory of it . . .

"What," I said lightly, "and no one's noticed? You're stealing schoolkids and killing them after, and it's not front page shock-horror news in every tabloid?"

"We only take runaways," she said, "off the street. Pick them up with a promise of food and shelter, it's easy; and no one much misses a kid who's already missing. I daresay there's a file on some police computer, but it'll not be much more than a list of names and queries. The bodies don't turn up."

"Why not?"

"I own a fishing trawler," she said, "under another company name, and the seas are deep."

"Okay, so you deal in flesh and butchery. What else?

Drugs, I expect? It must be a convenient way to shift them
around, in a fleet of security vans . . ."

"Actually," she said, "I didn't come here to answer your
questions, only to make sure you weren't going to be stupid
with your wife's life."

Perhaps so, but she'd seemed to enjoy answering the
questions none the less. The urge to confession is well
documented, as is the frustration of the clever criminal
who can't claim their just recognition; I thought perhaps
I could get away with just a couple more.

"That truck that nearly killed us," I said, "when I was in
the hospital. Was that your man did that?"

"Yes, it was. He was stupid. I'd set him to keep an eye
on you, and I had said that if he saw an opportunity to
finish you quietly, an accident I'd said, that would be all
right. Vernon would have written you off, I think, as a bad
investment, and simply cut his losses. But the man had to
go for the big gesture," *like with Jacky?* I wondered, and
thought probably yes. *So there's your revenge, Suzie love,
he died just as bad as your brother*, "and he chose to do it
while Vernon was in the room. That was unacceptable. I'm
very protective of Vernon."

Indeed. And that left me just the one more question. "Why
do you do it?" I demanded, as politely as I could manage.
"What's the point? It's not for profit, your legit business is
worth millions . . ."

"You should never turn your back on profit," she said
sententiously. "But largely, I do it because I enjoy it."

Yeah, right. Most people do only what they want to do;
at least she had the grace to admit it.

She left me, and I went back to sitting and thinking. Useless,
probably, but not fruitless: though the fruits of my thinking
were hard and ugly, bitter and misshapen and unwelcome.

*   *   *

After a while there were voices, again keys in locks and doors opening. This time two of Deverill's men had come to visit me, but not to talk. One carried a side-handled baton, with the casual ease of trained proficiency; the other was wrapping a length of inner tubing around his knuckles as he stepped into my cell.

"This is for Dean," he said. "First instalment."

"I don't think Vernon's going to be too pleased," I said, getting slowly to my feet, "when he finds you've beaten me up, just for your own private vengeance . . ."

The other man laughed. "Don't be thick, mate. Vernon sent us."

Oh, fuck. "Look," I said desperately, "before you do anything he'll regret later, would you take him a message for me? Tell him I really do need to talk to him, in private and right now . . . ?"

"He'll talk to you," the first man said, "when he's good and ready. When *you're* good and ready to be talked to. You're not, yet. You only think you are."

And then he lifted his hand, and kicked me. Very hard, very professionally, and right on the kneecap with his steel-tipped shoes.

Did I struggle? A little, I suppose. For the gesture, for honour's sake. But I've always been a realist, and never a willing fighter. They had the training and the equipment, and I don't believe I made a mark on either one of them.

They laid many a mark on me. The guy with the rubber knuckleduster didn't get to use it much, except when he dragged me up onto my knees purely for the sake of landing a punch or two; mostly I spent my time fœtal in a corner with my arms wrapped around my vulnerable head while they used their feet, pausing only occasionally for the other man to be inventive with his baton.

Pain is relative, I suppose, first cousin to an agony aunt

when you can't cry uncle, but this was the mother of all beatings. No time, no space to worry about my cracking ribs, or the deep damage those feet were doing to my gut; it was more instinct than sense that kept me protecting my head against the jabbing baton or the sharp stab of a shoe. I wasn't thinking. All I could do was hurt, and wait.

And scream a little, I think, until I had no breath left for screaming. I did hear screams, at least, though they seemed quite distant and not at all connected to me. I can't imagine anyone else was screaming, even in that place and on that night.

But screams went to grunts quite quickly, and I did know that I was grunting, because I could feel the grunts coming up and they hurt too, hard little bubbles of air and pain that burst in my throat every time a foot drove into my belly.

So I hurt, likely I screamed and certainly I grunted; and all the time I waited, and at last the thing happened that I was waiting for.

They stopped.

They spat on me, once each, I wasn't looking but I felt warm spit land on my cheek and dribble; and then they went away, locking the door behind them.

I was unexpectedly glad of that lock, so glad to be locked in and alone again.

For a while, for a good sweet while I didn't move a single voluntary muscle. My skin twitched and jumped a little of its own accord, my lungs and heart went on doing their individual things – though I rather wished they'd stop, because even my heartbeat hurt my ribs and breathing was like being kicked again, every shallow and irregular breath – but nothing shifted more than that. Even my eyes I kept closed, to save blinking.

There must be some still-primitive corner of the human mind, some enduring vestige of the hunter-gatherer soul which goes on believing that stillness equals safety. I lay curled in my corner, still as I could manage, feeling the edges of pain dull slowly as they sawed at my bones, feeling them fade into constant warning aches, *don't move or we'll all start up again, bright and new and refreshed*; and it wasn't only that I didn't hurt so much with my muscles slack and unresisting. There was something in my head also, and more than a simple relief at its being over. Over for the moment, at least; I held no illusions now. Nor wanted them: there was a contentment in being utterly still, perhaps a contentment in being itself, that I'd been too busy to discover until I was battered into it. And never mind if it was only a chemical state, some mix of adrenalin and endorphins conspiring to mush my mind so that I didn't care too much about the damage; feelings are real, as long as you feel them.

Sweet irony, of course, that I should finally learn to feel relaxed and easy with life, in what would most likely be the last few hours of my life. Unless it was better-grade irony even than that, and actually I was hurt worse than I knew and dying here: starting to drift, losing all connection with the world and that was why it seemed so good suddenly, all for the best in the best of all possible and not at all a burden simply to lie here and not hurt worse than I did . . .

Remembering all those people who claim afterlife experiences and the overall uniformity of their vision, I think I wouldn't have been at all surprised to open my eyes to a tunnel, a bright light and a figure of welcome, all suffused with this same sense of wellbeing. Be it God drawing His souls to heaven or just the common hallucination of a mind contracting, there were enough witnesses to give it credence, to make it again a genuine experience; and I think maybe I figured that I'd earned it, that I'd done enough, that it would be no shame to fail now . . .

But not God hailed me in that white cell, not God's voice

summoned or sent me back into my body, into my pain and fear.

Another voice altogether it was that snagged at me, light and dark, young and old and the most unlikely of voices.

"Jonty," it said; and that was all but that was enough, that was plenty. I opened my eyes.

Swirling giddy sickness and a stabbing white glare, the consequences of that deep vertiginous plunge from metaphysical floating into brutalised flesh, a cage of bones locked in a cage of light. My mouth flooded with an acrid saliva and I had to swallow hard, to spare my ribs the agony of throwing up; still didn't try to move, wasn't that stupid, only focused my mind on the impossible sounds of tearing above my head.

The walls were steel, I knew that, I'd touched them all; and there were steel bars also over the slit of a window; and still I could hear that steel being ripped away like cardboard, and I could feel the sudden rush of cool air into this airless box.

I closed my eyes again. Couldn't hope to recapture what I'd felt before, thought most likely that would be lost to me until the next time I slipped close to death, in reality or expectation; but it was easier, that was all, and right then what was easy seemed irredeemably attractive.

I lay in my own created darkness, in my pain and anticipation, listened to the sounds of destruction and didn't dare to hope. One moment at a time, that was all I could take now, and moment by moment I heard my undreamed-of miracle take shape.

Heard him tear a hole big enough to step through, then heard him do that thing: heard how he stepped into my cell, stepped over my prone body, crouched down and talked to me.

"Jonty," he said again, my unexpected angel; and this time when I opened my eyes all I could see was shadow, where his lean and perfect body was blocking out the light.

"Luke," I whispered; and if I hadn't been crying before with the pain and the fear and the brutal efficiency of the men who supplied them, I was certainly crying now, and he was all the excuse that I needed.

"You've been hurt," he said, showing again his major talent for seeing and stating the immediate, the clear nature of the world.

I just grunted, letting myself slip into his simple vision, not even trying to think through the pain any more. I lay like a child at his feet, waiting and trusting; and saw him move, watched how he reached out his hands to hold me.

Cold hands he had, and in all truth a cold heart to go with; but ah, there was magic in his touch. A cold magic also, I suppose, a hard magic with no kindness to it: if I'd been hurting before, his fingers dug away that pain to find a deeper, truer layer underneath. This was pure agony, he brought it to me like a gift and I was bathed in it. An icy fire filled my hollow bones, flowed like slow oil through all my veins and tissues, lit me up I was sure like a flaming glass. No screaming now: I needed to howl, and could not. If I gasped, if I whimpered, that was as much as I could manage.

He held me tightly, and it seemed that every steel-ripping finger was a conduit that channelled pain until I was more full of it than human blood and bone was built to bear. I writhed in his grasp, my eyes battered at him as my mouth could make no sense; and at last, at long last he let me go and I fell back sobbing into my corner.

Wanted to lie still again, to curl up with my back to him and the world and close my eyes and have it all, all of it go away. But that was a child's reaction again, and I could allow myself no more of that.

Slowly, slowly I stirred, I shifted on the hard flooring; I

put one hand and then the other down flat, and leaned my
weight forward till I was on all fours.

And my arms and legs held me up, and I found no
pain, only a terrible exhaustion. I lifted my head, and
that didn't hurt; I met him eye to eye, and that didn't
hurt; I took my weight all on the one hand and ran the
other clumsily over my wet cheeks and running eyes, and
even that didn't hurt.

Everything ached and tingled, but nothing worse. My
tongue felt fat and awkward in my mouth, each of my
teeth was separate and jittering and electric, but somehow
I worked them together to make his name, and a couple of
slow and slurring words more.

"Luke – thank you . . ."

"Can you walk?" he asked.

Big joke – and there was me, thinking all these years that
he had no sense of humour . . .

He'd learned to understand laughter, though, or some at
least of its many meanings. I wheezed at him faintly, and
his hands reached out to me again.

Not to hurt this time, not to heal; though I did flinch, I
couldn't help flinching. He ignored that and lifted me into
his arms – like an adult a child, I thought, and thought I
might resent that later; but then, isn't all gratitude only an
expression of resentment in different degrees? – and he stood
up from his crouch with all my weight costing him no visible
effort whatever. Of course not, why would it? His body was
made of star-stuff less tired than our own; he tore steel with
his fingers.

Stooping, he stepped out through the hole he had made
in the cabin's wall. Strips of steel curled and hung down
like apple-peel, where they hadn't pulled and stretched
like toffee.

Outside was clear and cool. With my head drooped against
his shoulder, looking up was easier than looking around; I

saw stars like shards of shattered light, and my mind was half ready to float again. It was an effort not to, with my body safe at last and too numbingly tired to hold me.

I frowned, and even that was a physical effort, took concentration to do it. I focused my eyes firmly on Luke's, and said, "What did you come back for?" Couldn't have been for me, I was sure of that.

And of course it wasn't for me. "I didn't leave," he said. "There were trees I didn't know. Over there, do you see?"

No, I didn't see. It was dark, and too much effort to squint, and my eyes weren't Luke's in any case to see clearly anything not obscured by a horizon. Twenty-twenty vision only goes so far. But yes, I believed there could be trees he wouldn't know: a park this grand, this old, whoever laid it out might have brought seeds or saplings from all over. And a new tree, yes, that could hold Luke here for days while he hugged it and loved it and learned it from root-tip to leaf-tip . . .

Just as well, for me. It all came together – his tree-hugging, his eyesight to see me from wherever those trees were, his hearing perhaps to pick up the sounds of my pain at the same distance, and his deceptive, inhuman body. Plus a sense of unexpected drama in him, a yearning for the big effect, that he chose to rip through the wall rather than simply pull locked doors open; and some equally unexpected and possibly quite random impulse to generosity, that he'd chosen to come and help when there was no obvious reason for him to do so. I didn't flatter myself that there was any tie of friendship that could draw him to my rescue purely on its own account.

Which being the case, neither would he go to war on my account; but he was a formidable war engine, and the only weapon that I had . . .

"I hope you enjoyed your trees, Luke," I whispered.

Didn't have the strength to shout; but all right, he was hearing me.

"Why?" He would expect a reason, of course, to shore up any such wish; simple generosity of spirit he wouldn't recognise, any more than I recognised it in him.

And quite right, too. "Because they won't be there much longer," I told him.

And had all his attention now: his stillness like a statue, his arms like stone beneath me, no giving flesh to cushion my weakness.

"Why not?"

"There's a woman here, the one who had me locked up in there? She's going to have all those trees cut down, to make room for another road across the park. That's one of the reasons she was holding me, because I said I was going to tell you, I thought you ought to know. She's the one who gave Dean his orders about that girl at Leavenhall, too. It's never been Deverill, you can see he's a tree-lover at heart . . ."

Not what he would have heard, of course, if he'd been stretching his clever ears to hear us talking, Mrs Tuck and me; but that wouldn't matter. Luke was a creature born of faith and destroyed by faith; Luke *believed*. He didn't understand about lies, and he'd never spotted one in all his long, long life. He saw sweet and clear and exceedingly well, and that was enough; a very Cartesian angel, he knew that what he saw was true. He never thought to look below the surface, that something might be other than it seemed.

And he was my friend, and so I used him.

And just in time, because there were voices suddenly in the night behind us, brief cries of surprise and running feet. Luke turned, and I twisted my head to see the same two men who'd spent such a happy time doing me over, coming at us fast.

Behind them were others, pale faces in the dark, Deverill and Suzie and Mrs Tuck.

Luke dropped me. I hit gravel, gasping; and rolled over the margin onto grass, not to be under their feet. For a moment it felt good only to be lying on springy stems and soft earth; but I pushed myself up onto an elbow to cry a warning, "Don't . . . !"

Too late. Of course, too late; what else were they going to do, under their employer's eyes? This was what they were paid for, after all, and they all too clearly enjoyed their job. They charged him; and even I could take no pleasure in their stupidity, though I'd suffered enough at their hands and feet. It seemed that I had no instinct for revenge or punishment, though I could draw little comfort from that just now.

Not so Luke, as I knew too well. He wouldn't punish them for hurting me, that was not his concern; but they stood in his way, and so he removed them.

They hadn't seen what his hands had done to corrugated steel. I don't like to remember what those hands did casually, in passing, to those men; but perhaps I do after all have an instinct for self-punishment, because the images are painfully bright in my memory despite its other failings, despite the dark and my exhausted weakness and my tear-blurred and reluctant eyes.

Like anyone, these men had their favourite moves. The one had his baton, and swung it as soon as he was in range; the other let fly with a kick. *Easy meat*, they must have been thinking, if they were thinking at all.

Me, I'd say they weren't thinking. They'd seen Dean's body, for God's sake; they'd doubtless seen the video also, whatever of that grisly execution had been caught by the security camera. They surely should have recognised Luke.

But they came on regardless, stick and kick and *watch him fall down* – only he didn't. The kick cracked hard into his knee, and I knew just how that felt; but Luke didn't seem even to feel it. Whatever, he ignored it utterly.

And the stick didn't make contact with his head, where it was aimed. Luke flung out an arm and met it with the palm of his hand; and the sound effects for that should have been the crunching of many small bones and the howl of pain after, but all we got was the grunt of surprise from the baton-wielder as Luke closed his unbreakable fingers around the shaft and tugged, wrenched it from the guy's hand and sent it up, up and away with a whirl of his arm.

For a moment then the two men stood and looked at him, in major reappraisal; and they still had a chance, I guess. If they'd only had the nous to turn and run, he would have let them. They didn't interest him. But something brought them on again, training or macho pride or simply fear for their jobs. *Still two to one* was in their heads, no doubt, and *we can take him out*, perhaps that too.

They knew the moves to do it, and Luke was no fighter; but they didn't know Luke. They closed on him from either side, consummate professionals, and the first swung another kick, aiming to sweep Luke's legs from under him and get him down on the ground for some more fancy footwork. But again he only stood there, something better than bone in his legs and wrapped around with matter that I knew too well could be very much harder than flesh.

It was the kicking man who yelled, who hobbled a pace back and then fell: broken shin, I thought, or broken ankle. The one still standing gave his mate a glance, total shock, I thought; and that would have been Luke's chance to belt him one, only Luke still wasn't interested. He just tried to walk straight through them.

The standing one grabbed him round the neck. *Big* mistake: you can't choke an angel. Luke looked at him, then reached up to grip him by the shoulders. Fingers that could puncture steel dug deep, and I swear that even through the man's bubbling scream, even under their heavy coating of muscle I heard his shoulder blades crack and splinter.

Luke tossed him aside then like something used and finished with.

The man on the ground, though, he was still flailing, still trying to fight. Wrenching at Luke's ankle, trying to topple him. Just instinct, it seemed, not knowing an end when he saw one.

He'd never see another. Luke bent down, picked him up; held him above his head, and hurled him down again; and then trod on his throat. The man spasmed, arched once and went limp. Luke didn't even look back.

He walked slowly and deliberately forward, and very much towards Mrs Tuck. She, no fool, was already moving sideways, heading for shelter, for the Portakabin.

No fool, she was taking Suzie with her: gripping her by the wrist and dragging my reluctant, resisting lover. Suzie wasn't fighting yet, but I thought she would, sooner than be hauled inside that particular steel cage by someone she hated and feared. Circumstances had changed now, she could see I wasn't exactly their prisoner any longer, obedience wasn't a prerequisite; yes, I thought, she'll start fighting any second now.

Strangely looking forward to that, I was, despite it all. My wife the cat as spitfire, all claws and teeth and hissing: she'd get my money any day, over the plump contented evil of Mrs Tuck. Not so contented now, I hoped, seeing her nemesis stride so steadfastly toward her . . .

But then she cheated, she changed the script; while one hand kept a grip on Suzie, the other delved into the handbag she carried slung over her shoulder.

Delved, and came up with a small gun. It was too dark for me to see, lacking eyes like Luke's, but none the less I saw her thumb work the safety-catch, neat and efficient and meaning this most sincerely, folks; I saw her level that little widower-maker at my Suzie's head; and no, Suzie would not be fighting now. She'd just been given another reason to be sensible.

As had I; but not Luke. What did he care for hostages? I sat up dizzyingly quick and screamed at him, "Luke, no! Stand still, don't go any closer, for God's sake . . . !"

He jerked slightly, but that was just at the word: he always flinched from any name of God, even from me who had no faith to back it. But then, when my doom-seeing soul expected him only to start walking again, he startled me by doing what I'd told him to do, standing still and going no closer. Mrs Tuck nodded her satisfaction, pushed Suzie against the Portakabin wall – this the untorn side, they wouldn't have seen the damage – and gestured with the gun, *stand still, girl*, while she reached into her bag again and came up with keys.

Luke, meanwhile, had turned his head to find me. "Why?" he asked simply.

Why. Right. Okay, explain compassion, desperation, love to a creature with no soul and entirely lacking in empathy; do it now, do it in a sentence . . .

Couldn't. I watched Mrs Tuck unlock the cabin door and thrust Suzie inside, and said, "Because she'll kill her if you go in after them."

He weighed that in the cold, accurate balance of his own judgement, and visibly found it wanting. Didn't speak to me again, only turned and walked toward the cabin.

"Luke, no!"

This time, he didn't so much as look back.

I saw Deverill take half a pace forward, presumably also wanting to stop Luke but for reasons entirely opposite to mine; only his path to Luke would lead him past his men, dead or unconscious on the ground, and I saw him check, consider, decide against emulating them. Wise man, he stayed where he was.

Not me, I couldn't do that. Not my man in danger: my woman, my wife, partner and lover and what more I needed time to find. So I thrust myself awkward and ungainly to my feet, and went staggering towards the cabin just as Luke reached it and stepped inside.

The door slammed, and I thought it was slamming on all my hopes of contentment. I ran, though I was in no condition for running; and arrived at that door only a couple of seconds behind Luke, only a couple of seconds too late.

I grabbed the handle, but it wouldn't turn. Locked or jammed or broken: I shook it desperately, pounded with my fists, and the whole cabin rocked.

I did it again, and it happened again, and it took my dull mind a while to catch up with what was happening beneath my hands. Then, gaping, I laid a palm flat against the door with no pressure. The cabin tilted ten, twenty degrees out of true, and crashed to ground again.

I stepped back, stunned and shaking. Before I could think to run around to the other side where the hole was in the wall, I saw one end rise a metre or so; and then the whole cabin went on rising at that angle, snapped free of its power lines so that all the lights in the windows went out at once, was lifted up like a shoebox toy in the unseen hand of a child.

How'd you get it up here? I'd asked, about Luke's new caravan.

I lifted it, he'd said.

And I'd wondered at the time what that had meant, and now I knew. Luke hates to fly, but when he must the air will bear him up; and his environment also, or so it seemed. Anything he chooses to take with him.

This was no easy, smooth ascension, going up nice and steady like a lift. The cabin jerked and swung and seemed to dangle from shifting, immaterial cables, so that anyone inside must be tumbling like dolls. Broken dolls, I was afraid. Not good territory for shooting, of course, I thought perhaps I needn't worry any longer about that; but not good for staying whole and undamaged either. Very likely not so hot for staying alive . . .

Sometimes as it tilted and turned, I caught a glimpse of Luke's dark hole where the wall was ripped open, and had visions of Suzie falling free. Nightmare visions, those: gone too high, she'd never survive such a fall.

But a fall was all there was in prospect now. What other way down? This wasn't an aircraft Luke had made, to fly unwilling guests back to his mountain in the Lakes. At least I guessed not, though in all honesty I couldn't be sure. I'd known him long enough not even to venture to read his mind. If that happened between us, it was strictly one-way traffic.

Up and up it went, till I was straining to see. Deverill was beside me now, both of us twisting our necks and squinting into the sky. He'd lost his anger, it seemed, in the stunning bewilderment of the moment; he said, "Jonty? What the hell is *happening* here?"

"Later," I grunted. Two stories I had to tell him, one of Luke and one of Mrs Tuck, and he wasn't going to like either one of them; but right now neither one concerned me in the least. Luke had Suzie up there too, and I cared for nothing and no one else.

And was totally helpless down here, could do nothing but stand and try to watch, not to be defeated by the night. I was seeing more by the absence of light now, how the cabin's shadow occluded the stars. Not so good, that, but good enough at least to show me one thing. I could tell quite clearly when the cabin stopped going up, and started coming down.

I could see the difference, too: that it had gone up lifted, awkward and effortful, and it was coming down freefall . . .

*   *   *

"Jesus, look out!" That was Deverill, his eyes a little older or his mind a little slower, lagging half a second behind mine.

"It's all right," I said dully, though it wasn't. "Not going to land on us."

Nor did it. Its erratic path into the air had taken it some little way askance from us, so that it crashed into the stableyard, or else into the stables; there was a high wall between it and us, I couldn't see.

Appalling loss stung at my eyes, I couldn't see.

Until he shook me, until Deverill's big hand closed on my shoulder and shook me hard, and I could vaguely see his other arm pointing.

Pointing up.

Then I dashed the back of my hand across my eyes, turned my aching neck up again, and peered into the star-sharp black of the sky; and saw a misshapen figure coming down, nice and slow and easy. Walking almost on the wind, finding it solid enough.

I thought I was seeing awry, not slender graceful Luke could look like that. Not until he was almost on the ground did I make out truly what I was seeing, my long-time angel with my new lover wrapped around him and clinging tight.

Luke hates to fly, but when he must – no, when he *chooses* . . .

He touched down like a dancer, and opened his arms like a man with a gift to present. Suzie broke free of him the instant that she could and came weaving uncertainly towards me, her feet hesitant on solid ground.

I ran to her and wrapped my own arms around her, half expecting to be rejected as Luke had been, no man's touch welcome to her just now; but her hands gripped my jacket, her face lifted and her eyes found mine. There were tears on her cheeks, I saw, and I wanted to kiss them away. She opened her mouth and whispered, "Sorry . . ."

I shook my head in denial, and simply kissed her sweat-sodden hair instead of her wet cheeks as she was violently, stinkingly sick all over me.

PHILOXENIA RENEWED

Not the formal rooms, these, downstairs in the big house. Deverill had brought us to his own private suite to get clean, to get as comfortable as we could manage, and then to explain.

There was no comfort in it, except the purely physical; but for me at least, for the moment at least, that was enough. Suzie and I shared the luxuries of his marbled bathroom with its gushing gold dolphin taps and fur rugs on the floor, and took our time in doing it. I offered her the choice, bath or shower, and she said, "Bath. And you, too." So we shared that also, a long soak in a deep tub and each of us soaping the other's trembling body with expensive unguents, me fussing over her cuts and bruises, she surprised to find none on me: "I thought they were giving you a bad time, something he said, I was so afraid for you . . ."

I didn't tell her about Luke's healing, hurting hands, not then, it wasn't the time. I didn't say anything, and she didn't pursue it. She only nestled close into my lap, spilling water out of the bath; I held her tight, all bones and skin she seemed, all nerves and terror too late allayed. I nuzzled dripping black hair and ears and eyes and cheeks, still tasting of Suzie despite the perfumed cleansers, and wouldn't let her

go until she'd at least stopped crying and those bones lay still
within that battered skin.

At last we moved, we climbed out of the bath and patted
each other dry with soft towels. Then I searched the cabinets
for medical supplies, plasters and antiseptic, though she
wouldn't let me use much of what I found: "I'm not going out
there smelling of TCP like a kid," she said, fending me off.

"Witch-hazel?"

"Not that, either. Stuff stinks. I smell nice," sniffing at her
wrist with the first, faintest touch of a smile.

"I just don't want you dying of blood-poisoning, that's
all."

"I won't. Uncle Han wouldn't let me."

She let me plaster the worst of her cuts, but no more
than that. We swathed ourselves then in a couple of heavy
bathrobes; combed each other's hair with delaying, dallying
fingers; finally touched lips in something more sigh than kiss,
only an exchange of air, and nodded an unspoken acceptance.
She took my hand, I unbolted the door, and we went out to
Deverill.

He was waiting in a sitting-room that had probably been
furnished by Mrs Tuck before she left him: slightly faded,
slightly chintzy, a motherly kind of room that looked oddly
cheap for such an imposing house. Looked cheap to me, at
least, until I'd walked barefoot across the carpet and sat
down on one of the sofas, felt its fabric under my palm and
its nurturing cushions engulf me. Quality like that, comfort
like that comes expensive.

What wasn't comfortable was Deverill's gaze, where he
sat in a chair by the fireplace. Bleak and grey he looked,
grey through to the bone of him. Miracles take people like
that, sometimes; but he must also have been busy while we
bathed, arranging for his men to clear up the mess in his
stableyard. His ex-wife, the mess. And not understanding
anything that had happened here today, knowing neither of

the stories, knowing only that Dean was dead and Mrs Tuck was dead and that neither death was the least bit natural. Small wonder if he looked zomboid and unbalanced.

He was at least ready to sit and listen, though, that was something. Actually, he looked like he never wanted to move again; drained, he looked, of more than human kindness. I picked a sofa and sat myself, was surprised by comfort and thought I understood him, thought I shared the feeling. Then I heard distant sounds of a heavy motor revving, chains clashing and men calling: noises in the stableyard, they were. And Suzie dropped down into my lap and nestled her still-damp head under my chin, curling up ridiculously small for a grown-up so that I could contain all of her within the circle of my arms; and I thought suddenly that no, I didn't share Deverill's feelings at all, probably couldn't come close to understanding.

To be honest, though, I didn't particularly feel like trying. A little sympathy I could manage, though that much tempered by my earlier knowledge of him, something at least of what he had done to other people. Empathy, not. Too much to ask.

Mostly, I wanted to be home. Didn't at all want to move: me, sofa, Suzie, bathrobes, that much was fine. They were just in the wrong place, that was all. I wanted the flat around us, and no Deverill.

So. Soonest begun, soonest over.

"You paid me to find out who had set up Lindsey Nolan," I said.

"I paid you a lot."

"Yes. That was part of it, I'll come to the money. Thing was, I already knew; only that I couldn't tell you, because you'd have told it straight to Mrs Tuck, and then Nolan and I both were in the shit."

"Why so?"

"We'd both be dead by now. Nolan's lucky, actually,

that he isn't yet. She probably wasn't sure of him, is all. Suspicious, but not sure. Maybe she was hoping that I really would turn up some third party with their screws into him, to prove all her suspicions false. I don't know that."

"I don't understand."

"No. I'm sorry, I'm not telling this well. I'm tired, and I don't want to be here. From the top, then: Lindsey Nolan wasn't set up. Not by anyone else," as he shifted irritably in his chair, ready to deny me. "He set himself up."

"What?"

"He panicked, I think," I said. "But he panicked in a smart way. What happened, he found out the truth about Scimitar Securities, or some of it at least – went sneaking into their computer files, most likely, snooped through their accounts and put the numbers together – and he got scared. If Mrs Tuck ever found out how much he knew, he was a dead man. Also I think he's a moral man, at least by his own lights; he'll have wanted to stop her, if he could find a way to do it safely. So he sets up a deliberately clumsy scam, tips the police off and does a runner to Spain. Where he makes sure the *guardia* pick him up, and what do you know? He's nice and snug in a Spanish jail for a few months, fighting extradition. One thing about jails, they're designed as hard places to get into. It's not ultimately safe, maybe, not forever; but for the moment it makes a pretty good hole to hide in. And he gets visits from Scotland Yard, very public, very legit; but I don't think they're only talking about a defrauded charity. I think he probably left plenty of evidence behind him, that he was running that scam in self-defence and deliberately turning himself in; I don't suppose it'll even come to trial, in the end. Likely they're negotiating about that at the moment, and meanwhile he's just been feeding them fragments of what he knows, holding the rest back till he's sure of his own position, that'll be why the police haven't busted the whole operation yet—"

"Wait a minute." Deverill held his hand up, physically to stop me. "Wait a minute. Why would they bust Dorothy's operation, what are you *talking* about? What does Lindsey know about her, that I don't?" *Nothing*, his voice was saying; and *whatever she's done, I've done worse, and Lindsey knows all about that and he's never tried to bust me. He's not a moral man, he's as bent as a three-bob bit* . . .

"I can't say for certain, you'll have to ask him; but what I know about for sure is kidnap, murder, trafficking in drugs and trafficking in flesh," working them off on my fingers one by one, with just a faint grunt from Suzie at losing even that much contact with me, "specifically organising sex rings for the abuse of children and then killing the kids after. Anything with the word 'traffic' in it, I suppose, that was their speciality: moving things about, whether it was people or other goods. Well, you know about that, they supplied your work-crews, didn't they?"

His eyebrows twitched an acknowledgement, though he was far too experienced a hand to admit it directly. Instead, "Drugs?" he said.

"Yes. I don't know the details; ask Lindsey Nolan. That would have been the most profitable, I'd guess, so it's most likely what he spotted on the account sheets. It's hard to cover up that much laundry. Especially from a specialist."

"I hate drugs," he said, and his face shifted. Odd, to see that in a man so professionally hard, ordinarily so controlled. "My first wife died from an overdose, did you know?"

No. First time around, probably I had known; my research would have thrown that up. But I hadn't bothered to make a note of it, discipline slipping by then, so no, I hadn't known this time until he told me. Made sense, though. That was when Mrs Tuck had wanted to stop answering questions, as soon as I mentioned drugs; those would be Vernon's scruples, and a problem to her if he found out. "Well, your second wife dealt in the stuff," I said, deliberately brutal.

"She dealt in anything she could get her hands on, so long as it was illegal."

"Why? Why would she need to do that? If it was money she wanted, I'd have given her more. I *offered* her more, but she wouldn't take it . . ."

"It wasn't money," I told him wearily. "I think it was the competition. Now she wasn't partnering you any more she needed to challenge you instead, to take you on and beat you at your own game. She couldn't hope to compete on money terms, you'd been at it twenty years longer and you had an empire already; all she could do about that was take half of it in settlement, and that would have been no victory at all. So she did some hard thinking, and found another way. She took just one company from you, and set out to be a better villain than you are, every which way she could. You're a bad man, Mr Deverill, but your ex-wife was a hell of a lot worse."

He grunted, was silent for a time, absorbing the news; then, "You're not so pure yourself. You took a lot of money from me, lad."

"Camouflage," I said. "Misdirection. All the information that came to you, went to her; I couldn't let her think I was onto her, so I let her think I was ripping you off instead. Stopped you mounting your own investigation, stopped you going to Spain yourself to talk to Nolan—"

"You stopped me. Told me to keep away."

"That's what I mean. Very useful to her, that would have been. I don't suppose he'd have talked to your emissaries" – and a shake of Deverill's head confirmed that – "but he might just have talked to you. She'd have been concerned. Besides," coming back to the money and being scrupulously honest with him now, as I couldn't have been before, "I'd ruined my career for this; and whether I was doing it for your sake or not, it all came back to you in the end. I think it probably seemed only fair to me, that you should put a little capital into my future. I wanted it to cost you something, I think, and money was all I could invoice you for."

Not all he'd paid, though, not now. His face reminded me of that; my turn to fall quiet.

Then, "So – tonight, then," he said slowly. "That – that conjuring trick, that *man*," though there was a suppressed shiver in his voice that said he knew neither of those labels fitted, "what was going down there?"

Mostly it was his ex-wife going down, I thought madly, in her Portakabin. But, "Different story," I said, "just a coincidence they both came together tonight. Luke's a road protestor, he's big into trees. Not big into people. That girl you were so vicious with, last time I was here? He killed her, for bulldozing trees at Leavenhall. Then he killed Dean, for making her do it. I guess someone told him it was all Mrs Tuck's idea, so he killed her too."

"Actually, it was my idea," he said; and his face said *don't tell Luke*, and I thought we had permanent protection there, against any retribution Deverill might decide to take from us.

There was a phone on a table by the sofa; I reached out an arm, picked up the receiver and dialled. When a known, husky voice answered at the third ring, I said, "Dulcie? Send someone to rescue us, there's a pet . . ."

Which she didn't, again she came to do it herself. By the time she arrived we were already outside the house, waiting barefoot on the gravel, still in those sumptuous bathrobes; "Keep them," Deverill had said, and I was happy to do that. Our clothes were disgusting, unwearable, and I'd sooner pinch a bathrobe than borrow a suit from this man. Suzie looked less persuaded, more inclined to discard any mementoes; but I thought the sheer heavyweight elegance of the thing might win her over yet.

Sitting in the back of the cab en route for home, with Dulcie asking no questions, Suzie put in one of her own.

"Are you starting to remember things, Jonty? A couple of times back there, it seemed almost like you weren't guessing any more . . ."

"I don't know. I did some heavy thinking when they had me locked in that cabin, and everything seemed to fall into place. I guess I persuaded myself; but I'm not sure what was just logical reasoning, and what was maybe a bit of memory slipping back. Could be I'm starting to recover things. I know I'm very certain about some of what went on, those missing months . . ."

So certain I was, next morning I left Suzie still sleeping while I slipped sneaky out of bed, out of the flat, out of the city.

God knows what Mrs Tuck's thugs – or Deverill's – had done with the Mini; maybe I should buy Suzie a new car? Just walk into a showroom, flash the gold card and drive out with something equally flashy? But no, the Mini suited her style so well; if it was lost, she'd probably want another just the same. And she'd want to buy it herself. She might let me keep Deverill's money, but I thought I'd not be allowed to spend much of it on her.

So I did the other thing instead, walked into a showroom and flashed the gold card and bought a car for me. A compromise car, the instinct for caution – *look after the ones you love* – fighting the anticipated pleasure of her approval.

"I'll take that one," I said, waving a cheerfully casual hand towards a low-slung sports model. Never mind Volvo's propaganda, BMWs had just as good a record for safety. Actually I'd have taken a Jag, only that Deverill drove one . . .

"Test drive, sir?"

"No, no need for that. It'll be fine."

That fazed the salesman, but only slightly. He produced a form, started asking questions about any extra features I'd like fitted before they delivered it. I smiled, and really fazed him.

"No, I'll take it as it is. And right now, please."

He wasn't happy, but gold cards are a wonderful persuader. One phone call to my bank, to check up on me – and I must, I really *must* go and see my bank manager – and he was suddenly all cooperation. The car had only been traded in the week before, so its tax disc was still valid; inside half an hour it had been insured and registered to me, and I was driving.

All the way across the country I drove, plenty far enough to test it; over to the Lakes and up the hill, up the track to Luke.

He was just where I knew he would be, crouched over his fire heating water.

"Jonty. I've been expecting you."

"Yeah, I know." I sat opposite him, waited quietly till he passed me a tin mug of steaming water, my breakfast for the day; and then I said, "It was you, wasn't it? Who made me crash that night?"

"Yes," he said, no thought of a lie.

I could see it, so clearly in my head. Returning memory or logical deduction, I couldn't say: but it was so easy, so obvious now. I'd come to see him, told him I was working for the tree-killer Deverill; and that was betrayal pure and simple, and enough to doom me as it had doomed the girl after me. Luke had his own attitude towards treachery. Bred in his bones, I guess, inherent in what he was. I'd driven off later, he'd tried and convicted me in my absence, and sentence was inevitable and immediate.

So there I was, there I must have been, heading back to the city; and suddenly there was Luke in the road ahead of me. Of course I'd stopped, and of course I'd turned around when he said I should, to take him home, to talk some more, something he had to tell me. Something important, it must have been; what else could make him fly to find me, and then accept a ride in a hated car?

We'd passed a kid on the way, the witness who'd seen me
with someone else in the car; and when there was no one else
to see, Luke had just lifted the car off the road as I'd seen him
lift the cabin last night. And stepped out then, no doubt, into
the supportive air, and let me fall . . .

Only that I didn't die, as I was meant to; luck, or physics
– a car comes straight down, maybe it takes less damage than
a car that flies off a road and rolls – or else some power or
principality beyond Luke looking out for me, sheltering me
from his judgement. Who knew? Not I. There was only the
fact, that I'd been meant to die but I'd lived regardless.

But my cowardly mind, so betrayed, had masked the truth
of it in a convenient amnesia. And masked so much else with
it, left me so confused I'd had to work the whole story out
from first principles, *Luke only sees what's on the surface,
he doesn't understand about lies and hidden motives . . .*

I'd come all this way to hear him say that one word, to
hear him confirm – as I knew he would, as he had to –
what I already knew that he'd done. And that word spoken,
I might as well leave my mug of water undrunk, get in my
scorching new car and scorch back to the city. What more
could I say, to a creature who'd tried to kill me for the sake
of some threatened trees and a perceived disloyalty?

"Thanks," I said. "For saving Suzie's life, last night. You
didn't have to do that."

And then, as he said nothing, I stood up and left my mug of
water undrunk, got into my car and drove home. Wondering
all the way whether, next time I visited the Lakes, I'd just
go to see my mother like a dutiful son and not detour up that
long-known track to visit my so-far-fallen angel.

Back in the city, back in the flat, I had a furious wife to
face. She was in the mood to hit me again, and with reason:
"Sneaking off, not saying, not even leaving a *note*, how could
you do this to me? Again? You must have known how scared

I'd be, I wanted you here, you bastard, and I didn't know where the hell you were . . ."

I told her where I'd been, but that wasn't enough; I told her what I'd said, what he'd said, and that still wasn't enough. I offered to take her for a drive in the car, and then she did hit me.

A hard slap on the cheek, a harder fist in the ribs, and I wondered if all our married life I'd be carrying bruises. But I wasn't prepared just to be a target; I grabbed her in a bear hug, too close for hitting, and whispered laughing love-stuff into her ear as she squirmed and kicked. I only had one of her arms trapped, though; her other hand wriggled its way under my belt and inside my jeans, and suddenly she was the one who was laughing as it closed tight around my balls.

I yelped, and she grinned savagely up at me. "What now, then?"

"Bed?" I suggested, ever the peacemaker, ever looking for the easy way.

"If you think you're up to it. Mini-dick. *Micro*-dick . . ."

I picked her up and carried her, and she was biting and scratching all the way until I dropped her onto the futon from a great height.

Later, after storm and tempest came the inevitable calm; and she lay with her head on my chest, idly licking salt from my nipple, and said, "Your mum phoned, by the way."

"Did she?" It was hard to drag my mind back, to start asking questions again. I was infinitely weary, infinitely comfortable; yesterday was behind us, and I wished it could stay that way.

"Yeah. She said she's been to see Nolan, and he told her everything."

Of course he did. She wouldn't have offered him the choice, any more than Suzie was offering it to me. My hand made a suggestion to her spine, *leave it till later*, but she just grunted, shifted a little and went on determinedly.

"They had this scam they'd been running, he told her, Deverill and Mrs Tuck between them, they'd been at it for years. Something to do with smuggling gold; they bought it on the continent, brought it into the country in Scimitar vans and then sold it here. That way they could pocket the VAT, she said. Only Nolan didn't trust Mrs Tuck, he thought she might be ripping Deverill off; so he hacked into her computers to check up on her, and figured out that she was bringing hard drugs in from Amsterdam on the same runs. He knew Deverill would go ape about that, he'd seen him kill a woman for dealing drugs on his premises, and another just for knowing about it and keeping quiet. But he was scared to blow the whistle himself, Mrs Tuck killed people too, if they were being a nuisance to her business. Any way this went, it was going to end with killing, he thought, and he just wanted to protect himself. So he set it up to look like he'd pinched all that money, and then he put this dossier together, apparently, with enough about Scimitar to get the Customs to run an investigation. He reckoned he'd got Deverill covered, he said, and he'd be safe enough himself in Spain. He thought she'd never know where the leak had come from."

"Uh-huh." That was more or less the way I'd guessed it. "So what did he do with the dossier?"

Oddly, she giggled; then, "He put it all on a computer," she said, "and then he sent it to a solicitor by e-mail. Anonymously. Someone he didn't know, someone dead straight, who he was sure would pass it all on to the right people . . ."

Oh, fuck. "*Me?*"

"Yeah. You. Ellie talks about you, you know. *Boasts* about you. Her son the solicitor. She wouldn't tell you, but she's dead proud . . ."

Hard to believe, but let that go. I was busy remembering.

"Wait a minute, I did get something – but that was months ago, before Christmas . . ."

She was nodding cheerfully. "Just at the time he flitted, yes? He said it was the last thing he did, before he went."

"Yes, but it was all encoded, I couldn't read it . . ."

"That's right. He's a computer freak, of course he put it in code. If Mrs Tuck ever heard that the leak went to the Customs just when Nolan went to Spain, his life wouldn't be worth fuck. He set it up with an engine, I think your mum said, so that it would all unravel itself later, when he was safely in jug and excommunicado and couldn't possibly be accused of leaking things he couldn't possibly have known about."

Yes. The gobbledygook had come with one instruction in clear, to save it all on a floppy until February, then put the disk into a cold machine and switch on. Weird, but solicitors do get asked to do some weird things; I'd done exactly what I was told, with a live tendril of curiosity running in my mind all through January to make sure I didn't forget.

And clearly I hadn't forgotten, though I didn't remember now. I must have run the program pretty much on the first day I could; seen the information decode, read the dossier, and . . .

"Bastard."

"What?"

"Lindsey Nolan, that's what." Chicken-hearted, chicken-shit Lindsey Nolan, who was so concerned about his own safety he can't have given much thought to my mother's. I did that for him. I'd have had two separate strands coming together in my head, in my life at pretty much the same time, Nolan's dossier and my own sighting of Marlon Thomas who was meant to be dead, for whom some other boy had died. And then, what, most likely my mother's traditional Christmas card arrived, traditionally six or seven weeks late,

with all her news to bring me up to date; and no question
but that the news would have included her screwing Nolan.
She'd have loved the notoriety of that.

And if Mrs Tuck ever learned that the leak that exposed her
had reached Customs via a solicitor whose mother had been
bonking Lindsey Nolan, she was going to add two and two
and come up with an answer that was totally, fatally wrong;
and the inevitable consequence of her mathematics would be
Ellie very quickly, very nastily dead.

So no, I hadn't passed the dossier on to Customs or
anyone else. I'd stashed it somewhere safe, undoubtedly –
*should've gone for that talk with your bank manager, Jonty,
he's probably got it in his vault* – and set myself up to look
like a patsy in her eyes, a man who knew nothing, was no
danger at all. Giving her a message, *like son like mother*,
neither one of us any kind of threat.

Meanwhile I'd gone on digging into Scimitar, learning all
I could, most likely stashing any physical evidence alongside
Nolan's to keep it safe until I had enough to be absolutely
certain. What I'd have been trying to put together would be
a dossier of my own, something that could go anonymously
to the police with enough facts and figures to have Mrs Tuck
and all her crew arrested and tried and sent to jail without ever
involving me. So much evidence, so many different facets
that I wouldn't have Nolan's worry, there'd be no obvious
track back to where it had all come from. And then maybe I'd
have taken Ellie off round the world and picked up some plastic surgery en route to make assurance doubly sure, change
our names and our faces both, *protect the ones you love* . . .

Now it was Suzie's fingers on my skin, making slow, gentle
suggestions that I was happy to fall in with. No hard
weather this time, everything leisurely, tender, laughing;
and afterwards she nestled close again, *going nowhere*, and
said, "Still wondering why you married me, then?"

"No."

She chuckled contentedly, and reached across me to where a half-smoked pack of cigarettes lay on the floor with an ashtray and too many stubs, evidence of how anxious she'd been this morning.

I watched her light up, and thought, *It was because I didn't love you, kitten. I'm sorry* . . .

That was another, the last and in some way the greatest of my recent insights, memory or logic doing its wicked and unwelcome thing in my head. *Protect the ones you love*, my overriding impulse: and I'd loved Carol, and had to protect her somehow from Scimitar's casual brutality. Even if she suspected me, Mrs Tuck had to be made certain I'd said nothing to Carol; and the best way to be sure of that was to leave her. Leave her big, leave her publicly and permanently.

And I'd been manipulating a friendship with Suzie, getting close to her to learn all I could about her brother and her brother's death; and Suzie had had the ill luck to fall in love with me, so what better way to be convincing than to seem to do the same with her, in a *coup de foudre* that had me marrying her in ridiculous haste?

Like mother like son, I thought acidly: sleep with the girl for information, marry her to win protection for someone else . . .

"You've gone all quiet. What are you thinking?"

"I'll trade favours with you," I said slowly.

"What?"

"I promise I'll never, ever tell you what I was thinking, if you give these up. Right now and for good." And my hand stretched out to encompass her cigarettes.

She looked at me, her face puckered, she blew a cloud of smoke right at me; she said, "I'll be horrible. For *months*."

"Nothing new there, then."

No fist this time, no kick on the ankle, not even a scowl and a promise of later retribution; just a longer pause for thought, and then, "Can I just finish this one first?"

"You can do what you like. You always do."

"Yeah. Right."

And she stubbed the cigarette out, barely smoked; and folded her hands around mine in a silent permission, and together we crushed those fags into a scrambled mess of card and cellophane, shreds of paper, shreds of tobacco.

Something else I'll never tell her, how surprised I was that she would do that, that she could let me keep my secrets and take me so utterly on trust. Lives pivot, I suppose, about such moments; or we find it convenient to believe that they do, that monumental changes hang on quite obscure hooks.

I don't want to kiss someone who tastes like my mother, I could have said in justification, only that she never gave me the chance. Watching us, watching her work my hands like a puppet's, I saw her again as someone unknown, unknowable, utterly out of my ken. Only a touch of existential wonder: another second and she was grunting, scowling, brushing and blowing the debris off my skin and off the sheet with a fierce concentration that was instantly and yearningly familiar to me, that had me laughing once again and reaching to redirect her hands, her mouth and her concentration too.

Even as I did that, though, I remember thinking that that moment must surely prefigure others, that there would never come a time that I could be completely sure of her; and there at least I was right, I had her absolutely.

Sometimes I like to think I'm getting to know her well, but *dream on, Jonty*. Some mysteries are fractal: doesn't matter how deep you go, they just go deeper. You can engulf the whole heart, but you never can come to the core.

Every day, every *day* I wake up with a stranger . . .